I0564013

Air Magic

Three Moon Falls
Book Four

Katie O'Connor

Air Magic

Three Moon Falls Book Four

Katie O'Connor

-Air Magic-

-Three Moon Falls Book Four-

This book is a work of fiction. Names, characters, places, and incidents either are products of the author's imagination or are used fictitiously. Any resemblance to actual events, locales, or persons, living or dead, is entirely coincidental.

Copyright © 2025 by Katie O'Connor

All rights reserved. No part of this book may be reproduced in any form or by any electronic or mechanical means, including information storage and retrieval systems, except in the case of brief quotations embodied in critical articles or reviews, without permission in writing from its copyright holder. No part of this document may be used in conjunction with or to train artificial intelligence.

Published December 2025 by Snarky Heart Press and Katie O'Connor

(katieohwrites.com)

ISBN: 978-1-997548-05-8 Digital Edition

978-1-997548-06-5 Alternate Digital Edition

ISBN: 978-1-997548-07-2 Print Edition

ISBN: 978-1-997548-08-9 Alternate Print Edition

Cover art by Crooked Sixpence Cover Designs

Copyediting by Terri St. Clair

Dedication

This one's for the girls in my high school. I was a total dweeb and too shy to reach out in friendship.

Know that I'm stalking you on social media, and wishing I'd been brave enough to befriend you. As an adult, I've learned that you probably shared many of my insecurities. I wish I'd known that back then.

About This Book

She believes she's the weakest of her magical line, and she's facing the biggest villain.

Lazuli Hawk has been in love with her deceased best friend's husband since the day she met him. He's everything she wants in a man, but you don't just jump your bestie's guy. Especially not when your family is the victim of a series of evil magicians intent on finding mysterious artifacts of immeasurable power and killing all of you in the process.

Frank Perrum's daughter is making him crazy. She keeps running away to visit the neighbors. There isn't a single nanny left in town who will put up with her shenanigans. The only solution is to have Lazuli look after her...if he can control his attraction. He'd like to date the beautiful witch next door, but he's incapable of loving her the way she deserves to be loved. And there are a lot of rumors about dangerous men stalking her family. That's no place for his daughter.

Rosie Perrum knows her dad is destined to fall for the witch next door, but she's getting tired of pushing them together. With the show-down imminent, they're running out of time. Can they find love in time and defeat the evil hunting them?

Chapter One

Unease thrummed through Lazuli as she stared out the kitchen window. The yard, which she loved so much, had an ominous feeling in the early dawn. Though the grass was still green, the trees were barren of leaves. Fall was here, and she'd swear she could feel snow in the air.

She'd been up for hours, waiting. Her nerves were strung tighter than a bowstring. Something wasn't right. Trouble was coming...her clairsentience, her visions of the future, were blaring and prodding her with vague and foggy images she couldn't put together into a cohesive vision, or even a solid premonition. It was going to be bad. Horrific.

Every psychic nerve she had was screaming. She'd had hundreds of premonitions in her life, maybe thousands, but nothing had ever set her nerves on edge like this. After waking from a disturbing nightmare, she'd crept downstairs and started breakfast.

Gramma Pearl, a light sleeper, joined her shortly afterward. She was already dressed in jeans and a brown striped sweater. The outfit complimented her hair and made her look younger than her sixty years. She didn't say anything, just clasped Laz on the shoulder and smiled sympathetically.

"I'm scared," Laz confessed. Her grandmother nodded. "Something big is coming. Too big. I'm not sure we can handle it."

"Try not to fret. Worry doesn't solve anything. All it does is sap your strength for the time you'll need it. Let's put that worry to work after breakfast. We'll make some healing cookies, and I have a new energy ball recipe I'd like to test out. It might boost power. Now seems the right time."

Laz nodded. She'd love something to enhance her magic. Of the four sisters, she believed her magic was the weakest. Hazel could do just about anything with water. Cynth moved earth and used its power to grow things and help her heal injuries. Amber generated and controlled fire.

What did Laz have? Visions. Freaking visions. Ya, she could move air. Big whoop. Any ten-dollar fan could do that. She admired the hell out of her sisters. Their skills were amazing. But jealousy still crept in now and then. A spell enhancer would ramp up her limited skills, maybe even turn them into something.

She pulled out the family recipe book. With luck, the busywork would keep her distracted. Sometimes the best way to clarify a vision is to stop thinking about it. Like when you can't think of something, and eventually you go about your business, then two days later, the thing you couldn't recall pops right into your head out of nowhere.

Her mom wandered into the kitchen, and after a quick hug, started a batch of pumpkin muffins. Their pumpkin harvest had been the best in years. They had enough to decorate the yard and to preserve for later. They had canned and frozen pumpkin just waiting to be used.

Before long, the rest of the family trickled into the kitchen seeking coffee and breakfast.

As the sun rose, morning sunlight streamed in through the kitchen window, bouncing off juice glasses and highlighting the elegantly mismatched, celestial-patterned coffee mugs and the nearly empty food platters sitting on the enormous, round, oak kitchen table. Lazuli stared down into her mug, nibbled on a strip of bacon, and tried to ignore the twanging of her nerves, like she was a harp, and someone was plucking her strings.

"I'm so glad you guys are finally home." She smiled at her mother and stepfather. After years away, Lily-Beth Hawk and her husband, Trevor Moon, had arrived home last night, though they still hadn't found the witch killer they'd been tracking. The current theory was that after he disappeared off their radar, he'd headed for Canada. Since Canada was home, they'd come back to Three Moon Falls to continue their work and spend some much-needed time with family.

"It's good to be home." Her mom's smile was soft.

"It is," Trevor agreed. "We've missed all of you."

The whole gang, all ten of them, four sisters, three boyfriends, mom, dad, and grandmother, were squished around the massive table designed to seat eight. Idly, Laz considered taking the table apart and rebuilding it to be expandable. If this family continued to grow, and it would once her sisters started having babies, they were going to need more space. Luckily, the kitchen was enormous and had plenty of room, almost as if the ancestor who built this part of the house had foreseen the need for extra space.

Lazuli's youngest sister, Hazel, and her fiancé, Dennis, were cuddled up against the kitchen alcove's window. Amber and Kody were on her left. To Amber's right, their third sister, Hyacinth, was holding hands with her fiancé, Earl. Even Gramma Pearl was smiling this morning, though something resembling unease wavered beyond her smile.

Lazuli's mind whirled with omens and premonitions, while her family chatted easily about nothing as they devoured the feast Lazuli and Gramma Pearl had prepped to go with the muffins. After last night's celebration of defeating evil once again, the whole family had stayed overnight at Hawk Manor, the family home. Luckily, the manor had seven bedrooms.

What an amazing, magical family she had. Lazuli didn't want to feel ungrateful, especially after everything that had happened in the last few months, but she was jealous of her sisters' happiness and of the love between her mom and stepfather. Aside from Gramma Pearl, Laz was the only single person left in the family.

Sure, she'd dated, but only one man had ever caught her heart, Frank Perrum, and he was out of the question. Her thoughts drifted to their handsome neighbor, and her chest squeezed, stealing her breath. She'd fallen for him years ago when he and his wife, Celine, her best friend from university, had moved in next door. Even though Celine had passed some time ago, Lazuli couldn't bring herself to act on her attraction to Frank. Going after your bestie's man was a hard no. Not that he'd ever shown any interest in her. Besides, she was only twenty-six. There was plenty of time to find her soulmate. Wasn't there?

"Frank is coming over today after lunch," Amber announced.

Lazuli nearly choked on her bacon. Coughing hard, she managed to avoid catastrophe and stop choking. You'd think that as an air witch, she'd have better control of her breathing. Apparently not.

"We're looking at the place where Kody and I are going to build. He needs to know the landscape. He and his designers are going to start on the plans for our house." Amber smiled sweetly at her fiancé. "We have so many ideas." Happiness rang in her voice and shone in her eyes.

"Do you want me to watch the store for you?" Lazuli asked. She didn't want to be around when Frank was here. It hurt too much to be near him and his adorable daughter Rosie.

"No, but thanks, Andi is coming in." The family had recently opened Four Seasons Metaphysical, a shop devoted to selling all things magical, spiritual, and paranormal. Business was good enough that they had hired Andi full time and were looking for more staff.

Laz nodded. Maybe she couldn't escape to the store, but she could hide out in her woodworking shop. She had plenty of commissions to finish before Christmas. She turned to her parents. "How long are you home for?"

"I'm not sure." Her mom smiled, "But I'm thrilled to be here."

Trevor jumped into the conversation. "We think the person we're looking for may be in Alberta, though we can't find him by scrying. We'll work from home until that is confirmed." He paused. "Or proven otherwise. Besides," he chuckled, "you girls need someone to watch over you. You get into entirely too much trouble when you are unsupervised." A teasing grin accompanied the words.

"Hey, I was supervising them," Gramma Pearl objected.

"None of what happened was our fault," Hazel growled.

"Okay then, catch us up." Not the Coles Notes, the full story." Their mother picked up her coffee, took a long, slow sip, and looked at each of them. She stopped at Amber, who sighed as if she didn't want to go first.

"Fine. This guy, Keres, was creeping around town. Turns out he was evil and looking for some kind of magic talisman. We fought. He tried to kill us and nearly managed to get Hazel with a swarm of magical wasps. After he killed his minion for more power, Kody and his grandmother, Abigail, helped us defeat him." She leaned back and crossed her arms. Kody reached behind her to massage her shoulders.

"I suppose I'm next," Hazel piped in. "After Keres was incarcerated, his son, Mathew Brown, came around stirring up crap."

"Don't forget my ex-fiancé was in on it too," Dennis added.

"Right. I nearly drowned trying to save Dennis from them." Hazel shivered in remembered fear. After drowning as a kid, she was terrified of water. Having to submerge herself fully in the lake to defeat Brown was the hardest thing she'd ever done. Her voice tensed. "Mom, it was the worst day of my life." She smiled shakily. "But, by the Goddess, I'm damned proud of what I did."

"You should be," Trevor exclaimed.

Everyone turned to Hyacinth, who grimaced.

"Riley was odd." She paused thoughtfully. "More than once, she said he'd kill her if she didn't find it. I'm not certain if she was truly evil or just under evil's influence. We're not sure who she meant by he, but we think it might be Vance MacElroy. She had a dossier on him. And on our family. Our fight with her was hard, not as hard as with Keres, but still hard. She had so many skills, casting burning light, fire, moving the earth, and water."

"I don't know much about magic, though I am learning," Earl piped in. "But it was like she was just learning all those things, too. Like she wasn't completely sure how to use them all." He shrugged.

Lazuli's mother and stepfather shared a long look. Laz almost swore they were communicating telepathically. Trevor was from a magical family and had very limited skills, so it was possible. After all, Laz could share basic emotions and some images with her family.

She swallowed a sigh. At times like this, even when surrounded by people she loved, she was lonely. "They were all looking for a talisman or a chalice. We did find a pendant with thirteen jewels on it. It's evil."

"How so?" Trevor asked.

He and her mother had been all over the world studying magic. An evil magic item wouldn't surprise either one of them.

"It compels you to wear it," Laz said. "I swear it calls you. It makes you angry and want to fight."

"Where the hell is this thing?" Her mom demanded.

"Well hidden," Dennis said. "And it's staying there. We've got pictures."

"I want to see them later today." Her mom pinned Dennis with an 'I'll get my way' stare.

"Oh no," Pearl exclaimed, derailing the conversation. "Here comes Rosie." She pointed out the window. She looked at Lazuli. "I guess you're up."

For whatever reason, Rosie adored Lazuli. At five, she was precocious and opinionated. Ever since her mother died just over a year ago, Rosie had taken to chasing off nannies and running away. Her favorite place to run was the Hawk's house.

Lazuli pushed away from the table and went to the kitchen door. She stepped into her work boots and, leaving them untied, went outside. She stood on the back deck with her arms crossed over her chest and waited for Rosie. It was chilly without a jacket.

One day, the youngster was going to get hurt on her misadventures. She raced across the lawn; her pink winter jacket unbuttoned despite the chill.

"Laz!" Rosie exclaimed and threw her arms around Lazuli's waist.

She kneeled. "Rosie, what are you doing here? Where is your father?"

"At home. Getting ready to go to work." Her father, Frank, owned the adjacent section of land, but it was at least a half mile from his place to theirs, and also was the one man Laz couldn't get out of her thoughts.

"Why are you here?" Laz looked Rosie right in the eye. While there had never been a wild animal attack on Hawk land, the possibility still existed. There were wolves, bears, coyotes, bobcats, and cougars in the area. That didn't even get into the elk, moose, and deer that could be dangerous if startled.

"I wanted to see you." Her eyes welled up. "I love you. I miss you."

"I love you too. But remember that we had a deal? If you want to come over, you have to ask first. You have my phone number. You should have called." She kept her voice calm and patient, though she was terrified that something would happen to Rosie.

Rosie looked at the ground and scuffed her feet. Her long black hair hung forward over her shoulders, hiding her expression.

"I don't have a sister. I want a twin, like Mandy and Jenny at school."

"When I was young, I always wished I were a twin. Sometimes, I'd dream about it." Those memories rushed back. There were times when she was sure she was a twin, and her parents had sent her sister away. Of course, they always denied it, proving it with baby pictures and family photos. It was just the imaginings of a young girl unsure of who she was.

"But you have sisters. I just have Dad."

Laz smoothed Rosie's hair back and placed her finger under her chin, gently pushing upwards. "Rosie, look at me." She waited until Rosie met her gaze for a few seconds. "I know that sometimes you're lonely. Please promise me you won't run away again. Sometimes, life can be dangerous. I don't want you to get hurt."

"I watched out for the bad man."

Lazuli's heart leaped in her chest. "What bad man?"

"There was lots of bad men. They hurt you guys. Lots of times."

"Where did you hear that?"

"At Daddy's work. The ladies in the store were talking."

"They were talking about bad men?"

Rosie nodded.

"The bad men are gone, honey. But you still need to stay safe. There are wild animals out there."

"They won't hurt me," she said with utter confidence.

Lazuli stared out over the yard, looking for a way to get her point across. Lucky for her, Frank came running across the grass. Seeing them together, he stopped dead. Slowly, he walked forward, his expression turbulent.

Oh, oh. Shit was going to hit the fan.

"Here's your father. I think you need to apologize."

Rosie's gaze darted left and right, and for a moment, Lazuli was certain the girl would run. Finally, her gaze dropped to her feet, and she twisted her hands together. Maybe this was the time Rosie realized they were serious.

"Frank. Hi. I was about to call you. She just arrived."

He paused at the edge of the deck. "Lazuli, hi. Sorry, she's being a bother again."

She rose slowly to her feet, her hungry eyes drinking him in. Tall, dark, handsome, broad-shouldered. He reminded her of storybook Gypsies. He had a Romany air about him. She loved his short, dark, neatly trimmed scruff. His brown eyes seemed to cut right into her.

Whew! The man was something else.

Her heart thundered.

He stared at her.

Oh yeah, he was waiting for her response.

"It's okay, Frank. She isn't any trouble, though I do worry about her getting hurt." She frowned at Rosie, who blushed and looked away.

"If you married my daddy, you could live with us, and I wouldn't need a stupid nanny, and I wouldn't have to run away to see you."

Frank gasped. Lazuli barely kept her mouth shut.

"Oh, honey. It doesn't work like that. Your daddy is my friend. Just like your mommy was my friend. We don't love each other like married people do. We're not getting married, but you and I can still be friends."

Rosie stamped her foot. "But I dreamed about you and Daddy getting married. *You had a short, puffy dress, like a tutu. It was white with sparkles, and the man said you were married.*" She paused. *"But you had your hands tied together with ribbon."*

She'd dreamed about a handfasting? What did a five-year-old know about handfasting?

"That sounds like a lovely dream, but that doesn't mean it will come true." Laz tried to let her down gently, even as she wondered if Rosie was having premonitions.

Rosie's mom, Celine, had possessed a small amount of magic. That meant that Rosie also had magical blood. Five was early for magical gifts to manifest, but some children got their magic around then. Anywhere from five to sixteen was normal.

Laz shook her head. There was no way it was a premonition.

It was more like one of Laz's fantasies.

She and Frank barely spoke. It was like she didn't exist to him, even if she was aware of every movement of his delectable body.

Chapter Two

Frank ran his fingers through his hair. He was at his wits' end. Now his daughter was trying to hook him up with Lazuli Hawk. That wasn't going to happen. It wasn't that she wasn't pretty, because she was. Her blondie-brown hair hung down past her shoulders, and her blue eyes sparkled, despite looking worried for Rosie. She was tall and muscular. She smelled of a delicious combination of wood shavings, cinnamon, and sugar.

Instead of her usual jeans and T-shirt, she wore a long flowing skirt in swirls of green and gold. Her bulky sweater was the same gold. The colors brought out the blue in her eyes and gold in her hair. She glowed like the sun shone from within her. She was lovely. And smokin' hot. Any man, except him, would be eager to date Lazuli. He often wondered why she never seemed to date...not that he was keeping track.

He apologized again. "Come on, Rosie. Time to go home. Mrs. Kirk is waiting for you. She was very upset when you disappeared." He turned his attention to Lazuli. "They were playing hide and seek."

Mrs. Kirk was their fifteenth nanny in just over a year. There was literally nobody left to hire, and neither of the local daycares would welcome Rosie back after she'd run away so many times. He was between a rock and a hard place.

If only Lazuli could watch his daughter. He'd be less stressed, and Rosie would be happier. Too bad he couldn't and wouldn't ask her. She had a thriving custom furniture business. Not to mention all the rumors about the Hawk family and some weird things happening around town.

Sure, they were magical. That wasn't a big deal. Around Three Moon Falls, where they lived, a lot of people were magical. There were probably as many magicals as there were mundanes. While he didn't understand why, his wife had been trying to improve her very limited magic skills. No way did he want Rosie to be tangled up in magic or the Hawks. Of course, he couldn't seem to stop her running over here at every chance. Once, she ran away from kindergarten and traveled four miles on foot to show up here. It was a wonder she hadn't gotten lost or hit by a car.

"Maybe Lazuli could be my nanny?" Rosie asked, her voice full of hope. "Then you could love her, and she could be my mom."

His breath hitched, and his anger skyrocketed. He reined it in with some difficulty. "Sweetheart, Lazuli has a job. She's a carpenter, not a nanny. And we don't love each other, and we're not getting married."

A heavy cloak of failure dropped over his shoulders. He was doing everything wrong. Why else would his daughter keep seeking love away from home?

"Rosie, why don't you go inside? I think Gramma Pearl has some cookies. I'd like to talk to your dad for a minute."

"Okay." She skipped inside.

As soon as the door was closed, and Laz's sisters waved to indicate they had Rosie, Laz turned back toward him. "Let's walk a bit."

He looked at his daughter and the Hawk family, indecision weighing on him.

"She'll be fine. They'll watch her. I don't want to risk her overhearing this conversation."

Her eyes were troubled, her brows pinched together. He wanted to kiss the wrinkles away. Nope. He was a married man. Okay, a widower. But he wasn't about to cheat on his dead wife.

"Fine. Let's walk."

She laughed lightly. "It's a walk, not a trip to the gallows." She waved to her left. "Let's head out by the greenhouses."

They walked along in silence until they were alongside the greenhouse. She walked past it and turned right. They walked into an alcove hidden between three long greenhouses set in a U-formation.

"Wow. I had no idea this was here."

"Most people don't know about it. Our family has a lot of secrets…nothing bad, just things we don't share with the whole world."

He nodded his understanding. "I'm sure most families do."

"Take a seat." She waved toward a wood and cast-iron bench set between a bunch of flowering rosebushes.

"This is a nice spot." He couldn't help but admire the abundance of roses, especially this late in October. It was a wonder the last frost hadn't taken them all. He sat, and she took the opposite end of the bench.

"Thanks. This was my great-grandmother's rose garden. Some of the bushes were imported directly from England." She fell silent.

Unable to stand the awkwardness between them and wishing he were better with women, he said, "Why are we here?"

"I didn't want to mention this where Rosie could hear, just in case you didn't agree. If you want, I can watch her after school. At least until you find a nanny she likes."

He huffed out a breath. "That's the thing. There are none left to hire. I don't know what to do. She doesn't want a nanny; she wants a mother. Marriage is so far off my list that she'll be twenty before I even have time to look."

"Okay, then, how about until the Christmas break? I can commit to a couple months." She stroked the petals of a pink rose beside her and shifted on the bench. "She's in grade one, that means it's only for a few hours a day, right?"

"Three-thirty to six. Maybe six-thirty by the time I get here. I've got a good manager for the evening shift at the lumberyard. And with the new mill going in, I've hired a mill manager."

"New mill?"

"I'm opening a service where I do rough-cut lumber for customers. They bring the logs they've harvested, and we cut to order, for a fee."

"Cool."

Frank owned Jenson's Wood Products. He'd purchased the company when he and Celine moved to Three Moon Falls. A small inheritance from his grandfather's estate allowed him to purchase the enormous lumberyard. It was one of the largest yards in the province. Probably *the* largest, independent of a major chain. He had a huge indoor warehouse of wood and building supplies, where he stocked basic tools, as well as an enormous outdoor storage area. He was doing okay, which allowed him to branch into custom cutting.

"There's been a lot of interest in the service. I hope it pays out." He studied her profile. She had a small nose and plump, kissable lips, and just like every time he was near her, he wanted to taste them. He was drawn to her in a way he didn't understand. She compelled him more than Celine ever had.

He'd met his wife when he was working on his graduate degree in business at university, and they'd hooked up a few times. Their relationship landed somewhere between friendship and hook-ups. They'd been faithful to each other, but not seriously looking toward the future. When she told him she was pregnant, he proposed, and they got married. When he graduated, they'd taken his inheritance and moved to Three Moon Falls.

Guilt roiled in his stomach. He'd cared for Celine the best he could. Sadly, he hadn't loved her more than friendship, and as Rosie's mother. She had deserved better. He shook off the memories.

"I can pay you to watch her."

"Oh, no need for that. Call it a favor. You never know when I'll need you to order some specialty wood at a great price. I can pick her up at school."

"The bus can drop her off."

"Honestly, Frank, I don't mind picking her up. It isn't far, and pretty soon the snow will be flying, and I'd feel better if I had her in my care instead of on the bus. I hated the bus as a kid."

"I thought Celine said you were home-schooled?"

"For elementary. We all started public school when we hit grade seven. The bus sucked."

"I'll pay for your gas."

"By the Goddess, Frank. Why can't you just accept the favor?"

"I don't know." Probably because it felt like friendship, or a relationship, and he wasn't mentally prepared to enter into a relationship with anyone. Especially not Lazuli Hawk. But what choice did he have? "Okay. I accept your gift. Please pick her up Monday to Friday. I'll let you know if there are days without school. I'll pick her up here after work."

Something inside him shifted at the thought of seeing Lazuli every day. A spark of joy. And maybe a bit of trepidation. He didn't want to get closer to her. Their distant friendship was enough. Wasn't it?

"What about her nanny?"

"I'll have to let her go. I don't think she'll be too upset." He didn't mind. Despite Rosie helping him select this nanny, his daughter didn't care for Mrs. Kirk. And Mrs. Kirk didn't much care for having to chase his daughter across the countryside.

"It's done then." Lazuli stuck out her hand to seal the deal.

He clasped her hand in his. Lightning shot up his arm and into his chest. Whoa! He barely managed to keep from jerking away in shock. Judging by the look on her face, she'd felt it too.

L azuli tried not to think about Frank; she did. A couple of times, she actually managed to banish him completely from her mind, but only for a few minutes. The jolt she'd felt when their hands clasped startled her. Her heart had leaped to life as if it had been jump-started.

She'd been attracted to him from the moment they met. It was as though the iron in her blood was drawn toward him, like metal filings to a magnet. Today's visceral reaction reinforced what she already suspected. Frank Perrum, her dead best friend's husband, affected her like no other man ever had. It was early to tell, but he might be her soulmate...his draw was that magnetic, and she'd spent five years fighting it. Out of loyalty to Celine, she would never date him. Ever.

Now, all she had to do was avoid thinking about him or being near him.

Simple.

Yup. Once this whole mess with the talisman was over, she'd find another man, one she could care about, even if he wasn't her one true love. Of course, there was always the possibility that the myth wasn't true. Maybe she'd be the first Hawk woman to have two true loves.

Her mother had nearly done it. Lily-Beth had fallen for Trevor Moon in high school. Somehow, they hadn't ended up together until decades later. Her mom had been in at least four serious long-term relationships with men. The proof was her and her sisters. Each was conceived, deliberately, by a man their mother cared deeply for. It wasn't until she and her sisters were in their teens that she rekindled her love with Trevor.

Pushing away her romantic worries, she sat in her blue Saturn outside the family store, Four Seasons Metaphysical, working up the courage to go inside. She always wondered why they didn't call the store Four Sisters, or something relating to Three Moon Falls, or even something more esoteric or magical. Three Moon Falls and Four Seasons Metaphysical was all a bit much...especially when filling out shipping labels. They needed to automate that process instead of doing it by hand. Only Gramma Pearl truly enjoyed the handwriting part of the job.

She needed to focus her mind and connect with the powers that ran through everything. She believed it was that interconnectedness of all things, like *The Force* in *Star Wars*, that gave her the ability to get glimpses of the future using things like tarot cards and rune stones, which was exactly what she needed to do right now.

Acting on instinct, she'd skipped the tools they had at home and came to the family store to choose new ones. Maybe the store deck, or a clean, new deck, unsoiled by past readings, would help her clarify the nighttime premonitions she'd been having. So far, there was nothing but a crushing sense of unease.

Giving herself a mental shake, acknowledging that there was no sense delaying the inevitable, she climbed out of her car and hurried through the chilly air into the shop. A happy song from wind chimes announced her arrival. The air was lovely, warm, and gently scented with sage, lavender, and vanilla. Stretching out left and right, the aisles were full of books, herbs, statuettes, trinkets, candles, and stones. Her nerves eased instantly in the familiar environment. The store had a bit of chaos, but for her, it was a positive, invigorating chaos.

"Afternoon, Andi," she greeted their employee.

"Hey, Laz. I thought everyone was busy at home today."

"We are. Or were." She forced a chuckle. "I've got a problem pestering me. I came to do some divination."

"Cool. I could do a Tarot spread for you." Andi did a lot of readings and was a customer favorite.

After a moment of consideration, Laz agreed. "Why not? I'm certainly not having any luck myself." They settled in the divination corner. She stroked the smooth, fringed table cover and admired the Boho chic style her sister Amber had created when setting up the area. It was pure fortune-telling without being cliché or trite. There was even a small display of crystal balls...some of real crystal, and some just glass or pretty stone. Above them, on a wall, a jar of gemstone chips sat beside one filled with feathers. Below that were another two jars, one with slivers of charred wood from a tree struck by lightning, the other with small seashells. The jars represented the four essential elements. Earth, air, fire, and water.

Andi handed her a deck of Tarot cards. It was a newer deck design with the art created by a family friend. "Shuffle these, and when you feel they're ready, cut once, and hand them back. While you're doing that, tell me what you're wrestling with."

She shuffled and shuffled again. "I've got this massive sense of unease. It keeps me awake at night. And when it isn't, it's filling my

dreams with sleeping premonitions. Or maybe it's just bad dreams."
She shrugged. "The trouble is, it's fuzzy. There's nothing concrete,
just vague images, like through fog, and a horrible sense of fear and
uncertainty. Every night. For weeks. I'm trying to clarify what they
might mean."

"That sounds awful." She pointed toward the deck. "Shuffle until
you feel the deck is ready."

Though she'd done thousands of Tarot spreads herself, she asked,
"How do I know when they're ready?" The candles flickered like there
was a breeze, though the room was still.

Andi laughed. "You should know, you do this all the time."

There was too much riding on this to make a decision. She kept
shuffling. Suddenly, she knew...like a bolt of lightning jolted through
her. She paused, cut the deck, and set it down before Andi.

"Wow," Laz exclaimed. "I've never been that certain before. It just
hit me that I was done shuffling."

"That's a good sign." Andi laid out a standard twelve-card spread
on the smooth, black tablecloth. "Here goes nothing." She flipped the
first card. The Tower.

Laz gasped. "That's not good. I'm going to be blindsided, or something is going to go wrong."

"Or the thing that blindsides you could be a pleasant surprise. There
are always alternative meanings, you know that. Every card has a positive and negative interpretation. And occasionally the cards cancel
each other out."

Card after card revealed darkness, fear, stress, and unease. And finally, death. The candle flames wavered and snuffed themselves out.

"Well, that was reassuring. Not." Laz snapped.

"Come on, Lazuli. You know this isn't about predicting the future.
It's about using each card's meanings, positive and negative, to help
focus your mind. Let the cards stew for a bit. Think about what we

saw. Or rather, let them flow to your subconscious, and let it help illuminate things."

Laz sighed. "I suppose. I was hoping for more clarity."

"Let's brainstorm this. What do you usually do when you can't focus on your presentient gifts?"

"Meditate. Stare into a crystal ball, or candle flame, or a bowl of water. Ignore the uneasy feelings. None of that is working." She couldn't remember the last time she'd been this frustrated. Her nerves were taut, and a massive headache nagged at the back of her neck and in her temples.

"I'm guessing this means the universe isn't ready to show you yet. Let it ride. It'll become clear when the time is right."

"Ya. I suppose. But I'm not good at waiting."

"Who is? Especially when there is a lot on the line. I can feel it in the air. Like something is going to happen. And it's going to be soon." Andi shuddered.

"I just hope we're ready for it. Whatever it is."

Chapter Three

The schoolyard was silent. Nobody was around. Even the wind had dissipated. Lazuli was super early to pick up Rosie. She wanted to get a good parking place for their first pick up. No other parents had arrived yet. She'd been ridiculous to show up like this.

The front door opened, and a man stepped out. He strode confidently toward her car. She rolled down the passenger window. He was tall, broad-shouldered, with neatly trimmed hair that matched his close-cropped blonde beard. She did like a man with a beard. Objectively, he was attractive. Too bad he paled in comparison to Frank.

"Can I help you?" he asked.

"I know I'm super early. I wanted a good spot." She laughed a little, trying to hide her embarrassment. "I'm Lazuli Hawk. I'm picking up Rosie Perrum. Her father said he'd let the school know."

"Right. Herb Tallus, principal. Frank did mention you'd be picking her up." He paused and gave her a questioning look. "Are you and Frank...um..."

"No. We're not dating. I'm helping out while he solves his nanny problem. We're neighbors. It's convenient." *By the Goddess, why was she explaining this to him? It was none of his damned business.*

"Good to know. Good to know." He smiled. It was friendly and welcoming, and set her nerves on edge. "Can I ask, are you dating anyone?"

"Mr. Tallus, do you really believe this is the proper venue for trying to get a date?"

His face went beet red. "Sorry. It's just that...I don't see you around much, and I've been wanting to ask you out since we met after the Founder's Day Parade two years ago."

"I'm flattered, but I'm not currently in the dating market." She tried to let him down easily. He showed no signs of being magical. Those who had magic gave off a nearly invisible sparkle that other magicals could detect. Dark or black magicals had the same sort of cue, but they sucked in all the light, almost like they were darkness itself. He had none of either, and magicals tended to marry magicals.

His smile slid into a disappointed frown. "Well, if you change your mind, you know where to find me. Did you want me to send Rosie out now?"

"No, but thanks. I don't want her to start thinking my babysitting means extra privileges. Nice to meet you, Mr. Tallus."

"Call me Herb. Have a good day, Lazuli." He gave her an unreadable look, pivoted, and walked back to the school.

She stared at him. Chills ran down her spine as she rolled up her window. Something about him put her nerves on edge. What kind of man asks a stranger for a date at an elementary school? Weird. So weird.

She pushed away the negative thoughts. Maybe he was just braver than most.

Without running her engine, she listened to a woodworking podcast while she waited for the dismissal bell. Cars began pulling in behind her, and parents and caregivers gathered in small clusters on the sidewalk and lawn. Recognizing a few magicals, she got out and went to talk to them while she waited. She wanted to ask them what they thought of the principal, but kept it to herself. No sense stirring up speculation.

The bell rang, and kids exploded out of the school. Rosie was in the first wave. She tore across the lawn, backpack dragging from her hand, and threw herself around Lazuli's waist.

"You came!"

"I told you I would." She ruffled Rosie's hair.

"Yay. I need a snack, please."

Laz laughed. "Of course you do, school is hard work for the brain, and that makes you hungry. Let's go to my place and find you something to eat. I think Gramma Pearl is making cookies."

Rosie chattered away about her day as they headed home. Abruptly, she fell silent. Laz peeked at her with the rearview mirror. She wasn't asleep; she was frowning out the window.

"Hey, Rosie Posie, what's with the frown?"

"Nothin." A blatant lie. Tears started streaming down her face.

"Hey, we'll be home in two minutes, and we can talk about it, okay?" The sudden mood swing worried her. Rosie was one of the most upbeat children she'd ever met.

"K." The response was surly at best and followed by a series of dramatic sniffs.

Lazuli parked the car and hurried around to help Rosie out of her booster seat. "Let's go get that snack and have a nice visit."

Gramma Pearl met them on the front step. "Oh, what have we here? Do I see tears? What happened?"

Lazuli shrugged. "It seems Rosie is having a hard day."

"Well, I have just the thing to fix that. I have peanut butter cookies and fruit-filled muffins. Plus, if Rosie wants to, we can decorate some sugar cookies I made for our friends at Athena's Seniors' Lodge."

"Okay." Rosie sniffed but seemed a little brighter.

They were past snack and well into decorating cookies before Lazuli felt it safe to broach the sudden tears. "Did you want to talk about why you were upset?"

"No."

"Sometimes, a problem shared is easier to handle. Who knows, maybe Gramma Pearl and I can help. Or you can talk to your Daddy later. Adults just want to help."

"Daddy doesn't understand."

"Did you talk to him?"

She nodded. "He says it's just a bad dream, but not real." Her frown was enormous. Her brows pinched together. "It is real. He didn't believe me about the ghosts in your store either. He NEVER believes me."

Laz took a moment to gather her thoughts. "Some people, most people, can't see ghosts. Only special, magical people can see ghosts. Your dad is special in so many ways, but he's not magic. That's why he doesn't see ghosts. Sometimes I see them, and Hazel does too. Sometimes they only let special people see them." Hazel was the family's ghost specialist. "What doesn't Daddy understand this time?"

"My dreams. I dreamed about a bad man. Lots of bad men. They're going to try to hurt us. I don't want anybody to die," she wailed.

"Who's going to die?" Pearl asked, sharing a significant look with Lazuli.

"I don't know, but when the bad men come, somebody dies, and I can't make it stop."

Fear raked over Lazuli's nerves. The poor girl's magic must be coming in if she was having premonitions. "You know what, sometimes I have bad dreams too. Usually, they are just dreams, but sometimes they come true. Mostly, the really bad ones never happen. Do you know why?" Rosie shook her head. "Because dreams are how our brain works out things we need to think about. Sometimes they're good. Sometimes they're happy. Or bad, or sad. Or confusing. I bet you've had some fun dreams too."

"One time, I dreamed I was a pirate. It was fun."

"But it didn't come true, right?" Another nod. "This scary dream is probably like the pirate dream and will never come true. The best you can do is try not to worry about it. And, think about happy things as you fall asleep. Do you think you can try that?"

"Okay." She didn't sound very convinced.

"That's what I do. It does help. And," she paused to be sure Rosie was listening, "I'll talk to your dad and make sure he knows this is serious. Now, what happy thing can you think about before you go to bed?"

Rosie's gaze shifted around the room, and she smiled slyly. "I have a secret trick."

"Wow, that's lucky. Can you tell me about your trick?"

"No. Daddy doesn't believe THAT either."

"I've seen some pretty special things. I don't think you can surprise me, and I will believe you if you tell me."

"I can make water dance."

"Well, that sounds cool. Show me."

"You don't believe me." She crossed her arms, smearing icing everywhere, and glared. "That yanks my skirt."

Laz did a double-take at the familiar saying. For months now, they'd bantered around the idea that Rosie was their great-grandmother reincarnated. 'That yanks my skirt' was her favorite way of cussing.

"I do believe you can make water dance, want to know why? Because my sister, Hazel, can do that too." Rosie's mouth dropped open.

"Really?"

"Absolutely." Laz glanced at Pearl, who had fallen silent but was obviously listening.

"I believe you, too," her grandmother added. "Moving water is a special skill, and it isn't easy. I'd like to see it."

Rosie's face screwed up tightly in concentration as she stared at her water glass. Slowly, one millimeter at a time, the water seeped up one side of the glass and spilled over onto the table. "See!"

After looking at each other, they clapped for her. "Very impressive. What else can you do?" Rosie was going to need someone to guide her magical skills before they got out of control, and she did something she didn't mean to. The younger a person was when their magic came in, the greater the chance of accidentally using it.

"Look." Rosie pointed at the glass. The water crept back up the side and into the glass, leaving only a small wet spot on the table.

"That is so cool." Laz clapped.

"Can you make it swirl?" Pearl asked. "Picture it moving in a circle, like water around the bathtub drain."

After a moment of concentration, Rosie grinned as the water started moving clockwise and a small water vortex formed in the glass. "I did it!"

They were outside playing with the cats when Frank arrived after work. Laz turned to Rosie and said, "Why don't you run inside and get Gramma Pearl to help you package up some cookies to take home. You worked so hard on them that you deserve to have them, and to show your dad."

Rosie raced down the driveway and embraced her father. "Daddy, we made cookies. I'm going inside to package 'em. K?"

"Sure thing. I could use a good cookie, but only after dinner. I brought takeout."

"Yay." She raced toward the house as Laz strolled toward Frank.

Sweet Mother Earth, he was glorious, despite the bags under his eyes.

"Hey, are you okay?" she asked, smiling softly.

"Tired, but good. Rosie had a rough night last night." He sighed and scraped his fingers through his messy hair. "Nightmares."

"About that..." she began hesitantly.

"What about it?" He looked down at her. His expression said he was bracing for something unpleasant.

"You know Celine had some magic, right?"

"She claimed she could see the future. Once, she had a vision that helped the police find a missing child. Though that could have been a coincidence. I've been around this town long enough to know that magic exists. Whether or not my wife was magic is up for debate."

"Actually, it isn't. She was mildly clairsentient. We were working on developing that talent and looking to see if she had other gifts."

"Okay, say I believe you, and I have no reason not to, what does that have to do with my daughter?" His earlier frown deepened, and his shoulders slumped.

"Magic is genetic." She let the statement hang between them.

Chapter Four

Frank jammed his hands into his pants pockets. "Are you saying…"

"Rosie has magic. And, unless I miss my guess, she has a lot of it. Magic comes in between five and sixteen. The earlier your magic arrives, the stronger it is. I was a late bloomer, magically. I think she's going to be a force to reckon with. She needs training and guidance."

"What am I supposed to do, send her to Hogwarts?" His voice was heavy with sarcasm. "I don't know anything about magic." He didn't need this crap.

"Normally, your family trains you. But with Celine gone…I, we, my sisters and I, can help her develop and control her skills in Celine's place."

He scraped his fingers across his face and through his hair. He stopped when they reached the back of his neck. "And these dreams? Are they part of that magic?"

"They could be. They might also be just dreams. But with Celine having some clairsentience, it is possible that Rosie has it too. Though there isn't always a direct correlation between parent and child. The child may have an entirely different set of skills."

He stumbled up onto the deck and flopped into a padded white wicker chair before his knees gave out entirely. "You've said that word twice—clairsenti-what? Tell me what that is. And is that why Rosie's so drawn to you?" He stared up at Lazuli, trying to find answers in her expressive face.

She sat beside him and patted his knee. "Honestly? It could be. I can't say for certain, but probably. Magical people can see the magic in others, though she wouldn't know that yet. At least not consciously. Clairsentience basically means to sense what others are feeling and understand why without being told." There was more, but she didn't think he was ready for a deeper lesson at this point.

He nodded because he didn't have words for the turmoil in his chest.

"With your permission, I will teach her about her gifts." Her hands tangled together until her knuckles turned white.

"What does that entail?" How in the hell was he even considering this craziness? "Is it a problem if she doesn't learn?" Maybe if he ignored this, it would just go away.

"Uncontrolled magic can explode at any time, maybe hurting Rosie or someone else."

"But what harm is there in dreams?" There was something she wasn't telling him.

Laz met his stare for a moment. "It isn't just dreams or premonitions, Frank." She paused.

He wasn't going to like whatever she was holding back.

"She has the power to move water and may have other untapped skills."

"And the fee for teaching her these skills?" he asked when he couldn't think of anything else to say. He could adapt to the idea of magic, and why not? There were millions of unexplained things in the universe.

"Fee?" She reared back like he'd slapped her. "There is no fee," she snapped. "She'll be here anyway. We can work with her on controlling her skills and understanding them. Most importantly, on the secrecy needed to keep her safe."

"Safe from what?"

"From herself, and from others. The witch burnings weren't that long ago. Being a magical is still considered heretical and dangerous."

"Can I think about it?" This was all too much for him to comprehend all at once.

"Of course. But at the very least, try to believe her, and maybe let her show you what she can do. She's quite upset that you don't believe her."

"Can you blame me? Would you believe her if you were in my position?" He hadn't grown up with this stuff, and he'd only learned about it after he and Celine married. It was a lot to swallow.

"I suppose in your position, belief would be difficult. And one more thing? Please advise her to keep her skills hidden from anyone outside the family."

"Ya, I can see why that's important."

"Think it over and let me know. Even if you say no, I'll still watch her after school, and I promise not to teach her without permission." She paused. "I did watch her work with water, just so you know."

"I appreciate the honesty."

H ours later, he lay in bed, staring at the ceiling. During bathtime, he'd asked Rosie to show him her skills and was astounded. She could lift water and float it across the room without spilling a drop and could make it swirl around like a whirlpool. He was as impressed as he was baffled.

Magic was always an ethereal concept. Logically, the brain was capable of way more than was known by science. It had to be...given the size of the brain and how much was mapped, and how much left uncharted...there had to be a use for the unknown portions.

Put that way, was it even magic? Or was it just another skill, like playing piano? Some people could, some couldn't, and others were gifted. The idea brought him comfort as he drifted off to sleep, only to be awakened by Rosie's screams.

He bolted out of bed, nearly tripping on the sheet wrapped around his body. How had he gotten so tangled up? He raced across the hall and into her room.

She sat on the bed, arms wrapped around her middle, sobbing.

"What's up, Rosie Posie?" He perched beside her and drew her into his arms.

"The bad man is here. Lots of them."

"Hey, it was just a bad dream. Nobody is here. I set the alarm. Remember how I showed you it would ring if anyone came in a door or window? You're safe, baby girl."

"Not here!" She glared. "Here."

What the hell did that mean?

"Call Lazuli. She needs to know. Get your phone."

"Whoa there. I'm not calling anyone at," he glanced at the kitty cat digital clock on her nightstand, "at four-thirty-two in the morning. We can talk to her tomorrow."

"No, Daddy, no! Now! It's important." Her words shuddered out on a wave of angry tears. "They need to know."

"I promise, at six-thirty, when we get up, I'll call. Okay." For a moment, he thought she'd resist. Instead, she climbed into his lap and wrapped her arms around his neck in a death grip. He eased her back enough that he wasn't being choked and rocked her back and forth.

After way too long for his peace of mind, her shoulders stopped shaking, her tears dried up, and she drifted off to sleep. Instead of tucking her back in, he lay down on her bed with Rosie tucked up against his side. He covered them with the blankets and lay back, wishing sleep would come.

Remembered rumors of strange happenings around town plagued him. How much was the truth? How many lies? How much was magic?

Trepidation crushed into him, turning his stomach to a churning pit of acid. If his daughter was right, something terrible was going to happen, and they could be right smack in the middle of it.

Lazuli had a point. Rosie needed to know how to control her skills, and he needed to know more about magic…what it could and couldn't do, what he could do to keep his child safe, and especially, just how often these 'visions' came true.

He didn't call in the morning. Rosie convinced him that it was better to talk to Laz in person, so at seven-thirty, they piled into his truck and headed over.

The gates at the end of the driveway opened as they approached. Someone must have seen them coming, even though it was a long way from the house to the gates. Maybe there was a camera. As he pulled up, Lazuli's truck was just backing away from the house. He waved, and she stopped.

"Morning," she greeted them. "I didn't know you were coming over this morning. What can I do for you?"

"Oh, someone opened the gates for us." He paused to gather his thoughts. He should have planned this discussion before they left home. "Can we talk? Is now a good time?"

"Sure, I was just headed to my shop." She nodded across the yard to her enormous shop, as if he hadn't been there dozens of times chasing his daughter. "Did you want some coffee?"

"Um. Sure. That would be nice. I didn't have any this morning. Rosie was anxious to see you."

She smiled down at his daughter; he'd almost swear he saw love in her eyes. Despite his attempts to keep Rosie at home, she spent a lot of time here, and the two had become friends. They headed inside. As always, stepping into the house was...odd.

It was like there was a barrier keeping him out...or something.

He shook his head and frowned.

"You did feel that." She grinned. "Now that you're in the know, as it were, I can tell you the house is magic. We're not sure how, but she's soaked up our magic and seems to be able to sense the intentions of people. The resistance you felt was her judging you. Apparently, you don't mean us any harm, so she let you in."

"I didn't feel anything," Rosie piped up.

Lazuli ruffled Rosie's hair. "I think the house likes you, Missy."

"Yay."

Frank shook his head but didn't comment on the idea of a magical house. He studied the room with new eyes. It looked like a typical family home. Books, pictures, knick-knacks. Maybe more candles than anywhere else, but no signs of magic that he could see. It was so...normal.

Five minutes later, they were sitting down with coffee. Rosie sat beside Lazuli, drawing pictures with the crayons and markers Laz pulled from a shelf in the living room. He stared around the industrial-looking kitchen. "Your kitchen is enormous." He'd been here before, but without her entire family hovering around, the size of the place was much more obvious.

Her light laugh tickled across the back of his neck like a physical touch. "We sell teas and lotions in our shop. In order to do that, we're a certified industrial kitchen. We abide by all the provincial regulations. We had to expand it to fit all our needs, and we certainly can't risk making anyone sick with our products. Celine used to love our coconut mango cold brew tea." She sighed. "I really do miss her."

He swallowed a lump of something he didn't want to think about. "Me too." Her sadness brought forth his guilt over not caring enough. Well, he'd make up for that by keeping her in his heart as best he could, and by keeping Celine's memory alive for Rosie. "That tea was good. I wasn't sure where she bought it."

"I'll give you a bag." She sipped her coffee.

"Where is everyone? Usually, there are people every-where." The question just popped out of his mouth.

"Mom, Trevor, and Gramma Pearl headed to the city for the day. They had a meeting of some sort. I'm not sure where my sisters are." She chuckled. "I didn't think I'd ever say this, but now that they're in solid relationships and not home as much, I sort of miss them."

"I can understand that."

Rosie slammed her marker down. "Daddy, tell her about the bad man."

"The bad man?" Lazuli's eyes opened wide, and she stared at him, then Rosie, and at him again.

"Rosie had another dream last night. She says there are lots of bad men…and they're here. She didn't specify what here meant. Not at our place, but here." He shrugged. He wasn't sure he believed her dreams were premonitions, but after seeing what she could do with water, he felt it best to give her the benefit of the doubt. "That's why we came over." He sipped his coffee, though acid burned in his stomach.

"Hey, Rosie. Want to tell me about it?" She rubbed Rosie's back.

"The bad men are here, and the bad girl is coming." She shrugged. "They're mean and they want a fight. They want the cup. And the pretty necklace."

C hills scraped down Lazuli's spine. Nobody outside of the family and certain select members of the magical community knew about the necklace they'd found in Chickadee Falls.

Nobody. At least nobody with good intentions.

Rosie shouldn't know about it.

"What necklace is that?" And a cup? She hadn't heard anything about a cup. Wait, hadn't Hazel mentioned Brown demanding a chalice? Shit. She thought they'd found what the people attacking them wanted when they found that damned necklace.

"You know. You guys read about it, then found it in the water. It has a bunch of stones." She scrunched up her face, counting to herself. "Thirteen stones. One big one at the bottom, and matching ones up the sides. But not all the same. It's gold."

It's a good thing Laz was sitting because Rosie had described the pendant perfectly. Even sitting, she felt like she'd topple right over. "That sounds very pretty."

"It is beautiful, but it's bad. Very bad." Rosie crossed her arms over her chest. "You shouldn't touch it. It will make you do bad things."

"That's very interesting."

"Stop pretending." Rosie glared. "You know. Don't touch it. Don't let the bad men have it. It's important that they don't get it. Or the cup. Find the cup."

"Rosie, stop being rude. Use your manners," Frank chided gently.

"But it's important. The necklace and cup make us fight."

"Oh, sweetie." Lazuli drew Rosie into her arms for a big hug. "We'll be super careful, I promise you. We'll watch out for the bad men, and nobody will touch the necklace. It's in a safe spot."

"Wait? What? There really is a necklace?"

Shit. She hadn't meant to let that slip. She swallowed a sigh. "Yes, we did find a necklace. It's weird, but beautiful."

"It's bad!"

"I don't think you need to worry about that. But I promise we'll be careful. And you be careful too, okay?"

"I'll keep Daddy safe."

"How about you call me if there is any trouble? I'll come help."

Frank glared at her. "What are you talking about? Does this have anything to do with the rumors flying around town?"

"That depends on the rumors." She got up and put a few cookies on a floral plate, carried them back to the oak table, and set them down. She refilled their coffee and Rosie's milk and slid back into her seat. She didn't want to reveal the past attacks, but if Rosie was having these visions, she was somehow involved. She nibbled a cookie as she stoked her courage.

Finally, she spoke. "Look, it isn't common knowledge, but our family has been attacked a few times since this spring. We're pretty certain things are finished." She almost winced at that lie. Nothing was even close to finished. "But if Rosie is having visions..." she trailed off, hoping he'd pick up what she meant.

It was bad enough that Rosie was having dreams, but there was no need to add more fear to the problem. At five, Rosie was still basically a baby. She didn't need to be pulled any further into her family's mess.

Frank nodded, appearing to have picked up on her unspoken worry.

She'd always liked that he was smart. Smart, good-looking, a solid family man. He really was everything she wanted in a husband. If only he hadn't been married to her best friend. And if only there wasn't this magical trouble brewing around them.

"I think…I think I want you to help Rosie with her magic. If she has it, she needs to know how to use it properly."

"We can teach her that. And the rules."

"Yay." Rosie bounced in her seat. "I get to be the magic princess."

"Take it easy," Laz placed her hand on Rosie's small shoulder. "The first rule of magic is that we don't talk about it with anyone but family, and we don't show anyone. That's very important."

"But I wanna show my friends." She pouted.

"Some people don't like magic. It scares them. They might get very upset. You have to promise not to show anyone except my family and your dad, okay. If you don't, Gramma Pearl can take your magic away."

Rosie's cheeks went pale, and Frank raised his eyebrow.

"Yes, magic can be contained. Once, when I used my magic to be mean to Hazel, Gramma Pearl took my magic away. So, you have to promise me not to share your magic or talk about it. If you promise that, I can teach you new things. Hazel's the best with water, but I know a bit."

"Can all magic people do what she does?" Frank asked, his fists were white-knuckled, like he was trying to hold back his emotions.

He was probably upset. Scared, angry, worried, and a little bit excited for his daughter. Odd that she couldn't read his emotions.

"Every magical has different skills. Hazel is a water witch. Hyacinth is an earth witch. I'm air, and Amber is fire."

"Fire?" His voice squeaked. "She can control fire. Jesus."

"It's a lot to take in. We'll begin at the beginning. We can work with Rosie on her skills, but you both must learn the rules, the history, and the cautions of magic. You'll need lessons too, even though you don't have magic of your own. You need to know what to watch out for."

"Okay." He sounded resigned to the whole thing.

"It's incredibly rare for a mundane to be raising a magical child alone, but we're here to help you both."

"I guess it's a good thing you're her babysitter now." The slight tremor in his voice revealed his fear and confusion.

She reached out and patted his hand. Electricity shot up her arm. Yikes! It was all she could do not to pull back. "We'll get through this, I promise. It won't be that bad." Even as she made the vow, she knew she lied. Whatever was coming, Frank and Rosie were about to get caught up in it.

Chapter Five

"Well, that was awkward," Lazuli grumbled as she climbed out of her truck at her shop. Usually, she walked the short distance from the house to her workspace, but she had errands to run later. Specifically, she had to run to Frank's lumberyard for some oak beams for table legs.

"It'll work out," she reassured herself. "You just have to stop lusting after Frank." As if that was possible. "He was your bestie's man. He's not for you, no matter how much he calls to you." People might think she was weird, talking to herself, but sometimes, it made it easier to work through her problems. Today, it did not.

Life sucked sometimes. She was twenty-six. She had a very successful business, but she'd always imagined she'd be married with kids by now. Being a carpenter would allow her to stay at home with her children, and she was looking forward to it. If only she found a man.

A vision slammed into her head, and she dropped to one knee as a sweet image of her, Frank, and Rosie staring down at a tiny baby wrapped in a pink blanket. A daughter. Her daughter. She struggled to her feet when the image faded, tears streaming down her cheeks. She couldn't believe her heart and the Goddess had pulled that vision from her dreams. It wasn't real. It wasn't a premonition. They'd never be her family. She'd have to accept their friendship...that's all it would possibly be.

Vision still blurry, she stumbled toward her workshop. One of the ravens who hung around the yard cawed loudly from the rooftop. She cawed back, and still looking up, she jammed the key at the lock and missed. The door pushed open.

"What in the world? Why is the door open?" She'd locked it last night. She was extra vigilant about locking up. It was a bit of an obsession since she'd purchased her first table saw. She had hundreds of thousands of dollars in tools, wood, and finished projects inside. She'd been woodworking since she was six, sold her first whittled statue at eight, and began buying her own tools at twelve.

"Someone's been in here." *Maybe one of her sisters?*

She paused in the doorway, deciding whether or not to call the police and report a break-in. She toed the door all the way open, but stayed in place, outside, as she studied her space looking for anything that might be missing. All the major equipment was where it should be.

Wait. Her belt sander wasn't in its designated slot, and some of her chisels were out. She never left tools out at the end of the day. Ever. There was a sheet of sandpaper on the floor. *Someone was here!*

She pulled out her phone and called Leticia Stone, a fellow magical and head of the local RCMP detachment. "Hey, It's Lazuli. Someone's been in my workshop. I don't think they're here now, and from the door, I can't see anything missing. But stuff's been moved."

"Move to a safe place and stay outside. I'm on my way. This could be connected." The chief was also a member of the Witch's Council and fully aware of all the attacks against her family.

"I'm not seeing any magic left behind. Not even on the doorknob. I can't see anything that says magic, light, or dark. It might be random, but they did get past my protective wards." Magic wards, created with a magic spell, flowers, ribbons, herbs, and sticks or wreaths, weren't perfect. But they did deter most people with bad intentions. Most non-magicals would be deterred from entering.

Whoever entered her space hadn't come through the front gate, that's for certain. Their main gate was full-on magical and only opened if a guest's intentions were good. It was impossible to protect large tracts of land, like theirs, so they focused protection on the obvious entry points and had thick hedges of thorny bushes running the entire perimeter. "Maybe it's not related?" she muttered to Leticia.

"Ha. After everything that happened, I'd wager on my Creole grandmother's grave that it *is* related. See you in ten. Stay outside." She clicked off the call.

Laz strode back to her truck. Might as well wait in comfort. Plus, she felt safer behind locked metal doors. Thinking about Rosie's dream, she pulled up her phone, opened a website in incognito mode, and called up the magical dark web. She'd look for chalice lore while she waited. If there was anything to learn about a random cup or chalice, she stood a good chance of finding it here. There were about a thousand chat rooms she could poke her nose into, looking for gossip as well. She'd have to see if Leticia had any magical cops who could do a proper search. Wood and air were her mediums, not technology. In recent years, she had heard rumors of technology witches; evolve with the times, she guessed, but she'd never met one. If such a thing existed, her friend would have access. Fifteen minutes later, she entered her workshop, right behind Leticia, who was in her casual clothing of jeans and a fuzzy jacket.

"You're right," her friend and police chief said. "No magic traces. I'm not picking up any magic juju either." She chuckled. "Juju, I can't believe people use that term. The correct term is *maji*." Leticia was a genuine bona fide Voodoo Priestess, complete with dreadlocks. Her brown skin had the clearest complexion of anyone Lazuli had ever met. She was stunning and incredibly powerful. She'd have to be to earn a place on the Witch's Council.

"Well, no signs of magic is a bonus. Probably some kids looking to prank someone. We've had a rash of break-ins and petty theft in town." Leticia turned to look Laz right in the eye. "Something's up. I threw the bones last night." She shuddered. "Evil. Whatever is after you is serious evil. Maybe more than Keres, Brown, and Rylie. It could be MacElroy, and he knows way more than he should. Some artifacts have been discovered missing from the Council's archives. Nobody knows how long they've been gone, but they suspect MacElroy took them before he was kicked off the council and imprisoned. The whole council is on high alert. It's a damn good thing your parents are back."

"Ya, I'm glad they're home. I've been thinking a lot, and I'm not going to stress over this. At least, I'm going to try not to worry." She chuckled wryly. "I'm going to let it happen, and hope I'm prepared for whatever is coming."

They walked past saws and lathes, and planers of differing sizes. The worktops were solid wood. Some were stained and chipped, but they were all dust-free. They circled the entire perimeter, then weaved through machines. Laz pointed out everything that was out of place. The only things missing were two wooden and stone Christmas/Yule ornaments she'd made to sell in the family store. *Who broke in and stole ornaments? Could this just be a scare tactic?*

"Do you know anything about a chalice?"

"Not off the top of my head. Why?"

"Brown was begging Hazel for it, Riley wanted it, and Rosie Perrum is having visions of a chalice. All she seems to know is that it is a cup...not what it's made of or what it looks like."

"Rosie has premonitions?" Leticia stood with her arms crossed over her chest and her expressionless professional face on.

"I guess I should have led with that. Ya. And once we convinced Frank that it was true, and that she could control water, he agreed to magic lessons."

"Good, we can't have any untrained magicals running around Three Moon Falls stirring up trouble accidentally."

"My thoughts exactly."

Leticia's phone rang and she answered it. After a few minutes of quiet conversation, she disconnected. "Well, gotta run. There was a break-in at the jewelry store, and another at the garden center. Seems we have a mini-crime spree happening. Strengthen those wards and let me know if anything else seems off. I'll get my tech wizards researching chalices. The only lore that comes to mind is Christian, as in the cup Jesus drank from, but that doesn't seem to fit."

"Thank you. And check with Danica. She can sometimes pick up things others miss. Maybe she can find something. Watch your back."

"You too." She strode away, leaving Laz alone in her workshop, her senses twitching, and nerves dancing. She needed to relax and focus, or she'd never get any real work done, and the mayor was waiting for her new dining room suite. The sideboard and chairs were finished, but the table wasn't done. That's why she'd planned on going to the lumberyard.

She used her intuition to select the right wood. Sometimes she would reject dozens of pieces before finding the one she wanted. Last week, she'd rejected every piece Frank had. Fortunately, she was a regular customer, she bought almost all her wood there, and he'd been willing to order more in.

Tea. Tea would help her calm down. And maybe crackers and cheese. Protein had a way of grounding her. Honestly, she really could go for a pork chop or two. And a cupcake. Too bad it wasn't even nine in the morning. Tea and meditation, it was. Once she was calmer, she'd head to town.

While she waited for the kettle, she went into the back room and checked that all her rock tumblers were working properly. A couple of batches were due for rotating to a finer grit. Rocks were a passion she shared with her sisters, especially Amber, who had a gift for gemstone magic.

Confident that everything in the rock room was working correctly, she settled at her small staff table in the corner with her tea and snack, then flipped on her battery-powered candles. No real flame here, not unless it was for a project. Open flame and sawdust were a dangerous combination.

She nibbled and focused on the plastic *flame*. Her mind drifted from thought to thought. She didn't try to control where it went; she just let her subconscious guide her. Her brain jumped from this morning's meeting with Frank, to Leticia, to the problems plaguing her family, to the wood she needed. It seemed like her mind would never become still.

She reached out with all her senses. Focusing first on what she could see, physically. On the things around her. The walls, the floor, the table, her teacup. She moved on to scent. Dust, fresh cut wood, the lingering aromas of stain and varnish.

The low growl of her rock tumbles edged into her mind, disturbing the relative silence of the workshop. Outside, a raven called, its squawk loud and penetrating. Ravens were her spirit animals. The strength of their wings and the fall of their feathers spoke to her power to move air.

The warmth of her cup seeped into her icy fingers. She savored the cinnamon taste of her tea and the salty herbs on her crackers. The plastic table cover was rough under the sides of her hands as she turned her full attention to the mock flame and let her eyes lose their focus.

The blur turned to fog, then mist, before clearing.

She gasped.

Through the wavering haze, she saw five people huddled around a table in a dim room. Mounds of books littered the table's surface, and the group argued among themselves. Men? Women? She couldn't tell for sure, just that they were angry. A bulky figure, dressed in black, slammed his very large fists down on the table, with a crack that echoed down her spine, and the vision vanished.

Chills raced across her skin, raising goosebumps. Creeping cold stole the warmth from her body. Even her tea went cold. Outside, the raven screamed again, as if echoing the dark warning of her vision.

Five people.

Holy crow.

Was that what they were facing?

Was this the future? Or could it be the past?

She'd caught glimpses of the past before. Like memories trapped in time. *Was that what this was? A random scene conjured by her stressed mind.*

Pushing out a heavy sigh, she stood and poured out her cold tea. There was no way to know what the vision was, or what it meant. She'd have to be content with knowing that it wasn't pleasant and *could* be a glimpse of the future. Nonetheless, her nerves continued to thrum.

By the Goddess," she grumbled aloud. "I can't let this get me down."

She reshelved all her tools and, after a quick final sanding, applied finishing oil to a bedside table she had contracted to build. Stepping back, she examined it from all angles, looking for flaws. Satisfied that it was perfect, she turned her attention to another project. Keeping her hands busy kept her from worrying too much.

The persistent beeping of her alarm warned her it was time to head to town. She'd hit the lumberyard to find the perfect four-by-four posts for the mayor's table and then pick up Rosie at school. Her stomach growled. "Dang. I need to stop skipping lunch." She grabbed a granola bar and her crossbody bag before she checked all the windows, carefully locked up, double-checking all three doors, and confirmed that everything was secure. She had doubled her wards earlier.

L az strolled up and down the aisles of lumber, inhaling the deep woodsy smell of cut wood. Every sheet of plywood, every two-by-four, even the cut-offs, had unseen potential. She could stay here all day. The posts she needed wouldn't be on the floor. Frank had promised to set them aside until she'd taken her choice. Though she only needed four, he'd ordered a half pallet. There wasn't much call for oak posts in Three Moon Falls. As far as she knew, there was only one other serious woodworker in town.

Frank was good that way. Last year, he'd ordered her some African Blackwood and some Sandalwood for a custom chess table. She didn't know if he treated all his customers so specially, but she made sure he knew she appreciated it when he went out of his way for her.

Footsteps sounded behind her as she was studying a slab of live-edge pine. She turned to make sure she wasn't in anyone's way, a soft smile breaking over her face.

"Frank. Hi."

"Afternoon, Laz." He smiled back, making her toes tingle.

She shoved her attraction into a mental box. "I just popped in on my way to get Rosie. Thought I'd pick up those posts." She couldn't help but run her gaze over him. He wore snug jeans and a black button-up work shirt with the lumberyard logo on the breast pocket. The outfit nicely emphasized his lean hips, long legs, and broad shoulders. Definitely droolworthy.

Give your head a shake, Hawk. She chided herself mentally. *Stop drooling and pick up your tongue.* She pointed to three of the live-edge slabs she had chosen. "I'll take these as well." The longest was twelve feet long, and perfect for the kitchen island Amber and Kody planned in their house. "I'll have to grab those tomorrow. I'll bring in my flat deck."

"Perfect. I'll have the guys set them aside for you. You're taking the posts today?"

"I am. Take me to your lumber."

His deep laugh rumbled down her spine and lodged in her belly. Her breath whooshed out unbidden. She'd swear the man got more potent every day.

"What do you have planned for my daughter today?"

They walked side by side, and she tried to ignore when their hands or shoulders brushed. "Um." She cleared the nervous lump from her throat. "We'll work on honing her skills." She paused. "I'd like to have you both over to discuss some basics and rules. I've also got a great book for you to read...if you want to."

"About," he looked around to be sure they were alone. "About her skills?"

"Ya, just the basics."

"I'd appreciate that." He stopped and turned to face her. He reached out and squeezed her shoulder. "Thanks for this. For all of it. For babysitting, for being there every time Rosie runs away. For teaching her the things Celine can't."

He blinked several times, and she realized he must really miss his wife. Her chest ached at the thought.

"I mean, Celine would really appreciate it." He squeezed her shoulder again and dropped his hand. "You're a good friend, Lazuli. A really good friend."

Irritation stabbed at her heart. She didn't want to be his friend. Of course, she couldn't be anything more, even if so much of her wanted to.

Chapter Six

F rank swallowed a mental groan. *Seriously, Perrum? You just friend-zoned her?*

It was the right thing to do. He wasn't interested in a relationship. He had a child to worry about. Besides, Celine deserved the respect in death that he hadn't quite managed in life. He should have tried harder to love her. He should have loved her more.

"Everyone needs more friends," Laz replied.

There was something in her voice that bothered him. She wasn't disappointed to be shoved into the friend zone...was she? Nah. He was imagining things. He led her through the store into the back room, where he showed her the posts. She had twenty to choose from.

"I ordered them from Ted Larson, from out by Little Smokey. He has a personal mill. He dries his own wood and cuts it himself. His great-grandfather planted a small oak forest. He harvested some of them a couple years ago. The logs are naturally dried, indoors, then cut."

"Wow. I had no idea we had anyone growing locally. You've got connections."

"I'll be happy to introduce you." He wasn't sure why he said it. He'd be cutting into his profit margin by eliminating himself from any future deals.

She considered the idea. "You know what? I'm quite content to order through you. It might cost me a bit more, but we've got a good personal and working relationship, and friends don't cut friends out. Right?"

Her generosity touched him. "I appreciate that."

He'd known she was kind. Celine had often talked about the good things Laz and her family had done. They'd been close friends, and his wife hadn't been one to tolerate crap from anyone. Frankly, he was surprised she hadn't left him, though after she passed, he'd discovered a letter from a lawyer that contained divorce papers. He was both hurt and angry at her, not that he didn't deserve it.

"Have at it." He gestured toward the pile.

She rolled the first one over and examined it from all sides. "Nice grain in this one. It's a definite maybe."

He chuckled at her self-deprecating smile. "Let me set it aside for you."

Twenty minutes later, she had selected eight pieces. "I'll take all of those."

"Perfect. I'll put those, and the live-edge slabs, on your account." She paid monthly. Having her not go through the register allowed him to discount her purchases without his staff knowing. Three Moon Falls wasn't tiny, but it was enough of a small town that people talked, and there was no sense stirring up trouble by having half the town realize not everyone paid the same prices. Laz was one of half a dozen people who were also commercial clients who got a discount. He'd prefer to keep that private.

"If you pull your truck into the loading bay, I'll have the guys load those for you. Or, if you give me the keys, I'll get them to pull it around, and I'll buy you a coffee. If you have time."

She glanced at her watch. Funny that it was an actual watch. Most of the women he knew wore fitness trackers instead. "I can manage a quick coffee. Here? Or did you want to run to Brewsters?" Brewsters was the local coffee and tea spot. They served all sorts of beverages and had several featured dessert items every day.

"Why not in my office, if that works for you?"

She shrugged like she didn't have an opinion, but her soft smile said she was fine with the office.

"I've got some great new coffee flavors for my single-serve brewer. There's a caramel pecan that's to die for. Especially with a shot of vanilla syrup."

Her laugh rang out, and several heads turned their way. "Why Frank Perrum, I never had you figured for a froufrou coffee guy."

"I blame Celine." He chuckled. Fancy coffees had been one of the few things he and Celine agreed on. He leaned closer to Laz to whisper, "Don't tell anyone, but I'll even drink…" he paused for dramatic effect, "fruity tea."

Immense pleasure over her second laugh filled his heart. There was just something about her…

He shoved the thought away and called out to a passing staff member, "Hey, Jamieson. Can you pull Lazuli's truck around to the loading bay?" He pointed out the posts she needed and then told him to put the three live-edge slabs aside and label them as sold. After that, the remaining posts could go onto the sales floor.

"Sure thing, Mr. Perrum," the red-headed twenty-something youth replied, as he took her keys, then hurried off.

"Didn't he graduate high school last year?"

"He did. He's doing his first year of university online. His mother is unwell, and his father is serving out his last few months in the military. He's stayed home to help out."

"Admirable. I'll have to make sure Gramma Pearl knows to check in on them. You know, to see if they need anything, or any extra help."

"I check in on them every couple of weeks, but I can see where his mom might feel more comfortable with a woman."

"True enough. How long has she been sick?"

"Since late summer. I'm not sure what, or how." He waved her toward a set of metal stairs. "Up here."

He watched her skip up the stairs, and it occurred to him that she must be pretty fit. There were days when dragging himself up the steps to the mezzanine was almost more than he could handle. Especially after Rosie kept him up all night.

After unlocking the door, he gestured her inside.

The room was brightly lit, and at twenty by thirty feet, it was more than enough room for an office. Eventually, he'd need to bring in another desk and hire a new assistant manager. His previous one had left when her husband had gotten a better job in the city.

"Wow! This place is enormous." I love that it's like an office and a mini apartment."

"We lived up here for a few months while we waited for our house to be built."

"I remember that. Celine grumbled that you worked all night, every night." She slapped a hand over her mouth. "I shouldn't have told you that. She told me in confidence."

He chuckled. "Trust me, I knew."

"Was it hard? Being newlyweds, with a baby, no home, and a fledgling business? I imagine that was a lot to juggle." She walked through his space, stroking her hand along the back of the leather couch, and peeking behind the room divider that hid the queen-sized bed he hadn't bothered to get rid of once they moved into their house.

She paused and looked out the window, down onto the sales floor. "Who's that?" She pointed.

He walked over to stand beside her. "Who?"

"That guy? In the black jacket."

He watched the man for a minute. "I'm not sure I've ever seen him before. Why?" She didn't say anything for several minutes, as if she was debating what to say. "Why, Laz?" He pushed for an answer since her silence was unnerving.

"Look, here's your first magic lesson. You can't see it, but magical people are easy to identify to other magicals. At least they usually are. That man," she continued to stare at him, "is dark. Like black."

"How can you tell?" He watched his customer, unable to see anything different about him. After a moment, the man headed to the front exit and left the store.

"Magic falls into three categories. Black, white, and gray."

"Okay. Coffee?" He interrupted because he needed coffee to steady his nerves.

"Yes, please. Anyway, white magic casters sort of sparkle; black casters, who usually don't care about what harm their magic might do, are dark, like they suck in all light. Gray casters are sort of a mixture, depending on which side they lean to."

He mulled over her words. "And he was black?"

"The blackest I've ever seen. Though the color is more like a shadow than true black. I wish I had a photo of him for the council."

"The council?" Clearly, there was more to magic than he'd ever imagined. "What's the council?" He tossed a pod into the brewer and hit the button.

"There's a Witch's Council. One of their roles is to police magical happenings. They rarely interfere, unless things are terribly out of control. There have been some things going on in town..."

"I've heard rumors."

She nodded. "The council is keeping track. They'll want to know he's around. Before now, there were no black casters in town, at least none that I know of. Though there are a few very dark gray casters."

He scraped his fingers through his hair and kneaded his neck to ease the tension there. He had a bad feeling about all of this. "How does this affect Rosie and me?"

"Rosie will learn to see the shimmer, or the darkness. I'll, we'll, teach her to avoid the darkness or the gray. You'll have to trust her to tell you who to watch out for."

"Watch out for? Why?" His fingers shaking, he added syrup to her mug. "Cream?"

"Sure. Please."

His unsteady hands nearly caused him to spill the cream while pouring. He passed it over.

She must have noticed his trembling. "Look, don't fret too much. All this has been happening your whole life. And probably since humans began to walk upright...depending, of course, on your world view."

She settled on the sofa, her body turned away from the windows. Her smile was reassuring, though he couldn't say why. "I suppose...." He trailed off, not sure what to ask next.

"The important thing is to keep Rosie safe and to train both of you properly. We can help with that. And if she says things that seem crazy, try to believe her. I don't think she's a fanciful child, at least not any more than most kids. She'll be sensitive to things you can't see, and quite frankly, can't even fathom."

"Like the moving water thing."

"Exactly."

Dread filled his heart. Being a single father was trouble enough. He snorted.

"What?"

"I was just thinking that I'm in over my head as a single father. Now, my kid controls water, and I'm drowning." He snorted again. "The irony is incredible."

"The Goddess has a sense of humor. And by Goddess, I mean the power that connects all things."

He nodded, appreciating that she was willing to simplify things for him. She was a good person. At least that's how it seemed to him. Sure, there were rumors about her and her family; some were probably true, but she'd been a good friend to Celine and was always there for Rosie. Look at how she stepped up to babysit. He couldn't think of many people who would do that for a neighbor.

"Here's what I propose for you guys." She took a slow drink from her mug. "After school, we'll spend time working with Rosie to build her skills. I'd like to spend a couple of hours a week with both of you, to learn the rules."

"That works. I have Tuesday and Thursday evenings free. I could maybe fit in some time on Sundays as well."

"Sure. I can work with that."

"Thanks." Again, he couldn't believe how kind she was being. Kind, generous, good-looking, smart, compassionate. If he were looking for a woman, she'd fit the bill nicely. Heaven knows, Rosie sure liked her. And her subtle, earthy sexiness was almost irresistible.

He pushed his attraction aside and, after taking a seat on the sofa, sipped his coffee.

An idea hit him. "I could check my security tapes for a picture of that guy. I have them focused on the front door, both inside and out."

And the back door and gates to the yard, but as that didn't play into what she needed, he didn't bother to mention it.

"Brilliant. I'd appreciate that."

He had a separate computer for security, not that there was much call for it in Three Moon Falls. Still, it had helped prosecute a habitual shoplifter last year. "Over here." He led her to a small cabinet in the corner. He opened the doors to reveal a computer and six monitors. He slid out the keyboard tray and started typing.

"That's cool. I had no idea, I thought it was an entertainment unit, though it is in a weird place."

He chuckled. "Exactly what I wanted you to think. My staff knows I have cameras throughout the store, but not where the video feeds go." He made some adjustments to find and save the feed he wanted.

"I'll run it at triple speed."

"Makes sense as we have no idea when he arrived."

He began playing ten minutes before they saw the man. Everything looked fine. People came and went. Some quickly, some more slowly. Two of his staff members helped a customer outside. Suddenly, the feed went fuzzy. "What the heck?"

He rolled it back and played it at regular speed.

"That is so weird," Laz said. "It has to be him." They watched for a few more minutes. The feed blurred again, just about the time he'd left. "Do you have other cameras inside?"

"I do. One for each aisle." He began checking them.

"Why so many cameras? It seems excessive for a lumber store."

"I inherited a large chunk of money. One of the caveats was that all my assets had to be protected by video. My grandfather was..." he hesitated. "He wasn't always on the right side of the law, or at least I suspect he wasn't quite on the up-and-up."

She made a sound of amusement.

"I debated rejecting the money...you know, blood money, or bad Karma, that type of thing. In the end, I donated half to the children's hospital. I figured the donation was a way to pay back the wrongs he'd done." He shrugged. I kept the rest, leaving me just enough to pay for university, buy a house, and buy the lumberyard."

"I like that."

"Me too. Though he's probably rolling in his grave over the donation. When I set up, I followed the caveat and put in cameras, here and at home. I just never got around to getting rid of them."

"Lucky for me. While there's no image of him, at least we're forewarned that he can mess up cameras. Any chance of me getting a copy of that?"

He shrugged. "Sure. I'll copy all the feeds for you." He put everything on a thumb drive and handed it to her, just as her watch beeped.

"Oh, gotta run. I don't want to be late picking up Rosie." She waved the small drive. "Thanks for this. I'll give it to the council. It might come to nothing, but it might help."

"Glad I could be of assistance."

"I appreciate it. Thanks for the coffee, and for having that wood loaded. I'll be by tomorrow for those live-edge slabs." She set her empty cup on a table.

"I'll walk you out, and I'll grab some dinner and bring it by your place after work, so we can get started on my education." Somehow, he knew he should be worried about the strange man and messed up video feeds, but instead, he was looking forward to seeing her again.

Another thing to worry about.

Chapter Seven

Lazuli couldn't help but laugh at Rosie's enthusiasm as she played with water, filling one cup from another without touching either. She was incredibly talented and a joy to work with. She could move it drop by drop, or in a river-like flow.

They sat on a denim blanket in the sun in the front yard. It was a beautiful fall afternoon, and Laz wanted to enjoy every second before winter reared its frosty head. It was warm enough to forgo a jacket, so they were both wearing long-sleeved fleece hoodies. Rosie in her favorite color, pink, and Laz in a green-gold tone.

"Listen, do you hear that?" Both cocked their heads to hear better.

"Chickadees, robins, and I think a blue jay," Rosie said.

"Perfect." They high-fived.

"Sometimes, when we come over, big black birds fly past the truck."

"Those are ravens. We have a family of ravens living by my workshop."

"They're huge."

"Yes, they are, but if you don't bother them, they won't bother you."

"When will the babies come?" Rosie asked.

"What babies? Oh, the ravens' babies have already left the nest for this year." Except for Cynthia, nobody she knew was pregnant, and neither were any of their cats. Her sister's dog had been spayed as well.

"Not the ravens, Miss Hazel's babies."

"Miss Hazel isn't pregnant. She's not having a baby any time soon." Idly, she wondered if this was a premonition or just a young girl fascinated with babies.

Rosie leaned in close and whispered, "She is having two babies. *I saw it.*"

"Did you dream about it? Sometimes dreams don't come true. So don't be disappointed when it doesn't happen."

"I didn't dream it." She glared and stomped her foot. "Why don't you believe me? I saw it."

"Tell me about seeing it." Perhaps it was a premonition. If so, her sister was in for a surprise. She wasn't trying for a baby right now; Hazel was still settling into her relationship with Dennis.

"Sometimes, if I sit very still and look at my toes in the bathtub, I get pictures of things that will happen. I saw my teacher being sick last week. Last night, I saw Miss Hazel holding two babies."

"Maybe they were someone else's babies. She does have friends with babies."

"Nope."

"That's interesting. Should we ask her about it?" Water divination was relatively common among magicals, so it could be true.

"No! She doesn't know yet."

Laz mimed zipping her mouth closed and mumbled, "My lips are sealed. I'll keep the secret." If her sister were pregnant, there was no sense spoiling the surprise for her or the family. If she wasn't...the 'vision' meant nothing, as they sometimes did. She'd definitely have to work on teaching Rosie to judge between dreams, visions, and hope. And to realize that not every vision came true.

"Let's try something new while we wait for your dad to get here with dinner."

"Pizza and salad." She wrinkled her nose at the word salad.

"You don't like salad?"

"He got the onion one. I like see-zur salad 'cause it has bacon."

"I love Ceaser salad too, but I like onions in my salad too." Unless she was on a very rare date. She didn't want to be kissing Frank...er, anyone, with onion breath. Her heart pinched in longing. Not happening. "Let's talk about the things you see...about your visions. How often do you see them?"

"Sometimes lots. Sometimes not much."

Typical of visions, except for the strongest seers. But, also, very uninformative. "When do you see them? What are you doing?"

"Sometimes the dreams wake me up. I don't like those. They're scary. Or I remember when I wake up." She sighed, and the water in the cup danced and bubbled.

Definitely time to teach her to channel her emotions, or she'd set off a reaction she couldn't control. That had been one of Laz's hardest lessons. She'd accidentally called in a small plow-wind that took out a swath of trees in the northwest corner of their property.

"Look at the water? See it bubble? That's because you are upset. It's important to know that your emotions can change water. Take a deep breath, Rosie."

She took an audible breath.

"Hold it in and let it out slowly." She demonstrated, and her young charge copied her. "See how the water goes still?"

"Ooh. Can you do that?"

"Not with water, but I do have visions. Sometimes lots of them. And I can make the wind blow." She called in a soft breeze and made it swirl the last of fall's leaves that lay on the grass where they worked. "Have you ever heard of a tornado, or been in very strong winds?"

Rosie nodded.

"That's what happens when I don't watch what I feel." She took a breath as she struggled to explain. "It's okay to feel things. Good things, bad things, scary things, angry things. That's all okay, but you have to watch...no, *we* have to watch, so that we don't let those feelings go crazy or we could damage things or hurt someone."

"Oh." She hung her head and sighed as she traced the patterns of their blanket.

"Did you do something like that? It's okay if you did, because you didn't know."

"I...I was mad. Nanny Grace got splashed by hot water when she was making tea."

Laz pulled Rosie into a snug embrace. "Oh, honey. That might have been an accident. People spill hot water all the time. I might not have been your fault."

"It was. I was glad, because she shouted at me."

"How do you feel about it now?"

"I feel bad."

"See, you learned your lesson. Now, you know better. Let's practice some calming breaths while we wait for your dad and our pizza."

They practiced for several minutes before Rosie spoke again. "Miss Hyacinth is going to have two baby girls."

"I thought you said Hazel was having twins." Laz raised an eyebrow. The odds of both Hazel and Cynth having twins were astronomical. There were very few twins in the Hawk line. They weren't nonexistent, just rare. "Well, let's just keep that our secret. We can tell Daddy, but no one else. It is a good secret, but it is Hyacinth and Earl's secret to share, not ours. Same with Hazel. We won't tell anyone."

"I know, good secrets, like when Grandma Perrum visited and we got Daddy a birthday present."

"Exactly. Now," she rubbed her hands together, "let's try a new thing. Did you know there's water in the ground?"

"Yup. From when it rains. But sometimes, it gets very dry because the sun and wind suck up all the water, and the grass hurts and turns brown."

"Exactly. Close your eyes and think about that water. See if you can feel it." After another ten minutes, Rosie could find the water but couldn't yet pull it from the ground. They needed Hazel here to help; she was the water witch. Rosie was getting frustrated. Fortunately, Frank's truck pulled up the driveway.

By the time Frank and Rosie left, Laz was exhausted. It was hard to make a young child understand the rules and why magic needed to be secret. Frank struggled hard to keep up, but disbelief could be difficult to overcome, especially when the subject of ghosts came up.

"How can my house be haunted? Rosie says there are wavy people she talks to."

"Ghosts are a tough one. We have ghosts in our shop. There's one in the bookstore. All those ghosts in the book we wrote about the Three Moon Falls ghosts are verified. But...ghosts aren't just attached to places; they can be attached to an object they were particularly close to. A favorite book or chair. A pendant. Basically, to anything."

All the color drained from his face. "I have my sister's rocking chair...from when she was three...before she died."

"That could be it."

"But why is she here? And not," he waved his hands in a vague somewhere else motion, not wherever."

"Some ghosts refuse to pass. Some have unfinished business." She took a deep breath and made sure Rosie was distracted by the Lego she played with. "The thing is, if they're around for too long, they can go mad. There are ways to help her move on. Hazel can help with that."

They had discussed the matter for a few minutes. In the end, Frank decided to sleep on any decisions. He was visibly upset, which made her wonder how he'd feel if he knew that her family believed that Rosie was their great-grandmother reincarnated. She didn't bring it up; there was no sense stressing him out. The Goddess had made ghosts for a reason, and while she didn't understand that reason, she wasn't going to question it.

She pushed the subject out of her mind. It was time to relax with a cup of tea and something sweet. Confetti squares, the ones made with colored marshmallows, peanut butter, and butterscotch chips, straight from the freezer, were a favorite treat. She piled a couple of squares, a sliced apple with dipping caramel, a piece of cheddar cheese, and two gingersnaps on a delicate plate patterned with bright purple irises. She carried her tea and snack into the living room and settled on her favorite end of the sofa. As much as she'd like to read, she opened her tablet and began searching for chalice lore.

Something poked at the back of her mind. Something she should remember. Try though she might, she couldn't bring the thought into focus. She let the pestering feeling float away and dove into her research.

If there was a chalice, she'd find it. Somehow.

Chapter Eight

"What's up, J.Z.?" Frank strode through the chilly fall air across the lot to his sixteen-year-old employee's side. "What can I help with?"

"Hey, Mr. P." The youth returned his greeting and nodded toward a well-dressed man with a sallow, gray-olive complexion. "This gentleman has questions that I can't answer. I thought maybe you could help him." His voice shook, like he was nervous.

Frank clapped the boy on the back. "Thanks for calling me." All his staff wore pagers during their shifts, including Frank.

He turned toward the man and offered his hand. "Frank Perrum, owner of Jensen's Wood Products. How can I help?"

"I was looking to get some work done." The man ignored his outstretched hand and seemed reluctant to meet his eye. "I've heard that the Hawk woman does woodworking. I was looking for her contact information."

Frank turned to J.Z. "You can go now. I'll handle this." He smiled so the boy understood he wasn't in trouble. "Please, come and see me upstairs after your shift ends." He'd reinforce the fact that J.Z. had done the right thing in calling him. He smiled again and waited until the boy nodded and walked away. "So, you need some carpentry done?"

The stranger nodded, but didn't offer anything more, not even a name.

"Unfortunately, we don't give out those numbers unless the contractor or business has added themselves to our list. It's available on our website." Something about the man set his nerves on edge. *Why would he approach a kid in the lot rather than come into the store? Intimidation?* "However, the Hawks haven't put themselves on that list."

"You must have her information. I know she shops here."

How would he know that? Creepy.

"I don't have anything I can share. I do know she works by referral. Perhaps you can find someone she's worked with to get one?" Total crap, but he was going with it. He wasn't sharing any personal information. Especially not after Laz was so worried about the strange man the other day. He decided not to add that Lazuli's sister ran the new metaphysical store. What the man didn't know wouldn't hurt Laz and her sisters.

"Was there anything else you needed? If not, you're welcome to check our website for other contractors." He made his tone dismissive, but not rude.

The man turned and walked away. Frank didn't move until the man left the yard and headed into the parking lot. Though he wasn't usually the nervous type, he hurried inside and upstairs to the office. "Who the hell are you?" he muttered as he fired up the surveillance system and scrolled backward to when the man first appeared.

"Well, at least you show up on video." He took a snapshot of the man's face and texted it to Laz. Maybe it wasn't important, but his gut feeling and inner chivalry told him to warn her.

Frank: *Hey, this guy was asking for your contact info. We didn't pass it on but thought you should know.*

He stared at the phone screen, waiting. Three dots appeared and disappeared.

Laz: *Weird. Thanks for letting me know.*

Frank: *Do you know him?*

Laz: *Nope.*

Frank: *Is he related to the weird stuff I've heard rumors about?*

Laz: *Not as far as I know.*

He was about to put his phone away when another message came through.

Laz: *You and I need to talk. Alone.*

Frank: *About the weird shit?*

Laz: *Yep. When's good?*

Frank: *After Rosie goes to bed tonight? Around 8. You could come over?*

His heart pounded. Why did this feel like a date...especially when he should be worried about the weird shit?

Laz: *8 it is. TTYL*

It felt like eight would never come. Rosie was grumpy. She'd wanted to stay for dinner with the Hawks. He couldn't—wouldn't allow that to become a habit. Eventually, after too many stories to count, she dozed off, still frowning.

He was just pouring hot water over some tea leaves when there was a barely audible knock at the front door. He hadn't even heard anyone drive up.

"Hi. Come in." He opened the door fully and stepped back. Laz stepped in and shed her forest green woolen fall jacket. She looked beautiful in snug jeans and a green and gold floral Henley. Green was her color.

"Hi. Cool night. Feels like it might rain later."

"That's what the weather app says." As he closed the door, he peeked outside. "Where's your truck?"

"I walked. It's only about half a mile. Maybe a mile."

"But...it's late. Wild animals."

Her light laugh made him grin.

She waved toward herself. "Witch...remember."

"That keeps off bears and cougars?"

She turned serious. "Not if they're starving or protecting their young. Scientists hypothesize that animals can detect magic. That's why we have familiars. They know what we are. Anyway, they'll stay clear, or at least not attack." Her shrug was eloquent and expressive.

"If you say so." He couldn't keep the doubt from his voice.

She made an X over her heart. "Cross my heart, I'll give up pie, stick a needle in my witch's eye." She waggled her brows. "Believe me now?"

"Fine," he said a bit petulantly. "But if you get attacked, don't come crying to me."

She clapped a hand over her mouth, but laughter spilled out anyway. "You sound like Gramma Pearl."

He rolled his eyes. "Come in." As he led her forward, he wondered what she thought of the fact that nothing had changed since Celine died. He didn't have the heart to remove the presence of Rosie's mother, though he'd dearly like to get rid of the feminine, floral furniture and replace it with something sturdier. Fit for a man and an active child.

"What do you want to know?" She settled herself at the kitchen table, her elbows and clasped hands resting on the top.

Unsure as to how much to ask and how honest she'd be, he'd fought with what to ask all afternoon. "Tell me about the weird events, especially any that might affect my daughter." He leaned back against the counter, waiting for her to speak and for the tea to steep.

She swallowed audibly and blew out a breath. "Our family is magic, but you knew that. Descended from the witches of Salem."

He raised a brow to show he was impressed by her lineage. Generally, people were either impressed or thought the claim was bullshit.

"It seems that our family possesses an artifact, probably acquired around the time we fled Salem. People are after it. We don't know why. We just know we had it hid until a dark magician, or sorcerer...if that term feels better for you, came looking for it."

"And?" He poured the water, then carried the teapot to the table and set it beside the cream, sugar, lemon, and honey he'd placed there earlier. He pivoted to grab a bakery box of assorted tarts from the fridge. "Help yourself." He slid a plate and a paper napkin toward her.

"Keres, the magician, attacked us after he blew up the falls."

"He did that with magic?" He snapped his mouth shut to cover his astonishment.

"No, the police think it was good old run-of-the-mill explosives. But his attack on us was magical."

She shuddered so slightly he barely noticed it. Whatever happened must have been traumatic. He recalled hearing something about someone dying.

"He used blood magic. He stabbed his friend to ramp up his own power. He attacked us all. Without Amber's fire magic and the help of Kody and his grandmother, we all would have died. Especially Hazel, he attacked her with a swarm of wasps. She's deathly allergic. The only way to defeat him was to burn him."

Her voice was heavy with regret, and she twisted her hands together. Her beautiful blue eyes turned dark with grief.

"Oh." He didn't know what else to say. "And what does that have to do with Rosie?"

She went on to explain the attacks by Keres' son, Matt Brown. And the one by Rylie, who tried to burn down Earl's bookstore, ending with, "Mom and Dad, he's my stepdad, are home from hunting someone who is stealing witches' power. They're starting to think this is related because someone, we're not sure who, nearly killed a newborn baby in town trying to steal her magic before it even manifested."

"And they could come after Rosie?"

L az jumped when he slammed his hand on the table.

"I won't let anyone hurt her," he declared, his voice heavy with anger and protectiveness.

"That's why it's so important that she doesn't show off her magic. That way, she'll likely go unnoticed. Her sparkle is small, almost nonexistent, and could easily pass unnoticed. Sometimes, a newborn gives a magical shout, if you will, as it's born. That could be how they found the baby, or they could have been stalking her magical mother. I know it's a lot to take in, but you have to listen to her about the people she sees, the ghosts, the visions. All of it."

She reached out and clasped his hand. "Frank, I wish I didn't have to scare you, but until this is all settled out and we find out why all these people are after us, you need to be on your guard. All the time. Every second." She couldn't emphasize it enough.

She didn't want to go on, but she did. "The man who hexed the cameras...he could be involved. He could be innocent. Even the stranger asking about me might be part of this...or maybe not." She was more scared than she let on, but there was no sense in terrifying Frank. It was enough that he was convinced to be cautious and vigilant.

"So, everyone's a suspect?"

"Yep. Basically. Don't trust anyone you don't know."

"How the hell does shit like this happen? Isn't there someone to police this crap? What about that...that council you mentioned?"

"The council has incarcerated everyone who was involved up to date." She took a deep breath before revealing the ugly truth. "Unfortunately, there was a break at the metaphysical prison, and they've escaped. Nobody knows where they are, or if they're still with the others who have escaped. But the Witch's Council is watching for them. All known magicals have been notified to be on the lookout."

"This is like a bad movie. Like all the Marvel and DC villains are working together. Shit. Shit. Shit." He scraped his fingers through his hair and across his beard. It rustled softly, and she wondered how it would feel against her hands, her lips. His arms and shoulders flexed under his heavy T-shirt, and she bit back a groan of attraction.

"You and Rosie are probably safe. Most likely." By the Goddess, she hoped they would be. She'd die if anything happened to either of them.

"And what about everyone else? How many people do I know who are magic? How many of them are going to get hurt? What's the fallout of this? Of your family stealing some damned artifact?" He stabbed a finger in her direction. "Whatever happens, this is on you...on the Hawk family."

His words were a slap to the face. He was one hundred percent right. She tried not to take offense. But her whole body tensed up in offense. Her back straightened, and anger rushed through her.

"You're right." She forced herself to let go of her ire. "But I cannot control what my ancestors did...not any more than you can control what yours did. For all we know, they didn't steal it. Maybe they created the dammed thing. All we can do is try and fix this moving forward. I'm sorry you became involved in this."

He closed his eyes and took several deep breaths before opening them again. "Sorry. I'm just..."

"Scared? Pissed? Frustrated? Terrified for your family?"

"All of the above."

"Ya, me too."

He nudged the bakery box her way, and she recognized the act of apology for what it was. "Thanks. I could use a snack. Strong emotions make me hungry. If I didn't watch myself, I'd eat my emotions until I was the size of a house."

"Your house or mine?" he joked.

"Probably the two combined." His house was only half the size of theirs, but it was perfect for the small family she knew he had been planning with Celine.

"Daddy, I got scared. I had a bad dream." Rosie stumbled in, rubbing her eyes.

"Come get a hug, Rosie Posie."

She climbed onto his lap, looking adorable in her bunny print foot pajamas, and stared at Laz. "Why are you here?"

"What did you dream about?" Frank asked, deflecting the question.

"A bear tried to eat me. It was blue and fuzzy and had big teeth." Her eyes were wide in either terror or excitement.

"That sounds awful," Laz commiserated. "How did you get away?"

"I ran and hid in the creek. I made the water bubble so he couldn't see me."

Not an impossibility, but not likely either. Especially the blue bear part.

"Great work," Frank praised Rosie and rubbed her back.

"You can always beat dream monsters with magic," Laz said.

Behind Rosie's head, Frank raised his eyebrows. Laz nodded subtly. It was true that if someone was pushing into your dreams, you could fight back. Having confidence in magic to envision the win, and to push back with could keep them out. She knew he'd have a hundred more questions once Rosie went to bed.

"Can I have a cookie?" She pointed to the bakery box.

"Not tonight, but you can have some apple slices and cheese."

She pouted. "No, thank you."

They cuddled a bit more. Laz watched, envious of their closeness. They were a dream she had no hope of achieving...at least not any time soon. Frank was a good father, and straight out of her fantasies...both in terms of a family and in physical attraction.

"Can you read me a story?" She looked at Laz.

"That's up to your father."

"A short one."

"Yay." She hopped down and grabbed Laz by the hand. "My room is upstairs. Come on."

Upstairs, she waited for Rosie to use the washroom and tucked her in.

"Read this one." She handed Laz a picture book from the stack on her night table.

Laz snuggled in beside her, trying to ignore Frank, who leaned against the doorjamb, looking entirely too content and sexy. "*The Green Fairy Princess...*" she read until Rosie dropped off, six pages later. She wiggled out from under her, and they went back downstairs and into the living room.

The room was just as it had been when Celine was alive. Delicate floral furniture. Flowery accents, family pictures everywhere. An overflowing bookcase of romance novels, mysteries, and children's books. Aside from the photos, there was almost nothing of Frank in the room.

They talked a bit about the power of dreams, though Frank seemed skeptical. It seemed to take him a while to get a grip on new concepts. She didn't push; she just let the idea rest and changed the subject.

He was entirely too easy to talk to. He listened and asked relevant questions, and talked freely about his life with Rosie, but changed the subject when Celine came up. *Did he still mourn her?* It was only about a year since she passed, and still well within a typical grieving season. Of course, she'd never lost anyone she was truly close with, so she really couldn't judge. She did know that everyone grieved differently.

All she knew was that she was jealous of the caring Frank had for her deceased best friend. She tried not to think about it. Wanting Frank was wrong on so many levels, and her jealousy was even more wrong. Reluctantly, she rose.

"I should go. It's getting late."

"Can I drive you?"

She shook her head in disbelief. "No. Of course not. Rosie's asleep. There's no sense in waking her. I'll be fine."

"Text me when you get home?" His concern for her well-being was touching and sent a jolt of warmth through her heart. "Better yet, talk to me while you walk?"

"Oh, Frank. That's not necessary." His caring was a cozy, warm blanket over her entire body.

"It'll make me feel better." He paused. "Just this once. Next time, you can just text when you get home. Okay?"

Next time? She liked that idea.

Chapter Nine

A chill wind heralded November First. Laz thought back to the quiet, private All Hallows' Eve celebration she'd shared with her family last night. They'd spent some time communing with their deceased relatives. The veil between the world of the living and the dead was thinnest on All Hallows' Eve. They'd asked questions and got no answers about what their foes were up to. It was disappointing to say the least.

Usually, they went all out with the celebration and made it a big party, sharing the season with their magical friends. This year, they'd kept it quiet, but it was still a lot of fun once the ritual of communing with those who had passed was finished.

Last night's celebration left her with a lingering sense of optimism. She wrapped her heavy woolen jacket around herself and tucked her hands into her pockets as she hurried down the street toward Lloyd's bar. She was ravenous. She'd grab a quick bite before heading back to work. She considered Flannigan's and their hearty Irish stew, but Lloyd's made better fish and chips, despite being a bar, and today felt like a deep-fried cod fillet day.

Up and down the street, shops were pulling down their Halloween décor. The witch in her hated to see it disappear. Any day now, Christmas would spring forth. While she wasn't Christian, she adored the love and caring of the season, and the beautiful sparkling lights made her happy.

After skipping breakfast, she dove into work. There were commissions to finish. She'd missed lunch while putting the final coats of finish on a set of bookshelves, then popped into town to grab some sandpaper and mahogany stain. It was pushing three, and she needed food before she got hangry. She was not a nice person when she was extremely underfed.

"Laz, hi."

She looked up. Frank strode toward her like a man on a mission. A large, welcoming smile graced his face below his red pompom-topped beanie.

"Hey, Frank. Where's Rosie?"

"She's at home with Mom. She popped in for the weekend. I thought I'd take the time to get some errands done before heading in late to work. Benefits of being the boss. What are you up to?"

"Lunch. I'm starved. Want to join me at Lloyd's?" The invite popped out before she realized she was thinking about it. In the past week, since he'd talked her home after being at his place, she couldn't stop thinking about him. The way he lingered in her mind was worse than usual.

"I'd like that. I could use a steak sandwich."

"I'm thinking fish and chips myself."

They walked the two blocks, and in no time were settled into a comfy booth on the outer edge of the spacious room. Though it was early afternoon, the place was hopping. Saturdays were always busy. Plenty of faces she knew, and quite a few she didn't.

She smiled as she looked around. She loved the typical bar décor. Solid wood chairs and tables. A few stools at the scarred wooden bar. Dimmable lighting, which was turned up until after five each day. The bar did good business with breakfast and lunch service. Things fell off during dinner, but picked up again early evening. It was the perfect time of day for food. Not too busy, not too loud.

They ordered and sat quietly while they waited for their beer. She did love a good IPA, though drinking was a rare occurrence. She was more of a tea granny than anything else. Slowly, their conversation rolled into memories of Celine. Once their food arrived, they chatted while they ate.

"She loved you," Frank said. "She told me that you gave her confidence she didn't have before she met you. She blossomed when we moved here, and you started hanging out more."

"That's sweet. I think having someone who could reassure her that her visions were real was comforting." She smiled at him. "She loved you so much."

He turned away and mumbled, "I know."

Why was he avoiding her gaze? Weird. Had they fought before she became ill? Laz didn't press the issue. She didn't want to disturb the pleasant atmosphere they were sharing at the moment. Besides, she had no right to delve into his secrets.

"Do you know those people?" He nodded to a table to her left.

"Which ones?" She feigned a stretch and looked the way he indicated.

"The two men. One's wearing a fleece-lined denim jacket. The other's in leather. They keep staring at us. I don't recognize either of them."

After stretching this way and that, she managed to get a good look and to catch both of them staring. "They're strangers. The leather guy is magic. Gray magic. The other is sort of hidden from me. I'm not getting a magical feel, or any other type of feel."

"What does that mean?" Concern etched his words.

"Gray means he doesn't hesitate to work dark magic, but isn't fully dark. Grays will often do magic without caring who it impacts but generally tend toward light or white magic."

"And the not getting a feel for him?"

"It's like looking through a two-way mirror when you know there's something on the other side. You know it's there, but you can't see it. He could be magic, or maybe not. Usually, if a person isn't magic, you can tell, but a few magicals can hide the signs. He could go either way. I just get a sense of him hiding something...but I couldn't say what, or how."

"I don't like the look of them."

She grinned. "There's nothing unusual about them. No bad vibes. I'm not worried." The lie fell off her tongue easily. She was worried. More than she let on. She was good at reading people. She wasn't able to read thoughts, except if her family 'sent' theirs to her. She did read strong emotions, and rarely was she able to catch more.

It was normal to catch a sense of magic, or the lack of it. Something was up with the duo because she couldn't read any emotion from them. Maybe she was just paranoid. All the events of the past few months had made her jumpy. *By the Goddess, was it really only six and a half months? It felt like years.*

She turned her attention back to her fish. It was perfectly cooked. The batter was crispy, and the tartar sauce had a delicious tang. "This is good," she said. "Sometimes I forget how much I love fish. Shellfish, on the other hand, I could eat every day. Coconut shrimp with mango chutney....to die for."

"That sounds good."

Without making it obvious, she kept half her attention on the other patrons of the bar. Most were innocuous enough, and she nodded greetings to those she knew. With a bit of effort, she could see the duo out of the corner of her eye.

"Don't look now," she muttered as she blinked to restore her vision after a blast of bright light when the door to the outside opened. "But the guy who messed up your cameras is here." It was almost comical the way Frank looked while trying not to appear to be looking.

"That *is* him," he grumbled. "What's he doing here?" The question was answered seconds later when he joined the duo. "None of them is the guy who was asking about you. Next, he'll show up and join them." The thought seemed random to Laz, but it was on Frank's mind.

"I wish I could get a picture of the three of them. If Vienna were here, I'd ask her for security footage."

"I didn't realize you knew Lloyd's wife that well." He groaned. "Magical, right?"

"I can't answer that. But she is aware of what's going on. It's too early for Lloyd to be working. He takes the late shift on Saturday. I'll text Vee and see if she can get me the images later." She pulled out her phone and shot off the message.

Her phone pinged almost immediately.

"She's dropping the kids at her mom's house and coming in. Apparently, she was on her way to work anyway."

His brows squinched together. "Is it always like that?"

"Like what?"

"When a Hawk calls, everyone comes running?" He sounded oddly irritated.

"I'm not sure what you mean?" She tried to figure out what was behind his bitter tone and failed.

"Lloyd's wife runs to do your bidding. You told me about how the Chief of Police rushed out, in person, when your shop was broken into. J.Z. stood up for you and later told me that it was important to protect you. You call; they obey."

Laughter bubbled out. First as a chuckle, then growing to a full guffaw. His frown grew deeper and more serious the longer she laughed...which only served to make her laugh harder. Around the bar, people turned to stare. Finally, she got a grip on herself.

"Oh, Frank. I'm so sorry for laughing." She tried hard but couldn't keep the mirth from her voice. "J.Z.'s parents are close family friends. So is Vee, and the chief. That's all. Wouldn't your friends come to your aid if you needed them?"

"I suppose. Are they," he waved his hands vaguely, "like you?"

"I can't and won't answer that."

"Fair enough." His acceptance of her secrecy was grudging at best.

His curiosity was interesting, and his ability to drop subjects he wouldn't get an answer to was impressive. She could see why Celine had fallen for him. "Look, I get it. You're stuck on the outside, looking in. It has to be frustrating. But there's a code, an unwritten code, people like us protect ourselves and each other. A lot of bad things have happened when mixed friendships or mixed marriages fail and people get chatty, or worse yet...vindictive." She did feel for him. Goddess knows she'd spent a lot of time on the outside as a teenager. The magical community in town was large, but not that large. Plus, she'd been homeschooled for years, and that often came with its own stigma. And feeling the least magical in her family was often lonely.

"I actually get it." He nodded toward the men. "What do you think they're talking about? Are they up to something? I have a bad feeling." His mouth dropped open, and he gasped. "Am I having a premonition?"

"Doubtful. Though I suppose you could have latent skills. However, most mundanes' intuition is real. Mother's intuition, women's intuition, a lot of men have it too. Intuition isn't related to magic."

"Okay." He was silent for a long time, and she let him consider all the things he was learning. She'd lived with magic all her life and knew how much there was to understand. There were still plenty of things beyond her comprehension.

Ten minutes later, as they finished eating and were debating dessert, he began asking questions. Simple at first, but growing increasingly complex as his knowledge grew. Fortunately, none of the adjacent tables was occupied and there was no risk of being overheard.

There were magical ways to eavesdrop, though she lacked the skill to use them, but with her senses on high alert due to the trio of men glowering nearby, she doubted anyone could get beyond her perception and listen in. If they did, they were already magical, so it didn't really matter.

"So, dessert?" She asked when he seemed to have run out of questions.

"I should go."

As he didn't sound super eager to leave, she checked her watch and added, "Me too. But, since it's pushing five, there's no rush now."

"Five? Really? Mom will be freaking. I'd better text her." He texted, got a response, and texted again. He looked up and said, "Mom says they're fine and not to hurry back. They're having a tea party. She says, Bring home cookies." He chuckled. "Apparently, I don't have the ingredients to bake with, and they want cookies. But first, dessert."

Vee, looking lovely with her short, curly, dark hair, and wearing a totally impractical and floaty dress, stopped by to ask who they wanted pictures of, and they placed their dessert orders while she was there.

Lloyd's didn't have an enormous dessert menu; after all, it was a bar. There was basic cheesecake with chocolate sauce, apple crumble, and chocolate cake. Vee made the crumble, and the rest were brought in from a grocery supplier.

With decaf coffee and dessert on the way, they sat and stared at each other. She wondered what he was thinking. A sudden chill washed over her, and something freezing brushed across her arm.

She whirled around to see who had touched her. Nobody was there. She glared toward the trio who hadn't left and were sitting around a table full of empty beer glasses. None of them looked her way. They were suspiciously disinterested.

"What's going on?" Frank whispered, barely loud enough to hear.

"Something touched me, and I got hit by a wave of icy cold."

"Nobody was near you." He seemed to grasp that it was magic. "What do we do? Do we leave? Do we stay?"

"We ignore it for now. If they try again, I'll be ready for it...I hope. Maybe I can figure out who it was."

"Funny that the guy who was asking about you didn't approach you. He claimed he needed a job done."

"Likely a story. I haven't received an email through my website. I don't publish my address, usually I meet clients at their place...not just for insurance reasons."

Under the unease of what happened, the appeal of dessert was lost on Laz. She plowed through a third of her apple crumble and asked for it to go when Vee brought them a thumb drive with the images they needed.

Frank checked his phone and looked up at Laz. "Rosie wants you to come meet Grandma. It's okay if you don't feel like it."

"It's no trouble. It's only a couple minutes out of the way. Barely any at all. I can do that before I go home and talk to the fam about those guys. Do we need to grab baking ingredients?"

Chapter Ten

Frank kept one eye on the rearview mirror as Laz followed him home. It was very gracious of her to agree to the visit, just to keep Rosie happy. She'd been an enormous help in purchasing baking supplies. He didn't bake, so he didn't know what they needed.

Rosie met them on the driveway and practically dragged Laz inside. "Grandma, she's here." Her voice warbled with excitement. She kicked off her shoes, flinging them halfway across the entry in her eagerness to get inside.

"Hang on," Laz said. "Let me take off my shoes." She removed her short tan leather boots and set them neatly by the wall. Rosie followed suit without being asked.

Silently, he admitted that his daughter was a bit feral since her mother passed. He hadn't been a stickler for rules at first, and half the time it felt like too much effort to begin enforcing them now. And he wasn't that great at putting his shoes away either. Maybe he could try to lead by example more often.

"Mom, we're here."

She came out of the kitchen, wiping her hands on a polka dot apron. Her hair was slightly mussed, and she had a bit of flour on her left cheek. Her smile was wide and engaging. "Come in, you're just in time for a tea party. You brought cookies, right?"

"And cookie ingredients." Laz stepped forward and offered her hand. "I'm Lazuli Hawk. I live next door. I get to spend time with Rosie after school."

Nice touch, he thought. Rosie hated it when he called Laz her babysitter. She was, she claimed, too big for a babysitter. Laz was her friend.

"Isabel Perrum. Frank's mom. It's so good to meet you. Rosie seems to adore you. It's very generous of you to help out."

His mom eyed Laz with a speculative gleam in her eye. She'd been nagging him to find a girlfriend, or better yet, a wife. While there were plenty of times when he was lonely, getting married again, even dating, wasn't high on his to-do list. When she glanced at him, he rolled his eyes.

"I'm excited for a tea party." Laz clapped her hands together like she couldn't wait.

In the kitchen, the main table was pushed aside to make room for Rosie's small wooden table and four chairs. Set with a tablecloth, dishes, mini-sandwiches, and plates of store-bought snacks, it was an adorable imitation of an honest-to-goodness high tea. His daughter needed more of this in her life.

"This looks ah-may-zing," Laz declared. "Where shall I sit?" She eased herself down into the seat Rosie pointed to.

"I'll grab those cookies." He put the perishables in the fridge and dug through the bags for the cookies. He put them on a plate and joined the ladies at the table.

"So, tell me, Lazuli, what do you do for a living?"

If she was startled by the question, Frank couldn't decipher it. She just talked about making furniture, ornaments, rock jewelry, and a few other things. She rolled with his mother's questions like she was accustomed to FBI-style interrogations.

"Well," his mother said an hour later, "she's lovely. Very nice. Rosie adores her. You could do worse for a second wife."

"Mom! I'm not looking for a wife. I was happily married to Celine. That's enough for me."

"Oh, bull cookies," she snapped. "You were miserable. Oh, you did a good job hiding it. But you married out of duty, and you were never truly happy. The best you achieved with Celine was not miserable, though you hid it well."

"You knew?" *How had she seen it?* He put a lot of effort into hiding his ambivalent emotions. No, he hadn't loved his wife, but he'd respected her, and he was grateful to her for giving him a daughter. He'd treated her well...with caring and compassion, just not with love. Who knows, maybe he wasn't even capable of actual love beyond what he felt for his mother and daughter.

"Son, I don't see you often, but I'm not an idiot. Celine loved you; that was apparent. But it was clear that you did your best, though you didn't love her. I'm proud of you for that, but you can't force love when it simply isn't there."

"Do you think Rosie would have been better off if we hadn't married?" He picked up two floral, china teacups from the table and carried them to the sink. The cups had belonged to Celine's grandmother, but his wife had always used them for tea parties with Rosie.

"I think that's a moot point. We can only do our best. Looking back and wishful thinking serve nothing. I don't even think that Celine noticed, but you're my son. I read the discontent in your eyes."

"Celine knew. After she passed, I found divorce papers dated before she got sick. I don't know that she loved me either. Obviously, she'd had enough."

"Or she loved you enough to let you go." She squeezed his shoulder. "Now, Laz on the other hand...she likes you. I see it in the way she watches you."

"Mo-om."

"Franklin Charles Perrum, don't you *mom* me. She likes you, and I know the feeling is mutual. You should date her."

"Mom, there's a lot of stuff happening right now. Her life is chaos at times." More than he'd ever admit. His mom would freak out if she knew about all the Hawks had been through. He just hoped Rosie didn't tell her about magic.

She sniffed. "I wasn't wrong about Julie Steinbrenner when you started dating her in high school. That girl was just trying to make her ex jealous and used you to do it. I'm not wrong about this. You mark my words." In an abrupt change of subject, she added, "Go spend time with my adorable granddaughter. Supper will be a snack. After that tea party and all those treats, we don't need a full meal. It'll be ready in an hour." She made a shooing motion toward the door and turned her back on him.

Midnight rolled around before he headed for bed with his mother's words ringing in his head. He stood in the bedroom doorway, glaring at the feminine, floral bedding Celine had purchased for their room. He hated it. He always had, though he hadn't complained. If frou-frou bedding gave her pleasure, he wasn't going to grumble. The only piece of furniture he'd put his foot down about was the bed. No poles and canopies allowed. He'd insisted on a solid wood bed. Nice and sturdy. Manly.

In a fit of sorrow and self-recrimination over how badly he'd treated her, he balled up the bedding...comforter, sheets, blankets, decorator pillows, and all...and stuffed them into garbage bags. He flopped down on the bed and cried angry tears for not loving her enough.

He woke with Rosie cuddled into his side; both of them covered with her favorite fuzzy blanket.

"Daddy, you're awake."

"What are you doing in my bed, Rosie Posie?" He tickled her side until she laughed and tickled him back.

"I had a bad dream. I came in. The light was on, and you had tears on your face. Why were you sad?"

"Oh, baby girl." He hugged her tightly. "I was just missing your mom. I loved her so much." The lie was easy. He'd never let her daughter know about his lack of love.

"It's okay." She patted his cheek. "Sometimes I cry too. I miss her." She paused. "Maybe you could get a new wife, and she could be my mom. Maybe it could be Miss Lazuli." Though Laz had told her to call her Laz or just Lazuli, Rosie slipped into formality on occasion.

A new wife...if only it were that easy.

"Mommy really likes Miss Laz."

For the life of him, he couldn't make himself ask if that was a memory. Or if she was talking to her mother's ghost. He couldn't stand the thought of Celine watching him screw up parenting their daughter.

Chapter Eleven

The next night, Laz looked around the kitchen table. Her whole family was there. Her mom and dad, her three sisters and their men, and her cousin Cecily. Gramma Pearl was finishing up dinner and had sent them all to the table to sit while she served. "I'm going to have to take this table apart and make some leaves for it. It's getting crowded," Laz hypothesized aloud.

"We all fit," her mom said.

"True, but sooner or later, babies are going to start coming. And with Amber and Hyacinth in serious relationships..."

"And maybe you'll find a man," Hazel interrupted, teasing as always.

She wouldn't mind finding a man. Maybe someone like Frank. Laz shoved away the vision she'd had of her, Frank, Rosie, and a baby. It was one of those images created by wishful thinking, not a psychic vision. Frank was not for her. "Anyway," she said, "yesterday, I ran into Frank and we had a late lunch at Lloyd's. There were three men there." She explained about the strange video footage, the men, and the stranger asking about her. "I sent the images and footage to Leticia. She's putting her tech guys on it." She sipped her juice. "While we were in the bar, someone, maybe one of those men, touched my arm...though they weren't even close."

Everyone looked shocked or gasped. Her stepfather looked angry.

"It only happened once, but it was definitely a psychic touch." After the outrage died down, she explained how it felt, and then passed around her phone with the downloaded images of the three men. "We have to keep an eye out for these guys. The other weird thing is I can't read anything on them. No thoughts, no emotions. Nothing. If the idea wasn't so ridiculous, I'd say they weren't real."

"Come on, dear," her mother chided, "zombies and the undead don't exist."

"Maybe so, but that's what Keres was trying to do; he was trying to resurrect his dead wife. Who knows what he's up to, now that he's escaped, and who knows who he's with or working for?"

Their unhappy thoughts buffeted her. Reading the family was easy. Too easy, and sometimes their unfiltered thoughts were overwhelming. Everyone had their memories of what they'd been through, and snippets played in her head like movies on fast forward. Usually, it was relatively simple to block the stray thoughts of others, especially family, whose thoughts basically became background noise, like the white noise people used to fall asleep.

"Stop!" She covered her ears, though it was no defense against the thoughts. "You're all projecting too loudly. Tamp it down." Their thoughts were like punches to the brain, and the pain of it all was making her physically sick. Her stomach rolled, and she bit back a dry heave.

One by one, the voices winked out or dimmed. She and her sisters had been taught to guard their thoughts–theirs winked out first. The men's thoughts took longer to fade.

"Thanks." She massaged the pain in her temples. Maybe dinner would help. She'd burned a ton of calories in the few minutes she'd been magically blocking them.

"We also have to research a chalice," Hyacinth, the oldest of her sisters, said. "Rylie kept going on about a chalice."

"Brown did too," Hazel, the youngest, added.

"Isn't it enough that there's a creepy necklace? One that's evil. Why does there have to be something else?" Amber said, her green eyes flashing with anger.

"I can ask my grandmother about chalice lore. She's a bit of a history buff," Kody said. "She loves a good research project." Following the conversation was like watching a ping pong match with six players and three balls.

"What I really want to know," Laz said, "is what's the end game? What is all this leading to? There's more to it than Brown helping Keres reanimate his wife. And what about MacElroy?"

"Refresh my memory on him," Earl said.

"He was caught stealing magic artifacts. He was on the Witch's Council with access to everything. Then he went rogue and blew up an airplane and torched an elementary school with fireballs. Luckily, no one in the school was hurt. But eight people died on that private plane. All of them magical. Three were on the council. Things were in a freaking mess until they captured him. He served eight years and broke out. There are still artifacts missing." Gramma Pearl said, setting a dish of gravy on the table beside the mashed potatoes. "Rumor has it that he had several men working for him, and one managed to get himself assigned to the prison and was instrumental in his escape. I don't know anything about a chalice, though."

Random visions of mud flying, wind howling, water rushing, and people falling assaulted Laz. She groaned in dismay, clutching her head between her hands, the vivid imagery a barrage of color and sound. Mostly screaming. Dozens of visions coalesced into a debilitating cacophony of noise and pain.

L az blinked her eyes and groaned. Her head hurt like she'd been hit by a truck.

"Hey, there you are," her mother whispered. "How are you feeling?"

"What..." she trailed off, her head hurt too much to formulate a question.

"We were talking, and you were overcome with a vision. You blacked out, and we carried you into the living room. Everyone else is in the kitchen. We were worried. You've been out for an hour. *Was* it a vision?" Her voice was soft, compassionate. Laz wanted to crawl onto her lap for a special mom-hug.

"More like a thousand visions all at once." She massaged her head. "I need drugs."

"Gramma Pearl is steeping some willow bark tea."

"Something stronger." It was all she could do to force the words past the agony. She closed her eyes. "Please."

The couch shifted, and her footsteps went away, then came back. Something warm nudged her hand. "Tea's ready, and cool enough to drink. I grabbed some painkillers too."

She accepted them without comment, downed the pills, and chugged the bitter tea. Gramma Pearl refused to add sugar or honey to medicinal teas, claiming it reduced their efficacy. "So sleepy."

"Get some rest. We'll be here when you wake up. You're safe at home, Lazuli. We'll watch over you."

At that moment, she didn't care about anything but sleep and freedom from pain. Later, she'd try to sort out what she'd experienced, though she doubted she'd get far.

Sunlight streamed in the living room windows, and Laz turned her head away from the blinding light.

Whoa! Wait!

It was suppertime last she recalled. Her stomach growled.

Had she been out that long? All night?

"Welcome to the land of the living," Hazel said from the chair across from the sofa. "How's the head? Do you need tea? Drugs?"

"I need to pee." She tried to stand and wobbled on her feet. "Holy broomsticks, I'm weak."

"Whatever vision you had, you screamed and passed out. Here, let me help you."

It was a tribute to how worried her family was when Hazel was being solicitous and not teasing.

Leaning heavily on her baby sister, she made her way into the bathroom and, when she was finished, went back to the sofa. Her mouth tasted like death, but she didn't have the strength to brush her teeth. She'd swished some mouthwash and called it good enough.

Her grandmother bustled in with a heaping tray of food. Hazel pushed a folding table closer, and the tray went on top. "Eat," Pearl demanded. "Food, water, then we'll talk."

She was extremely thirsty, so she picked up the water and started chugging.

"Food too," Pearl demanded, hands on her slender hips. For a woman in her early sixties, she looked darned good. She barely looked forty-five. Magic kept you young. Today, she had dark shadows under her eyes and seemed excessively worried. "You'll give yourself an upset stomach with all that water."

Laz picked up her fork and dove into the delicious plate of leftovers. Too bad she'd missed the roast chicken dinner when it was fresh last night. Hopefully, they'd saved her some dessert. After what turned out to be an early lunch, she rested on the sofa, sleeping off and on all day.

Between naps, she rummaged through what she remembered of her visions but couldn't get anything to come into solid focus. The only certainty was that there was a whole horde of people, magic flying everywhere, and so much mess and blood. And maybe...people dying. She couldn't hone in solidly on that, but she knew it deep in her bones.

Chapter Twelve

"Try again, Rosie." Laz encouraged from where she sat on the deck swing beside Frank. It was a warm fall day, unlike when she was in town the other day. The sun was shining and there were no clouds. It wasn't going to last. Winter would roll in any day now. They'd already had a skiff of snow, which melted, but real snow was due next week, though you couldn't tell by today's temp. It was thirteen Celsius or fifty-five Fahrenheit. Rare for the second week of November. Rare and very welcome. She loved the outdoors, and today was the perfect fall day.

"I can't find the water." She stomped her foot in the grass. "I don't want to."

Laz's heart hurt for Rosie. She'd been trying for half an hour and had yet to succeed in pulling water from the ground. Laz knew the frustration well. It had taken her six months to learn to create a vacuum in a sealed box. She'd never understood why she needed that particular skill. She had never used it, except to stall Dennis's truck. Sometimes it felt like her skills were like learning beginner calculus in high school. Useless.

Hazel, who was guiding Rosie, knelt beside her. "I know this is hard. I think using water is the hardest gift." When Rosie frowned, she hid her smile, though Laz picked up on Hazel's amusement. "It is a gift. Not everyone gets to move water like we do. Laz can't do it. Neither can Amber nor Hyacinth. You are special."

Rosie's frustration was palpable. It beat against Laz like ocean waves...like the water she was struggling to control. Surging and ebbing over and over.

"Hey, Rosie," Frank called out, his tone light. "You do this, just once, and I'll take you for ice cream." In a low voice, he added, "She rarely gets to go to the ice cream place. Maybe that will motivate her. I don't want to discourage her, but we've been here for nearly two hours. While the lessons were fascinating and humbling, I'm getting bored."

"Me too. I don't know how Mom managed training four of us at once. Her frustration must have been off the charts. I do remember her threatening to bind our magic." She chuckled. "I can't say I blame her."

Happy memories flowed over her. And some very rare, shameful ones, where they'd pushed her mom's buttons until her frustration swept over the top and she lost her temper.

Funny, she couldn't feel any frustration from Frank, though he'd admitted to it. She turned her gaze to Rosie and Hazel, but turned all her senses toward Frank, searching for stray emotions. Mundanes couldn't usually control their emotional leakage. Sure, some tamped down their feelings, but there was always spillover.

She got nothing from him. Not one tiny peep or stray feeling.

No joy. No anger. No frustration. No boredom.

A big fat nothing. She focused harder, turning just enough to see him out of the corner of her eye. Reminding herself not to get lost in his handsome profile and broad shoulders, she studied him. Still nothing.

"What's wrong?" he asked.

"Nothing. Why?" She stopped concentrating and tried to relax.

"Your face is screwed up and you're frowning like you want to bite someone's head off." He squeezed her hand where it rested on the swing's padded seat between them. She squeezed back and left their hands joined on the seat. "Are you worried about the strangers?"

"Ya. A bit. And some other stuff not worth mentioning."

"Well, if you ever need anyone to talk to, I'm a good listener."

The offer was appreciated, more so because it was unexpected. "Thanks. I'm good for now, but I'll keep your offer in mind." She focused back on Rosie, in her little blue sweater, her eyes scrunched tight, and her nose wrinkled in concentration.

"Feel the water in the ground. Just like you feel it in a kitchen glass. Ignore the dirt."

"I see worms," Rosie muttered in a disgusted tone. "I hate worms."

"I'm not a fan either," Hazel agreed. "But they are important to Mother Nature. Ignore them, too, and all the other insects."

"There's rocks." Rosie's hands clenched into tight fists, her knuckles going white. "I feel it!" She hopped up and down. "Oh, no. I lost it."

"Yay," Laz and Frank cheered from the deck. She'd done it. Finding the water was a huge step. "I'm proud of you," she called.

Rosie's smile was gigantic. "I'll try again." Her face bunched up.

Laz held her breath, wishing she could do it for Rosie. It was hard to watch her fail over and over again.

"My feet are wet!" She danced around, kicking up the tiny bit of water she had extracted. "I did it."

Learning to push the water back came much easier after having pulled it up.

"Okay," Hazel interrupted the pushing and pulling. "It's time to focus on making it the way we found it. Remember that magic is about balance. We don't want to mess with what Mother Nature created. Push the water back, just so it is where we started. I'll help."

Laz suspected that her sister didn't actually do anything, except supervise.

"Let me know when you think it's right?"

"There. I think," uncertainty filled her voice.

"You got it right. It's just how I remembered. This is why I told you to look carefully before you started."

"I'm proud of you both," Laz called. Hazel was good with kids. She always had been, but working with a frustrated child was no easy feat.

After a quick, nutritious snack to refuel, father and daughter headed out. Laz stared down the driveway long after they passed out of sight.

"You should just ask him on a date," Hazel said, slinging her arm around Laz's shoulders. "You like him. He likes you."

"He was my best friend's husband. Friends don't poach on their friend's man."

"That friend has been dead for a year. I think she'd be happy if you two were together. Who better to raise your child than your bestie? Go for it, Laz. He's a good man."

"Ya, he is."

L az and Frank paused in the doorway to City Hall's meeting room. A podium was set up at the front. It was flanked by chairs on both sides. There were rows of chairs across the floor. People sat and mingled in small groups. The excited chatter was off the charts. The emotions ricocheting around were even worse, but Laz forced herself into the room. She took a seat near the back, and Frank slid into the chair beside her.

"All these people are magic?" he whispered. "Holy shit."

"They are." There were thirty people in the room, including Mayor Quinton, Leticia Stone, two other police officers, and two town councilors. Closer to her heart were all ten members of her family, including her cousin, Cec, who was visiting. Her friends, Mel and Jerry, and Danica sat across the room. To her surprise, Earl's sister, her husband, and their newborn daughter, Anna, were there as well. There was even a face or two that surprised her.

"Okay, let's get this started," Mayor Quinton tapped on the podium. "We'll keep this short and sweet. I'll turn this meeting over to Officer Stone."

Leticia, in full uniform, including flashlight, radio, and pistol at her side, stepped up to the mic. "As you may or may not know, I'm on the Witch's Council. It is my job to keep them informed of local happenings of note. Not the day-to-day stuff, but the big stuff." She took a deep breath and looked around the room. After a moment, she spoke again. "I've called you today to keep you in the loop. None of you is unaware of the major events that have been happening around here. It seems that someone is after the Hawk family. They've done nothing wrong and can't understand why they've been attacked."

A low murmur went through the crowd. Once it died down, she began again. "The council has asked me to report that Vance MacElroy has been seen not far from here."

Laz's heart dropped to her toes and sprang up into her throat. The crowd's fear battered her, heightening her own.

"Mind your emotions," the mayor snapped from her seat beside the podium. "Rein it in."

The punishing feelings ebbed somewhat.

"It isn't confirmed. They're looking into it. But be aware that he may be close." She flipped on a screen, and an image appeared. On the left was a young man in his mid-forties, on the left an older man. "The left is what he looked like when he was incarcerated. The right is a computer-aged and enhanced image of what he could look like now. If you see him, or anyone you think might be him, contact me immediately. Day or night. Don't hesitate. Don't delay. I'd rather chase a hundred false leads than miss him."

"What does he want?" A man yelled.

"Honestly, we don't know. He does have some artifacts he stole from the council, which were never recovered. The people who attacked the Hawks, and then escaped prison, are looking for at least two artifacts."

"How do you escape magical prison?" an unfamiliar female voice shouted.

Leticia raised her hands for quiet. "The security problem they exploited has been rectified and won't happen again. The escapees are looking for two items. One has been called a chalice. The other is described both as a pendant of some sort or simply a talisman. Those are the only details we have on what they're looking for. So, if you have something like that or know of something, let me know. Chalice lore would be particularly useful. I'm talking to you history buffs." She looked directly at a couple of people before going on. "When found, the items will need to be properly secured to prevent them from being stolen." One hand resting on the butt of her gun, she surveyed the crowd.

"Rosie talks about both of those things," Frank whispered, his face so close his breath whispered across Laz's ear.

"Sh. Don't let anyone hear you. Aside from Leticia and one non-magical jeweler, the pendant is a secret."

"Wait! You have it?"

"Sh," she hissed.

His eyes went wide, either at his shock over her potentially having the relic or over her reprimand. She didn't care which, as long as he shut up. There were a few chairs between them and the other people, but some people had what her grandmother called 'long ears'...perhaps even magically enhanced hearing.

The meeting dragged on after the initial reveal. Everyone had questions, dozens of questions. Nobody had answers. It appeared that the mayor and chief of police had only been doing the attendees a courtesy by keeping them in the loop. Plus, a few extra eyes watching for that MacElroy guy wouldn't hurt.

Since his mother had decided to hang out for a couple of weeks, Frank had a bit of free time. He'd been surprised when Laz invited him to the meeting they'd just left. He hadn't known what to think when Celine revealed her interest in magic and developing her growing skills. He sure hadn't expected his daughter to develop the talents she was showing. And now all this other stuff. He had a feeling he was in for a bumpy ride. Especially if he and Rosie kept spending time with the Hawks.

Someone could hurt his daughter to steal her power, and they had that damn pendant, which must be the artifact she'd mentioned when they'd talked in his kitchen.

He should pack up his daughter and get the hell out of town. Get away from what was shaping up to be a showdown. He sighed as they walked toward Laz's truck. He had a business to run; he couldn't just leave. His new assistant manager was good, but not that good. He'd only been on the job for three days.

And, he had Rosie to think of. She needed to learn magic properly. How in the world would an ordinary guy like him find a magical to teach her? Plus, she adored the Hawk sisters. Even though his mom was visiting, Rosie still went to Laz's three days a week. It was a good balance; it kept her happy, and it didn't overburden his mother. In her mid-sixties, his mom claimed she didn't need a rest, but he saw how sometimes Rosie's enthusiasm wore her down. Hell, it could wear him down, and he was only thirty-one.

Besides, a Perrum never ran from a fight...even if they wanted to. He just wasn't sure he was ready for this fight. Was there even a way to win?

Chapter Thirteen

"Did you want to grab some food and go for a picnic?"

Her question startled him. He assumed she'd be headed home for a family discussion after the morning's meeting. Perhaps, no, probably, her family hadn't learned anything new at the meeting since they were at the center of all the action.

Did he want to go on a picnic? He'd rather go hide in a hole until all this was over.

It was incredibly hard to distance himself from Lazuli, even with all the stuff going on. He liked her. A lot. More than he should. And his mother repeatedly encouraging him to spend time with Laz wasn't helping him resist her charms. He gave in to the inevitable. Until this...whatever it turned out to be...was over, he was stuck with the Hawks, so he might as well enjoy himself. "A picnic sounds nice."

"What do you feel like? I could eat anything." She rubbed her stomach like she was starved.

"Greek? There's that new place that opened last month, Pandora's Pantry. I've heard they're good."

"That sounds delicious. I haven't had Greek in years." She beeped the truck open and climbed in.

"Any good picnic spots around here?"

"I know the perfect place. It's close to home." She laughed lightly. "In fact, it's on our land. We can drive right up to it. I even have a blanket behind the seat. I'm always ready for an impromptu picnic."

"That sounds perfect." More so than he wanted to admit.

After picking up food and heading back to her family's land, Laz drove slowly down a rutted path.

"It's a good thing you drive a truck."

"We've been out here with cars, but it's been years. I often walk out. It's gotten overgrown. It's probably time to have the road serviced again. But it's worth all the bumps." She slowed to a stop and shut off the truck. "It's a two-minute walk." After he got out, she flipped the seat forward and pulled out a very flat, clear plastic bag containing an indigo blue blanket.

"Is that denim?"

"You betcha. Burrs don't stick to it, and it's easy to shake the dirt off. Plus, it's super durable and washable." Her smile was radiant. "I sound like an infomercial. But I did make it in high school sewing class. I'm pretty proud of it." Squares and triangles in various colors of denim, from pale blue to navy, were sewn together like a quilt.

"I didn't know you could sew."

"I do. I sew a lot of my clothing. If I'm not wearing jeans, I'm probably wearing something I made myself. I'm pretty good at modifying a pattern into something slightly different. Almost like an instinct. I knit too. And there's probably a lot you don't know about me."

"I'd like to fix that."

She paused and looked over her shoulder. "I'd like to get to know you better, too." Initially, her smile was warm and welcoming, but it faded to perplexion before she resumed walking.

As he followed her down a narrow path, he was torn between looking at the beautiful trees around them and staring at her backside. Those jeans did all the right things for her.

It was a bit creepy to be following her without comment, but the only things his mind would focus on were the weather and what he'd heard at the meeting.

They entered a small clearing with a creek flowing through it. A chill wind blew across his face. It was a good thing they wore warm clothing. The sun shone down weakly, but brightly, and helped take a bit of the chill from the day.

"This creek runs a long way in both directions. Eventually, it feeds into the one that becomes Chickadee Falls."

He paused to look around. The grass was short, not short enough to have been mown, but not super long either. The clearing was oval, about fifty by sixty feet. It was surrounded by a spruce and pine forest. There was even a bench hidden in the trees. She must really like to come out here if she'd brought out that bench.

She flipped open the blanket, and it drifted to the ground nearly perfectly flat.

"Nicely done." He wondered if she'd used her air magic to keep it flat.

"I come here a lot. It's a good thinking space when my shop feels claustrophobic." She sat and kicked off her shoes. "Well, are you joining me, or do I have to wrestle you for the food?" She made grabby hands at the food bag.

He laughed, and she launched herself at his legs. He barely stepped back in time to avoid the tackle. "Whoa. Easy there. I'll feed you. No need to go all starving lion on me. Why are you so hungry?" He sat beside her. Closer than was probably polite, but not as close as he'd like to be.

She looked thoughtful as he handed her one of the takeout boxes. They'd ordered the same thing. "I used a fair bit of magic at that meeting. It's hard to block psychic noise when a group is riled up. Even those of us trained to keep our thoughts to ourselves have—leakage, I guess. And there was a lot of stray emotion at that meeting. People were scared and upset...not that I blame them."

"You're saying you can hear what people are thinking?" He reared back a bit. "Can you read my mind?"

"I pick up stray emotions from people, but from you, I get nothing. It's surprising. I do not get a single peep."

He'd heard of mind readers but assumed they were just pulling a fast one over their audience. He opened his box and inhaled the rich scents of lamb, herbs, garlic, and onion, before taking a bite. "That's a relief. Do you get thoughts, like ideas, or just emotions?"

He watched out of the corner of his eye as she thought about her answer. It was hard to read what she was thinking. She'd probably be a great poker player. Her expression didn't change much at all.

"I can get images, and sometimes actual thoughts, but those are usually only from my family...if they send them to me. We've been trained to ignore each other...like background noise. I get emotion from others. Getting an actual thought or image is incredibly rare. But like I said, I don't even get emotion from you. It's totally weird. I've never met anyone who didn't give me something. Except those guys at Lloyd's. It's actually sort of perplexing."

Relief washed over him. He detested the idea of someone listening in on his brain. "Can other people 'hear' me?" He made air quotes around hear.

"Actual mind reading? I've heard it can be done, but I've never met anyone who can do it. At least not full thoughts. Your emotions can be picked up. Some people, who don't know they're magical, can feel overwhelmed in groups because they don't know that they're picking up strong emotions. We talked the other day about people having just a bit of magic and how everyone's skill level is different. I hate to use the word, but it's about purity...how many magical ancestors you have versus how many mundanes."

She paused for a second. "It's like those DNA tests. You're one-third Egyptian, one-third Viking, and one-third something else. But it's the percentage of magical that gives you your abilities."

He grunted a response. He didn't have words. It was a lot to understand, even though he'd been reading a lot on his own. He finished his meal in silence, then lay down on his back, hands behind his head, looking up at the sky. Laz lay beside him, propped up on one elbow, looking at him.

"I'm sorry you got pulled into all of this." Regret colored her voice.

"It's not like it's your fault. I mean, besides the fact that you're a Hawk and people are after your family. I was mad the other day when I barked at you. I was pissed, to be honest. But this isn't something you can control. Just keep me in the loop and warn me if I need to be warned. Of anything. Not just the things you think I should know about. I need to decide for myself what's best for Rosie and me."

"I can do that."

He hoped she was telling the truth. She seemed honest, but then he didn't really know her that well. He was half relying on Celine's opinion.

L az lay down on her side facing Frank. She tucked her arm under her cheek, so she was lying flatter than she had been but still facing him. Frank rolled toward her without saying anything, and they just looked at each other.

The man had the most incredible, deep brown eyes. Not solid brown, but with lighter shades swirled in, and tiny gold flecks sparkling at her. They were expressive, too. She'd known people whose brown eyes were unreadable. Not Frank's. He wasn't transparent, but she saw reflections of what he was feeling in his eyes.

Right now, she'd almost swear she was reading attraction...but that couldn't be right. *Could it?* Maybe she should kiss him. Just to know what it felt like. He wasn't available for a relationship. He had loved his wife and was probably still in mourning. Otherwise, he'd have dated someone else by now. She saw how women flirted with him at the lumberyard. Certainly, Celine had never complained about any marital troubles. She always seemed happy, though sometimes it seemed that she wasn't thrilled to be in Three Moon Falls.

"Are you okay?" His concern showed in his eyes and voice.

"Just thinking about things." She didn't finish the thought aloud. *About how much I like you, and how the more time I spend with you, the more I care about you.*

He reached out and touched her cheek. "It'll be okay, Lazuli. Rosie told me that we'd be fine. You. Me. Her. She said there'll be fights, but we'll be okay."

She leaned into his soft touch instead of telling him that visions, especially those of a young, untrained psychic, could be wrong...they often were.

He lifted on one elbow and stared down at her, indecision clear on his face.

"What?"

"I'm about to do something incredibly stupid." His voice was low and emotional.

Could he be thinking what she was thinking? Impossible. Suddenly tongue-tied, she just looked at him. Waiting. Anticipating. Hoping.

"You should stop me." He leaned closer.

Her heart pounded loud enough that she was sure he could hear it. She studied his face and found her attention drawn to the pulse thumping rapidly in his neck. She watched it for ten beats and looked back up at him, shaking her head.

"Is that no, you won't stop me? Or no, don't kiss me?"

"Shut up and kiss me, Frank."

She expected a response. A laugh or maybe upset that she was rude.

Instead, he swooped forward until his lips were so close she could feel their warmth. "This is such a bad idea. Why do you compel me? Why am I so attracted to you?"

And then, like a miracle out of her dreams, he kissed her. Long and slow and sweet.

The first touch of his lips was like a live electrical wire. Her entire body jolted to life. She arched toward him, deepening the soft caress. Heat unfurled in her belly...a slow-burning heat like a spark on wood. She cupped his head with her free arm, threading her fingers through his short hair as their tongues danced. His embrace was warm, safe, comforting, but mostly...invigorating.

His hand slid from her cheek to her neck, sliding to cup the back of her head.

A raven cawed loudly, and Frank jumped back, a look of surprise in his eyes. He sat up. "I should apo—"

"Don't you dare apologize, Frank Perrum." She rose on her elbow and turned toward the origin of the crow's call. There he was, sitting pretty on the large boulder at the edge of the clearing, his head cocked to the left. "And you," she pointed her finger at the bird, "you have terrible timing."

He cawed again and took off into flight.

"Did it just sound like he was laughing?"

"Yup, pretty sure he was. I think that was the male. The female is probably around here somewhere."

"How do you know?"

"I sort of have an affinity for ravens and crows. There's one pair that hangs out by my shop. Occasionally, they follow me around."

"Cool. Was he a raven or a crow?"

"Judging by the size and beak shape, I've decided this pair is ravens. There's a family of crows that nest close to the house as well. Both the ravens and the crows sometimes bring me treasure. Pretty rocks, bits of metal they find."

"I've heard they like shiny things."

"That's actually a myth. Or more accurately, some like them, but most corvids don't collect shiny things. They don't seem to like the reflection. I'm not sure why they bring them to me." She grinned. "Though once, the female of that duo brought me a broken gold chain." She floundered to a stop. *Why was she talking about birds when she could be kissing him?* Maybe if she lay down, he'd kiss her again.

He stared at her for a full minute, his eyes shadowed and unreadable, making her wish she could sense his emotions. It annoyed her that she couldn't.

"I guess I should get home. Mom's probably wondering where I am." He stood and brushed off his jeans, though she couldn't see any dirt on them.

"I suppose…" Dammit. She wanted another kiss. *Too bad he was skittish. He's your best friend's widower. He's not for you.*

Maybe not, but she sure enjoyed that kiss.

Chapter Fourteen

A week passed without incident. Lazuli's skin was crawling with nerves. She'd swear the fearful anticipation was worse than the event...whatever that event turned out to be. By the Goddess, she just wanted this whole freaking thing to be over.

She lay in bed, debating getting up, but she could hear voices in the kitchen, fighting. Again. She and her sisters had been snapping at each other for no reason. Gramma Pearl was bitchy, and even her mom and stepdad were bickering. If something didn't happen soon, her family was going to disintegrate.

She didn't feel up to facing them. Maybe she could dress and sneak out without being noticed. Unlikely, but worth a shot.

Careful not to make a sound, she slid out of bed and pulled on her work clothing. She'd shower when she got home, or in the emergency shower in her shop. She paused at her closed bedroom door, listening for anyone who might be nearby. Silence.

So far, so good.

Dammit! Her mouth tasted terrible. Could she skip brushing her teeth? Along with not being susceptible to a lot of minor ailments, witches weren't prone to tooth decay, but she couldn't go around with bad breath. Especially if she was sneaking into town for breakfast.

She crept out of her room and into the bathroom. She let a few drops of water fall on her toothbrush and cleaned her teeth. Rinsing it without making noise was harder, but she managed. Poised at the top of the stairs, she listened again. Aside from the bickering, it was silent.

Step by step, she crept downstairs, carefully avoiding the squeaky step. You'd think that a house that magically repaired itself would fix that squeak, but no. She snorted to herself. Probably left it there to catch people like her in the act of sneaking out.

At the bottom of the stairs, she paused once more. Heart racing, she peered around the corner into the living room. The coast was clear. She tiptoed to the front door. Her work boots were on the front step. She rarely brought them inside...too much sawdust. She reached out and grabbed the doorknob.

"Where are you going?" Gramma Pearl demanded.

"To work?" She meant to sound authoritative, but the words came out as a question, as she whirled around to face her accuser.

"Not without breakfast." Her grandmother was a stickler for three meals a day. Her dark brows pulled together in a frown.

"I have food in the shop." Resigned to not escaping, because no matter how hard she argued and used logic, she wasn't going to win an argument with Pearl.

"Do you think I get up early every day and cook just so you can sneak out and let the food go to waste?" She didn't wait for the answer to what was clearly a rhetorical question. "No, I do not. I'm not doing this for my health; I'm doing it for yours. I'm sixty-five years old. I'm no spring chicken."

Laz let a derisive laugh out. There was something about magic that kept a person young. While her grandmother was in her mid-sixties, she looked younger and had the constitution of someone in their thirties. She wasn't getting old anytime soon.

"Don't you take that tone with me." Her grandmother's tone softened. "Come and eat, dear."

Resigned, she followed her grandmother into the kitchen. Her mom and stepdad were at the table, looking like two people who wished they were anywhere but here. She knew the feeling well.

"It smells good in here," Laz offered the words as an apology. Her stomach growled, and she laughed. "I had no idea I was this hungry. What's for breakfast?" She smelled maple sausages, something eggy, and melted cheese.

"Bacon, cheddar, broccoli quiche. With sausages, waffles, fresh fruit, and whipped cream," Pearl said. "Your sisters are on their way over for breakfast. I thought we could use another strategy session."

Another strategy session? Like the nine they'd had since the meeting weren't enough. It certainly explained why Gramma Pearl had gone all out and made everyone's favorite breakfasts.

"Well, I might as well grab a plate." She ignored the fact that breakfast was set up as a buffet, indicating that they'd serve themselves once everyone arrived.

"You can wait for your sisters," her mom said. "Your father and I have to wait. But at least there's coffee."

"Thank the Goddess for that."

"Thank me for that," Pearl snapped.

She was really a bear this morning. She'd never seen her grandmother so out of sorts. Usually, she was only grumpy when kept out of the loop on something. When Laz and her sisters had been teens, only the worst behavior had garnered this attitude. Something was up, and probably not just the stress of the unknown.

She walked over to the stove where Pearl was cooking sausages and threw her arms around her grandmother. "Gramma Pearl, you are the best. We'd be lost without you. I appreciate everything you do for us. All of it. Sorry, I tried to leave without having breakfast."

Pearl patted her shoulder. "Grab a coffee and sit down, dear."

As Laz slid into her spot at the table with her coffee, Hazel, Hyacinth, and Amber strolled in. It was interesting that none of them had brought their fiancés. That didn't seem fair, since they were equally wrapped up in this mess. On the plus side, she didn't have to watch their happiness. As the second oldest, she thought she'd be married before at least her two younger sisters. And while she didn't begrudge their happiness, she was jealous, though careful not to let it show. Her turn was coming. She knew it.

Somehow, since their kiss, Frank had managed not to be around. He'd skipped their teaching sessions, claiming problems at work. She hoped he wasn't just avoiding her.

It wasn't until halfway through breakfast that their opponents were brought up. Laz wished Hazel hadn't broached the subject because she had no great desire to rehash things.

"I'm taking today off," Hazel declared. "I'm spending the day reading grimoires and journals. Everyone seems to think we have the stupid chalice. We found clues to the pendant there. Maybe I'll find clues to the chalice."

"I doubt it, but good luck," Pearl said, sounding unusually snippy.

Again, with the unusual attitude. Laz frowned. "I'll help look, as soon as I get a coat of varnish on the mayor's table."

"How's that coming?" her stepfather asked.

"Really good. Frank ordered some wood for me. I found great posts for the legs. The grain is exquisite. Mayor Quinton is going to love it. I'm so pleased with how it's turning out."

"I'd love to see it."

"Come with me when I go to the shop. I'll show you what I'm working on." Trevor supported them in everything they did. More so now that he was home. It was hard enough to stay in touch while he and her mom were away on council business. Keeping updated on projects and other nonessentials was almost impossible.

"Oh, can I come too?"

"Sure, Mom. The more the merrier."

"Well, that took a lot of time and solved nothing," Laz grumbled as she walked to her workshop with her parents.

"I think talking makes your grandmother feel better," her mom said. "I am surprised that there hasn't been any news. Someone, somewhere must have seen them."

"You'd think so..." Laz trailed off. She stopped in the middle of the path and cocked her head as she looked at them. "Do you think Gramma Pearl is acting weird?"

"She's a bit off for sure." Trevor's tone was contemplative. "What do you think, Lily-Beth?"

"Mom gets like that sometimes," Laz's mom said. "Usually only when she's super stressed about something. The last time I recall is when my sister, Topaz, left Three Moon Falls. Pearl was horrid for months."

"So, you agree then...something's up with her. Does it feel like more than just being antsy over waiting for shit to hit the fan?" Laz was really concerned. The last thing they needed was to worry about a family member being out of sorts.

"I do, but I've learned that the best thing we can do is let it ride. She'll either talk or calm down when she's ready. Pushing only makes it worse. Mom is one of the most stubborn people I've ever met."

"You know what," Laz grumbled to Hazel, "our family records way too much crap. Reading these old grimoires and journals used to be my hobby. Now, I swear if I ever have to read another one, I'll drown myself to escape them. They record every single solitary boring detail. This one goes on for pages about eggs. I might never eat an egg again, just in spite."

Hazel laughed. "This one waxes poetic on making perfume from roses and lilac." She fake gagged. Lilac was her least favorite floral scent, though rose was okay. She preferred lemon, vanilla, and sweet spices like cinnamon.

Laz leaned back in her wingback chair and set her book on the side table, its top patterned with a tree of life. She loved this room with its big windows and bookshelves. The room itself was an enormous circle, twelve feet across. It had three multi-paned stained-glass windows. Six comfortable-looking chairs were set in two-chair groupings with sturdy mosaic tile tables between each pair. The walls were lined with grimoires and journals. Some dated all the way back to Salem. Each was magically treated for protection against aging, dirt, and fingerprints. It was a book cache from every historian's dreams.

They were focusing on the oldest books, and reading was slow due to trouble converting the older books' language. English had changed a lot since the 1600s.

"This book is riddled with bad rhyming poetry," Her mother groaned. "Not even for spell work, but just random poems about gardens, trees, and three pages about bees. We have some unique ancestors." Her tone changed from exasperated to contemplative. "You know, I'm impressed that you girls spent so much time combing the archives to find the details on the pendant. I do wish you'd let me see it in person."

"Not happening," Hazel declared, crossing her arms over her chest. "That thing is evil. Pure and true evil. Nobody gets their hands on it. E-ver."

"I just want to see it."

"You've seen the pictures, Mom. That will have to suffice." Hazel and Dennis had taken the pendant away from the family. Hazel was the least affected by it, and even she didn't know where Dennis had chosen to hide it. They'd put it in a Faraday box to block its magical calling. It had helped, but not enough. Though he hadn't told them how, Dennis had further shielded the pendant from discovery. Wherever it was, it was well and truly hidden, and they weren't pulling it out for anyone.

"It's not fair. I'm part of this family, too."

"That's just it, Mom. You only saw pictures, and you're lusting after it. It pulls you in and takes you over. Whatever it was designed for wasn't good."

"Should we turn it over to the council?" Her mom's tone was softly inquisitive.

"We decided to keep it. Depending on what happens, it might prove valuable to us. Once this is over, they can take it with our blessings," Hazel decreed.

Laz nodded her agreement.

"I wonder how we ended up with it?" Lily-Beth asked. "Why us?"

"I get the impression that we, our ancestors, stole it when they fled Salem. How or why is unclear. But why they hid it is obvious. Though

I can't understand how Rosalie managed to resist its pull and hide it, is beyond me," Laz said. "She must have been very strong."

"Or she spelled herself to forget about it." Hazel threw in. "Can you spell yourself?"

"Probably not, but if her spouse were magic, he could have done it for her, and her for him. So many questions, so few answers." Laz sighed and picked up her book again. "Wake me if I fall asleep."

Chapter Fifteen

"Thanks for coming with us," Frank looked over at Lazuli. They were walking downtown with Rosie between them, holding both their hands. It still amazed him that at six years old, she was still willing to hold hands. He sure wouldn't have been at that age. He'd have been running ahead, demanding his parents hurry up. So many differences between little girls and little boys.

"How could I not join you? This is a celebration."

Last night, he and Rosie had completed what Laz called Grade One Witchery. They'd learned so much, and his daughter was finally realizing why it was so important to keep her skills a secret.

"I can't think of a better way to celebrate than with ice cream. I think I'll have a banana split." Laz rubbed her tummy with her free hand.

"Can I have one too?" Rosie asked.

"I don't know, that's a lot of ice cream. We'll see." Frank frowned. Hopefully, by the time they walked the two blocks to Get Iced, the ice cream shop, she'd have changed her mind. She loved bubble gum flavor.

"They do have a mini version for kids," Laz added. "I get it sometimes instead of the big split."

"I can't believe we're going for ice cream on November seventeenth. It's freezing out here." Light snow drifted down, melting when it hit the sidewalk. "I'm pretty sure this coming storm marks the actual start of winter." He shivered inside his winter coat, thankful that he hadn't had to pull out his full parka yet. It was a fight every day to get Rosie to wear mittens. He'd given up on a toque for now. Hats could come later.

"It's never too cold for ice cream." Laz's upbeat tone made him smile. She was always so positive, even when he knew she was worried.

"We need to hurry." Rosie rushed them down the sidewalk, pulling them along by the hands, and dragged them into the store. "I'm starved."

"Oh," Laz exclaimed, "it looks amazing in here since the renos." The floor was the same classic black and white checkerboard. The walls had been painted a warm pale green and had been decorated with murals of grazing cows. The tables and chairs had been updated from chrome to white wood with black legs. There was a new shelving unit with boxes of ice cream cones, candy, and dairy-themed trinkets.

"Look at the stuffies." Rosie ran to a bin of stuffed animals. Mostly cows and ice cream cones. "They're so cute." She looked up hopefully.

"Not today, honey. Christmas is coming."

Her hopeful expression slid to a disappointed frown, but she didn't object.

Frank chose a simple caramel sundae topped with toasted pecans. Rosie had the mini banana split, and Lazuli selected the full split with brownie bites. When it came, it was twice the size of the supper he ate last night.

"You aren't going to eat all of that, are you?" He stared at the massive bowl of food.

"Darn rights. Just watch me." She scooped up an enormous bite and stuck it in her mouth. Her eyes closed in obvious bliss... just like he imagined they would if he kissed her again.

Don't go there, Perrum.

He forced his attention to his bowl and away from her ecstasy. Lazuli Hawk was pure temptation, and the more time they spent together, the further he fell under her spell. Not that he believed it was an actual spell. More than once, she'd reiterated that forcing someone to do something against their will was a no-no. He took great reassurance from that tidbit of information.

"My teacher is nice. I love her," Rosie declared between bites. "On Fridays, we get to read for a whole hour. And sometimes, we get to have popcorn for a snack. But only if everyone is being good." She frowned. "Sometimes the boys are stupid."

"Stupid isn't a very nice word," he reminded her. "But I see what you mean."

"I don't like the principal, Mr. Tallus. He's weird."

"I've met him," Laz said. "He's nice. Maybe you just don't know him yet."

Frank bit back a comment on him not liking the man either. He tried to keep his opinions of teachers and staff to himself. No sense setting his daughter up for failure by coloring her perception of someone. "Laz is right, give yourself time to get to know him."

Rosie inhaled her treat, which was one scoop, a quarter of a small banana, strawberry sauce, and sprinkles. "Can I go play?"

"I don't see why not. Be nice to the other kids," he reminded her, not that she had mean tendencies, but a little reminder went a long way.

"Thanks, Daddy." She picked up her bowl and carried it to the gray bus bin and set it gently inside. She walked to the play area, slipped off her shoes, and climbed carefully through the opening in the mesh surrounding it. He'd expected her to run in excitement. Sometimes, she surprised him.

"She really is adorable. You're doing a good job of raising her."

"Thanks. Some days are tough. Especially right after Mom goes home, when she has Grandma-Syndrome. It takes a while to get back to routine, but the visits and the connection they're building are worth a few tantrums."

"I hope I'm as good a mother as you are a father."

Being only friends, who shared one kiss, he was surprised she brought up children. It felt like a deep conversation. They were barely more than acquaintances. "I'm sure you will be. You're kind and patient, and kids seem to like you. Do you want a lot of kids?"

"I think that's up to the Goddess. Though given my choice, I'd like four. Definitely an even number. Odd man out is never easy. Not as a kid, not as an adult."

"I'm an only child, so I wouldn't know. Mom stayed at home, too, so there was no daycare. And only one or two incidents at Scouts is all I can recall."

"If you ever married again, would you have more kids?"

They were headed into uncharted territory here. He wasn't sure what to make of it. "I'm not actively looking for a relationship. Though I suppose I wouldn't turn one down if the right woman came along. But kids?" He paused, thinking about the questions. Strangely, he could almost picture himself married to Lazuli with a handful of kids. "I guess that would depend on how old Rosie was, and who the woman was. Who knows, she could already have kids and not want more. Really, there are too many variables to consider."

She nodded. "I can see that. I suppose some of the same factors come into play for me. My partner would have to be content knowing that Hawk women only have girls. It's some kind of genetic thing. Never, since my family started keeping records, has there been a male child."

"Wow."

"I've considered adopting, because I'd like to have a son." She shrugged. "That decision is a long way away at this point, though I am open to a relationship."

A frisson of excitement rocked him. *Why did that statement make him feel so good? I'm not considering taking this friendship further, am I?*

To his surprise, he realized he was. Despite the potential danger looming over her, and perhaps them, he was considering dating Lazuli. The idea had sort of crept up on him. Over the last few weeks, they'd spent at least twenty hours together. When he added that to the time he'd spent with her and Celine, it wasn't a lot, but it felt like enough to get a good feel for her character and values.

"What's on for you this weekend?" He was considering asking her out. On a date. If he could find a sitter. Maybe one of her family members would watch Rosie.

"Saturday, I'm headed to the Catholic church for the morning. It's the start of preparations for holiday food hampers. I like to help every year."

He tried to bank his surprise and apparently failed.

"Don't look so shocked. Just because I'm not of their faith, it doesn't mean that I don't have compassion." Her laugh was light and without any mocking. "We help out with a lot of things, though obviously, Halloween events are our favorites. You should join us at the church on Saturday. I'm sure Mom and Dad would love to watch Rosie."

Over the days they'd met for lessons, they'd spent time with Laz's parents, both of whom doted on Rosie and treated her like a grandchild. "I think I'd like that." He told himself this was friendship, not a 'relationship'.

"Great." She whipped out her phone. "I'll ask if they have time." Her fingers flew over the keyboard, and she set the phone down and picked up her spoon. "This is so good."

"The ice cream is half melted. Gross."

"Nope. Brownie bites in sweet cream sauce. I love mostly melted ice cream. Delish." Smiling widely, she took an enormous bite.

He had to admire her zest for life. He looked toward the ball enclosure to check on Rosie. As he looked, she bolted out of the pit and raced toward him.

"Hey, no running indoors," he chided gently.

"The bad men are here!" She grabbed his arm and pulled. "Come on, Dad. Laz, we have to go."

"What are you talking about?" He tried to be calm, but her firm insistence was worrisome.

"Come on, Lazuli. I can feel them. We...have...to...go." She tugged on their arms with each word.

"I think we should listen." Laz slid out of the bench. She grabbed their dishes and rushed to the bus bin. She was back before he was on his feet. "Come on, Frank. Time to go."

Her brows were pinched together, and for the first time, she looked worried. It was enough to get him out of his seat. There was no sense resisting, even if he didn't have one single clue what the hell was going on. They hurried outside.

Rosie paused, looking left then right. "This way." She dragged them across the street without looking and into the jewelry store. She weaved through the displays and through a doorway marked Staff Only.

"Where are you going?" a woman demanded.

"Sorry, Kate. Just ignore us," Laz called out.

The woman's eyes went wide, but she gestured to the back door. "Catch you later, Laz."

Her words were heavy with meaning even he couldn't miss. Thank goodness she knew Laz.

"I'll call you," Laz shouted as they exploded out the back door into a paved back alley.

Rosie raced ahead and stopped between two dumpsters, panting.

"Want to tell me what this is all about?" he asked, his hands on his hips in his best upset father pose.

"Calm down, Frank. Something, or someone, obviously spooked her." She placed her hand on his arm and gave him a look he couldn't quite interpret. She turned to Rosie. "Where should we go, darling?"

Rosie looked left and right. "To your store. They won't look there. Yet."

The final word sent a chill down his spine.

Geez, having a psychic kid was going to take decades off his life...if it hadn't already.

"Let's go this way," Laz suggested. "It's only a few blocks to the store. Follow me." She looked both ways, then stepped out of the bins' protection. She headed left down the alley.

Every few feet, she glanced back to ensure they were behind her. What the hell had happened? Why had she been unaware of the presence of danger? And why had Rosie, neck deep in a ball pit, noticed it?

She paused at every intersection, making sure she felt nothing and that there was no traffic. She pounded on the shop's screen door. Maybe they needed to add an actual lock to it, something with a key, rather than the hook and eye fastening inside. She laughed quietly at the idea of a lock on a screen door. Like it would do any good. The hook was more to keep Sasha, the shop cat, in than to keep people out.

A moment later, Andi, with her long dark hair in a ponytail, popped the door open. "What's up, Laz? Why didn't you come around front?" She looked up and down the alley. "Where's your truck?" Her green eyes held questions.

"Andi, hi. Long story. We're just going to hang out here for a while. Is Amber here?"

"You betcha. Just sit tight, little chickadees, I'll send her back." She gave Frank a questioning look and headed through the door to the front of the shop.

"Wow," Frank muttered. "This place is even more crowded than it was after the break-in. Business must be good."

"We're doing well," Amber said, coming into the room. Her green eyes sparkled, and her long blonde hair was up in a messy bun. She wore an unbuttoned smock over a forest-green maxi-dress. "Mail order business is almost more than we can handle. Who knew?"

"Obviously, you did." Laz rolled her eyes. "The online shop was your idea."

"Any-who. What's up?" Amber looked at each of them in turn and stepped back. "By the Goddess, your auras are insane."

"I felt the bad guys," Rosie said, her voice trembling. "I'm so mad. I was in the ball pit with my friend. We were playing Magic. I like her. She sparkles."

Laz made a mental note to find out who she was playing with because her friend was obviously magical. Learning who Rosie's new friend was could come later. They had bigger concerns.

"Really? A warning premonition?" Amber looked at Laz for confirmation.

"Yeah. I totally missed it. But they're still close. Now that I know they're here, whoever they are, I can feel them."

"I'll make some tea." Amber put the kettle on and turned back to them. "Any idea who it is?"

Laz reached out with cautious mental fingers. She got close, but not too close. She didn't want them to realize she was on to them. Plus, if they felt her inquiry, they might be able to find her. After a moment, she revealed what she'd found. "Um...it's not Keres as far as I can tell. I wasn't as close to him as you were, but I know how he felt in the fight. All I get is men. Five dark men."

"Like magically dark?" Frank asked.

She nodded. "I need a minute to think." She flopped onto the red sofa, leaned her head back, and closed her eyes. Slowly, the feeling of her adversaries faded, like they were moving away. She sat upright. "I don't feel them. Sit down, guys. We need to talk."

Frank took a seat in the chair, and Rosie climbed onto his lap.

"First, we have to let the council, particularly Leticia, know that they are here. Whoever they are. And that there are at least five of them." She looked at her sister. "Amber, can you let the family know, while I talk to Leticia?" She took a few steadying breaths. "Rosie, Frank, you have to be super careful around people you don't know." Later, she'd tell Frank to watch acquaintances as well. Sometimes, people weren't what they seemed. She was accustomed to carefully vetting everyone she met, but she doubted he was.

"Are there any magicals at the school who can keep watch on my daughter? Or should I pull her from school?"

"Yes, there are. I'll talk to them. I don't think you need to keep her home. There are only a couple weeks left until school's out for Christmas."

He nodded.

"My family is their focus. At least that's how it seems now, and the crap that happened over the past months bears that out. So far, this group hasn't done anything. It could be that they're just dark magicals who are in town for another reason."

"They aren't," Rosie interrupted.

"You could be right," Laz said, not wanting to upset Rosie. "But you might be wrong. Sometimes, what psychics *see* and *feel* doesn't come true. Sometimes, we're wrong."

Rosie frowned but didn't argue.

"So, we go about our lives, but we're careful. If anything changes, I'll let you know, Frank. And if you, or Rosie, see anything questionable, call me right away."

"Hey, Rosie," Amber said, "Have you ever seen our shop? Want to come look at all the cool things we have?"

"Can I, Daddy?"

"Sure thing. Be careful not to break anything."

"I will."

Amber took Rosie by the hand and led her away.

"What's the truth?" Frank asked.

"Honestly, I have no idea. I only have the certainty that this is going to be ugly. And judging by what's already happened, messy and probably violent. I'm not sure that you guys will be involved. Often, the psychic, or seer, as some people call us, only sees what happens. They don't become part of it. I'm hoping that's the case here."

"Dammit." He slapped his hands on his knees.

His actions and tone revealed how upset he was, but she still couldn't feel his emotions. "Are you blocking your feelings from me?"

"How the hell would I know how to do that?" He sucked in an audible breath. "Sorry. I'm worried and upset. I don't know how to block, and at this moment, I don't care if the whole world knows how pissed I am."

"Fair. I haven't foreseen anything involving you guys, though I admit my visions are vague and at the moment very rare."

"I guess that's reassuring."

She couldn't help but chuckle at his wry tone. "Frank, you make me laugh. I love that you have a sense of humor during all this. It can't be easy learning your kid is magic, can move water, and see things nobody else can."

"It isn't. And don't forget the ghosts." He scraped a hand across his beard. "On one hand, I'm at wits' end, on the other, I'm a bit proud of her skills."

"You should be."

They lapsed into silence. She had no idea where his thoughts went, but hers were on the mystery men.

"What do you think they're doing out front?" he asked at last.

"Probably looking at books and jewelry."

"Harmless, I guess."

A few moments later, Rosie skipped back in. "Look, Daddy. Amber gave me a necklace." She held up a necklace of round beads. "The black one is tourm…" She stumbled over the word. "Tourmaline, and the red one is garnet. And she gave me these rocks." She poured them from a bag into his hand. "This is tiger's eye; it helps make visions stronger. This is quartz, and this is amethyst for protection. And this pretty black one that shines green and blue is labradorite to help me sleep. And this one is a moss agate. I like it because it's pretty. See the dip in it. That's for rubbing. Rubbing it helps you relax. It's my new pocket rock."

"I love them. They're very pretty. Here, slip them back into your bag so you don't lose them. I'm very impressed you know their names. That's a lot to remember." Hell, he'd already forgotten half of their names.

Smiling widely at his praise, she placed them, one by one, into the purple velvet bag, and with her tongue between her teeth, carefully tied it up. She looked up at him. "Tying a bag is harder than tying my shoes. The strings are teeny."

"They are small." He looked at Amber. "What do I owe you?"

"Absolutely nothing," she said, sounding a bit affronted. "They are a gift."

"Thank you so much."

"Ya, thanks," Rosie agreed. "I love them, just like I love you guys."

"We love you too," Amber and Laz said in unison.

While not everyone believed in the power of gemstones. Laz did. One hundred percent. She'd seen them work. There was a reason why she made jewelry from wood and stone. Though she knew they'd help protect Rosie, part of her wondered if it was going to be enough.

The girl knew too much about things she shouldn't. She'd had visions of the book where they'd found the pendant talisman. She'd described it perfectly without seeing it, and she'd known it was evil. She'd also had visions of a chalice, which Rylie had been screaming for when she attacked Cynth and Earl.

She sighed. Things weren't looking good. The nagging sense of danger hanging over her made her chest hurt. She wanted to weep.

Chapter Sixteen

G ray, dismal, angry clouds began to dump huge flakes of wet snow on Frank as he pulled into the Hawk driveway. The gates rolled open as he approached, so someone had seen him coming. Laz's truck wasn't near the house, so he drove the short distance to her shop. If she wasn't there, he'd head home.

He could do without the snow, but they were due. Probably overdue. Snow was piling up on the grass and atop the fence posts, but was still melting on the asphalt driveway. There was no doubt that it would start sticking there, too. If he were inside by the fireplace with a book and a snifter of good brandy, it would be beautiful. Right now? Not so much.

Pulling his jacket tight and resetting his ball cap, he hopped out and hurried to the shop door. Jazz music flowed around him as he got close. Jazz, huh? He never would have expected that. Of course, she didn't seem the boy band type either. Come to think of it, before this minute, he wouldn't have pegged her as leaning toward any specific genre. As the music lulled, he knocked, softly at first, then more loudly.

Snow piled up on his shoulders as he waited.

The door popped open without warning. He was hit with a wave of sawdust-smelling warmth.

"Frank, what are you doing here? Is everything okay?" She peered around him like she was expecting to find a horde of ghosts behind him. "Come in, come in." She grabbed his arm and tugged. "It's too cold to stand outside."

He didn't blame her; it was barely below freezing, but she wasn't wearing a jacket. Her long-sleeved T-shirt was snug without being uncomfortable, and her jeans fit in all the right places. She was feminine, even in her work clothing.

"Just a sec," he cleared his throat to swallow his attraction. "Let me brush off all this snow." When his clothing was clear, he stomped his feet and stepped inside. "Should I take my boots off?"

"No, it's okay. Just give them a good wipe, please."

He scrubbed them as dry as he could on the long runner. He noticed she had winter boots by the door, but was wearing work boots.

"What's up? You want coffee?"

"That would be great, thanks." She waved him forward, and he followed her to a small kitchenette in the far corner. It was just a couple of cupboards, a mini fridge, and an old table and chairs with stainless steel legs. Judging by the seats on the chairs, he'd guess the table had a Formica top. Very retro, but also cute...not that he was a judge of decorating.

"I've got tons of tea, but just regular, decaf, and salted caramel coffee to choose from. And I hope you drink it black, because I'm out of cream."

"Black, decaf will be perfect." It took only minutes to brew two cups. The salted caramel scent of hers was almost as enticing as the deep, rich darkness of his. "It smells great, thank you."

They sat across from each other. "What can I do for you?" There was no impatience in her tone. She flipped open a box of Hedgehog chocolates and pushed them his way.

"Um." He scrubbed his hands down his thighs before taking one. "I have no idea. Rosie is at a sleepover with a friend. He named the girl. "This friend sparkles. I guess that means she's magic. That's okay, right? Should I have asked first?"

"It's fine. You're her father. You don't need my permission. But, until this mess is over, maybe check first...if that's not a problem. But they're a nice, magical family. They won't steer her wrong." She looked at him expectantly.

"Oh, okay. I did warn her not to do anything magic or talk about magic. I was on my way home, and I just had this urge to stop by. Someone let me in the gate."

Her amused grin was breathtaking. "To a point, the gate is magic. It can sense the intent of the visitor. If you'd been bent on mischief, it wouldn't have opened. People who haven't been here before never get past."

"Are you telling me your property is impenetrable?"

"Not even close. The two main gates are magic, but beyond that, if you were determined, you could get in. It doesn't take much effort to scale the fences. Sometimes the cats, both the tame ones and the feral, will warn us of visitors. So do the ravens and crows."

"That's so cool." He rubbed his hand up and down the hot side of his mug. "But also, quite intimidating."

"Nothing to fear, unless you decide to stir up trouble."

"This is a nice space." His mind was jumping like Rosie hyped up on sugar.

"Thanks, it's taken a long time to get where I wanted it to be. After uni, I hired a company to build the shop itself. I had a bit of money I inherited from a relative. I had savings from my earlier, much smaller works, which I used for more equipment. It's nice to be out of the family garage. I've been working with wood since I was a kid. The whole rock thing is relatively recent, just the past couple of years, but I've been picking up pretty rocks since I was a kid. I sell jewelry, polished stones, and stone slabs. Anything my muse tells me to create. My favorite are the stone wind chimes."

He admired her business sense. She seemed to know exactly what she needed and where she was going. Certainly, her work was highly valued locally, and she had some exquisite pieces for sale on her website...not that he was stalking her website. He just looked out of curiosity.

They talked about running a business. Though hers was small, and his employed over twenty people, they had a lot in common, including being eco-friendly and sourcing locally where possible. Conversation flowed easily between them. She was intelligent and a good communicator. Add that to her good looks, and she was a temptation he was having trouble resisting.

Sitting here, talking so casually felt like a date. His errant brain kept drifting back to their kiss. He kept wondering why she didn't smack him, and he kept wanting to do it again. Her lips were a siren song. "I should go," he said when he finished his second coffee.

She glanced at the clock. "It's almost dinner time. Why don't you join us for supper? There's no sense rushing home to eat alone."

She seemed as surprised at the invitation as he was.

"That would be nice. As long as your family doesn't mind." He didn't want to intrude on their evening, but he also hadn't planned anything for dinner. And who wouldn't want to spend time with a beautiful and charming woman?

"It'll be delish. It's ham and scalloped potatoes, with salad and roasted butternut squash. The veggies are from our gardens and greenhouses. Mom said it'd be ready for six. We've got just enough time to get there."

"If you're sure..."

"One hundred percent. Just give me a minute to put some things away." He followed along as she walked around the shop, reshelving tools and unplugging equipment. She checked that none of her tumblers were bulging or leaking, explaining what she was doing as she went. She swept up a tiny pile of wood shavings from a bench and disposed of them. Lastly, she checked the second man-door and the rollup garage-style door. "All locked up. I'm ready."

"You're very meticulous."

"I have to be. Woodworking is a messy business, and I can't risk a fire. Plus, my tools are expensive. I treat them as best as I can." She wedged a bit of paper between the door and the jam as she closed and locked it. "If that doesn't drop when I open the door, I know someone was here, again."

"Smart."

"I stole it from *Fahrenheit 451*." She looked around. "Look at the snow. It's really coming down."

"Hop in your truck, I'll brush it off for you."

"I'm sure I can manage." She double checked that the shop door was locked.

He pushed the remote starter on his truck. "Hop in, I'll do yours first. That'll give you time to get to the house before me and warn them I'm coming."

"Thanks. I appreciate it, but no warning is needed. Friends are always welcome."

Her grateful smile made him wish he could sweep her vehicle off more often.

He cleared the snow from her driver's door with his gloved hand and took the snowbrush she handed him when she climbed in. Slowly, he cleared off the accumulation. There had to be a full inch here. *How long had they been talking? He dropped Rosie off at four. Holy cow. That was two hours. Time flies!*

He gave back the brush and waved her away. Though it was cold out, he was enjoying the lazy fall of the heavy flakes. He brushed his truck off and followed her to the house. If this kept up, it could potentially become a blizzard. Good thing he had four-wheel drive to get home with. Of course, if it were a blizzard, he wasn't about to risk driving unnecessarily.

As he pulled up to the house, he was struck by the idea that this moment felt like a man meeting his date's family for the first time. His nerves jangled, and his mouth went dry.

"Ridiculous," he chided himself. "It's not a date, and you've met this family dozens of times. You've even shared meals with them." He wasn't as familiar with her parents as everyone else, but they seemed nice enough. They sure liked Rosie.

"Frank, good to see you." Hyacinth stepped back to let him inside.

The uncomfortable feeling of the house judging him creeped him out a bit, even though he knew what it was. *What if he failed to pass its inspection?*

"Mom's just setting the table." Cynth took his jacket and hung it in the closet before leading him to the kitchen.

"Hi, Mrs. Hawk. Trevor." He greeted Laz's stepfather more casually, as they'd had several business dealings in the past.

"Oh, Frank, call me Lily-Beth, please. We don't stand on formality now. Especially since you've been dragged into the magic realm." She turned to Hyacinth. "Is Earl coming?"

"No, something came up at the bookstore. He asked for some leftovers."

"I'll fix him a plate. I'm disappointed nobody else could make it. I made a ton of food."

"I told you to check with them first," Trevor teased, "but you didn't want to bother them. We were gone most of the past ten years, honey. They've grown up and have their own lives."

"A mother wants to spend time with her children." She sniffed, though Frank thought she was acting a bit.

"Mo-om," Laz groaned. "We had family dinners for the past five nights."

"True, but you'd expect my mother would have hung around. I'm not that terrible of a cook."

"Darling, you're a wonderful cook. Your mother and Leticia are having dinner."

"See, everyone abandons me." She swooned and placed the back of her hand on her forehead.

"Give it up, Mom." Laz laughed. "Your melodrama is too much."

Frank grinned. This family had great dynamics. Grumbling out the truth but doing it with a sense of humor. They were so connected as a family that he was jealous. With only his mom and daughter as family, he'd often longed for more, especially after his father passed when he was very young. As a kid, he'd wanted brothers to play with. He could see how being part of a large family could be both good and intrusive at the same time.

"What brings you our way, Frank?" Lily-Beth asked. "Take a seat, son." She waved toward the table. He sat, and Laz sat beside him.

"Nothing, really. I'd dropped Rosie off in town and stopped to say hi."

"Nice." Lily-Beth's tone implied that it was more than nice, and weirdly, like she thought maybe something was going on between him and Laz.

Dinner was casual with conversation that flowed easily. Nothing was mentioned about magic or the troubles that plagued them. It wasn't so easy for him to compartmentalize things.

He asked Laz about it as they sat alone in the living room together after dinner. Everyone else had vanished upstairs.

"We try not to focus on the negative at mealtime, though we are far from perfect. And magic has always been part of our lives. It's like laundry...it's just there for us. I'm sure that if we were new to it, we'd talk about it all the time. All of us, Trevor included, were born into magic families. We've been surrounded since birth.

"Did you have more questions?"

He thought about it. "Nothing pressing. If I think of anything, I'll call or text. Right now, I'm just happy to sit and visit with you."

His comment invoked a warm smile. "It's kind of nice, isn't it?"

As it had earlier, their conversation flowed back and forth. They touched on magic, movies, books, local news, and even the state of the economy. He could talk to her for hours and never get bored. She was smart, insightful, and funny. She was a lot like Celine had been, only warmer, and not so distant. He hated himself for comparing them.

Laz was exactly what he wanted in a woman.

The idea had him shaking his head. What made him think he'd be a better man for her than he had been for Celine? He had grown and changed since he and Celine had been hook-up friends, but was that enough? Life wasn't so casual now, even without his daughter in the mix.

Could he be ready for a relationship?

What did it matter? With the trouble looming over them, nothing personal was moving forward. But perhaps, later.

Chapter Seventeen

Sunday morning, Lazuli's phone woke her from a dark, disturbing dream. She looked at the clock beside her bed. Like the watches she wore, she preferred old school and used a bedside clock rather than her phone. *Eight o'clock? Who would call this early?*

A glance told her it was Frank.

Adrenaline surged through her, waking her more thoroughly than two pots of coffee. She snatched the phone up.

"Frank, what's wrong?"

"Um. Laz. Hi. Nothing's wrong."

"Thank the Goddess for that." She leaned back against her pillows and pulled the blanket up to her chin. "What can I do for you?"

"Rose and I are going sledding. We thought you'd like to come. It's going to be beautiful. It's cloudy but warm, barely below freezing. It's the perfect day to be outside."

Rosie shouted something unintelligible in the background.

"We're having a wiener roast too. With marshmallows."

She did need to work. "Sure, I can spare a few hours." Life wasn't all work, and a wiener roast sounded great. "I'll bring chocolate and graham crackers for s'mores. When should I be there?"

They agreed to meet at ten. Since she was going outside, she didn't shower. Freezing temperatures were brutal on wet hair. She'd shower later. She washed up, put on a watch with a snowman center, and sticks to mark the minute and hour hands. She grabbed a quick bite to eat in the silent house. Either everyone else was up and gone, or they were still asleep. The rising sun was brightening the yard as she sat at the table with her cereal. A pair of mule deer wandered through the yard. She made a mental note to throw some grain out for them. Feeding them for hunting purposes was illegal, but she had no intention of turning them into food. She just loved watching the animals stroll through. The entire family did.

Rosie exploded out of their front door when she pulled up. "What took so long? I thought you'd never get here."

"Oh, am I late?"

"You're exactly on time. Ignore little Miss Impatient."

"Daddy," Rosie complained. "There is no Little Miss Impatient book."

"Maybe there should be." He tugged her braid where it hung out from under her thick pink and purple toque, which matched her jacket, pants, and mittens.

Frank wore a red snowmobile suit, black mitts, and a hat. "I'll fire up the snowmachine to pull you two to the hill. It's a bit of a walk, and this will be faster and easier with the gear." He nodded at a plastic tub that sat on a long toboggan, which rested alongside three saucer-shaped sliders.

"Sounds good to me. Let's do this."

The hill was only five minutes away. Laz and Rosie watched as he built a fire with the kindling he brought, and fed it logs that had been under a nearby pine. "I stack wood here in the summer, just for this." His light attitude turned sad.

"What?"

"Nothing. Let's get sledding while this burns down to usable coals."

"That face isn't nothing. We're friends. We can share things that upset us."

"Thanks. Come on, Rosie, let's go."

She leaped up from where she was building a snow fort. "Yay."

Laz watched them go, frustrated by the sudden distance between them. Rather than dwell on it, she grabbed her sled and followed them down the hill, laughing in delight as the fresh snow blew up in her face. Sledding brought out the kid in her, and she loved it.

They chased each other up and down the hill, usually with Frank hauling Rosie behind him, and riding in front of him.

"Time for lunch," he called as they trudged up the hill after over an hour of fun. "The fire should be ready." He'd been stoking it between rides, and there was a nice pile of coals.

"Wonderful, I'm starved." It seemed like much longer than three hours since she'd eaten her cereal.

"I brought buns and wraps. I wasn't sure what you'd prefer."

"Oh, a wrap would be perfect, thanks." His consideration didn't surprise her. Through her friendship with Celine, she'd learned that he did small, kind things for those he cared about. She was thrilled that he'd gone out of his way for her.

"Can I have a wrap too, Daddy? Please and thank you."

"You certainly can."

They roasted the wieners on collapsible sticks he'd unearthed from the plastic bin.

"Why does food outdoors always taste so good?" Laz asked.

"Is it the outdoors, the treat, or the massive effort we just put in going up and down that hill?" He groaned in mock exhaustion.

She laughed. "Maybe all three. But come on, that hill isn't that big. It's kid-sized and perfect."

"There's another one a bit further on for those who are more daring, but I don't think all of us are ready for that."

"I know I don't want to walk up anything bigger."

"Can I have another one?" Rosie asked a few minutes later. Her right cheek was smeared with ketchup.

By the time she finished two hot dogs and two s'mores, Laz was stuffed. "This was fun. But I think we should get going."

The wind had picked up, and dark clouds had rolled in quickly. "So much for a mild winter. Looks like Mother Nature is going to slam us with more snow."

"That's odd. I checked the forecast before we left. Nothing but light clouds for the next three days." He frowned. "Never trust the weatherman."

Laz had only glanced at the temperature earlier. But if what he said was true, it could mean someone was messing with the nearby weather. "I guess you're right, though I hate to see the day end."

"Me too." He began kicking snow on the fire.

They covered it, stirred it, covered it again. By the fourth covering, not one ember remained. The fire was well and truly out. "I guess we're good to go." He tied the bin to the back of the toboggan, on top of the saucers. Like on the way out, Rosie climbed on. Laz sat behind her and wrapped her arms around Rosie to hold her on. She gave Frank a nod, and he slowly pulled out and headed back to the house.

Snow began falling. Tiny light flakes at first, and growing heavier. In the few minutes it took to get back to the house, the sunny morning had turned into a full-on snowstorm.

"Wow!" Laz exclaimed. "This is awful. I can barely see."

"Come inside, let's see if it lightens up a bit before you try and drive."

They bundled into the house, leaving the snowmobile by the steps instead of putting it back under its cover in the side yard.

"Whew." Frank brushed snow off Rosie and helped her out of her gear before taking his own off. "Come in. Let's get warmed up. The temperature really dropped. I thought thick clouds meant warmth."

"Ya, me too."

He raised an eyebrow in question.

She shrugged.

They settled Rosie in front of the TV with a princess movie and a small snack and headed for the kitchen for coffee.

"Can people control the weather?" he whispered.

"Yes. Though it takes great effort. It isn't easy."

"Could this be...."

After a moment of thought, she said, "Anything is possible, but I can't figure out a reason why. And rapid weather changes aren't rare around here. Mom always jokes that if you don't like the weather, wait five minutes, it'll change." She was more worried than she let on, and his expression made it clear that he thought so too.

"So, hypothetically speaking, if someone were doing this, why would they change the weather?" His fingers tapped an unsteady rhythm on the kitchen table. He leaped up. "Coffee?" He stood and went to one of the two brewers. He pulled the pot from the fast-flow pot.

"That would be great." She peeked out the kitchen window. The early afternoon light had faded to dusk due to the clouds and thick falling snow. "By the looks of things, I'm not leaving any time soon. I need to let my family know where I am."

"You check in?"

"Always. It's a magic family thing. Especially now." She didn't go into reasons. Frank was smart enough to figure it out on his own.

"Couldn't you just *think* them a message?"

"I could, but generally, we only do that in emergencies. Like when Riley attacked Hyacinth and Earl, Cynth *called* us to come help. For day-to-day messages, we try to be normal." She shrugged. "Want help with that coffee?"

He stood there, pot in hand, staring at her, as if he'd forgotten what he was doing. He glanced down at his hand. "Right." With swift, smooth motions, he prepped the pot and hit the switch. Almost instantly, the rich dark aroma of fresh coffee filled the room.

"Pardon me a sec while I text home." She shot off a text to their newly formed family chat string. She let them know where she was and why. Her phone immediately began chiming with an explosion of responses.

"Wow." Frank rejoined her at the table and stared at her phone.

"Ya, we're a chatty group." She read the texts. "The weather all over town is like this, and the radio station is grumbling about it being completely counter to what weather apps say is happening."

"Meaning?"

She inhaled deeply and blew out a slow breath. "Meaning my family thinks this is magical. I'm not sure I agree. I can't feel any magic." He looked worried, and she wanted to reassure him. "For right now, I'm going to assume it's just freak weather. No sense getting upset over what is potentially nothing."

"And if it is something?"

"Then I'll face that dragon when it appears. And no, dragons aren't real. It's an expression."

"I'm trusting you on this one. What do you want in your coffee?"

"Cream, if you have it."

"Coffee cream, whipping cream, or caramel flavored syrup?"

"You're certainly prepared."

He shrugged.

"I'll take the regular coffee cream, thanks." She watched while he poured coffee and cream and stirred. For a moment, her mind flashed to Hyacinth's delivery of Earl's sister's baby and the magical attacks that happened to Baby Anna. "I'm not trying to jump topics all over the place, but you need to keep a close eye on Rosie. Watch for her to be extra sleepy, in pain, or acting out of character. She explained the attacks where someone was in Anna's mind. "We don't know if it is related, but there is someone, or more than one person, who is out there stealing magic from other witches. Some are left magicless, some are left with damaged brains, and some have died."

Frank's mouth opened and closed and dropped open again. His eyes bulged and his brow dipped down into a frown. He carried the two heavy black mugs to the table.

"Again, not trying to freak you out, but it is a very remote possibility."

"And this weather is a cover for that?"

She hadn't considered that. "I doubt it. I'm just saying, be aware, okay?"

An assault on someone's magic wasn't likely to be blatant, like this weather change. It would be subtle and almost unnoticeable, like the attack on Hazel. By the Goddess, there had been way too many attacks on her family. This bullshit had to end.

"Let's just enjoy the quiet as we watch the weather. It's a good time to get to know each other better. We're neighbors and friends after all." And she'd like to know everything about Frank. His likes, his dislikes. If he were ticklish. If he preferred meat or seafood. All the things. Despite the tiny kiss they'd shared on their picnic, she doubted she'd ever get another. Frank certainly hadn't made any moves on her. She wasn't going to approach him—there was still the voice in her head nagging about 'poaching on your friend's man'...though it wasn't as loud as it had been.

"I'm going to go check on Rosie. Why don't we go sit with her?" The worry was clear in his voice and expression, and honestly, she didn't blame him one bit. She was on the edge of freaked out herself.

Chapter Eighteen

F rank tucked Rosie into bed and stared down at her. She looked so peaceful lying there, like she didn't have a care in the world. So sweet and innocent. He should probably take her ease as a good sign. Today was the first day in months that she wasn't grumbling about the bad men. That had to be a good thing.

The poor girl was exhausted. Sledding had tired her out. She had napped until supper. After they ate, the three of them played board games like a real family. He and Rosie had loved every minute of it, and he was pretty sure Laz had too.

Outside, the snow continued to fall. It had lightened up a lot, but it was still coming down and piling up. Judging by the low Mugo pines in his front yard, they'd gotten nearly a foot. He couldn't remember a single day in his entire life when that had happened. He should be enjoying being snowed in with a beautiful and entertaining woman, but the fears lingering in the back of his mind kept intruding and making him restless.

Rosie mumbled, rolled over, and pulled her favorite stuffed bunny to her chest. She sighed like she was releasing all her stress. A slow smile spread over her face, letting him know that she was finally well and truly asleep. The roll and sigh were how he knew she wasn't faking when he put her to bed. Some nights, she faked sleep, and when he was gone, would read with her flashlight. When she was older, she'd realize that her little light never ran out of batteries. He loved that her idea of rebellion was sneaking in time with a book. At least she wasn't running away to the Hawk's place anymore.

Stepping back, he eased the door shut and returned to the living room.

Laz was curled up on the end of the sofa under Rosie's fuzzy blanket. "Is she asleep?"

He grinned. "Finally. Though I suppose I shouldn't have expected her to go to bed on time after a two-hour nap."

"True enough."

"Would you like a glass of wine? I've got a white and a red that's not too dry."

"Red would be great."

In the kitchen, he grabbed the wine and two glasses and set them on the elegant wooden tray he had made for his wife for serving guests. He added some cheese, some sliced sausage, pickles, grapes, and crackers, and carried them to the living room.

"I fixed a snack to go with the wine." Suddenly, without Rosie around, this felt entirely too much like a date, leaving him feeling unaccountably nervous.

"Oo, a charcuterie board. Nice." She snagged a piece of cheese as soon as he set it on the table.

"Why do women insist on a fancy name for everything? It's snacks."

"You don't like the word charcuterie?"

"I can't even say it." He laughed. It was one of the few words he tripped on. "And don't even ask me how to spell it."

She looked at him for a second before bursting into laughter. "You sound like my dad. He just asks for a meat and cheese snack when Mom asks what he wants."

Frank bowed. "Lazuli Hawk, I give to you my best charred cutlery board."

She laughed again, her eyes sparkling in the dim lamplight. "That tray is exquisite. The grain, the wood, the carving, the glossy finish."

"Thank you. I made it."

"I'm impressed. This snack is perfect, but it would be even more perfect if you lit a fire." She gestured to the fireplace.

"It's gas, not wood."

"I don't mind. It just feels like the perfect night for a fire. Blizzards and fires just go so well together."

A moment later, the fire was flickering away and sending lovely warmth into the room. He handed Laz her wine and sat on the opposite end of the sofa. If he stretched out his arm, he'd just be able to caress her neck. Instead, he fisted his hand and kept his arm at his side.

"Tell me about that picture." She pointed to a picture on the bookcase in the corner. "Is that you?"

"Don't remind me," he groaned. "Celine loved that picture. It's from university. I needed a Phys Ed credit. I took a mixed martial arts class. That's me, and my opponent in my only win in three years of classes."

"You took it for three years? It doesn't sound like you enjoyed it."

"I liked the physical activity, but not so much getting punched and kicked. But the girls seemed to like it. I was young and stupid."

"So, lover, not fighter then?" Laz teased.

"You know it."

The silence that fell between them was simultaneously comfortable and nerve-racking. He wanted to talk about everything. He wanted to pull her into his arms and taste her delectable lips again. "Are you seeing anyone?"

"You mean like dating?" She shifted on the couch to face him fully and rested her arm on the back. "No. I'm not dating. I was, for a while. That was last year. It didn't work out. Are you?"

"I'm not. Celine's only been gone a year. It feels...early."

"Oh."

He didn't care for the disappointment in her tone. She had let him kiss her. Okay, after he bungled his attempt, she'd taken over. *Did that mean she was potentially interested in him? If so, what did that mean to him? Was he ready for something or someone new?* Or maybe it wasn't a matter of being ready; it could be a matter of being capable. He hadn't given his first wife the love she deserved. Did he have it in his heart to truly love anyone beyond his mother and child?

Then again, he had no intention of bringing someone into Rosie's life unless it was permanently.

His brain happily added that Lazuli was there already. Neighbors and friends. Rosie's childcare provider, at least until the end of the year. So being around her wouldn't upset his daughter. Surely the friendship would remain if they dated and didn't find themselves compatible.

He almost snorted at that. Compatible. He liked everything about her, and while it wasn't the be-all and end-all of a relationship, his physical attraction to Laz was off the charts. It didn't feel like a proximity thing. It felt like...more.

"Frank?"

"What?" He turned to look at her, sipping his wine to clear the sudden frog from his throat.

"Where did you go?" Concern filled her gaze. She swirled her glass but didn't take her eyes off him.

"The past? The future? Honestly, everywhere, and nowhere." He shrugged like it didn't matter, but it did matter. He was lonely. Laz could fix that. But he didn't want to start anything, in case it failed.

"Want to talk about it?"

"I didn't love Celine," he blurted. "I don't know if I'm capable of loving anyone." Embarrassed, he drained his glass. He set it on the table and pulled the food tray onto the seat between them, all while telling himself he wasn't putting a physical barrier there. He nibbled a cracker and refilled his wine before he looked at Laz.

"Frank, you were very good to her. You cared for her. You looked after her and your child. You gave them a stable life and home. You showed kindness and tenderness. She had everything she wanted."

"Except love," he snapped. "She deserved better."

From Laz's expression, he could read that she was formulating her words.

"Perhaps not. But you did the honorable thing and married her. You didn't have to do that, and she appreciated it. She told me that more than once. She did love you. And I believe she understood that you gave her all that you could."

"So why was she divorcing me? I found the papers after she passed."

"That I don't know. She never told me she planned to do that."

He swallowed back bitter anger before it consumed him. "There was a custody agreement. She was leaving Rosie with me. How could she do that? How could she abandon her child? Me? I get that one hundred percent. But her daughter? Never."

"I don't know. Did she keep a diary, or journal?"

"Not that I ever found. The only time she ever held a pen was to make a shopping list. She was always on her phone. Or out back in her She-Shed."

"Did you look there?"

"I haven't set foot out there. I...I...I can't." There was no way he could force himself to breach her private domain. She stayed out of his tiny home office, and he stayed out of her shed.

"After this storm ends, and the rest of this," she made a vague gesture, "this stuff, settles out, I can go with you. I miss her too. She was my best friend, but I can help you get through this." She blinked several times.

Tears?

"I know that she was writing letters for Rosie. For when she's older. Life advice and that type of stuff. It wouldn't surprise me if she had journals, too. You might get some insight there."

"How does that work? She was abandoning her child and leaving me, and she was writing letters for after she died?" The words snapped out. He was furious. Leaping to his feet, he paced the living room. "Why did she have to go and die?"

"I don't understand it myself. Good people die and evil people live on. It isn't fair, but I'm not sure life's supposed to be fair. I think the challenges we face define us, as does our reaction to both good and bad turns of fate." She fell silent.

Weary to his core, he dropped back on the couch, knocking the wine bottle off the tray with the force of his landing. Luckily, it was capped, and Laz caught it before it could hit the floor.

"I had a friend who got cancer in high school. She thought she was going to die. She reevaluated her entire life, how she did things, how she treated people. She didn't die and became a different person. Kinder. Softer. More generous. As far as I know, she still is. We haven't talked since last year, but I doubt she'll revert." She stacked some cheese and pickles on a cracker and stopped with them just in front of her mouth. "I believe that the reason there is both a divorce notice and a letter to Rosie is that Celine must have had a change of heart after she knew death was inevitable."

"Maybe." He drew the word out thoughtfully. "I didn't look at the date on the letter. Maybe I should."

They talked for hours about Celine and the things they'd done together. With all three of them, and each with her alone.

"You know what, Frank?" Laz set the nearly empty food tray onto the coffee table. "I think you did love Celine. I hear it in your voice; in the way you talk about her. You might not have been 'in love' with her, you know, romantic love, but you did love her as a dear friend and family member."

"It's still unfair to her." He leaned forward with his elbows on his knees and buried his face in his hands. "I should have done better."

The couch shifted. He felt Laz's arms wrap around his shoulders. "Frank, you can't control who you love or how they feel about you. You did your best, and Celine knew that. It's time to let the guilt go. To move on. To show Rosie that you can love and lose someone, then love again. Love isn't limited to just one partner. Celine would want you to be happy."

He leaned into her embrace, resting his head on her shoulder. Her words and the soft strength in her arms offered comfort. The tears he hadn't shed after the funeral fell silently.

L az held Frank tight. His shoulders shook as he released his grief. She suspected that his guilt had kept him from expressing it fully before now. She was honored that he trusted her enough to let his emotions out. Most men wouldn't. There was something cathartic in tears. Helping him find that brought her peace, and unfortunately, it reinforced her love for him. When she first met him, when he and Celine were in the hook-up phase of their relationship, she should have run as fast as she could.

Instead, she'd stuck true to her friendship, doing her best to ignore the incredible spark of life she felt every time he was near. It was that damned Hawk curse to only love one man. And hers was out of reach.

After a few moments of silence, without his shoulders shaking, Frank sat up and moved slowly out of her embrace. "Um. Sorry. But thank you."

"No apologies needed. We all grieve in our way, in our own time. I was honored to help you."

He nodded and got up. He walked slowly out of the room, like he was exhausted. Strong emotions had a way of sucking all the energy out of you.

She leaned her left side against the back of the couch and sat motionless, still sideways. Her body was still warm from their embrace. Moving might dissipate that heat and the feeling of closeness warming her heart.

The sound of water running floated down the hall. Moments later, he was back with another bottle of wine. He held it up to her. "More?"

"Sure." She wasn't a big drinker; she'd only had two glasses. She glanced at her watch. Two glasses in nearly four hours. She could handle more. Maybe another glass would dull her attraction to him.

He poured the wine and sat beside her, just close enough that her knees brushed his thighs. He shifted slightly so he was facing her and cleared his throat.

"I know the timing on this is bad. Or horrible. But are you open to dating?"

"In general, or specifically?" It was a weird time for the question. Especially after he'd told her he wasn't looking to date.

"Specifically." He paused. "I'd like to take you out to dinner." He cleared his throat. "On a date. To see where this friendship could go."

She didn't answer immediately. She couldn't...her heart was stuck in her throat and her pulse thrummed in her ears. She almost bolted off the couch.

Before she could moisten her mouth enough to speak, he went on. "I'm attracted to you. Rosie likes you. I like you, Lazuli. A lot. I mean, I hope that isn't creepy since you were my wife's best friend." His shoulders slumped.

"The best friend thing is awkward for me." A certainty fell over her that to pass up on this opportunity would be a mistake. "I'm...um. Sure, I'd like to go on a date with you."

"You don't sound certain." He took her hands and squeezed them between his. "It's fine if you aren't interested."

"I think...I think I am interested." He had no idea how interested.

"Good. I think Celine would approve. She cared a lot about you."

"She loved you." She smiled softly, remembering her friend.

"She loved you, too." He leaned back, still holding her hands.

She wiggled one hand free to reach her wine. A few sips dislodged the lump in her throat. She'd fought her attraction for so long that this fragile new relationship felt unreal. She needed to stop dwelling on what could go wrong.

She needed a distraction.

"Movie?" she asked.

He stared at the floor for so long she thought she'd said something to upset him.

"Sure. What's your poison?"

"Action. Upbeat. Something I've seen before."

"How am I supposed to know what you've seen?" He picked up the remote and turned on the TV. He scrolled for a few minutes without landing on anything.

"How about the guide? It's probably faster."

"Women! Scrolling is the only way."

She snatched the remote out of his hand, making him laugh. She changed to the guide. She paused at an old Bruce Willis movie. "How about this? It's action, it's fun, it's light."

"Good enough for me."

Putting the remote on the table and picking up her wine, she settled back into the softness of the couch, leaning just a little toward him. When he put his feet on the coffee table, she did the same. Minutes into the opening scene, his arm slipped behind her on the back of the couch.

Her heart did a little happy dance before settling back into normal, if slightly faster beating. "This is nice."

"Ya, it is."

She leaned fully into him, and his arm dropped down closer. His chest rose deeply and fell slowly, like he'd sighed. From the corner of her eye, she saw his soft smile.

Ya, this was good. Really good.

Slowly, the fun of the movie and being at Frank's side erased her tension, and she relaxed fully.

"Laz? Laz? Wake up, hon."

She smiled. He called her hon. "What?"

"The movie's over. You've been asleep for an hour. "Bedtime." He pulled his arm off her shoulder and flexed it repeatedly.

"Oh. Did I crush you?" She should feel bad, but it had been so long since a guy held her like this, she couldn't work up the energy, or the sympathy.

"Naw. I'm good." He flexed again. "You can sleep in my room. I'll sleep on the couch."

"Don't be silly. You need to be where Rosie expects you to be. I'll take the couch. Besides," she yawned. "I'm shorter. I'll fit better." She stood and stretched.

"Do I get a goodnight kiss?" He rose in front of her, a roguish grin on his face. "I mean...we are dating, right?"

"You move fast, Perrum."

"Too fast?" He backed up half a step.

"Nope. Just about perfect." She inched forward and slipped her arms around his neck. Rising on tiptoe, she pressed her lips against his and was rewarded by a groan of submission. His left hand cupped the back of her head. The right landed on her hip and tugged her closer.

The kiss was sweet, and not quite chaste. Heat burned everywhere she touched him. It was all she could do to keep her hands in a neutral place. If he pushed, she'd let him seduce her. But he didn't. After a moment of soft kisses, he eased back and ran a finger down her cheek.

"As much as I'd love to take this further...it's too soon."

"Ya."

His grin said her disappointment was obvious and amusing. "Bedtime. I'll get you blankets." He trailed his hand down her arm and clasped her fingers in his for a second before heading for the stairs. "Be right back." He winked.

She fanned her face. The man was lethal. And delicious. And that ass.... She was still staring at the stairwell when he came back into view.

"Miss me?" He winked again.

"Yup." She slid her arms around his waist as soon as he dropped the bedding.

"Good."

He cupped her face in both hands and lowered his mouth to hers. BOOM!

The noise was deafening.

She was knocked onto the floor, her wrist slamming into the coffee table. The house shook around her. Frank was on his knees beside her.

"What the hell?"

Rosie's terrified scream penetrated her pain. "Daddy!"

Frank looked at Laz.

"Go! I'm fine."

He bolted up the stairs as smoke filled the room. They had to get out!

"Frank, hurry," she screamed up the stairs. "We have to go!" She grabbed her jacket and keys from by the front door.

"Coming." He rushed down the stairs, muttering comforting words to Rosie, who was wrapped in a blanket.

"Let's go." They slammed into their boots and jackets and headed out into the snow.

The half-moon shone down on them. Sometime during the movie, the storm had passed. It was freezing out.

The snow dragged at her knees as she trudged to the truck as fast as she could, breaking a trail for Frank.

"Daddy, look!"

Laz turned toward them. Behind Frank, the house was in flames. "Get in the truck," she demanded, opening the door for them. She shoved it shut and raced to her side, got in, and started the engine. She was parked behind Frank on the driveway. They weren't in immediate danger from the fire, but she slammed the truck into four-wheel drive and backed away, not bothering to scrape off the windows.

The driveway was sixty feet straight back. They were safe for the moment.

"Okay, is anyone hurt?" She asked after she stopped.

"Daddy, I'm scared."

"Me too, Rosie Posie. Me too. Are you hurt?" He pulled her closer, and Laz was momentarily jealous of the attention he gave his terrified daughter.

Crying, Rosie said, "I-I-I'm okay. I'm scared."

Frank soothed her before turning to Laz. "Are you okay?"

"My wrist," she groaned. "I think it's broken." She fumbled one-handed and managed to pull her phone from her jeans' pocket and hand it to him. "Call the fire department. I'll brush us off so we can get out of their way."

Frank stared at his house, now fully engulfed in flames. "How can it even burn under all that snow?" he muttered.

"The bad men did it," Rosie sobbed, tears streaming down her face.

"Maybe not," Laz tried to lie. "Maybe it was the furnace, or something. The firefighters will let us know." Rosie's frown cut deep. "We'll find out." She turned away from the child. "Frank, call the fire department!"

Twelve minutes later, they were still sitting in the brushed-off truck when three firetrucks rolled up the driveway. It could have been longer, but apparently, the plows had come out as soon as the snow stopped. One of the mixed blessings of living a couple of miles from town was the separation from everything. Privacy was good. The distance from emergency services...not so much.

"My toys," Rosie cried. "I want my toys."

"Oh, honey," Frank said, patting her back. "We'll get you new toys."

She sniffled. "K." After a moment, she said, "I saved my rocks." She held up the purple bag.

"Good job, honey."

The fire chief came and took their statements. Laz couldn't tell if he was magical or not. She could barely think beyond the pain in her wrist. It was bruised and quite swollen.

"You need to see a doctor for that. The ambulance is on its way."

After the medics checked the three of them, he declared Frank and Rosie fine. They hadn't even inhaled enough smoke to do damage.

"Go to my place," Laz demanded as they rolled her away. "You can stay there. Send someone to the hospital to pick me up. They'll be worried." They'd better send Hyacinth. She was the healer. With luck, she could do some healing before the professionals managed a proper exam. Since the firefighters had seen her injury, she hadn't been able to go straight home. If Cynth didn't get there fast enough, Laz would be stuck in a cast.

Her wrist was probably broken. She wouldn't have thought her bones weak enough that falling would bust them, but clearly, they were.

"Send Cynth," she called, peering around the medic to see Frank.

His eyes widened. He must have realized that she'd sent a telepathic message to her family.

Hell, she'd sent several. Despite her final mental message that everything was going to be okay, that she'd be okay, they were upset, though they were trying not to bombard her with thoughts. She didn't have to explain to him that this wasn't the furnace, or some other random explosion. This was an attack.

The question was, were they after her, or Rosie?

And why hadn't they continued the attack when they left the house?

Chapter Nineteen

Lucky for Laz, Hyacinth was stuck in town after delivering a baby during the blizzard. She met the ambulance at the door.

"Fix this," Laz hissed. "Before some doctor sees me."

"Chillax, your agitation is interfering with me reading the injury."

"Ladies," Dr. Carter greeted them, auburn bob swinging as she entered the ER cubicle. "I hear there's been an accident." She straightened her lab coat as she waited for an answer.

"Thank, the Goddess it's you," Laz declared gratefully. "I was worried it would be someone else." Dr. Carter wasn't magical, but she came from a magical family.

She asked questions, as if she were examining Laz and taking a medical history, but let Cynth do her work. It took intense focus and serious energy to heal a bone. After ten minutes, Cynth flopped back into the bedside chair.

"That's all I can do. It's still got slight cracks, but a sprain brace should do the trick, and since several people saw your injury, you'd need to wear that anyway. I healed the inner bruising but left the top layers and a bit of swelling." She kept her voice too low to hear outside the small space.

"Now that we know nothing else is injured," she whispered before raising her voice. "Let's get you to X-ray."

"Thank you, Dr. Carter." Laz smiled at their family friend. "I hope it isn't too serious."

"My guess is a bad sprain, maybe some torn ligaments. Let's get that X-ray, and hopefully you can be home before breakfast." She slipped Cynth a chocolate bar. "I saw you coming," she whispered.

"Thank you."

"I'll send someone in with real food. I know you need it to recover."

One thing about her hometown that she loved was how quickly they got the plows out after a storm. Most of the roads had already been cleared.

Despite the blizzard, the entire family had gathered by the time they got home. The noise inside was deafening. Even Abigail, Kody's grandmother, who was staying with Kody until she could find a place in town, was there. She swore she wasn't going to let her great-grandchild be born without her assistance...though as far as Laz knew, Amber wasn't even pregnant. Cynth was. Or, maybe her sister was keeping secrets.

For a moment, she was upset that Amber might be hiding something. And a bit jealous too. Someday, she'd like to have children of her own. Despite her envy, she rejoiced in the idea that there might be another baby on the way. She'd find out soon enough.

"Girls, how are you holding up?" Their mother rushed to the door to reassure herself that they were fine. Funny, she could be gone for years and not fret too much, but when she was around, she hovered like a mama bear over newborn cubs.

"Good." Laz hugged her mom. "Tired and a bit achy. I have a few bruises from where I hit the floor." She waved her brace-wrapped wrist. "Luckily, Cynth was able to fix most of the damage."

"Wonderful." After another hug and a peck on Laz's cheek, she turned to Cynth. "And you, did you refuel? Are you okay?"

"I need to eat. Dr. Carter had some food brought in. I expect it was as much as she could swing without causing questions. But I do need more. Take me to your buffet."

"Come, come." She ushered her daughters past their siblings and into the kitchen. "We didn't know how long you'd be, so we went ahead and ate."

"Your breakfast is almost ready," Gramma Pearl added. "I started cooking as soon as you said you were on the way."

"Hey," Frank said from behind her, "are you okay? I was worried." He stepped around Cynth and her mother and came to Lazuli's side. He looked her up and down, then gently lifted her wrist. "How bad is it?"

"Cynth healed most of it. Just a couple of not quite healed small cracks and some bruising. I've got a worse bruise on my ass." She forced a laugh, and sobered when he didn't join in. "Really, Frank, I'm okay. I'll be fine. Mostly, I'm tired from lack of sleep. How are you? How's Rosie?"

"She's okay. Better now that we're here. I'm..." he swallowed hard. "I'm...I'm less fine. I've lost my home. The fire chief says it's a total loss. The house. The garage. My truck. The snowmachines beside the house. I guess Celine's shed is untouched, as is my yard equipment shed. They are, were, further from the house. I'll get insurance out after the fire investigation is complete. Chief says it was likely a gas explosion."

"I didn't smell any gas." The only thing she'd been able to smell was Frank and the delicious spicy soap he used.

"Me either."

"I'm guessing magic attack," her father jumped into the conversation, and then hugged her. "I'm glad you're okay. After you eat, we'll need to brainstorm."

"Again," she sighed. She was sick to death of attacks, danger, and mostly brainstorming. "We're going to have to find that damned chalice and destroy it."

Pearl gasped. "You can't just destroy magical relics. They have cultural and historical value. They were created for a purpose."

"How do we even know that purpose was a good one? How do we know it wasn't for destruction, or evil?" Laz glared.

"Hey, now," Frank squeezed her shoulder. "Take it easy, Laz. We'll figure this out. You guys have solved all the other issues that came up in the last few months. I'm sure we can get to the bottom of this and neutralize this bad guy as well."

"If neutralize means end his life, I'm all in."

Frank reared back at her words. His eyes went wide. "You don't mean that?"

Her whole body drooped with exhaustion. Her neck and head ached. She sighed. "No, not really. I'm just sick of all this. I'm done."

He opened his arms and raised an eyebrow, welcoming her into his embrace. She stepped into the warm comfort of his arms. He closed them around her, and he whispered, "Hey, hon, we'll get through this. We'll be okay."

"How can you be so calm? You've lost everything." She stared up into his eyes.

"Easy. I still have Rosie. I've got insurance, and I still have you. I might have lost a few trinkets and photographs, but we're all alive and unharmed. Mostly unharmed," he corrected. "I really can't ask more than that."

His words penetrated her anger. He was right, they'd been lucky to get out alive. If they'd gone to bed earlier, they might not have. "You're right."

"Come, sit. Your breakfast is ready." Pearl ushered them to the table, and her family gathered round.

Dennis and Earl brought in a couple of folding chairs to ensure there was seating for everyone. Rosie tried to climb into Frank's lap.

"Here, little missy," Kody said. He was sitting beside Frank. "Sit on me. That way you're close to Dad, but he can still eat." She pouted a bit but climbed onto Kody's lap.

The conversation was deceptively casual until they finished eating. Then, her father spoke up. "Laz, honey, tell us what happened. We've heard from Frank and Rosie. We need to hear it from you."

Events of the night whirled through her head, the bad ones pushing out the happy memories like kissing Frank. She struggled to organize the images into a coherent picture. From the moment she'd climbed into the ambulance, she'd avoided thinking of what had happened. "I don't know. Frank had just gotten me blankets, so I could sleep on the couch. He wanted me to take the bed and let him have the couch, but we finally agreed that because I'm short, the couch was better for me."

"Anyway, he'd just handed me the blankets when all hell broke loose. Something exploded, and we were knocked to the floor. Rosie screamed. Frank ran to get her. The room began filling with smoke." She shuddered at the memory. She still smelled like smoke. She probably should have showered, but she was starving.

She cleared the lump of emotion from her throat. It was mostly remembered fear. "We managed to grab boots and coats and get outside. We only had a phone because mine was still in my pants' pocket. By some miracle, my keys were in my coat pocket, not my purse." She groaned. "Ugh, I have to get all new ID and bank cards."

"Did you notice anything odd? Or magical?" Her mom asked, her tone kind and undemanding, but still managing to convey quiet pressure.

"Nothing. I mean, the storm was unexpected, and it dumped a lot of snow. But I can't imagine why anyone would cause a storm like that. But honestly, I was too panicked and worried about all of us getting out and to a safe place that I didn't take the time to look."

"Elton was there," she added. "Maybe he caught something." Elton was one of the emergency crew that came to the fire. He was also magical and would know what to look for. There were magicals amongst the fire department, the police department, the medics, on the town council, at the hospital. Basically, with a large portion of the town being magic, they were involved in everything.

"It's good that we had a magical there for the first look," Amber said. She leaned against Kody, who had his arm around her.

Laz took a moment to eat a few bites of sausage and waffles. "I don't know. I'm so tired of all this. I'm exhausted, I'm smelly. I need to rest before I try and muddle out the problems of the world."

"We'll talk more after you shower and rest," her mom said. "All three of you are going to bed and resting. We'll talk more later."

"I'll be at the shop for a while," Amber said, and everyone else explained their plans for the day. It was clear that nobody wanted to do anything except solve the problem, but they respected her need to rest.

Trevor and Lily-Beth led Frank, Rosie, and Laz upstairs. Frank trudged along, Rosie in his arms. Despite his worries and all the unanswered questions plaguing him, he was beyond exhausted. The deep circles under Laz's beautiful blue eyes betrayed her exhaustion. As did the pallor of her skin. If he were honest with himself, he'd admit that he didn't want to be separated from her, even for sleep. He'd just connected with her, but he had strong feelings already.

"Laz, you're in your room. We've put Frank and Rosie next door in Hazel's old room."

"No," Rosie snapped.

"Hey, Rosie Posie. It's okay. We'll be fine here."

"No. I want Laz."

There was no way he'd let his daughter out of his sight. "Sorry, sweetie. Laz needs sleep, and so do we."

"Yes!" She burst into loud sobbing tears. "Yes!"

"Hey, hey." Laz ran her hand down Rosie's back. "Tell you what. What if we all sleep in my room? I have a queen-sized bed. We'll all fit."

"That isn't necessary. She can't have everything she wants." As much as the idea appealed to him, he knew the value of keeping rules intact for his daughter. She was a handful already. Giving in to her whims wasn't going to help.

"I think," Laz said thoughtfully, "that, just this once, it might be okay to share a room. We've all been through a lot." Behind Rosie's back, Laz mimed waiting for Rosie to fall asleep and then creeping out of the room. The idea had merit.

He turned Rosie to face him. "Look, munchkin. This is a one-time thing. We'll sleep in Laz's room. Once. Only once. Do you understand? We can't be messing up everyone else's life because we're still upset."

Laz's parents watched the exchange with interested grins. Great, now they were speculating on his relationship with Laz...before it had even started.

"One time." Rosie nodded.

"Come, let's get Rosie washed up." Lily-Beth pointed to the washroom. "Laz, go shower in our room. I'll find Rosie something to sleep in." She'd already been kind enough to find them clean clothing and to let them shower off the smoke smell.

"I'll be fast." Laz dashed into her room and came out with a handful of clothing. "Five minutes, Rosie. Okay."

Rosie nodded. "'Kay."

Laz as good as her word. She was back in six minutes. He hadn't meant to time her, but he'd caught a glance at the large alarm clock on her nightstand.

"How do you want to do this?"

"You and Rosie get in. I'll sleep on top on this side." She pulled a vibrant red and gold quilt from a wingback chair in the corner. "I'll sleep under this."

"Can you sleep beside me? Under the covers?" Rosie pleaded.

This was shaping up to be a disaster. He looked at Laz and shrugged, reminding himself that this was platonic. This was two adults comforting a girl who had just endured a traumatic explosion. She'd been beside herself until Cynth had texted that Laz was fine. Even then, she'd been antsy and worried.

"Okay, but I get up pretty early, Rosie. I'll probably be gone when you wake up in the morning." She returned his shrug with a look that told him she was uncomfortable with what was happening.

Rosie wiggled out of his arms and hopped onto the bed. "Thank you." Her response was much more subdued than he expected. Maybe this wasn't just pure manipulation. Maybe she was more upset than she currently seemed. Walking around the bed, he pulled down the covers and tucked her in.

Someone knocked, and he turned toward the door. "Here's a pair of my pajamas," Trevor held out a pile of Santa print clothing. "Sorry, Christmas is all I have."

"Thank you." He'd been wondering if he'd have to sleep in his borrowed duds. This family had been so good to them since the fire that he hesitated to ask for more. He was already wearing Trevor's jeans and sweater. "I'll just pop into the washroom and change."

"There are a couple of new toothbrushes on the counter for you and Rosie. Help yourself to anything else you need. Our home is your home. After all, you are sleeping with my daughter." He chuckled and walked away.

"Dad!" Laz laughingly chided Trevor for his joke. "I'll get even," she called out into the hallway as she stood shaking her head. She was still smiling when she turned back to Frank and Rosie. "Go ahead and get cleaned up. I'm not going any—" A massive yawn interrupted her words.

"Don't yawn. It's contagious." Unable to help himself, he yawned. "Come on, kiddo. Time to clean our teeth."

Torn between delaying as long as he could and his eagerness to get back to Laz, he made short work of their final bedtime preparations. Rosie looked adorable in one of Hazel's old T-shirts. After they woke up, he'd have to go to town and buy some basics. And look for a temporary place to live until his house could be rebuilt. With all the worries pressing down on him, it didn't even make sense to go to bed. There was no way he was going to sleep. Beyond that was the irony of finally having this beautiful woman in his bed and being unable to take advantage of her. God, the Goddess, Karma, the Universe...someone had a cruel sense of humor.

Frank lay facing Laz, with Rosie snuggled between them, hugging a stuffed bear Laz had unearthed from a box in her closet. Slowly, his daughter's eyes drifted shut. After she did her little sleep shuffle, the one that proved she was asleep, he looked at Laz.

"Sorry to invade your bed. And your house."

"No problem. This isn't a big inconvenience." She yawned. "I'm so tired." Like Rosie, her eyes drifted shut. She blinked them open. "I should go."

"Go to sleep, hon. You're safe here." It was all he could do not to reach out and stroke her face. Even in exhaustion, she was lovely. Her willingness to sleep like this was just more proof of what a good person she was. Her entire family was generous and caring. He'd lucked out when he ended up with the Hawks as neighbors.

After a few moments, both Laz and Rosie were fast asleep. It felt wrong to let down his guard, even though they were safe in this protective home. Still, he drifted off.

Chapter Twenty

L az drifted slowly towards wakefulness. She was hot, and something heavy pressed down on her waist. She peeked her eyes open. The room was fully dark. Her alarm clock and the nightlight out in the hallway were the only visible lights. How long had she slept? It had been mid-morning when she went to bed.

With Frank.

She almost jerked upright but caught herself just in time. She didn't want to wake Frank and Rosie. Clarity came slowly. The unusual heat was from her bedmates. Barely moving, she flexed each of her muscles to see what hurt. Ow! Her butt was really sore. She'd landed hard. Her aching wrist was probably what woke her. Despite the healing, it was still painful. Not as bad as it would have been, but sore enough.

She didn't want to get up and face reality.

She sighed silently.

Life goes on.

She either had to deal with it or...well, basically, she had no choice but to deal with it. If it was already dark, that meant her family would be back and waiting for their strategy session.

Slowly, she rolled from her left side to her back. The weight on her waist didn't lift. She rolled on her side toward the center of the bed, expecting to find Rosie fast asleep.

Instead, she was greeted by Frank's sleeping face. Rosie was gone!

About to bolt out of bed, the light sound of Rosie's giggles came from downstairs. Okay. Rosie was fine. Then what was the weight on her side?

Holy shit!

It was Frank's arm!

She was cuddled up to Frank!

She had to get out of bed before he woke up!

He looked so peaceful in sleep that she took a moment to stare. His dark hair was sexy and sleep-rumpled, his chin sported an entirely too attractive five o'clock shadow, and his lips practically whispered for her to kiss them.

Get up, Laz, she mentally chided herself. *Get up now!*

One of Frank's eyes peeked open.

She jerked backward, nearly falling off the bed.

"You're kind of a wiggle bug, you know that?"

"Um. Ya. Sorry. I didn't mean to wake you."

"Laz. Relax. Come back over here. I was enjoying having you in my arms." He winked.

She blinked.

How could he be so chill about them being in bed together...without Rosie? "You were awake? How long have you been awake?"

"About two minutes before you started breakdancing. Rosie just snuck out and went downstairs."

"Why is your arm around me?"

"No idea how it got there. Rosie was on the outside when I woke up. I'm not complaining." His voice was low and heavy with sleep, and too sexy for her comfort.

"We, I, should get up."

"Five minutes, Laz. We deserve five minutes of peace and quiet...and cuddles." His smile was slow and sexy.

Dang! This man did things to her heart and libido that nobody should be able to do.

"We are dating, right?"

She raised an eyebrow at his bold question. "You asked me out. That doesn't mean we're dating." She really should get up or at least move his hand off her waist.

"You said yes. That means we're dating."

"I don't cuddle on the first date. I don't even kiss on the first date." Her heart danced a little, and her pulse hummed in her ears.

"We went on a picnic. That could be our first date..." he trailed off like he expected her to seriously consider the idea. "We went on a picnic. Plus, we went to a movie last night."

She chuckled. "We watched a movie last night."

"I'd have taken you to dinner and a movie if I could have. That counts, right?"

She looked him right in the eye. Was he serious? Did he really want to cuddle, or was he just teasing, trying to get a rise out of her?

She'd been dreaming of scenes like this for years. Since long before Rosie.

"Oh, to hell with it." She slid closer. "You know they're going to come looking for us now that Rosie's awake."

"Two minutes, Laz. I just want two minutes alone with you." He squeezed her waist and smiled. She realized he had just the tiniest hint of a dimple on his left cheek.

How had she missed that before? Probably because she never looked too hard, she was too busy trying not to let him notice that she noticed him. "You have a dimple." She touched it with her finger. "It's cute."

"I am not cute. I'm manly. Masculine. Tough."

"Maybe so, but the dimple is adorable."

"And you are beautiful."

Heat flooded her face. "Thank you." She scooted forward and pressed her lips to his. His surprised gasp was nothing more than a puff of breath on her lips. Then, he was kissing her back, and she swirled away from reality on a wave of sensual bliss.

"Ahem."

Her father's voice intruded on her pleasure.

She jerked away from Frank.

"Am I interrupting something?" Her dad asked wryly.

"Ya, Dad. You are. Go away."

Frank leaped up. "Um. Sorry, sir. I meant no disrespect, sir."

"Jeez, Frank. Get back in here." She glared at her father. "Dad...go away. We'll be down in five minutes." With a smirk, her father wandered away.

"Five minutes," he called back, "and then I'm sending up Pearl."

"Shit, no. She scares me." He grabbed the clothes he'd piled on the chair last night and bolted from the room.

"I hate my family." Resigned, she got up and dressed. Her father's casual attitude surprised her. Of course, he was very observant, and while he hadn't been home much lately, he probably realized how attracted she was to Frank. He also trusted her to take care of herself.

T he rich scent of melted cheese and tomato sauce led Frank to the kitchen. The table was set with two plates, and Pearl was busy loading the dishwasher. Apparently, the rest of the family had already eaten. The kitchen was still busy, but not as busy as it had been when he went to bed. Pearl, Lily-Beth, Trevor, Hazel, Dennis, and Amber were sitting at the table. Everyone else must have left or not come back. Honestly, Frank had no idea who lived where. Did any of the girls, besides Laz, still live at home? He'd have to ask her if she ever came downstairs. He suspected she was hiding, and he didn't appreciate her leaving him to the metaphorical wolves. He was tough, but her family could be damned scary.

"Evening, everyone. Something smells delicious," as he poured himself a cup of coffee.

One by one, they returned his greeting. Lily-Beth added, "There's lasagna for dinner. I'll serve you as soon as my errant daughter arrives." Her voice was full of caring, and he thought maybe even understanding.

Nobody, not one single family member, mentioned Trevor seeing him cuddled up to and kissing Laz. Frank kept waiting for the bomb to drop, and he was downstairs a full ten minutes before Laz showed up.

She strode up to him at the table and kissed his cheek. "Evening."

"Oo," Hazel teased. "Are you two like dating, or what?" Her tone was pure sisterly taunting.

"Or what?" Laz tossed out casually, picked up his coffee, and took a large drink.

"Hey, get your own. That one's mine." He winked so she'd know he was joking. "Want to come to town with me. I need to get some basics for Rosie and me. I want to hit the stores before they close for the night. I can't believe I slept all day. It's nearly six p.m."

"You'd better check out the bags and boxes in the living room first," Trevor advised. "People have been dropping off donations all day."

"We're storing the household goods at the shop for now. The bags are mostly clothing," Trevor added.

"Why would they do that?" Frank looked from one Hawk to the other. All of them were grinning.

"Because everyone in town knows what happened. You run a local business that many of them rely on. People can be incredibly generous." Laz sat beside him with her coffee. "Plus, the magical community knows we've taken you in. We don't do that with just anyone. That means you have our support and approval."

"I don't know what to say." His chest hurt from the kindness. He'd never known generosity like this.

"Say thanks. Take what you can use and pass the rest on to charity. There are several to choose from." Laz nudged him with her elbow. "But yes, I'll go shopping with you, after you check out what's here."

"I should go by the house too."

"You can," Trevor said. "But you won't be able to get close. Along with the fire investigation, the Witches Council is doing an investigation of its own. Your yard is cordoned off until they're finished."

Just like that, his mind was taken away from his blessings, and from Laz's arm around his shoulders, and thrust back into the reality of magical bullshit.

"While you shop, the rest of us will be researching that damned chalice." Lily-Beth slid into a seat beside Trevor and leaned against him.

While Laz and Frank ate supper, which felt like breakfast to him, the family recapped everything they knew. Rosie colored quietly at the end of the table. They'd discussed having her play elsewhere, but in the end decided she probably needed to be included. Nothing was discussed in graphic detail, but he learned more details of what had happened previously.

"You can't be serious?" He stared at Laz. "He's trying to reanimate his dead wife? Like a fricken zom... Z-o-m-b-i-e?" He spelled it quickly, hoping Rosie wasn't fast enough to catch what it was. "Can you even do that?" *What could possibly go wrong?* The sarcastic comment rang in his head.

"There's no proof, but we found a spell in Keres' computer that seems designed that way. What stumps me," Laz frowned, "is what Keres, Brown, Rylie, and all the other escapees are planning to do, and how it fits in with MacElroy."

"I'm just hoping Leticia's guys can find something on the dark web about the chalice." Hazel sighed and tapped her fingers on the table. "I do not want to have to read any more musty old tomes to find information. Our ancestors were boring."

"Excuse me, I have to run." Pearl got up and left the kitchen. A moment later, the front door slammed, and a car started up.

"Still," Lazuli said, "research has to be done. About the chalice, and maybe I can figure out why my presentience has virtually disappeared. And Rosie hasn't seen anything for a couple days either. It's weird."

Chapter Twenty-One

Two days later, Laz sat on the small red sofa in the back of Four Seasons Metaphysical with her three sisters. She inhaled deeply, taking the soothing scent of sage deep into her lungs and holding it for a moment. This was their private work area. There was a tiny kitchenette with a table and stove. A couple of chairs, and the sofa. Off to the other side were shelves of stock and the ingredients for making candles. The whole place had a homey workshop feel that was comforting to her artist's soul.

"Anyone else think it was odd the Gramma Pearl took off right after supper last night?" Laz wondered aloud.

"Ya, and the night before as well. She ate and took off like her underwear was on fire." Hazel said.

"Gross. Don't ever talk about our grandmother's panties. Ick. She's been acting weird. Jumpy or twitchy," Cynth said with a frown. "It's like she's got a secret. Or something."

"Oooh. Hot gossip." Kansas, one of the two shop ghosts, materialized.

"Hush," Ev, the other ghost, popped into view and elbowed the younger ghost in the ribs. "Haven't I managed to teach you that you learn more from stealth?"

Kansas, a young drug addict who had died outside the shop, just glared at the former owner of the pharmacy that used to be in that location.

"Hush up, you two," Cynth grumbled.

"Maybe she's got a boyfriend." Laz laughed and snagged a snickerdoodle off the star-shaped plate on the coffee table.

Andi, one of their best employees, came into the back room. "Who has a boyfriend? Aren't all of you taken?"

"Yup, we are," Laz said. "Well, Frank and I are sort of together. We're dating. But we were talking about Gramma Pearl. She's being weird."

"Ya, I saw her at the library in the back room." The back room was where the actual magic and metaphysical texts were kept...away from mundane eyes. "She had a huge stack of books. I called out to her." She shook her head in puzzlement. "She looked at me, then rushed away without saying anything."

"That's odd."

"Yup," Andi agreed. "And when she came into the shop this morning, she took a bunch of stuff without putting it through the register. I noted what I could, but I thought I'd ask her about it...before stirring up trouble. I mean, she is part owner. Usually, she pays for what she takes."

"So, not a boyfriend then?" Hazel asked, spinning her silver and amethyst bracelets round and round on her arm. "Do you think we should confront her?"

"Hell no. I'm not that brave," Laz laughed, though she wasn't feeling amused. A horrid thought crossed her mind. "Do you think... nah, never mind."

"Oh no, you don't, Laz. You can't start a thought like that and then zip your cake-hole. Out with it, little sister," Hyacinth said.

"You can drop the big sister lingo. We're all adults now," Laz snapped. "And you're not the boss of me."

"Mature," Amber laughed. "Real mature." The amusement slid right off her face. "Seriously, what were you thinking. I'm actually rather worried."

"Fine." Laz took a moment to gather her thoughts. "Suppose...what if..." she sighed. This was going to sound stupid. It was just a random thought that tried to come out without permission. "What if, with all this shit going on, and a high-level magician like MacElroy..."

"There's no such thing as a high-level magician," Cynth corrected.

Laz flipped her the bird. "What if she's under someone else's control?" She blurted the idea, hoping like hell she was wrong.

"Don't be ridiculous," Hazel said. "She's too strong for that."

"I'm just saying...they came for all of us, and Baby Anna, and there was magic found at Frank's after the fire. Rylie torched the bookstore. There's a shit ton of power hanging around here. The council is afraid of MacElroy."

Her sisters fell silent. Nobody looked at each other. They all stared at the floor, frowning.

"It couldn't be," Amber whispered. "No way. She's too strong."

Laz looked up. Everyone's attention was on Amber.

Andi threw her hands in the air. "I'm out of this one. Keep me posted." She whirled round and left the room.

"Now Andi's acting weird. When have you ever known her to run from a problem, or from gossip?" Laz said. Andi didn't share gossip, but she loved listening to it. She loved being in the know.

"Never." Cynth tapped her toes on the floor and jumped up. She took a double chocolate chip cookie off the tray. "What if they got to her, too?"

"I think she's just scared," Hazel said. "She's not the bravest person I've ever met."

Everyone talked at once; their voices blending into a concerned cacophony, their uncontrolled emotions battering her like pellets of hail.

"Whoa! Wait! Shut up!" Laz shouted. When they stopped chattering, she said, "Your emotions are off the chart. And we can't start thinking our friends are against us. That just feeds the chaos. I'm beginning to think chaos is at least part of the goal."

"Oh." Hazel slapped her hands on her knees. "And when there's chaos, they can sneak around doing any damn thing they want. You're right, Laz. We need to be careful."

"What do we do then?" Amber rose and paced back and forth behind the small sofa. "Do we control Gramma Pearl? Do we tell Mom and Dad? Do we let it ride? Maybe I should run upstairs and grab Kody. He might have some insight."

"Possible," Laz agreed. "He's not as close to the problem as we are. Maybe the separation will help. Do we need Dennis and Earl, too?"

Amber jogged up the stairs that connected the apartment she shared with Kody to the shop. Cynth ran down the block to get Earl, and Hazel texted Dennis. Laz wondered if she should call Frank, too. After a moment of consideration, she decided to call him, even though the poor guy was overwhelmed already. He'd been hit by so much over the past few weeks. Knowing he probably didn't have the mental space to be there to talk this out didn't stop her from asking him to join them. He'd asked to be kept in the loop...though this was more a tangled ball of yarn than a loop.

Sasha, the shop cat, strolled through the room. She had first appeared when they'd just opened the shop. Pregnant, dirty, and starving, she was demanding and had scared the living hell out of Kody when she first talked to him. "You guys need to keep it down," she hissed. "I'm trying to rest."

Hazel scooped the cat up. "Oh, hush. If you want to nap, go back upstairs." She set the black cat with the white stripe on her chest back on the floor. "You've got a darned good life here."

"It'll do," she said, her voice dripping disdain, as she ambled back toward the stairs.

"What's up, ladies?" Their mom strolled into the room, with their dad right behind her, his hand on her lower back. When Laz was young, she thought their constant touching was gross. Now, she understood the simple touches were acts of affection, and she envied them.

"Nothing's up," Laz lied.

Her father snorted, and her mom outright laughed. "Honey, please." Her mom shook her head. "Why do you think we're here?" She looked around, "Where's Mom? I thought she'd be right in the thick of this."

"That's the thing." Laz stood to give them a seat on the sofa. She pulled over a chair from the tiny kitchen table and straddled it backward, resting her arms on the back. "Apparently, she just left. She took some stuff, without paying for it, and took off."

"Well, she is part owner," her dad said. He waited for his wife to take a seat before sitting close beside her and taking her hand.

"True, but it was odd." Laz had no great desire to lay out the whole thing. Honestly, she'd been hoping they could solve it without involving anyone else. "I don't want to go over this multiple times, so I'll just wait until everyone's here. Anyone want coffee?"

"On it." Hazel jumped up and started the pot, just as Earl and Cynth came back in with a bakery box. Frank and Rosie tagged along behind them.

"No heavy discussion goes right without treats," Earl declared.

Laz waggled her fingers in a gimme motion, and he passed her the box. By the time everyone had a cookie or brownie, the first pot of coffee was ready. Amber and Kody came in from upstairs, and two minutes later, Dennis arrived from the greenhouse.

"Andi can watch Rosie for you, Frank," Laz suggested. "We've got some great kids' books in the kids' area out there, and of course, coloring books."

Laz and Frank led Rosie to the front and introduced her to Andi. "We'll be in the back," Frank said. "You guys have fun."

Andi grinned. "Guess what, I have juice and cookies." Both of which the shop kept on hand for snacks and visiting children.

When Rosie was comfy, they returned to the back.

"We are gathered here today," Hazel joked. Of all of the girls, Hazel had the most irreverent humor and the least serious demeanor. At times, it was annoying. Right now, the glib comment caused a laugh, and some of the tension ebbed.

"I'm going to cleanse the room," Lily-Beth declared. "I think we need a protective circle, too." She lit a bundle of sage and walked around the room, clearing the negativity by wafting the smoke into every corner with flicks of a large raven feather. Tradition would have dictated using eagle feathers, but recent laws made the possession of eagle feathers a crime.

"Do you really think this discussion is going to go that far astray that we need a magic circle for protection?" Kody asked, crossing his arms over his chest and shifting closer to Amber.

"Probably not, but I've picked up a new trick." Lily-Beth grinned. "I can create a muffling barrier. If we're all inside the circle, I can make it harder for anyone outside to listen in. I can't stop them entirely, but if we keep our voices low, it'll be almost impossible for them to hear. Even magically."

"Where did you pick that up?" Laz could hardly believe such a spell existed.

"Istanbul."

"When were you in Istanbul?" Hazel demanded.

Dennis patted her shoulder. "Chill, hon." She glared at him. Kansas snickered and blinked out of view.

"Last year," Trevor said. "It was just a stop on our way to Paris."

"Great, my parents are travelling the world and I'm stuck in Three Moon Falls," Hazel grumbled. Her father gently shushed her. She curled her lip but fell silent.

"To be clear," Trevor said, his expression dead serious, "it wasn't all fun and games. The stop at Istanbul was at a paranormal medical clinic to have your mother cleansed of a memory-erasing spell. It took them four days to heal her. After that, they taught us a couple of new things."

"Geez, Mom." Laz felt like her heart would stop beating. *What the hell?* She'd known they were on a dangerous mission. But having her memory erased? The idea made her sick to her stomach. "You might have kept us informed."

"Oh, you mean the way you girls kept us informed of all the action here?" Lily-Beth raised one eyebrow."

"Ya, Laz, lay off." Cynth wrinkled her nose in a so-there gesture.

"How about you back off?" Hazel grumbled. "You're always so bossy."

"Stop it," Earl demanded. "Look at you. You're bickering like a bunch of toddlers. How are we going to solve anything with you guys fighting and taking offense at every second word?"

He was right. Laz clamped a hand over her mouth to keep from arguing back. "Maybe," she said after a moment of absolute stunned silence by everyone, "maybe we need to up the wards here, and at all our homes. Can we find or create something stronger? I don't know if it's just the tension we've been under for so long, or if we're being influenced somehow."

Her mom raised her hand in a stop motion. She mimed zipping her lips, then mimed casting a circle.

Wordlessly, the girls got up and began to work. Trevor closed and locked the inside back door and then asked Andi to stay out front and keep anyone from coming into the back room. Their mother gathered a bunch of items from the stock shelves and set them on the coffee table as Amber laid out a circle of short white candles. Outside of that, Cynth laid another circle of stones, alternating between amethyst, selenite, and citrine. Between the candles and stones, she laid a circle of thirteen tall quartz crystals.

With a large bag of salt in her hands, Laz prepared to lay the final circle. Her mom's hand on her arm stopped her. Lily-Beth held up a bundle of herbs. While they all waited, their mom crushed the herbs into fine powder and, after taking the salt from Laz, mixed the salt and herbs before handing them back with a go-ahead nod.

Everyone stepped into the center of the circle as Laz poured the mixture around. When the salt circle was closed, Amber lit the candles with a single snap of her fingers.

"Yikes." Earl gasped. "That will never not freak me out."

Working together, they called on the Goddess and her consort to aid them. Then they requested the presence of Soteria, the Greek goddess of protection, Secellus from the Celtic tradition, Roman goddess Minerva, and Isis. In a quiet, reverent voice, Laz invited all the gods and goddesses who were listening to join them. A soft wind shifted through the room, and then everything fell still.

"Here we go," Lily-Beth said, circling the inside of the circle with a small bell. She made three rounds deosil, or clockwise, to non-magicals. "Mother Earth, Father Sky, all our lordly friends, thank you for being with us today." With a final shake of the bell, she began chanting in a foreign language, maybe Turkish or Greek. With a low bow, she lit the charcoal brazier.

The sisters hummed along, and after a moment, the men joined in. Energy pulsed through the room, and Laz's heart slowed to beat in time with the chant's rhythm. The hair on the back of her neck stood up. Beside her, Frank had goosebumps on his arms. The energy was incredible and invigorating.

By the third repetition of the lyrics, Laz had memorized them. It was a benefit of often using rhyming poetry for spells, you learned to memorize quickly. She chanted along. Her mom moved into the center of the room and dropped more herbs into the brazier. Still speaking the other language, she recited something lyrical and quite pretty. Falling silent, she faced west and clapped her hands three times. Then she did the same to the south, east, and north.

The soft music coming from the front of the shop became muffled.

"Whoa," Laz muttered, "it's muffling sound from outside."

"And it works better the other way. It will be incredibly difficult for anyone to eavesdrop on us now, normally, or magically."

"So cool," Hazel muttered.

"Where do we begin, Mom?" They'd cast the circle big enough to enclose the couch and four kitchen chairs. There wasn't enough seating for everyone, so Laz plopped down on the floor, gently pulling Frank's hand so he joined her. Her parents took the kitchen chairs. Dennis and Hazel sat on the couch, while Earl and Cynth took the two armchairs. Amber and Kody took the last two kitchen chairs.

"First, all our homes and businesses will need new wards. Floral, amulets, and painted."

"Wait, I can't go painting magic symbols around the greenhouse," Dennis objected.

"Yes, you can. Clear nail polish. Nobody will even see it. Up high, down low, under tables. It will be subtle. Like we did at your house after Brown attacked us," Hazel reminded him.

"That's a relief." Frank sighed heavily. "I'm definitely not prepared for this. A man doesn't fight with symbols. He stands up for what he believes in and protects his own." He took Laz's hand and squeezed it gently.

Her body warmed at his declaration. "This is how you protect them." She leaned into him.

He muttered something under his breath, which she ignored.

"We have a few things to address," Lily-Beth said. "First, why is my mother being so secretive? Second, what happened at Frank's place? Third, is anyone seeing, hearing, or feeling something odd? Fourth, how do we proceed from here?" She looked at each of them in turn.

What little joy or pleasure there was from the exciting new spell fled in an instant. Everyone sobered.

"I don't feel like Gramma Pearl is possessed." Laz made air quotes around the last word. "It's more like she's sneaking around, hiding something or doing things she doesn't want us to know about."

"Ya," Hazel piped up. "She never goes out without telling us, and the past few nights she's just up and disappeared. "She's hiding something."

"The other night, she went totally white when you were discussing the chalice," Frank said. "It thought it was odd, or maybe that she had an upset stomach because she just jerked up and left the room. But when she left the house, I didn't know what to think."

"You don't think she knows something about the chalice? Do you?" Laz directed the question at her mother. "You know her best." They discussed all of Pearl's strange behaviors and decided that Lily-Beth would confront her that evening.

"I want to be there," Laz said. "I'm the most psychic. Maybe I can pick up if she's lying, though she is super-good at hiding her emotions."

Her mom nodded. "We'll all be there. About Frank's place, there is magic residue. Not much, but some, and it's dark. Frank, I know you planned on moving into a hotel for the time being. But I think it's best if you and Rosie stay with us for protection. At least until we determine why you were targeted, or if they were actually after Laz."

He was silent for a full minute. "I don't like it, but we'll stay."

Laz hid her smile as it wasn't the time for happiness. But she was thrilled to have Frank close for the next while. They seemed to be really connecting. Even now, he was holding her hand when, a couple of weeks ago, he could barely look at her. "And what about anyone feeling anything weird?" Laz asked. "I'm not getting visions. I mean, I was never inundated, but I usually had a couple a week. Now, I get nothing, but I'm not feeling anything weird, just that my clairsentience is silent, or sleeping." She was worried someone was suppressing her visions, but she didn't mention it. "Anyone else feeling off?"

They went around the room, and nobody was feeling anything. "Rosie isn't having bad dreams since the fire, though it's only been a couple of nights," Frank added. "Does that mean whoever's out there is doing nothing, or are they...what do you call it...blocking us?"

"Could be either," someone muttered.

"Well, that cleared up nothing," Hazel grumbled. "I say let's make those wards and paint those symbols."

"Why did we need the fancy ritual?" Kody whispered to Amber.

"Because we're going to discuss which protective runes are best, and what to put in the wards. If you know how a ward is created, it's easier to undo it," Lily-Beth replied. "And because we're going to brainstorm how to trap our opponents."

"What?" "That's crazy." "Are you insane?" "No fricken way." The comments came one atop the other, and Laz couldn't distinguish which came from whom.

"I was reading about protection on my new phone last night," Frank said. "Could we create and use sigils for protection? What I read is that you can design them yourself. Maybe we could set them up against specific people...you know...the ones we know broke out of jail."

They tossed around ideas, then put Frank and Laz in charge of sigil creation while everyone else worked on new warding. Wards weren't perfect; they couldn't keep out people with the ability to defeat them, but a ward could slow down someone bent on harm, and they could warn of problems.

Suddenly, Laz shivered. "Oh, weird."

"What's weird?" her father, who was working beside her, asked.

"I just felt a shiver...like someone poured icy water over me." She shivered again just thinking about it. "Not in my head, but on me." *Creepy as hell.* "Like someone touched me...like in the bar the other day."

Rosie burst into the back room. "Daddy!" Tears ran down her face.

"Sorry," Andi came in hot on her heels. "I couldn't stop her. She just started crying and ran."

Chapter Twenty-Two

F rank's heart leapt into his throat when Rosie burst into the back room crying. What the hell had happened? He never should have left her with a stranger. He scooped her up and carried her to the sofa. Dennis and Hazel got up immediately and let them sit.

"Thanks, Andi. And don't worry about it. She's been upset lately. What's up, Rosie Posie?" He stroked her back and tried not to be angry or freaked out. He was still muddling his way through single parenting, and tantrums always threw him for a loop. Probably because Rosie rarely had them, especially now that they were nanny-free.

"Tell me what happened?"

"She just started crying," Andi said. "We were coloring fairy pictures, and she burst into tears, threw her marker down, and ran. She was in such a rush, she tipped over the table." Her voice was heavy with apology.

"It's okay, Andi," Laz said. "We'll figure this out. We were about done here anyway."

They'd been making wards for two hours; it was surprising she hadn't already come looking for snacks because she was bored.

Slowly, Rosie's tears abated. "Daddy, I got scared." Her voice shook. "We were having fun. I like Andi. But something touched me. I couldn't see it."

His gaze flew to Laz, who looked as shocked as he felt. "Could it be a bug?" he asked. "Like a big old fly?"

"No!" She glared. "It toucheded me, everywhere. All at the same time. It was so cold."

Laz knelt before them. "Me too, honey. It touched me too. It was ice cold. It was awful."

Rosie nodded. "It was bad. It was the bad man."

Lily-Beth joined Laz on the floor. "Tell us about it. What did you feel? Did you see anything?"

"It was cold. I didn't see anything. Nobody."

"Did you feel anything or see anything in your head?" she asked gently.

Rosie squished tighter into his arms and wrapped her hands around his neck, nearly cutting off his airflow.

"A little lighter, baby. You're choking me." She relaxed just a touch. "That's better." He rubbed her back over and over, in small soothing circles.

"It was the man. The one who bosses them around. He tells them what to do."

"Jeez," someone muttered.

Frank glared.

"Did you see him?" Laz asked. "In your mind."

"I don't know what he looks like. He's big. And dark. I'm scared." Her entire body trembled.

After half an hour of gentle questions, they didn't learn anything new. Everyone, except Frank and Rosie, returned to what they were doing. He'd never felt so helpless and useless in his life. He was in way over his head, and he was drowning.

Anger flared within him. It was all he could do to bite it down. He was like a bent willow, just waiting to whip back up. He wanted to punch something. Like beat the ever-loving crap out of something. Pummel it until there was nothing left. His heartbeat climbed along with his anger.

Lily-Beth, who had been making tea, walked over to him and put her hand on his shoulder. "Son, calm down. She can feel your rage. She'll think you're mad at her."

Shit.

He inhaled a rough, noisy breath and tightened all his muscles and forced them to relax all at once. He was still furious, but slightly calmer. He needed to get out of there. He needed to get away from the magic and these people.

He had work to do. There was a meeting with the insurance company in less than an hour, and a daughter to protect. But he felt frozen in place. Held captive by feelings he couldn't deal with.

"Frank, Rosie, and I are going back to the house," Laz declared without consulting him.

"We're what?" *Who put her in charge?*

"We're going back to the house. I know some relaxation games we can play." She gave him a look pleading for understanding...at least that's what he thought it was. Who knew for sure? "We're just going to chill for a while. We'll make some lunch too."

Just like that, they were bundled into the truck the insurance company had rented for him and on their way back to the house. Rosie sat in the back, humming an unfamiliar song while they talked about the weather and how Christmas was getting close.

"Do you celebrate Christmas? Isn't that a Christian thing?"

"We put up a Yule tree, but yes, we exchange gifts. Many magicals do. Yule is about celebrating the return of light and acknowledging the change of seasons. Like many people, we find it a time of peace and joy. Love and sharing. So, yes, in a sense, we celebrate. And we do share gifts, but on Yule, not Christmas day."

She managed to make it sound reasonable, not like it was a commercial event. He'd never been much into the holidays until they'd had Rosie. Now, he loved watching her joy in the seasonal celebrations. They used each as an excuse for a small party or celebration. Everything from Christmas to St. Paddy's Day to Valentine's. The small parties broke up the monotony of life. Not that life with Rosie was ever boring.

The discussion helped him relax. Having something besides anger to focus on drained his ire, though he was certain he would never stop wanting to massacre the person who 'touched' his child. Given the chance, he'd end them. Laws, morals, karma...none of them mattered at this moment.

He glanced at Laz, who was frowning. "What? I can practically hear you thinking," he said. She gave him a sidelong glance. "Not like that." He took a second to formulate what he meant. "I see your expression. Your shoulders are tight, and your knuckles are white from where your hands are clenched. Obviously, you're thinking really hard."

"But you don't 'sense' anything? Right?"

"I do not. I'm not sure I'd want to listen in on people's thoughts. For a moment, I thought it would be fascinating. Then I realized I have no desire to know what people think about me, if they think about me at all."

"I love you, Daddy," Rosie piped up from the back, clearly intent on making him feel good.

"Love you too, Rosie Posie."

"I know. But sometimes, when you don't say anything, you're mad."

Her comment startled him. "How do you know that?"

"I feel it." She giggled. "Right now, Laz is laughing at you."

"Not laughing at him...at least not exactly. I'm laughing at his surprise. Neither of us realized that you didn't just get visions, you felt things too. Your magic is very strong."

"I'm going to do something important."

In the rearview mirror, he saw Rosie frown.

"I just don't know what yet."

"You'd do something important, even if you didn't have magic," he said. "And I know you will do something valuable without magic, too."

"Prolly."

"Probably," he corrected her gently. "Say all the letters."

"'kay." She giggled.

"Brat."

"I loooove you." She laughed again.

He glanced at Laz and rolled his eyes. What could he do? His daughter was too dang smart for her own good.

I nitially, he'd believed that Laz had just been trying to distract him when she suggested returning to the house. Boy, was he wrong.

"Yoga?"

"Yup." She grinned. "Even if you suck at it, and you will, it will help you relax. We'll mostly work with easy poses, child's pose, mountain pose, and dead man's pose. Easy poses and breathing."

"Nanny Becket used to make me do yoga. I hate it."

Frank tweaked her nose. "No, you didn't like Nanny Becket. We'll try Laz's yoga and see if we like it."

She led them through a series of poses, focusing on breathing and keeping their shoulders relaxed. "This isn't real yoga," he complained. "Where are all the pretzel moves?"

"We can try those, but the six I've chosen are the best for removing tension."

"I can do this one," Rosie bragged and stood on one foot, wrapped her other leg around the one she was standing on, and twisted her arms together. You try, Daddy."

Laughing, he gave it his best effort. He could twist his arms and stand on one foot, but there was no way he could balance with tangled legs. He kept falling over.

Laz grinned at him. "Even though you can't do it yet, it's good for you, and you're much more relaxed."

"Somebody's at the gate," Rosie dropped her other foot to the floor and stared out the window. "Somebody not good."

The house trembled.

"Earthquake?" Frank asked, trying not to panic.

"Hang on. I'll check." Laz closed her eyes. Her brow wrinkled. "Nope. Not an earthquake."

"An a-t-t-a-c-k?"

"At-tack. Attack," Rosie clapped for herself. "No, Daddy, the house stopped them at the gate. It took a lot of energy, so the house shivered." She looked thoughtful. "We should feed the thing?"

"What thing?" Laz asked, obviously perplexed.

"Ya, kiddo, feed what thing?" *What the hell was this now?*

"The thing in the basement."

"You have an animal in your basement?" He stared at her.

"The only animals here are wild ones, and the cats. There isn't an animal in the basement."

Rosie laughed. "It's not an animal. It's magic. And it's hungry now. It used all its energy."

Jeez. Cheez Whiz on burnt toast and a ham sandwich. He wasn't ready for magic things that needed to be fed...whatever that meant. Laz didn't look impressed either.

"What is it?" Laz asked.

Rosie shrugged. "I dunno. But it took a lot of magic to stop them at the gate. Now it's hungry."

"How do we feed it?"

"It eats magic. It likes leftovers."

"The thing in the basement, not an animal, eats magic leftovers?" Laz asked. She took Rosie's hands and led her to the sofa. She sat down and looked Rosie right in the eyes. "Honey, I'm going to need you to tell me everything you know about the thing in the basement. Do you know where it is?"

"In the old part. In the dirt." She scrunched up her face. "I can feel it, but I can't see it. We should feed it. It's too tired to fight again. Let's do magic!"

Chapter Twenty-Three

*W*hat the ever-loving universe was she talking about? Laz tried not to flip out. *There was something in the basement that ate magic? How had she not known that, and what the hell was it?*

"Is it bad?" When Frank opened his mouth, Laz gestured for him to be quiet. He glared, but didn't speak again.

"Nope. It's good. It p'tects you. We should feed it."

Laz's mind boiled with questions and partial thoughts. Could this thing, whatever it was, be part of the reason their house had a mind of its own? It protected them, it repaired itself, it kept out strangers. How did it get there? Who had put it there? And why the hell was it hungry?

"Can it wait a bit to be fed?"

"Not too long. Somebody is snooping. It's stopping them. I can do water magic. That will help."

"And you're sure it's good, and not tricking you?"

"Yes." She sounded exasperated.

"Can you tell it to wait?"

"It doesn't think like us. It just...knows. It doesn't talk, but I can feel it."

Half panicked, Laz sent an urgent message to her sisters to get their asses to the house. She mentally reinforced the rush part but added a no immediate danger ending. Affirmative replies flooded in.

"You called your mom," Rosie said in awe, her eyes wide with surprise.

How the hell had she known that? "I did. I'm not afraid to ask for help when I'm not certain what's going on. Even though sometimes I don't want to admit I don't know, or I'm worried. It helps to share problems."

"It sure does. And I, for one, am glad they're coming. Smart move, Laz." Frank offered his hand for a high five.

Clearly, he was exaggerating his enthusiasm to prove it was okay to ask for help. A father's way to keep his daughter from isolating her problems and fears. An admirable trait for sure. He was a good father. The image she'd seen, before her visions faded, of the three of them with an infant popped back into her head. She wouldn't object to Frank as the father of her daughters...however many they ended up with.

It wasn't long before her family came in, talking amongst themselves and calling out greetings.

"What's up?" Her mom asked when everyone was settled in the living room. They were all seated, but nobody was still.

"Rosie," Laz said, "Tell them what you told us."

"The thing in the basement is hungry. It worked very hard to keep them out of the gate. It needs magic. It eats leftovers." Her tone was a bit belligerent, as if she expected disbelief.

"Interesting," Lily-Beth said, clearly confused. "What else do you know?"

She rehashed their earlier conversation, ending with, "I can show you where it is, in the old part."

"I don't understand what she means by old part," Frank grumbled, his fingers tapping restlessly on the arm of the chair.

"Our house started as a cabin. It's been built onto at least three times that we know of. Part has a concrete basement, some have wooden, and the oldest part is just dirt. Probably an old root cellar."

"That explains the way it looks." Earl grinned. "It's kind of a hodge-podge of styles, but it works really well." The house was a blend of Victorian and Colonial styling, two stories tall, with dormer windows in the attic. An octagonal turret graced either end. Flawless white woodwork was balanced with brick trim. It radiated comfort and welcome.

Laz was struck by the fact that Gramma Pearl didn't answer her psychic call. "Where's Gramma Pearl? She should be here."

"Her car is here," Trevor said.

"I'll go check her room," Laz's mom sounded worried.

"I'll come too." Laz followed her up the stairs. They knocked once and opened the door.

Piles and piles and boxes of books and magical items filled the normally pristine room. Every flat surface was covered, and there was barely room to walk between the stacks of boxes. "When did she turn into a hoarder?" Laz asked.

"It wasn't like this last week when I vacuumed. By the Goddess, what is going on here?"

Laz pushed past her mom and picked up a book. "I can't even translate this title. It looks like Arabic. This one's French."

"Lavender, sage, willow bark, mustard seed, cumin, sesame seeds." Laz turned. Her mom was digging into a box. "Ground rubies, ground garnet. Opal chips. Gold dust. Silver wire. Copper chains. Holy royal pantheon. Look at the size of this diamond. It can't be real." She held up a two-inch faceted stone. "There's a fortune in gems here. What in the ever-loving fudge is she doing?"

"How is that any of your business?" Pearl demanded from the doorway. "You are invading my privacy. Frankly, I'm appalled." She snatched the stone from Laz's hand.

"Mom, what are you doing? What's all this stuff?" Lily-Beth asked softly.

"Are you in trouble, Gramma Pearl? Are you even you?"

"For the love of the Goddess. Yes, I'm me." Her indignation fled, and she deflated visibly. "I'm trying to..." Footsteps sounded on the stairs, and she turned around. "Let's finish this downstairs." Her voice cracked as she shooed everyone back downstairs. She closed the door behind herself.

Nobody said anything. They just watched Pearl pace back and forth in the living room. The waiting was making Laz crazy. The urge to dig into her grandmother's thoughts was overwhelming. She wasn't as much concerned about what she saw upstairs and what was going on in Pearl's mind as she was worried that someone was controlling her mind and using Pearl as a tool. She clenched her hands and curled her toes in her fuzzy bunny slippers until she felt she had better control of her urges. Peeking was morally and socially wrong and reprehensible, but fear for the rest of her family drove her to temptation.

She leaned on the doorjamb between the kitchen and the living room. Waiting. Frank came to stand behind her, placing his hand on her shoulder. "Hey, relax," he whispered. "Give her a moment to explain."

"I'm trying to be patient," she whispered back, grateful for his support.

"Okay, Mom, out with it," Lily-Beth demanded. "We've all seen your room. What the hell is going on with you?"

"I didn't want to tell anyone until I found a solution."

"Solution to what?" Amber asked, taking the words right out of Laz's mouth.

"Well...um...the thing is..."

Laz had never seen her grandmother at a loss for words. Not once. And rarely had she ever paused to find the right words. She wanted to shake the truth out of her grandmother.

"The thing is what, Gramma Pearl? Quit hedging around and looking for lies. Tell us the truth," Laz demanded, unable to keep silent a second longer.

"Zip it, girl. I'm your grandmother, and you will respect me."

Laz reared back at the rebuke. "Actually, unless you can explain this to everyone's satisfaction, you get no respect. Not now, not ever."

Pearl glared, sniffed, and straightened her shoulders. "The thing is..." she swallowed hard, "I know where the chalice is."

"What the fudge?" Laz blurted. Everyone talked at once until her mom whistled.

"Mom, how does that explain the books and the spell ingredients in your room?" Lily-Beth's voice was soft, but definitely no-nonsense.

"And what about those jewels? And where is the chalice?" Laz threw in, tired of waiting for answers.

"If the chalice is what I think it is, it's in the basement."

"I told you," Rosie declared. "And it needs magic." She stomped her foot.

Frank gently hushed her. "Not now, sweetie. Let Gramma Pearl finish her story. Then you can tell us again."

"And the books?" Trevor prodded.

Everyone nodded at the question and leaned forward in their seats in anticipation of the answer.

"I was trying to duplicate the chalice's power."

Stunned silence filled the room.

"Oh, get over it," Pearl demanded. "The thing is, the chalice is magic."

"No shit," Frank whispered.

Pearl whirled round to glare at him. "My research tells me that Petunia Beryl Hawk worked with a blacksmith and jeweler to create the chalice. It's designed to funnel stray magic bits. Unless I'm wrong, it's what protects and heals this house. It uses leftover magic for the benefit of those who live here."

"I told you," Rosie declared.

Nobody paid any attention to her.

"I believe that if the chalice leaves, the house loses its magic. I wanted to replicate what they did. I've done some silversmithing. I can create a cup, and I have magical skills. With the right ingredients and spell, I can make one to replace this one."

"Why make a fake one? It's not like we're giving away the real one." Trevor said.

"Wouldn't it be easier to create a forgery and let the fake be found?" Frank asked. "You know, keep the real one protected." He snorted. "I can't believe I'm talking about magic cups like they're real."

"It is real, Daddy," Rosie said, tugging on his arm. He gave her a quick hug.

"We should look at it," Hazel suggested.

"We should leave it buried." Just thinking about unearthing it made Laz squeamish. "No good will come from unburying it." Where that certainty came from, she couldn't guess. It was more than a premonition; it was a full-on bad omen.

"I think we should dig it up again, so I can replicate it," Pearl said. Something about her grandmother's attitude set Laz's nerves on edge.

She wasn't usually prone to irrational actions like the one she was suggesting.

"Again," Laz squeaked. "You've already dug it up once?"

"I suspected something was protecting our home. I didn't know what. When we were looking for clues to the artifact, before we found the pendant, I found a reference to the item in the basement. It is a cup, by the way." She looked entirely too smug.

"So, you've known about this for weeks and kept it to yourself through all of our discussions about what it was and where to find it? Why, Gramma? Why?" Laz's knees went weak at the depths of Pearl's betrayal.

"I don't suppose you know anything about our would-be attackers, do you? Are you in cahoots with them? Can we even trust you not to hand over the pendant and the chalice?" Hot anger flooded through Laz. Her face burned, and her nerves tingled. This was beyond unbelievable. Her hands burned like they were on fire. She channeled a breeze to cool them.

"Watch your mouth, girl. I might have kept a secret, but I am still your grandmother." Her glare would normally have quelled any backtalk.

"Zip it, old lady," Laz snapped. "You lied to us. To our whole family. You, who preaches truth and protects the family. You lied. You planned to forge a new chalice without telling us. How in the name of the Goddess can you justify that? How, Gramma Pearl? How?"

Frank massaged her shoulders, but she shrugged him off. She didn't want to calm down. "Are you blocking my visions, too?"

Rosie tugged on her arm. "Gramma Pearl isn't bad," she said, her face a mask of confusion and concern. "She's good, Laz."

Could Rosie be right? Could her grandmother just have made a huge mistake? For the life of her, Laz couldn't decide. "Okay, honey," she lied, "I believe you."

Rosie glared.

"I'll try to believe you," Laz corrected.

"I think we should leave the chalice where it is," Frank suggested.

His words seemed to release everyone from their stunned stupor. They all began talking at once.

"So, if we dig this thing up and take it from the house, the house loses its power?" Amber asked.

"Yes," Pearl said. "At least I believe so. That's what the journal readings seem to indicate. Somehow, and I'll be jiggered if I can figure out how, it takes the leftover and unused magic from our spells and channels them."

"That's why it needs fed," Rosie yelled. "It fought off the men at the gates. It protected us so much the house shook. It's empty."

"Seriously?" Laz knelt in front of Rosie. "That's what shook the house?"

"Yes!"

"How long have you known it was there?" Frank asked her.

She shrugged. "I just knowed."

"How could she know that?" He turned to Laz.

"It is possible that she might be our reincarnated great-grandmother."

"W hat the..." Frank barely stopped himself and stared at Lazuli, "are you talking about? The hits just kept on coming. A magic house, magic attacks, a magically burned-down house, now this. Laz was out of her mind. Reincarnation wasn't real.

"For months now, we've believed that Rosie is our great-grand-mother. She uses her same mannerisms and speech patterns. She knows things she shouldn't."

"Okay, I don't believe in reincarnation, and coincidences happen all the time." Frank's insides shook. "That's what this is."

"We, I, believe it's more than that," Laz said, her soft voice not in the least soothing. She fidgeted with her watch, a plain gold one this time...fidgeted like she was trying to keep something from him.

They were trying to bamboozle him. "Fine, give me examples." He crossed his arms over his chest and pinned her with his toughest stare. She didn't seem cowed by his anger.

"She uses a few of my grandmother's favorite phrases like 'that yanks my skirt', she knew the clue to the artifact was in a purple book. She knows about and understands the chalice."

"It's not an artifact, it's a pendant. It has thirteen stones, and it is very pretty, but it is bad," Rosie declared.

"And..." Laz gestured to the girl, "and that. There's no way she should know that."

"She probably overheard you talking about it."

"Frank, we don't talk about it. Nobody knows about it. We were super careful to keep her from knowing. She's a child. She'd be easy to coerce or trick into revealing something we wanted hidden. She's psychic like our grandmother was. There's just so much."

He stumbled to the couch, flopped down, and buried his head in his hands. This was more than he could take. Magic was tough enough. Magic sucking cups? Not likely. But reincarnation? That was too far out there. It was like something from a B-grade movie.

Laz sat beside him. "I didn't believe it at first, none of us did. But it seems undeniable."

"What's that mean to me? And how come she remembers things from before? Assuming I buy into this."

"I've done some reading. It's believed that some memories slip through when a soul comes back. Maybe it's random. Maybe it's the Goddess leaving them on purpose. There's no way to know. Some researchers believe déjà vu is memories from previous lives popping up."

Rosie came up to Frank and kissed his forehead. "It's okay, Daddy. I'm just me."

"Of course you are, honey. Things are just...weird."

She patted his cheek and smiled. "It's going to be okay. I promise."

"I hope you're right, baby."

"Don't dig it up. The bad men want it. They don't know where it is."

He didn't even bother to question her assertions; he just believed her. What choice did he have? Her having magic had already shown him there was a whole world he knew nothing about. Why wouldn't reincarnation be part of it? He was torn between believing the concept and thinking it was total insanity.

"Does everyone come back?"

"No. Great Gramma is the only one of our relatives we can't call from beyond the veil," Las reassured him. "Not everyone comes back. I'm thinking it's probably pretty rare, or we'd hear more about it. Even the Council doesn't know much. Or at least they aren't sharing what they know."

She turned to her family, who stood clustered across the room, talking in low voices. "What are we going to do?"

"I don't know about you guys," Pearl declared, "But I'm going to eat something, then I'm going to work on creating a decoy chalice. They want a cup. I say we give them one. But it has to be magic, or they'll know it's fake."

As much as Frank wanted out of the whole situation, it was clear he and Rosie were in up to their necks, and he couldn't think of a better plan. "Somebody order food. I'll go pick it up."

"I'll go with him," Laz declared. "Just don't make any decisions while we're gone. Your truck or mine?"

"Mine has newer winter tires than yours," he said. "Let's take it. There are still a few icy patches after that last snowstorm. We want the best grip possible."

Chapter Twenty-Four

Even in the passenger seat, Laz kept scanning the ditches and the road ahead. This time of day, there was a decent chance of seeing deer or elk. She wouldn't want to hit one. Frank kept his eyes on the road and occasionally on the rearview mirror. The sun was going down, but the sky was blessedly clear of snow clouds, and there wasn't much traffic, though there were a few spots of black ice on the highway.

"This is a ton of food," Frank grumbled, making Laz laugh.

"We're a ton of people. There are twelve of us, and Cynth is eating for two. Gosh, I can't believe my baby sister is pregnant."

"That was fast. They haven't been together long."

"Nope, but they have a history. If you take that into account, it doesn't seem far-fetched, though I still don't want to think about them bumping uglies." Okay, she was jealous that all three of her sisters were in relationships, and what she had with Frank was tenuous and unsteady. Never mind that Cynth was expecting, and Rosie's claims that

Hazel was pregnant with twins. She hated being jealous and vowed that her sisters would never know how she felt, because her jealousy didn't mean she wasn't thrilled for them.

"Me either. I don't want to think about any of your sisters having sex." He shuddered and swerved slightly. "Holy shit. That guy behind us came out of nowhere. Bloody zoomer."

Laz glanced out the back window. Another vehicle, a tall one, maybe a truck, maybe an SUV, it was hard to tell which, was right on their tail, its LED headlights nearly blinding her. "He's way too close. Pull over and let him pass."

"I can't, there's snow on the shoulder. I don't know how deep it is. I'll slow down so he can get by."

As their speed ebbed, the other vehicle got closer. Laz covered her eyes to reduce the headlights' glare and peeked through her fingers. "He's gaining on us."

"He can't pass on this hill."

They were headed up a steep hill to a sharp turn. "I think he's going to hit us," she shouted. Their bumpers met with a deafening crash. Her head whipped forward and back again. Snow whirled up around them, and everything went white. Then dark.

Agonizing pain in her head woke her. She nearly gagged on the intrusive smell of ginger chicken.

"Hey, you're awake," Frank murmured, his fingers stroking her face.

"Sh. My head." She shifted her head and groaned. Agony spiked down her spine and up across her head.

"Don't move. Help's coming."

"What happened?" Even as she asked, memories rushed in. "He did that on purpose."

"Yes."

"How long was I out? Was I out?" She closed her eyes to block the pain. "My chest hurts." Her nearly healed wrist was killing her, too. Everything hurt. Every damned molecule in her body was on fire.

"Mine too. Seatbelt bite. Good thing we were buckled in."

Wailing sirens exacerbated the pounding in her head. "Make them shut it off."

"Don't move, baby. I'll be right back." He backed away and disappeared from her sight. His door eased shut almost soundlessly. She appreciated him not slamming it.

She started counting to distract herself from the relentless pounding. She got to thirteen when the siren abruptly cut off. The blinding lights continued to flash. Those things were enough to give a person a seizure; thank the Goddess she wasn't epileptic.

The door opened, and he popped his head back in. "I'll be right outside. Here's the medics." He backed out again.

"Hi." A dark-haired man with a clean-shaven face stuck his head in the truck. "I want you to stay still for me. Can you tell me your name?"

"Lazuli Hawk." He asked her a battery of questions, including the date and who the prime minister was, and seemed satisfied with her answers. *That was good, right?*

"I'm going to shine a light in your eyes. Try not to move your head. Spine damage is unlikely, but we're not going to take any chances."

She winced at the bright light. "Son of a—" He flashed it repeatedly in both eyes.

"Can you wiggle your fingers?" She obeyed. "How about your toes?"

"I feel fine, except for this damned headache and my chest."

"Your side of the vehicle hit a boulder. We're going to take you out as carefully as we can and put you on a backboard. But first, a cervical collar."

"But nothing hurts. I'm freezing, though." She looked down. "Gross, I'm covered in food."

"We'll get you a blanket and clean you up once you're in the ambulance. The collar is a precaution, ma'am. Hold tight, Lazuli. That's an interesting name." His smile and words were reassuring, but she had no interest in conversation.

"Is Frank okay?"

"The gentleman you were with is being examined, but aside from bruising from his seatbelt and a tiny cut where his head hit the side window, he appears okay. We'll make sure."

"Can I call my mom?"

"Not right now. Did you have a purse? We'll bring it along. Your phone, too, if we can find it." As he chatted, he fit her neck with a grossly uncomfortable and movement limiting brace.

"This thing sucks," she grumbled. "I can't move."

"That's sort of the point." His light chuckle was reassuring.

"Where's Frank?"

"You can see him in two minutes, just hold tight."

She needed to see him. Needed to know he was alright. Panic swelled in her chest, stealing her breath.

"Lazuli, take a deep breath. Try to relax. Your friend is fine. This might hurt a bit, but we have no choice. We're going to have you wiggle into this rescue seat and ease you out."

"Can't I just climb out?"

"Let me check with my supervisor. Don't move."

A minute later, he was back. "Policy says to use the seat."

"Let me do it," she demanded. "I can move."

He had another fast discussion with someone behind him and then nodded. "Take it slow. If anything feels unusual or stops feeling, freeze, okay?"

Wincing at the increased pain in her head, she slowly eased her backside over the bin between the seats and onto Frank's side. Thank the Goddess she was flexible. She paused to catch her breath. The damned seatbelt bite was killing her, and her mouth was dry from the airbag powder. She hoped it wasn't toxic.

"What's this white shit?"

"It's probably talc or corn starch. It won't hurt you."

"Sucks to breathe it. My mouth is full."

"You probably gasped when you hit and inhaled a bit. The hospital will check it out for you. For now, don't worry." Someone spoke to him. "Okay, Lazuli, hold still. Try not to change your position as we pull you out."

After some agonizing pulling, the medic and a firefighter had her out of the truck and sitting on the stretcher.

"I'm fine," she grumbled, "I just want to go home."

"Be patient, Laz," Frank called. Wherever he was, she couldn't see him without twisting her body, which the medics wouldn't let her do.

An unfamiliar police officer stepped into her field of view. "Your friend has contacted your family, and they'll meet you at the hospital. I'd like to take a quick statement before the medics finish with you." He bombarded her with a dozen questions. "Okay, then. I'll get a better statement at the hospital." He patted her leg and stepped back.

The medics rolled her through the night, she closed her eyes against the blinding lights, and grunted as they bumped her into the ambulance. Frank climbed in beside her.

"Are you hurt?" she demanded, her throat still dry from the powder. "Can I get a drink?"

"No food or drink until the doc checks you out," the medic said, buckling himself in.

"I'm okay," Frank said, reaching out to take her hand. His thumb caressed her palm. "You got the worst of it. Your mom will meet us at the hospital. She's going to call your doctor."

"I'm glad you're okay." Unable to keep her eyes open due to the pain, she let them drift shut. "I need drugs." She didn't often take over-the-counter meds, but the biting pain was more than she could bear.

"After the doctor," the medic declared.

She was pretty sure they were able to medicate patients, but her muddled brain wouldn't let her formulate the question. Frank's gentle massage lulled her to sleep as the two attendants talked around her.

"Lazuli Hawk, I'm getting tired of seeing you in my emergency room." Dr. Carter slipped through the closed cubicle curtain.

"Ya, well, I'm tired of being here."

"I'm going to run a few tests, then you can see your mom while we wait for the results." She began her examination.

"Where's Frank?"

"The man you came in with is waiting in the waiting room."

"I want to see him."

"After the exam."

"Now, or I'm leaving." She struggled to sit up.

"You've always been stubborn." She stuck her head out of the curtain and told whoever was outside to find Frank.

Relief flooded through her when he stepped inside. There was a small bandage on his left temple, but otherwise, he looked okay. He was covered in airbag dust.

"Are you okay?"

"I am. Apparently, my long legs kept me further from the airbag, so I didn't sustain many injuries from it."

"Good." She sighed and nodded at the doc. When Dr. Carter began her examination. Frank slipped into the bedside chair and held her hand again.

Eventually, she was declared fine except for the seatbelt bruising and a very minor concussion. "Why does my head hurt so damned bad?"

"Everyone experiences concussions differently. Take some over-the-counter pain killers, and if they don't give you relief, call me for a prescription, okay?"

"Sorry about supper," Laz said as she inched her way into the house. "It's all in the ditch." She really didn't care, because all she wanted was sleep. "I'm going to shower and go to bed."

"Not until I examine you," Hyacinth declared. "I'll relieve some of your pain, but I don't like that someone ran you off the road. I want to check you out for magic. There was dark residue at the crash site."

"After I shower."

Frank helped her upstairs. "I'll wait out here." He closed the bathroom door.

She leaned against the wall, tired from the simple climb. Gathering her strength, she used her ability to control air to create a small vacuum and suck the airbag powder and bits of food from her clothing and hair. Some of it was stuck fast. The takeout bags must have exploded. She might never eat ginger chicken again. Gross. She funneled the debris into the trash, downed two pain pills, and stripped.

Her shoulder ached with every movement, but she managed to clean herself up. The furnace was running when she stepped from the shower. Rotating her body slowly, she channeled the warm air from the floor vent to dry herself. She wrapped her body in a towel and called out, "Frank? Can you come in?"

The door cracked open. "What do you need?"

"Can you wrap my hair? It's dripping down my back. Or do you hurt too much?"

"I'm okay. I took some meds earlier. Turn around."

Wrapped up tightly, she let him lead her to her bedroom. Amber waited on the edge of the bed. "I've got this, Frank. We'll meet you downstairs after she's dressed."

"I'll wait in the hallway." He slipped out and closed the door.

As Amber helped her into some comfy jammies, she said, "That man has it bad for you. He's worried sick."

"He's a good guy."

"He cares about you a lot. Turn around, let me comb your hair." Unlike when they were kids and helped each other with their hair, her strokes were gentle. She combed out the knots and pulled Laz's hair into a low ponytail. "Let's go see Mom. She checked out the crash site."

"I need Cynth to do something about this headache." Nausea was growing in her stomach...either from hunger, the accident, or both.

Surprisingly, the only people around were Cynth and her mom. Amber disappeared as soon as she and Frank helped Laz onto the couch.

Cynth set to work right away, gently placing her hands on Laz's head. "I'll ease the pain where I can. There's some bruising, too. I'll deal with it. I'm going to check if anyone was in your brain."

"How could that happen?" Frank demanded. "They didn't stop. They rammed us off the road and kept going."

"Just because you didn't see them stop, doesn't mean they didn't mask their stop, or meddle from a distance."

"Son of a bitch!"

"Sh. My head."

"Sorry, babe," his voice dropped to a whisper.

Funny, he was using endearments now, when only days ago, they were just friends. Any other man would have bolted, what with all the magic and shenanigans going on. Maybe that was because he was familiar with magic from his first wife. Her eyes drifted shut. It hurt too much to think.

Cynth's fingers were so light on her scalp; she could barely feel them. As she worked, the pain ebbed, but didn't go away completely.

"Someone brushed through, but didn't linger," Cynth whispered. "I feel, residue, like windblown dirt?" She sounded unsure. "I can't find any indication that they dug deeply. Either they were rushed or immediately found what they needed."

"Are you saying they could know where the chalice is?"

"I'd say only if that was foremost in your mind. If you were thinking of something else, that's most likely what they'd find." She kept working, her breath slow and steady. She worked her way all over Lazuli's head and down into her neck. "Lie back, and I'll ease the pain from the seatbelt."

"Eat this," her mom commanded. "Energy ball," she explained to Frank.

"I can't take the bruising away; half the town will know about the accident, and they'll expect bruising. But I can ease the discomfort, for both you and Frank."

"You can do that for me?"

Laz opened her eyes to look at him. "Ya, Frank, she can ease your pain. I'm feeling better already." Mostly, she was relieved that their assailant hadn't left visible marks in her brain. "She'll need to rest a bit first."

Cynth stepped back, and her mom guided her to a chair. "Food coming up," Lily-Beth declared and hurried into the kitchen. She came back with a heavily laden tray. "Restorative tea, cheese, crackers, pepperoni, cookies, and energy balls." She balanced the tray on her daughter's lap.

Laz sat up. "I could use some food too."

"Amber and Kody went to get supper."

"Hopefully they make it back," Frank muttered.

"I think this was a scare tactic," Laz said, sitting up slowly, careful not to jostle anything. Her head was a thousand times better, but still hurt. It was important to balance magical energy use. Enough to feel better, but not enough to totally deplete Cynth's energy. She explained that to Frank.

"Does this *healing* leave residual energy?" he asked, worry coloring his voice, and a deep frown on his brow.

"Some. All magic leaves traces and residue. There are ways to use most of it up, like channeling it into a spell. Hazel can use it to heal plants. Most of it is left alone to dissipate back into the universe where it came from."

"Could the thing in the basement suck it up?"

Laz jerked with the reality of his words. "That's exactly what Gramma Pearl said." She looked around. "Where is she anyway?"

"Upstairs in her room, researching."

"I'm worried about her."

"I tried to sneak read Gramma Pearl," Lily-Beth said. "I'm not the strongest at reading these things, but I didn't find anything. I'm debating calling Cecily for a proper reading, but I'm not sure I want to involve anyone else."

"Makes sense," Laz agreed. "If shit goes south, we need someone left behind to protect the world."

"Geez. Crap on toast," Frank muttered.

"Hey," Laz said, getting up and going to his side and patting his shoulder. "There are always wars, it's just that you weren't aware of the magical ones."

"Like Salem and all the other witch trials." He nodded his understanding.

"Except they started long before that. People persecute what they don't understand. And evil exists everywhere," Laz said, sadness for the state of humanity wearing her down. "Like the men in Salem going after mundane women, calling them witches to get control of their land. A lot of mundanes have died due to false accusations."

Everyone went silent for a few minutes. Cynth stood up, set her tray on her seat, and brushed her hands together. "Which is why I say find the joy. Every moment, good or bad, has joy. Our joy here is that you two are okay. And since we know they're coming, we can defeat them." She gestured to the couch. "Okay, Frankie-boy, lie down and I'll fix your chest."

He went without visual hesitation, though Laz suspected he was wary, and why wouldn't he be? Easing his discomfort went quickly. Checking his brain took a bit longer. He stood and flexed his shoulders, moving them left and right, bending and stretching. "Wow. That's so much better. There's very little pain left. Thank you so much. How can I repay you? Can I pay you? I know you do your midwifing for pay."

"No. This one's on the house. I don't heal just anybody." She smiled. "A proper witch doesn't charge for her work. Some take donations. The midwife thing is different. It's a normal career, and I rarely need my special skills."

"Understood. Thanks again." Gratitude rang in his voice and showed in his smile. "I have so many questions." He chuckled. "Though I'm learning that things become clearer if I pay attention. Except I can't quite wrap my head around the thing in the basement being helpful, but not sentient, or at least not truly sentient. How can a not-alive thing collect and use magic residue? And how do we know it's not evil itself? And how does it know who to trust?"

"Those are faith questions. We don't understand how it works. But we take it on faith."

The front door opened, and Amber and Kody came in. "Food's here," Amber called. "The accident is all cleaned up. Leticia was there. Looks like she was checking things over. I expect we'll see her later."

Chapter Twenty-Five

"What are our plans for Yule this year?" Laz asked her sisters. "I can't believe it's already December eighth." She leaned against the counter in the shop's back room, enjoying the cranberry-vanilla tea in her mug.

"I'm having a sale on candles, gift items, and books," Amber said, taking a seat at the small kitchen table. She smoothed her hands over the surface, as if ensuring it was dust-free.

"How long will it run?" It was tough to find the right length for a sale. Too long, and people would delay coming in, and might forget about it. Too short, and Laz knew they might miss potential customers who were busy with the holidays. With this being the store's first Christmas/Yule season, they were playing a guessing game.

"I'm thinking December 13th to the 23rd. We might catch a few extra Christmas shoppers that way. Like everyone else, I'm closing Christmas Day, Boxing Day, and New Year's Eve."

Laz nodded in agreement. "I noticed the new angel statues and the Bibles. The statues make sense, but Bibles?" They seemed counterintuitive. Typical Christians tended not to visit their shop.

"Bibles in a magic shop. Ridiculous," Ev snapped derisively, her ghostly form sliding into view for a moment before fading away.

"Actually, the first Bible was by request, sort of. There's a book that compares Pagan beliefs with Christianity. There's a lot that's the same." She chuckled. "And, a lot that's different. The customer considers herself a Christian-Pagan. She believes in God but also believes and works with the powers within the earth. I ordered the book and the Bible she requested. Then I decided, why not get a few? I made sure I can send them back if they don't sell."

"Earl sells Bibles in the bookstore," Cynth said.

"I suggested that. She doesn't like the bookstore. I didn't ask why, I just accommodated her." Amber looked at each of her sisters, one after the other. "There's something else. I don't know if it means anything or not. I can't decide."

"What?" Laz's senses went on high alert. Pressure built behind her eyes as a vision poked at the back of her mind. She closed her eyes and let it come. *Two men and a woman. Outside the shop, clustered together, talking? Maybe chanting?* She had no sound. *A fire. The woman looked frantically left and right, and they bolted...leaving the fire burning against the building.*

"A fire!" she declared, opening her eyes. Her legs trembled as she stumbled toward a chair. "They were here. I couldn't see faces, but I felt them. And since when do I get visions after the fact? They're almost always before." She moved to the couch and sank into its welcoming cushions.

"Fire was my first thought. I thought it was ash, but there were no burn marks, so I chalked it up to dust. I didn't say anything sooner. I knew you'd all be in this morning."

"When was this?" Hazel demanded, peering toward the front of the store.

"This morning. I went out to sweep the walk."

People shed the energy of their emotions. Sweeping sideways with intention cleared away negative energy. They swept outside both doors every day. Sometimes more than once. And at their homes as well. Lingering negative energy could affect anyone and ruin their day.

"I'm going to check if Earl's security camera caught anything, but I doubt it. Our shop is probably out of range." Hazel started punching a message into her phone.

"How could they do that?" Laz asked. "Wouldn't our wards keep them from doing mischief?"

"Well," Amber said thoughtfully, "they were interrupted before they did any damage, and the fire put itself out. That's protection of a sort, just not what I imagined."

"Ya, but the Goddess always does things her way." Laz's shakes were going away. "I wonder if they did anything to the lumberyard or garden center."

"Why would they? Every attack so far, except on Baby Anna, has been directed at us. I'm sure that was just to grab her power. At least that's how it felt to me," Cynth said.

"Still, I'll check with Frank. Amber, check with Dennis. Brown knows you and Dennis are a thing." Laz frowned. "Hell, after Rylie and seeing the dossiers she had on us, they probably know more about us than we do."

"I think this is all about testing our powers," Hazel said after she texted Dennis.

"Hang on," Amber said. "I need an antacid. All this talk of evil and stalking has given me heartburn." She stood with one hand on her chest, the other on her belly. Rummaging through a drawer, she extracted a roll and popped one into her mouth.

"If they know about us, they know about our friends too. Does this mean everyone we know is in danger? What the hell does MacElroy want?" She groaned. "I'm sure he's the ringleader. It's not a premonition; it's just a knowing. She blew out a breath, making the flame on a candle on the coffee table dance back and forth, without extinguishing it. She pushed the air away from it and watched it dim, then flare when she let the air back in. It wasn't as impressive as the way Amber started fires with a flick of her fingers, but it was impressive enough. Besides, everything needed air to live. Engines needed air to run. People needed air to breathe. And when it was hot, she could call up just the right amount of breeze to cool off without changing weather patterns. Her favorite was channeling air from the heat duct to her slippers, so her feet stayed warm when she got out of bed.

"What are you thinking about, Laz?" Amber's question interrupted her game.

"Air, mostly. The chalice? Why didn't Gramma tell us about it? Why did she keep it a secret? And why was she trying to duplicate it? Wouldn't a decoy just have to *feel* magical and not actually be? Why would it need to be the same?" She set her tea beside the gold-tone candle and crossed her arms. "I can't get away from the idea that she's still lying to us."

"Why would she do that?" Cynth grumbled, rubbing the smooth surface of a polished stone she pulled from her pocket.

"Why would she suddenly start peeking into our boyfriends' minds? But she's done that, more than once, too." Laz frowned at the memory.

Blinding pain slammed into the center of her forehead. She groaned in agony as wave after wave of images washed over her like a tsunami of dirt. Nothing came into immediate focus as the images jumped from one to another and on to another.

She clutched her head. The images settled to a single focus. *Keres, with a man she could only see from behind. MacElroy! Arguing.*

"I say we start killing them," Keres demanded. *"They'll give it up to protect themselves."*

"And bring the damned law down on us. There's value in waiting. If we take them out, they could retaliate and destroy it." Keres snapped. His shoulders tensed. Even from behind, Laz could read his barely checked anger.

"I don't believe they have it," Keres sneered. *"I couldn't find it. I read her mind, and she knew nothing about it. I still have a tenuous connection with her. I could go in again and search."*

"Stay the fuck out of their heads. Bad enough you ran that one off the road. I should kill the two of you for disobeying. What part of fucking secrecy don't you get? We keep low and don't show ourselves. Gossip and subtle questions will reveal more than alerting them to our search. Stay away from them."

Abruptly, the vision vanished, and the room, and her sisters' concerned faces swam into view. She groaned. "Drugs," she whimpered, not even caring how weak her voice was. "Cold." Her teeth chattered.

A soft, fuzzy blanket draped over her shoulders, and two pain pills floated across the room on their own. Something thumped softly, and something rustled. *The kettle?* Clutching her head in her hands, she mumbled her thanks.

"A vision?" Amber whispered.

"Gimme a minute." She wanted to tell them everything she saw, but the pain was too debilitating. She fell backward on the sofa with her arms crossed over her head and eyes trying to shield herself from the light and noise. Across the room, her sisters whispered among themselves, concern heavy in their voices. Slowly, everything faded as she drifted into a worried sleep.

"Hey, wake up, honey," her mom's voice murmured.

"No." The throbbing had ebbed but was still horrid. She needed sleep.

"Drink this." A mug was thrust into her hands. The ceramic was cool and smooth under her fingers in direct contrast to the jagged pain in her head. Lifting just enough to get the mug to her mouth, she chugged the drink, barely holding back a gag.

"You trying to kill me?" She coughed at the bitter aftertaste.

"You'll feel better in a few minutes." Nothing was worse than her family's remedies for pain-killing teas.

"Where is she?" Frank demanded in a harsh whisper. "Rosie said Laz needs me."

"Sh," someone hushed him. "This way."

Frank settled on the couch beside Laz with Rosie on his lap. Jeez, Laz looked like hell. She was beyond pale. She had all the color of a damned zombie.

"Laz, are you okay?" Rosie whispered. "You're hurting." The childish compassion in her voice nearly broke his heart.

Laz cracked her eyes open and smiled weakly. "Hey. I'm good. I just have a headache. I'll be okay in a bit. Sometimes what I see hurts."

"Your heart hurts too." She climbed onto Laz's lap. "Your head and your heart. It's okay. Daddy says that sometimes life hurts, but it always gets better." She pressed a soft kiss on Laz's cheek, hugged her, and climbed back onto Frank's lap.

"She's okay, Daddy. Stop worrying."

Someone chuckled.

"I think the kiss and hug were just what I needed," Laz declared. "And food."

"I'd offer to go get something," Frank said, "but we all know what happened last time." His blithe comment made everyone chuckle.

"I'll order in," Kody said.

"Pizza and Vietnamese hot soup," Laz mumbled.

Frank sat back, out of the way, with Rosie on his lap while they fed Laz beef jerky, energy balls, and fruit juice. Finally, she straightened up and started talking. In a shaky voice, she related her vision. When she finished, they peppered her with questions. She answered as best she could, and when the food arrived, she shoveled it in like she hadn't eaten in weeks, all the while answering the same questions again and again.

"Enough of this," he said. "She's exhausted. This isn't getting us anywhere. I'm taking her home to sleep."

"But we haven't figured this out," Cynth said with a hint of petulance.

"Figure it out without us. Come on, Rosie." He set her on her feet. "Time to go."

Laz stood and wobbled a bit until he grabbed her arm. "See you guys at home." Without a backward glance, he led her through the store to his truck parked out front.

He helped Laz in, buckled her and Rosie in place, and climbed in. "Relax, ladies. We'll be home soon."

"And hopefully they won't show up en masse."

"Let's hope."

They were almost home when she whispered, "I couldn't tell if it was the past, the present, or the future." Her voice shook, and her hands trembled in her lap. "I'm scared, Frank. I've never been this scared."

He reached out and squeezed her hand and pulled it over to rest on his thigh so he could keep holding on. He didn't know if he was comforting her or himself. "I'm scared too, but we're going to get through this...somehow. I have to believe that."

Chapter Twenty-Six

"I'm going to use air to move the water, Rosie. I want you to keep the water from moving." Without moving her mouth, she channeled the air to ripple the water. Instantly, Rosie pushed back, holding it flat.

"Good. That's the way. I'm going to blow harder now." It had taken two days to fully shake her last vision's aftereffects.

She increased the wind pressure on the water until tiny waves formed in the bowl. "Flatten it. Keep it from moving." They worked on that for a while. Increasing and decreasing the effort she put into moving it.

"Now for something harder. I'm going to use the air to dry up the water. Then you pull it back into the bowl."

At Laz's insistence that he not distract his daughter, Frank sat silently, watching but offering no comments or encouragement. He was jumpy, like he wanted to comment or step in to help, but aside from fidgeting in his seat, he was resisting the urge.

A tiny cloud formed above the bowl, growing bigger and bigger as the water level in the bowl dropped. "Pull it back down," she encouraged. "See it dropping back in. One drop at a time. Pull out the rain."

Rosie's face curled up in effort. Her eyes squinted and her cheeks puffed up, making her look like a half blind pufferfish. One drop fell from the cloud. Then another and another.

Laz praised the effort, though she wasn't resisting or holding onto the cloud too hard. Training came in increments, and at times, a series of small successes, to build confidence, was the best path forward. "Well done, take a rest now."

"I want to finish."

"Okay, push the water back down." It all dribbled back into the bowl, and Rosie slumped when she was done.

"Can I have a cookie?"

"Snickerdoodle or hot cocoa cookie?"

"Hot cocoa, please."

Laz got up and grabbed the cookie jar and the energy balls from the fridge. "Lemon, vanilla, or matcha?" She slid the divided tin across the table.

"Matcha."

"Gross." Frank laughed. He hated the taste of matcha, but Rosie decided she loved it after learning that most of Laz's sisters enjoyed it.

"Daddy, it's good. You should try it again. You have to try something seven times before you can say you don't like it."

Laz laughed at how she parroted her father's wisdom. "She's got you there."

"The cup feels better. It took our magic leftovers."

"Did it now, Miss Rosie?" Laz asked.

She nodded and mumbled, "Yes," around a mouth full of cookie. "It's very strong now. It hasn't had to push anyone away for a while."

Under Rosie and Pearl's insistence that the chalice was good, and not evil, they'd returned to normal life and returned to using simple magic. Lighting candles with a snap. Teleporting things from the cupboard to the table. Creating warming breezes inside the house. Shoveling snow without a shovel. Flipping book pages with a thought. Hands-free filling and turning on the kettle. The usual things.

"Can I water the plants?"

She couldn't turn on the tap magically, but she could use her skills to get the water from the jug to the plants without too much mess. "You'd better wait for Hazel on that," Laz said. "She's the plant expert."

"Okay." Rosie frowned.

"I have to hit the workshop today for a couple hours. My mom and dad will watch you while I'm there and your dad is at work."

Frank left at the same time she did. He went right toward town, and she turned left. Neither of them intended to put in a full day, and she knew he was relieved that Rosie enjoyed being with Lily-Beth and Trevor.

An eerie feeling dropped over her as she stepped out of the truck. The sky was clear, and the air should have been colder than it was. Stepping forward, she hit a wall of warmth and stopped dead. This wasn't right.

A raven screamed from the roof and swooped toward her, veering left and hopping along the crest of a snow pile. It screamed and swooped again, going back to the same pile. After the third time, she muttered, "Okay, I see you." She stepped into the deeper snow, grunting when it passed over the top of her boots. "Crap." It was only ten feet to the snow pile she'd created when shoveling after the last storm. She'd pushed it further back toward the trees to allow for more shoveling as the winter progressed.

The raven hopped in front of her, just out of reach, and then over the pile to the other side.

"Whatever you want, better be important." The bird's fear pecked at her heart. It was terrified and worried. Getting emotions from animals was more Cynth's thing than hers, though the nearby ravens, hawks, and crows seemed to prefer Laz's company.

She crested the five-foot bank and looked around. "By the Goddess!" She rushed down the other side. A small cat, one of the newer feral ones and barely more than a kitten, and a raven lay at the foot of the bank.

"What the ever-loving crap?" The raven hovered over the bird, totally ignoring the cat, which would normally have become his food. "What happened?"

The bird's wing was twisted at an unusual angle, and the cat's chest barely rose and fell. The healthy bird cawed loudly.

"Okay, I get it." She whipped out her phone and called Cynth, who said she'd be right over.

Here, behind the pile, the temperature was more what it should be. But neither of the animals would last long in this cold. "Do I take them inside, or what?" she muttered to herself.

The healthy raven squawked and fled back toward the shop. "I guess I'm moving you." While it was obvious that the bird was in agony, the cat seemed worse. She shrugged out of her jacket and gently wrapped the unprotesting cat in it. It didn't make a sound as she took it inside and placed it in an empty cardboard box she lined with scraps of fabric.

The messenger raven watched her every move, even standing in the doorway she'd left ajar and keeping her in his sight. "Okay, your friend is next." She expected a battle. Ravens were known to protect their mates and their young. This one stood by, cawing softly as she lifted his friend and took him inside.

Cynth pulled up in her SUV. "What do we have?"

They went inside, and the messenger followed them, seemingly unfearful of being indoors. "Okay, buddy," Cynth said. "We're going to look after him."

"Let me know if you want out," Laz told the bird and slowly shut the door. He hopped over to the workbench where his friend lay atop Laz's jacket.

"I called Evan Hardy. He's coming out. I'm not as good at healing animals as people, but I can see what ails them." Evan Hardy was the local vet. He had no magic they were aware of, but he was the best person to treat an animal that might need meds or more than just a magical boost.

She focused on the cat. "Her leg is broken, and she's starving. I don't know how long she lay there. She's suffering badly from the cold. She needs warmth, and that leg needs mending. I don't sense frostbite." She turned her attention to the raven.

"The bird's wing is twisted. It's a male, which probably makes the other a female. A couple. They do mate for life." Cynth examined the bird with soft touches. "There's magic here. Both of these animals have been hurt by magic." Her voice went dark with anger.

"How? This land is protected."

"No, the gates protect the driveways, and the thorny hedges protect the rest. It isn't impenetrable. Obviously, the assholes can come and go as they please. This shop is too far from the road for either of these injured animals to have made it alone. They were hurt close." She turned to the healthy bird. "Okay, Missy. I want to examine you, too."

The bird cocked her head left and right and stepped forward slowly. At the last second, she flapped her wings twice and landed on the bench.

"Holy shit," Laz exclaimed. "She understood you."

The crow nodded.

With slow, steady strokes, Cynth examined her. "I think you're okay. But watch what you eat and stay away from strangers." She looked at Laz. "We should start feeding them close to the house. Just so they have a safe food source."

"We can't possibly protect all the animals in the area."

"No, but we can protect cats and birds. And I'm guessing these two birds are the ones that hang out around your shop. They were probably targeted for a reason."

The crow's raucous caw startled both women.

"Jeez. You're inside. Tone it down." Laz chided, and the bird ducked her head in acknowledgment.

"I think this was a scare tactic aimed at you."

"Ya think?" Laz snapped sarcastically.

"Hey, don't bite the hand that heals you. I'm just trying to muddle this out."

"Ya, I get it. I'm just frustrated. This has been dragging on way too long. I want it over with." The raven cawed, and Laz was struck by a certainty that the end was coming before the new year rolled around. By the Goddess, she hoped she was right...however it ended.

The vet knocked, and the guardian bird flew up to a top cupboard and huddled down to watch. Smart bird.

"Weirdest thing I ever saw," Evan said after examining the raven. "It's like he's been tangled in a net or something. Reminds me of a bird that got caught up in a kite string. But there's no string, and no bits left over. He's lucky you found him. I can set the wing, but he needs to be caged for a few weeks. I'll take him back to my office."

"Could he stay here? I have an old cat carrier that might work. Or a budgie cage. He'd have room to move but not fly. I'll follow your instructions exactly."

"I don't know."

"Look, his mate's around here somewhere. If I set the cage in a window, they'll be able to see each other. But I'm sure the cat is better off with you. Cats are easier to domesticate than ravens. The bird might do better away from other animals."

She crossed her fingers behind her back for luck, praying to the Goddess that Evan would agree. She'd prefer to keep them both, but having the cat might ease his conscience.

"A cat carrier is too small," Cynth said. "What about Hazel's old parrot cage? That one she got from a garage sale before Mom said no way to a large bird. It would have plenty of room for him to move and stretch, but not fly."

"That's probably a better size," Evan agreed.

He did a full exam on the cat. Then, using plaster and bandages from his kit, set the leg. "She needs a cone, too. I'll take her to the office, and email feeding and care directions for the raven...if you promise to let me know if anything seems off." He was talking to Cynth, not Laz. "I know you have medical training."

"I, we, can keep you updated," Laz agreed. She got a hint of pleasure from the healthy bird who seemed to agree with the decision.

"I'll come back in two days to check on him." After a long lecture on the care of wild animals, Evan departed.

Cynth spent ten minutes pouring healing energy into the bird with very little improvement. "I'm sure this injury is magical. There is the smallest bit of residue, but it is microscopic. I helped a bit, but he's going to have to heal naturally. I'll come by every day and give him an energy push...it might help."

"I'm going to get that cage," Laz told the bird, standing with the door open. "You in, or out."

The raven hopped down and settled beside its mate.

"No pooping on my stuff. If you need to go, do it here." She spread a couple of layers of thick paper on the floor. Got it?" The bird nodded, making Laz shake her head. "Back in ten minutes."

She walked out with Cynth. "Wow, it's warm right here. Must be a thermal downdraft or something."

"No breeze though," Laz countered. She channeled in a breeze to stir up the air, mixing the warm with the cold, doing her best to return it to normal. "That's better." She shivered and shook her head as they headed back to the house in their own vehicles. She'd swear someone was messing with the temp around her building. But who? And why?

After situating the bird in its new cage, she headed to town. Time for a talk with the police chief.

"**A**ny word on what caused Frank's fire?" she asked after the pleasantries were finished. She sat in Leticia's utilitarian office at the station. The only personal effect was a family picture of Leticia and her siblings. Leticia preferred to keep a solid line between personal and public. The exception being her few friendships within the magical community. That included the Hawk family.

"Magic. There was magic all over your friend's house. White, black, and gray. I expect the white was from the daughter." She shook her head, and the beads on the ends of her dreads rattled together. "She might be casting without knowing it. Especially if she's afraid. You said she controls water, right?"

Laz nodded.

"One of the upstairs bedrooms survived better than the rest. Almost as if it was protected, and it's where the white energy was focused."

"Wow, she tried to protect her things."

"Impressive, but futile. There's nothing left; it burned to the ground. Just that one section was less destroyed." She shook her head. "It was gas-fueled."

Like the Hawk family, and many rural properties in the area, heat was provided by piped-in natural gas.

"I was surprised the line didn't rupture. They often will."

"Thank the Goddess for that. It could have injured the firefighters."

"Honestly, the house could have fully exploded, not just the small explosion you mentioned. You got lucky."

Laz's stomach rose in her throat. It took all her will not to empty her stomach in the small garbage can beside the desk.

"You need to watch out. I can't find any substantive evidence, but MacElroy and Keres have been seen in the area. Not in town, but nearby." She turned serious. "You have my number. If any shit goes down, you call before you start to fight. I've got your back, and there's council backup in the area. And I don't just mean your parents."

The Council was large, though Laz didn't know the full extent. They had research facilities all over the world, at least one magical hospital, several incarceration facilities, magic vaults, research facilities, and who knew what else. They were self-funding through investments and business dealings. They were big, and at times mired in bureaucracy, but not as much as some governing bodies.

"Good to know they're around. I was worried nobody would take this seriously. There wasn't much concern when Keres, Brown, and Rylie attacked. At least not enough to suit me."

"I agree, but they have a policy of letting things work out themselves...like fights between toddlers."

Laz rolled her eyes at the idiocy. "Here's hoping they show up for the next battle."

Chapter Twenty-Seven

"Are you sure this is a good idea?" Laz looked around the living room. Balloons hung everywhere. The air was heady with the aroma of fresh-baked chocolate cake and the savory scents of hot appetizers. Her stomach growled in anticipation.

"It's Hyacinth's twenty-eighth birthday. Of course, we have to do this." Hazel poured barbecue chips into a star-patterned bowl and set it on the table next to the cheezies and a plate of seasoned crackers she had made earlier.

"But inviting all our friends over? It just seems risky to me. Having a large number of Three Moon Falls' strongest witches all in one place with MacElroy and Keres in the area seems like an unnecessary risk to me."

Her mom strolled into the kitchen with a case of sodas. She set the box on the counter by a large plastic container of ice. "Of course, we're doing this. I've missed too many birthdays, and we're not skipping any more. We'll celebrate Cynth today, and you in January. All of us. Every year from now on. We're not skipping another birthday celebration. Are you having premonitions about today?" Her tone turned compassionate with an undertone of worry.

"No. I'm just getting jumbles of weird images. Nothing concrete. And there's nothing about today specifically, at least as far as I can tell." She couldn't shake the unease pressing on her shoulders. Her chest was tight with worry, and her fingers ached from clenching her fists against unknown, invisible assailants that weren't even real. At least not yet.

She was beginning to understand why some political attacks were called terrorism. It wasn't the attack itself that was the problem; it was the fear and terror of what might be coming afterward that instilled fear. She shook off the negative thoughts. Today was a celebration.

"I'm not getting anything either. How about Rosie?" Her mom asked, and just like that, the negative thoughts were back before they were even gone.

Laz sighed and began putting the soda into the ice. She might as well give up. This party was happening whether she wanted it to or not. She'd attend, but she wouldn't let her guard down for a minute.

Her father and Frank came into the kitchen. Trevor immediately went to his wife for a kiss. Frank smiled at Laz and came over to her. He stroked a finger down her cheek. "Are you okay? You look tired."

"I didn't sleep well last night." Or any night for the past couple of weeks, but she kept the last part to herself.

"Maybe you should take something for that. I have some over-the-counter sleeping pills. I can give you one tonight."

"I don't think so, but I appreciate the offer." No way in hell was she taking sleeping pills. She needed all her senses intact. She kissed his cheek, and he wrapped his arm around her shoulder. Aside from wanting to stay safe, there was no apartment readily available before the new year, so he and Rosie were staying at Hawk Manor for the time being.

Seeing him every day, sharing meals with him, and talking for hours had brought them closer together. There had been no formal dates, but family board game nights, and time alone had built a sweet intimacy between them. Though she hadn't said the words, she was fully and solidly in love with him. The declaration would wait until she was more certain of his feelings. His caring was obvious...that didn't mean it was love.

With the few men she'd dated seriously in the past, she'd always been able to read their emotions. Their frustration, their caring, their boredom. All their emotions. She got nothing from Frank. Research told her that being unable to read your partner was often a sign that they were meant for you. Knowing everything your partner thought made white lies impossible, and no marriage would last without the ability to hide petty things that were annoying in the moment but were unimportant in the big scheme. Everyone needed mental privacy. Funny that her mom seemed to be able to read Trevor's mind. But maybe that just came from knowing him so well after being married so long.

"Let me know if you change your mind. They're out in my truck."

"I'll do that. Thanks, Frank."

"Now," he grinned, "what can I do to help get this party going. People will be here soon."

"I've got several cases of pop and beer in my trunk," Trevor said. "Can you help me carry it in?"

They took off outside, and Laz busied herself setting up food trays with Hazel. The party was a surprise. Earl was bringing Cynth over once all the guests had arrived. Of course, it wouldn't end up being much of a surprise with a dozen cars in the driveway. As Danica, the first guest, arrived, Laz found out her mother had a plan. Everyone was parking out of sight, down by her workshop.

Danica was followed by Mel and Jerry, Leticia, and a couple of magical cops. Amber, Kody, and Kody's grandmother were next. The house was filling fast. Mayor Quinton and her husband came in. Then Andi from the store, and Jeri, who worked at Earl's bookstore. Though they were already friends, Jeri and Jerry made a joke out of greeting one another.

"Hi, I'm Jeri," she said with a laugh.

"Hey, I'm Jerry too." He bowed low. "This handsome man is my partner, Mel. Nice to meet you, again."

Before long, the house rang with laughter and conversation. Most of the guests had some form of magic and were well-versed in shielding their emotions. Earl and Dennis didn't have any magic, but her sisters had shown them how to keep things to themselves, or at least tone down the broadcasting of their emotions.

"Here they come," Amber announced. "Earl just texted."

Everyone scrambled into the kitchen, out of sight of the front door.

"Hello?" Cynth called when she entered a few minutes later.

"In the kitchen, dear," her mom called back. "Just making a snack."

"It smells good in—"

"Surprise. Happy Birthday," everyone shouted all at once.

Cynth's hands flew to her chest. "Oh, my goodness." Her cheeks turned pink as Earl urged her forward into the gathered guests.

"Happy Birthday, babe." He kissed her cheek and stepped back so her guests could greet her.

"I said I didn't want a party," she grumbled, but her smile showed that she was touched by the attention.

Happy conversation bubbled through the room as everyone chatted and loaded plates with hot and cold appetizers, chicken wings, and salad. Laz leaned back against the kitchen sink, taking it all in.

Danica, with her hair styled into a purple pixie cut, flirted with one of the police officers. Mel and Jerry held each other's hands as they laughed with Lily-Beth and Trevor. All her sisters and their men mingled with smiles on their faces. Rosie hopped from group to group, listening and sometimes talking to the other guests. She had a great time watching and holding Earl's niece, Baby Anna. It was the perfect party.

"What are you doing out here alone?" Frank asked, setting his empty plate on the counter. "You should be socializing."

"I should. I'm feeling...I don't know...overwhelmed maybe?"

"Because you're exhausted?" He slid his arm around her and pulled her to his side.

"Probably."

"Why don't we step out back for a bit. It is warm in here after the oven was on for so long, and with all these people crammed in."

They grabbed their jackets and went out the back door just off the kitchen. The evening was warm, and the sky was cloud-covered. "I wish I could see the stars," she grumbled, leaning against the deck railing. "Why does clear skies have to mean cold in the winter?"

He stepped behind her and wrapped his arms around her waist. "I could explain it, if you wanted me to."

She swatted his wrist. "I know why. That was a rhetorical question, Frank." She leaned into him, loving the feeling of peace brought by having his arms around her.

"Yup." He pressed his cheek to hers. "It is beautiful out here. It's a lovely night. And you're beautiful. Inside and out."

A soft smile crept over her face as his comment pushed aside her worries. They fell silent. A snowshoe hare hopped across the lawn, just barely inside the light cast from the windows. An owl dove at the hare, barely missing it before swooping back into the trees. In the distance, one coyote's howl was answered with a series of yips.

She shivered.

"I thought you loved that sound."

"I do, but tonight it feels lonely to me."

"You're not alone," he whispered against her ear, "I've got you."

She turned in his arms. "I appreciate that." She pressed her lips to his. Softly at first. Then more firmly as passion rose and her love threatened to pour out. She lost herself in the warmth of the kiss and the comfort of his embrace. Finally, she stepped back. "I suppose we should go back inside."

"One more minute."

He kissed her again. Long and slow.

When he eased back, she resisted the urge to pull him closer again. "Thanks," she whispered. "I feel much better now."

"You are very welcome. Happy to help, anytime." He winked, pulled her to his side, and turned her toward the house. "Get ready for chaos."

Three hours later, Laz climbed the stairs. The guests were all gone, and the house was tidied. She contemplated how blessed she was that her family had so many magical friends. People they could count on.

Frank met her at the top of the steps. "She's finally asleep," he whispered. "I didn't think she'd ever stop talking about the party."

"She was adorable, hopping from person to person, getting to know them all."

"She's turning into a real social butterfly. For a while, with all the changing nannies, I worried she'd end up disliking people or would draw into herself. I'm glad that didn't happen."

"Being a father must be very hard at times." She grabbed his hand and pulled him into her room. "Come, sit with me for a few minutes."

He hesitated. "Will your parents mind?"

She shrugged. "I don't know. I've never taken a man to my room before. At least not until you and I ended up in bed with Rosie." She tugged again. "Come on. I need to be with you."

His eyes went wide.

"Not like that." She absolutely wanted him in a physical sense. But, right now, she just wanted more time with him without her family around. "I want to sit with you."

He glanced around furtively.

"Nobody else is even awake." She chuckled.

He followed her in and eased the door shut behind them.

"Turn your back for half a sec, please."

He turned away and asked why.

"So I can get out of this dress." She slipped out of the knit dress she'd worn to the party and into some fuzzy flannel pajamas. "Okay, you can turn back around." She folded the dress and set it on the chair in the corner before climbing up on the bed. "Come, sit with me."

He hesitated and stood staring at her.

It sure would have been nice to know what he was thinking.

He walked around to the far side of the bed and joined her, sliding his arm around her shoulders. She snuggled in close with a happy sigh. "I needed this. I needed you." She brushed a kiss across his cheek, loving the roughness of his late-night scruff.

On impulse, she pivoted out from under his arm and onto his lap to kiss him again. She couldn't remember ever wanting to be with a man this badly. Heedless of her entire family being nearby, she silently set about seducing him.

Chapter Twenty-Eight

"Anyone seen Laz this morning?" Frank asked as he poured himself a coffee. He tried not to catch either of her parents' eyes. After they'd made love last night, he'd fallen asleep in her bed. She was gone when he woke, which hurt a bit. Thankfully, it was early, and after a late night, Rosie was still asleep and didn't notice that she'd slept alone.

"Not yet," Hazel replied. "She's probably at her shop. Some mornings she likes to get an early start and eat later. She could be checking on the birds, too."

"You should take her a coffee," Trevor said. "There are travel mugs in the upper left cabinet."

"Hang on, I'll pack you some muffins for breakfast. You probably need them after last night," Lily-Beth said.

He froze. Was she talking about the party, or their...extra-curricular activities? "Um. Sure. That sounds good."

Lily-Beth came over to where he stood and pulled some muffins from the pan on the counter. "Relax," she whispered, "we approve." She hesitated for a heartbeat. "But know that if you hurt her, we have enough land to bury you where nobody will e-ver find you." She smiled broadly.

"Um. Ya. Okay. Yes, ma'am." *They knew!* He knew giving in was a mistake. He should have resisted harder, but dammit, she was irresistible.

Her laugh was light and carefree, almost like she'd been joking. He was sure it was one of those jokes people make, but don't actually mean. He hoped.

"I really like her. A lot." What else could he say?

She snapped the lid on a container of buttered muffins and scooped some fruit salad into another container. She put two forks and the containers into a cloth bag as he filled two stainless-steel road cups. "Thank you." He did his best to smile before snatching up the items and fleeing the kitchen.

Outside, he paused in the early morning light, trying to get his heart to stop pounding. How could a woman be so nice and so terrifying all at once? He walked slowly toward the workshop and decided to stop sleeping with Laz in her parents' home. To stop sleeping with her at all...at least until he had a better understanding of how he felt toward her.

She was special, and he adored being with her. She was smart, talented, and kind. She was wonderful with his daughter. They seemed to connect on so many levels and had a lot of interests in common. They liked the same books and TV shows. He'd been attracted to her for years. Almost since he'd met her, and the more time he spent with her, the deeper he fell. Besides, she was as hot as hell. It would take a better man than him to resist her charms.

Was it love? Maybe, but he couldn't be certain, and he was wary after not loving his wife enough. Was he even capable of loving a woman, of loving Laz, the way she deserved to be loved? He needed to sort things out, sooner rather than later. He should back away gracefully, without hurting her. If it wasn't too late already. He was more than aware of the caring in her eyes when she looked at him. Just last night, Mel and Jerry were teasing him about Laz being in love with him.

A skiff of snow had fallen overnight. One set of tracks led away from the house. He followed them to her workshop and knocked before letting himself in. Laz had her back to him and didn't turn, so he shut the door behind him.

A soft breeze brushed past him, first warm, then turning cool as it blew the other way. A sheet of paper shifted off a nearby table saw and floated in the currents. It flew around and around the room. He ducked as it went past for the third time.

Her shoulders looked stiff, and the paper began moving faster and faster, each rotation getting smaller and smaller. Tighter and tighter.

Jeez! It was a tornado in here. Small tools began to rattle in their brackets on the wall. More papers lifted, and a stack of sandpaper rustled in its cubicle before the sheets flew out and joined the chaos. Small metal tools rattled in the wire hook wall holders.

He pressed his back to the door. In a cage in the far corner of the room, two crows watched and squawked.

It hit him like a piece of wood thrown from a saw that she was doing this. Laz was creating the tornado. This was way beyond using a small breeze to turn water into clouds. If she could do this, what else could she do?

The wind stopped abruptly, and she whirled round. He must have made a sound to draw her attention.

"Frank. I didn't hear you come in."

"Um. Ya." He held up the snack bag. "I brought you food. And coffee." He lifted the mugs he held in his other hand. It was a miracle he hadn't dropped them or tipped them and spilled the coffee. He fumbled for something to say as he wiped off his boots. Her pure power had stolen his ability to reason. If he wasn't certain of her innate goodness, he'd be so scared his balls would shrivel up, fall off, and roll away like marbles.

She took one coffee and the bag from him. "Come in. We can sit at the table and eat." She set them on the table. "Just let me let Brenna and Corbin out of the cage. Corbin's doing much better with Cynth's daily energy boosts. It seems to be healing him faster."

"Corbin, I know means crow, but Brenna?"

"Brenna means raven as well. Kind of a play on words."

"Cute. Are they okay loose?" He stared nervously at the enormous birds. "How big are they, exactly?"

"Corbin, the male, is the biggest. I'd guess his wingspan is over three and a half feet. Brenna is much smaller, only thirty inches. She let me measure her."

"Aren't you afraid of them?" It hurt his masculinity to imply that he was afraid.

"They've been hanging around for years. They can live for fifteen years. I always talk to them when I see them, and sometimes I leave them food. They seem to understand me when I talk, but maybe that's just me wishing it was true. Watch."

She walked up to the cage and said, "If I let you out, will you be good?"

The duo nodded.

"Promise not to scare my friend, Frank?"

They nodded again. She opened the cage, and the smaller of the two stepped out and hopped to the floor. It walked up to Frank and stared at him as it tilted its head left and right.

"You can pet her. She likes her neck scratched at the back."

Somewhat in awe, he stroked the soft feathers. The bird preened before walking back to her mate.

"That's so cool. Can you do that with all birds?"

"This is a first for me. Cynth is our animal person. Animals and babies. This is new. Let's eat. I skipped breakfast. Sorry, I left without waking you. I was up at four. I couldn't sleep. It was either that or wake you in the naughty way." She grinned.

He had wondered if she was having second thoughts. "What were you doing when I came in?"

"I started thinking about all the things air can do. Air's my element. I decided to try a few new things. Before today, I've sucked the air out of a vehicle's engine and made it stall. I've used wind to snuff candles and to shift papers. Breezes are a cinch. I can kick up a dust storm or blow one away. I've used it to keep the front of my jigsaw clear while cutting. You saw me evaporate water and turn it into clouds."

"That was impressive, but it was nothing like the tornado I just saw. What else does air do?"

"Accelerates, or inhibits fire." She looked giddy for a second. "I used air to move some of the grit I use for my rock tumbler and channeled it to round the edge of a piece of wood. It can cut stone, too."

"Holy smokes." He wondered if she would have shared all those skills if he hadn't caught her in the act.

"I was just...practicing. I accidentally discovered that I could light a fire too." She set a candle in the middle of the table and held both hands over it. Her face wrinkled up, she squinted, and with a small pop, the wick burst into flames. Just as quickly, it snuffed out.

"Shit. Can you do it again?"

She lit it and snuffed it without moving. "I can't let it burn. Candles are dangerous in a woodshop. Can I tell you something?" she asked, not meeting his eye. She sipped her coffee and stared at the candle.

"Sure. Anything."

"I'm freaked. I've never managed more than a slight whirlwind before...no matter how hard I tried. I've always felt...weak...in my skills." She sighed. "I shouldn't be able to create fire, and I sure as hell couldn't do this." A long, thin stream of coffee lifted through the opening of her travel mug. It hovered in the air and slid back down, one drop at a time.

"Is that unusual?"

"It's incredibly rare to be able to control more than one of the elements. I'm almost afraid to try moving earth. What if I can? Gramma Pearl can do a bit of most things, but she's unusually strong."

"I think you should try." He took a moment to put his thoughts together. "I think you need to experiment with things, figure out what you can do. Test your skills." He didn't add that he was afraid that his daughter's prediction was going to come true, and he wanted the good guys to have as much power as possible.

After thinking about the things air can do, he said, "High-pressure air can power tools, move vehicles, lift things, and clean away dust. It can keep a diver afloat...holy shit, Laz. You're amazing. What if you could make it do that stuff?" His insides shook with fear and excitement.

"I'm almost afraid to think about it. I've spent half my life wondering why I got the sucky power. Cynth can hear animals and heal people. Amber can control fire."

"Apparently, you can too."

She grinned at the compliment. "Hazel can grow anything or stop it from growing and talk to ghosts. Mom can control fire and hear animals. But me, I just got air. I never stopped to think about all the things air could do. I've wasted so much time by not experimenting. I just focused on my psychic visions and on being able to sense what people are feeling. I feel like I cheated myself by not respecting my power and trying to learn more."

"Aren't those enough? Seriously, they're crazy skills." By rights, he should be afraid of her, but when he looked into her worried blue eyes, all he felt was caring and compassion for her mixed feelings.

"Can you talk to animals, besides these birds?" The second raven had hopped out of the cage and sat beside its mate on the counter. "If he can't fly, do you worry about him falling off the counter? Maybe he should be on the floor, walking around?"

"You might be right." Abandoning her muffin, she moved the bird to the floor. "Don't you make a mess, Corbin." He bobbed his head. She lifted the cage to the floor. "Go back in if you get tired."

"How can we test your skills? What else might you be able to do?"

"Earth's the only main element missing from my new repertoire. Maybe I could..." She walked to a flowering plant in the corner by the window and carried it back to the table. With one hand on each side of the pot, she stared at the dirt for several long moments. Finally, a tiny puff of dry dirt spurted in the air. She swirled it around and tamped it back into the pot. She leaned back.

"Whew. That was hard." She sounded giddy. "But I did it." Her voice dropped to a worried whisper. "I don't understand why. I shouldn't be able to control more than one element. That skill only surfaces every third generation. Gramma has it. My kids might have it, but probably not all of them, likely just one, if history repeats. Something's messed up here. Why me? Why now?"

"Can someone give you their powers? Is that a thing?"

"No. Definitely not. They can give me their energy. Earl did that when Baby Anna was dying. He pushed his energy into Hyacinth.

Together, their energy saved Anna's life. But that's not the same as giving power."

"I think we should talk to your parents." He winced.

"What?"

"I'd rather I never saw them again...I think your mom knows about last night."

Laz's cheeks went pink. "Oops. Sorry about that. Well, sorry she found out...not sorry I seduced you. We'd better face the music and solve this riddle."

"How about I go to work, and you talk to them?" He gave her his best pleading grin.

"Screw you, Perrum. We'll face the music just like we enjoyed ourselves...together."

"Can I at least have my coffee and breakfast first?"

She snorted. "Men, always after some kind of carnal pleasure. Fine. Eat."

As much as he'd like a leisurely coffee with her, she was barely containing her excitement and worry. She wiggled in her seat, paced, talked a mile a minute about the possible reasons she had such a wide skill range, and about her excitement and plans to develop those skills.

He drained the last of his coffee. "Okay, let's go."

"Thank the Goddess. I didn't think you'd ever finish. Let's go." They looked at the birds. "You guys okay in here if I leave you out?" She moved their food and water bowls to the floor. "Be good now."

Her family had zero insight into why she was suddenly developing new skills.

"I've heard of witches stealing other witches' magic, but not passing it off on purpose," her mom said. "We spent a decade chasing someone down who was stealing powers. We always arrived too late." Her face was a mask of frustration. "I've never heard of just giving it to someone. Have you, Mom?" Lily-Beth looked at Pearl.

"Never. I've spent weeks in those grimoires. Nothing like that was even hinted at. Of course, I wasn't searching for that either. My focus was...elsewhere."

"Ya, on sneaking around behind our backs and pretending you didn't know about the chalice," Laz snapped. She was still furious at her grandmother's deception and didn't like the way Pearl didn't quite meet anyone's eyes.

"I had my reasons."

Laz bit back a rude reply. Being rude wasn't her usual way, but Pearl was still acting sketchy. Hanging out in her room. Refusing to return the books to the library. Skulking around on the magical dark web. Hauling in bags and boxes. She'd put a hasp and padlock on her door to keep them out, and told them if they didn't like it, they could damn well move out. As the family matriarch, the house was in her name.

"Well, I'm not going to sit around and listen to you guys bicker over nothing," Amber declared. "I've got a storage room full of new stock to put out. "If any of my sisters is interested, I could use a hand to get them into the sales system and out on the floor." She pushed away from the table and levitated her dirty plate to the sink. With Kody following behind, she left the house.

"I'm with her," Laz said. "I need to do something to take my mind off this crap."

"Don't you have commissions?" Frank asked.

"I finished most of it this morning when I woke up. I'll just swing by my shop and check on Corbin and Brenna. I've got some decorative items, jewelry, and gifts for the shop's inventory. Are you coming, Frank?"

"I think I'll take Rosie and head to work. I'm behind on my paperwork, and I've got an appointment with a builder about my new house."

"I'll come to the shop and sort stuff," Cynth said, but I'll take my vehicle." Driving herself was normal for Cynth as she often had to take off unexpectedly when a patient went into labor.

"I'll hitch a ride if you can drop me off at the garden center when we're done." Hazel chugged the last of her coffee.

Once the kitchen was tidy, they set out, leaving Gramma Pearl, Lily-Beth, and Trevor behind. Laz hoped her parents could talk some sense into her grandmother. The last thing the world needed was another damned magical trinket. Having two in their possession was more than enough.

They made short work of the new stock, finishing just after one that afternoon. "How about some lunch? We could go to Lloyd's for a burger," Laz suggested. Her muffin and fruit breakfast had vanished hours ago, and if she didn't get some coffee soon, she was going to fall asleep where she stood.

It was a short walk to the bar, which did as much restaurant business as it did in booze. They bundled up and walked over. The icy air was refreshing, and Laz perked up a bit. Inside, it was quiet with only three other tables occupied. Two by locals, and one by a mixed group Laz didn't recognize. Likely people just passing through, though she gave them a good, long look in case any of them were Brown, Keres, Rylie, or MacElroy. She had no idea what any of the other escapees looked like. The council was keeping a lid on who they were and whether or not they were believed to be in the area. Their secrecy made her wonder if perhaps some people on the council might not be entirely honest. Why else would they keep the information under wraps?

They were waiting for their meals when the door opened and someone stepped into the bar. It swung shut before Laz got a look at the newcomer. She stared across the room, waiting for her eyes to readjust after the bright flash of light from outside. The lone figure strode through the bar, swerving left and right around the tables, headed right for them.

"Heads up," Laz muttered. "Incoming." The person's face came into focus. "Holy shit," she barked the words out. "It's fricken Natalia."

"What the fuck!" Hazel jumped to her feet. Natalia had been working with Brown when he fought Hazel and Dennis. If she hadn't turned against him at the last second, they'd both be dead. She'd done time in magical prison but was released on parole.

"I never thought I'd see her again," Amber said, crossing her arms.

"What do you want?" Hazel snapped.

Natalia pulled up a chair from the neighboring table, leaned forward, and rested her elbows on their table. "Look, I know you guys don't like me."

Hazel snorted derisively, but she sat back down. Laz squeezed her sister's shoulder to show support.

"I don't blame you," Natalia said. "I deserve your distrust. I bought into Brown's lies. I was flattered by his attention and the power he promised me. I've learned my lesson. My magic's been bound for two years. After that, I get limited powers until I prove myself. I won't stay. I just came to warn you that shit's about to hit the fan. I caught wind of some rumors." She nodded discreetly towards the strangers. "Those guys...they are, for lack of a better word, MacElroy's minions. There's some infighting going on."

"How the hell do you know that?" Laz demanded, trying to sound bold in direct opposition to the river of icy fear running down her back.

"I have friends who have friends. They think I'm just biding my time before I turn back to the other side." She paused and looked each of them in the eye. "I swear on my magic that I'm not. I'll never go back." She shuddered and looked ashamed. "And those four are with him. I'm not sure if they're the ones grumbling or not. But I'm damned certain they're going to be a problem."

"None of them show any indication of magic," Cynth said. "I know, I've been studying them since we arrived. After the last shitshow with Rylie, I'm not taking any chances."

"That's just it. It's rumored that what MacElroy stole from the Council was a way to block signs of magic. He can magic the fuck out of someone or something, and nobody would ever know. If that's true, he could have cloaked them. We'd never know. But my source tells me they're working with him. I've been watching them. And when you came in, I decided I should warn you. It never hurts to know the face of your enemy."

"I still don't know why we should believe you," Hazel snarled, her hands bunched into fists on top of the wooden table like she was set to attack their uninvited guest.

"Look, I did my part. I told you what I know. If I hear anything else, I'll pass it on. I can't make up for what I did to you guys. My greed and lust for power controlled me." Her voice was heavy with regret. "I'm still in mandatory psychology retraining classes to get past that. Believe me, I never want to go there again. I'm on your side. Take the information or not." She eased back from the table and stood. She looked down at them. "I know you have no reason to trust me, but I felt I had to share what little I know." She pivoted gracefully on her heel and headed back toward the door.

Her walk was slow and measured, and Laz picked up on her irritation and uncertainty. "She's upset with us, but there's more. I can't quite put my finger on it." She sipped her cola. "I feel like my regular skills, the visions, my ability to read emotions, are fading as my new skills grow. What if I lose them?"

Her sisters stared at her in shock.

"The Goddess giveth, the Goddess taketh away," Hazel quipped, sounding more perplexed than amused.

"Zip it," Amber said. "This is serious. But magic cloaking? Sounds like something out of a science fiction TV show."

A commotion near the door drew their attention. They turned in unison toward the sound. Two of the men from the strangers' table stood between Natalia and the door. Something glinted in the man on the left's hand.

Chapter Twenty-Nine

"He has a weapon," Laz whispered. "We have to help her."

"It's nothing, probably just hitting on her," Cynth said. "Don't get involved."

The third man, and a woman from their table, moved to stand behind Natalia.

"We can't just let her get hurt." Laz looked around. It was early, Lloyd's bouncer probably wasn't on shift yet. He usually didn't come in until after seven. Lloyd and his wife were nowhere in sight. Neither were the two servers. "Everyone's gone. Where did they go?" There was always one staff member in front of the bar. Always.

The other patrons sat at their tables, seemingly oblivious to the standoff. Nobody moved. They seemed frozen.

"I can't ignore this," Laz declared, bolting from her seat fast enough that her chair flew backwards and crashed into the next table. She strode toward Natalia. "What's up, Nat?" she asked.

"These *gentlemen* won't let me leave."

"Ignore them, come have a beer with us." She stepped around the pair furthest from the door to stand beside Natalia. To her credit, Natalia played along.

"I think I might just do that. I feel a sudden thirst."

"Nobody's going anywhere," the tallest of the men said, using his scarred fingers to brush his greasy hair back from his ashen face.

"We were just about to have us a conversation," the woman put in. Her eyes shone with unholy glee.

"Cool. Come. Join us."

Nat stood motionless, like she was reining herself in.

"Fuck you, bitch. Mind your own damn business," the shortest of the men declared, puffing out his chest in a ridiculous display of masculine bravado.

"Honey," Hazel piped in, moving to stand beside Laz, "Ain't none of us gonna fuck a pig like you."

Hazel was always up for a smart comment or a verbal fight, but now wasn't the time. Laz sent her a psychic message to shut up, but her sister showed no signs of receiving it.

Natalia's warning that these men had masked magic pushed to the front of Laz's mind. They were here for a reason, and their excitement for a fight pounded off her like mental fists. It was all she could do not to recoil from the assault. At least not all her skills were gone.

She looked for staff, but they were all still out of sight.

Something pushed her to increase the tension. The idea wasn't hers. Someone was trying to manipulate her. She might love fighting and teasing her sisters, but she typically walked away from disagreements with strangers. The idea must be from these men. Had they *encouraged* the staff to leave? Were they pushing ideas into her head?

"I think I will join you for that drink," Natalia said at last. She seemed to be shaking off some sort of stupor. She edged towards the sisters. Their antagonists stepped forward in perfect synchronization as if all dancing to the same beat.

"You bitches will stay right where you are until we're done with you," the short one's eyes squinted with menace.

Laz shouted mentally for her family. Hazel hadn't seemed to hear her, but maybe her other sisters would. She opened the family channel and shouted for her mother, adding a mental image of where she was and what was happening.

She got zero sense that anyone had heard her plea. Usually, in an emergency, she got at least a faint response.

"My friends and I are gonna play a game with you *ladies*," he sneered the last word.

"Not interested," Laz said. "We're just going to grab our friend and enjoy our lunch."

The man's fist lashed out and caught her in the stomach. She dropped to her knees. She hadn't been in a serious fist fight since tenth grade, when Alisha Peterborough stole her purse. Gasping for breath, she struggled to her feet and faced him again.

It took a second to remember that she was an air witch. She channeled her powers to pull much needed air into her lungs. The ache in her chest eased. He'd caught her just below the sternum, forcing her lungs to empty.

She twirled her fingertips in a fast circle, envisioning a whirlwind. Faster and faster, she charged the small burst and with a flick of her fingers, slammed the point of the wind into his nose. He went down like an exploded building, crumpling slowly, one joint at a time, his air whooshing out in a rush. Blood gushing from his nose.

"What the fuck?" The man beside him growled. She slowly pulled the air from his lungs until he clutched at his throat.

The other two backed off. Three glasses floated off a table and dumped themselves over their heads...no doubt brought there by

Hazel. Dirt swirled up off the floor and smeared itself into their faces. Laz bit back a smile at Cynth's contribution.

Amber stepped up, a red ball of fire in one hand, a blue one in the other. She juggled them back and forth, staring menacingly at their foe.

"Take your sorry asses back to your pathetic boss and tell him he's going down. And if we ever see any of you in town again, we'll end you." Laz focused on each until they cowered, one after the other.

"And next time," Cynth drawled, "we'll show you exactly what we can do. No more of these pathetic playground games."

"Do we make ourselves clear?" Amber asked, still juggling her fireballs.

"And stay the fuck away from our friends," Hazel added, always the one to get in the last word. "Now get the hell out of here."

The foursome scrambled around them and shot out the door. Amber launched her fireballs through the opening and over their heads. They landed harmlessly in the snow and extinguished themselves.

"Geez, someone could have seen that," Laz reprimanded her.

"My new trick. I found a cloaking spell. I can't hide myself, but I can hide small objects."

What was with her family discovering new spells and not sharing them?

"Thank you," Natalia said, her voice shaking. "They heard me warn you about them. They were going to... never mind what they planned. They'll be back. With friends."

"And we'll be ready for them," Laz said. "Come and have a drink. I think we all need and deserve one. I'll go check on Lloyd and the crew. See what happened to them."

She pushed through the doors into the kitchen and pulled a smoking pan off the grill. Lloyd, his wife, the servers, dishwasher, and the cook were in the office.

"Lloyd. Dude, what's up?"

He shook his head. "Laz, what are you doing back here. This is staff only."

"Ya, we got thirsty and couldn't find our server. Come join us for a spell." She put a subtle emphasis on the last word. His wife, Vienna, blinked and looked at her. "Sure, for a spell." Obviously, she'd picked up on Laz's hint.

Slowly, everyone else regained their senses.

Lloyd and Vienna joined them out front. After making sure the other patrons, who had seemed oblivious to the action, were back to normal and didn't need anything, they sat with the sisters and Natalia. They shared a hushed conversation about what had happened.

"By the Goddess, I can't believe that happened in our bar," Vienna grumbled. "Your meal is on us."

"Not your fault. There's a lot of shit going on right now," Laz reminded them. Vienna had strong enough magic that she had to be one of the people the council had set up to watch for oddities.

"I should have noticed them."

"It's that cloaking spell," Nat explained. "Rumor has it that he has a powerful arsenal of spells. Right now, MacElroy's still weak from being in prison and not being able to practice his magic. I hate to say it, but you guys have to provoke a confrontation before he gets any stronger. It might be the only way to beat them."

"It's only days until the winter solstice. He'll be stronger during Yule." The idea sickened Laz. She sat at the table, jiggling her knees. Her fight or flight response was making her twitchy. "We need to find out where they're hiding, and make this happen."

"Get real, Laz. As if Mom and Dad will allow us to confront them first. Speaking of which, why didn't you warn us what was going down? We only stepped in when we saw things going south for you," Cynth said.

"Dammit. I did shout for you, and for Mom too. I didn't get an answer."

"Ya, because we didn't get the message. What's going on with you, Laz?" Amber said. "You're all messed up. Your aura is, too, and not just because of that confrontation. I noticed it when you came in from the shop. You're usually peaceful greens and perceptive blues. Earlier, you were sparking rainbows of all shades, sprinkled with this weird royal blue I've never seen before. Right now, you're black and red with anger and rage...but those crazy rainbows are still there."

Laz shrugged. Auras weren't her biggest gift.

"I need to go," Natalia said. "My contacts will want to know what happened. They'll want my side of the story."

"Are you sure that's safe?" Laz asked.

"I don't have much choice, but it works in my favor that those twits have a reputation for abusing ladies. If they doubt me, I'll tell them I was trying to worm my way into your lives to spy on you." She turned to Vienna. "I'll email a spell to you. Something I heard about in prison. It'll make the doorway glow when anyone hiding their magic enters. Only the spell caster can see the glow."

"I'm going to need that for the shop," Amber said.

"And for Dennis's house," Hazel piped up.

"I'll send it to the shop too. You guys can sort out who needs it. Thanks for standing up for me. I know you had no reason to, and I appreciate it."

Hazel leaned over and hugged her. "I'm still pissed at what you did on the island, but you turned it right and helped save my life. That goes a long way."

"Watch yourself. I expect you'll be targeted along with us," Laz advised softly. "We appreciate you putting yourself in danger for us. Give us your number, and we'll try and keep you updated on things."

"You'd trust me like that?"

An undeniable certainty came over Laz, not a premonition, but a calm sense of right. "Yes. I would. I do." Her visions had become sporadic and less clear. She wasn't hearing her family. Her magic was totally wonky, but she knew she could trust Natalia. She hoped. "Watch your ass."

"I'll do that. You watch yours. They're gunning for you. They want that chalice and the talisman. I never learned exactly what either was. They're working on rumors and believe you have both. MacElroy's bent on revenge for something, and Keres intends to help him get it.

Chapter Thirty

"I can't believe we haven't seen a single sign of anything from MacElroy," Laz grumbled to Frank as they sat in the café waiting to meet his builder for the second time.

"I'm surprised too. You said the winter solstice is a likely attack time, and it's coming up fast. One week. We have one damned week to figure this out."

"I don't think there's anything we can do or figure out. It's a waiting game. We need to stay rested and fueled up. As much as I'd like to drink myself into a stupor so I can fall asleep, I don't dare. A hangover could be disastrous."

"True enough. I'm not much of a drinker, but I sure could use something to take the edge off."

"I thought we did that last night?" She winked. Making love to Frank was the highlight of her day, though they were more careful to keep quiet and try to avoid having her family notice. So far, nobody had mentioned anything beyond that first morning.

"Let's not go there right now."

"But later?" She raised her eyebrows. Flirting with him was such fun. "Tell me again why I'm at this meeting?"

"I had plans for a new house drawn up. I need a woman's perspective. You might catch things I missed."

Her heart dipped. Would just any woman do? This wasn't because he was thinking of a long-term relationship with her. She hid her frown. "Happy to help you. I'll give the plans a close look."

"I'm going with a bungalow instead of a two-story."

"Why's that?"

"After Rosie was upstairs in the fire, I wanted to make sure that she could easily get out in an emergency. She can crawl out a first-floor window."

"You can buy emergency escape ladders that are super easy to use."

"I considered those. I decided on a bungalow, but the layout has room for a staircase in case I wanted to add a second floor in the future."

"Thinking ahead, I like that."

"I hope you like the plan."

His words barely sank in when they were joined by the contractor, who rolled his plans out on the table. They went over all the details together.

"Okay, I have questions. First, if you plan to run the stairs to the second floor through this storage room, where's the utility corridor going up? Second, there isn't enough storage space, and you don't even have a linen closet."

"What second floor?" The contractor said.

"I sent your office a message. I guess you didn't get it. I'm hoping to leave the possibility of a second-floor expansion.

Las looked at their guest. "Can I mark this up?"

"I guess."

She pulled out a pen and started sketching. "If you pull this wall out here," she made a couple of quick lines, "you can expand this small bedroom, add the utility corridor, and a linen closet. Move it another two feet, and you could expand the bedroom closets, which are too small if you ask me. Aside from that, I love this floorplan. The kitchen is enormous, and having a living room and den allows places for a family to separate from each other."

"That was the idea." Frank's smile was enormous. "Can we make those ideas work?" They discussed the redrafting fees and the increased costs for the extra space and pouring a bigger basement. "I'm good with that. When do we start?"

"First thing in the spring would be best."

"Not any sooner?" Frank frowned. "I was hoping to start right away."

"Building in winter has its issues. Working in the cold, digging a basement, and getting the concrete to set properly. It takes a lot of heaters, which are expensive to rent and to run." He listed several other potential issues.

Frank's face was a study in concentration as he considered the costs and ramifications. "I think we should start first thing in January. I'm eager to get my life back in order. Living at your girlfriend's parents' house is awkward."

She hoped that's all it was, not that he just wanted to get away from her and her magical problems.

The contractor laughed as he rolled up his drawings. "I'll send you a revised estimate, and if you agree, I'll have a crew ready to go the first week in January." He stood, and they shook hands.

"Are you that eager to get away from me?" she teased when they were alone.

"Not in the least. Eventually, all this 'tension' will end, and life will get back to normal. I'm hoping to spend a lot more time with you."

Her heart tripped a happy beat, and she couldn't help smiling. "I'm looking forward to that too."

"Is there any way you could...*mitigate* the cold temperatures to speed up work?"

"Probably, but I wouldn't. The physical cost would be much too high. Messing with major things, like weather patterns, and disturbing the natural order can backfire. And then there's the whole no personal gain rule."

"But don't you violate that when you levitate food and change the air to warm slippers?"

"It's a gray area. Those tiny acts don't affect anyone else. But altering an entire building site would be massive in terms of energy. We believe there is a balance. Everything is interconnected and shares the same energy pool. Large uses would take from that pool, and something, someone, somewhere would suffer for it. And large spells cast for personal gain almost always backfire in some manner."

He caught on right away. "Ya, I wouldn't want my house to cave in two days after it's finished."

"Exactly." She finished her tea. "Do you want to go Christmas shopping? I want to get something for Rosie. Two things, actually, one for Christmas, one for our Yule celebration." She sobered. Yule and the solstice were closely tied together. This year, the New Moon fell the night before the Solstice...meaning it was going to be basically full dark on the solstice. The dark of the moon was a perfect time to perform dark or evil magic.

Yule might not be fun this year.

In her family's tradition, the moon was considered full for the day before the full moon through the day after. That meant three days. The same went for the new moon, which gave MacElroy some leeway for his magic. If she had to guess, she'd assume the attack would be the first day of the new moon, allowing him time to finish his preparation for whatever he had planned. It was so odd that there were no rumors beyond the small bit Natalia had shared. Of course, there hadn't been any rumors surrounding the previous attacks either.

She pushed the negative thoughts away. "So, shopping or what?"

"I should get back to work, but I haven't even thought about Christmas. I guess I should at least start looking."

They were in the new toy store when Laz felt the first chill of something being wrong. She paused and, being careful to seem casual, looked all around her. Everyone was going about their business. "Let's tour all the aisles first, then start making decisions."

Frank gave her a questioning look but agreed.

In the third aisle, she feigned interest in a firetruck. Out of the corner of her eye, she saw a woman step into the same aisle. Dark hair, dark eyes, and a sallow complexion. No purse, a summer jacket despite the freezing temperatures outside. The woman glanced furtively left and right and backed out of the aisle.

"This way," Laz hissed, pulling on Frank's arm. "I need to follow her."

"Follow who?"

"Just come." With her arm on his elbow, she hurried him along. The woman walked up the next aisle. Laz increased her pace. She didn't know what she would do when she caught her, but she just knew she needed to talk to her. Confront her.

The woman bolted for the front of the store. Laz abandoned Frank and raced after her. Even from this distance, her aura was dark, practically black, but laced with the yellow-green of fear...and for Laz to read an aura that clearly, something was up. Laz caught her in the doorway.

"Why are you following me?" Laz grabbed her by both arms.

"I...I'm not. I'm just shopping for my son." Her shaking voice had a hint of Australia in it, and her entire body was trembling.

"You were. I saw you. I felt your intentions. Don't lie to me. Why were you following me? Who sent you? I can see your lies. Tell me the truth." She slowly pulled the air away from the woman. Her face went pale, and she gasped. "I said, tell me." She let the air flow back in, her stomach roiling with agony at basically torturing the woman. This wasn't who she was, but she needed to know...for her family's safety.

"I don't know his name. He has my son. I'm new here. I needed work. He's paying me. Not enough to survive, but some." Tears rolled down her face. "I have to tell him everything you do, or he'll hurt my boy." Sincerity rolled off her in waves.

"Jesus," Frank muttered.

Laz hadn't even realized he'd caught up to her.

"I believe you," Laz said, releasing the woman's arms.

"If I...if I don't bring back information..." She buried her face in her hands. Her shoulders shook with sobs.

Laz looked helplessly at Frank. What the hell did they do? They couldn't give MacElroy information, but they couldn't let him hurt her child either.

"I have an idea," Frank blurted.

"What?" Laz stared at him.

"We'll help with your son. Stay here." Grabbing Laz by the arm, he pulled her out of earshot. "We go about our day, doing normal things, but buying weird things. Things that could be used for spells. Weird shit. Chicken feet, broken glass, and herbs. We grab stuff at the second-hand store. A cup, some jewelry."

Laz kept one eye on the woman as he explained his idea. "We misdirect her. Let her follow, but buy potentially magical stuff. She can report back on everything she saw. We can have someone follow her. Find out where they are, or how she reports to him. Double-cross."

Laz grabbed him by the cheeks and pulled him in for a kiss. "Brilliant. But she can't know, they might pull it out of her."

"Good point."

The woman hadn't moved; she stood there looking petrified as they returned to her side.

"I'm not sure how, but we'll help you get your son back. You know I'm powerful, right?"

The strange woman nodded. "He's delirious with anger and fear that you'll defeat him. You can't get my boy back."

"I know people on the council. I'm friends with the head of the local RCMP. My family is one of the most magical in the country. We'll get him back. You just have to follow us around and report what you see."

"I can't."

"What have you got to lose? He's expecting a report. You give it to him, and I promise we'll help with your son."

"You swear?"

"On my life. On my magic."

"Just don't volunteer that you talked to us. If he asks, don't lie. Say you talked to us, because we approached you, which is true. Then say we talked about toys and the weather. I'm looking for a toy for my neighbor's daughter, and the weather is unseasonably warm today. Again, if you tell him that, no lie."

"What if I fumble or mess up?"

"Do your best. What's your name?"

"Marcy. Marcy Martin." Her brown eyes lit with hope. "Can you really help?"

"We'll do our best for you, Marcy, for you and your son." Laz patted her shoulder. "Now, I believe I have some shopping to do." She walked away without another word.

They bought a few toys and then, after texting Leticia for assistance with following Marcy, started on the list of things Frank suggested.

They made a big deal of acting secretive and checking the list Laz had in her wallet. It was a grocery list, but Marcy had no way of knowing it and would report that there was a list. They bought herbs, oils, rubbing alcohol, a tin mug, several pendants, earrings, chicken feet and livers, and five pounds of chocolate. The last item was pure impulse, but it would imply that they'd need a lot of energy after the spell.

They drove back to Hawk Manor. Marcy followed in her car. Hopefully unaware of the car that was following her. Perhaps Leticia's contact would be able to learn where MacElroy was.

Chapter Thirty-One

"I'm not really up for a party," Laz grumbled, pulling on a red sweater dress. One good thing about using magic was that it burned a lot of calories. She'd been eating away her stress, but practicing her new skills was burning them up as fast as she took them in. The dress clung to her curves down to her waist, where it flared out slightly. The hem fell just above her knees. She hated stockings in all their varieties, especially those that went up to her waist. They always felt like they were choking her. But knowing it was freezing, she slipped into silk stockings with stay-up tops. They'd keep her legs warm, and Frank might like them later. She smiled to herself, carefully keeping it from her youngest sister.

"I don't want to party either," Hazel agreed.

"I'm surprised you're here, and not at home getting ready with Dennis."

"He's getting a new house key cut. I can't find mine. Plus, most of my clothes are still here. I came to pick up this dress. She ran a hand down her sides. "I love the velvet because it's warm. Mayor Quinton's place is always cold." The deep Christmas green of the dress accentuated Hazel's brown eyes and eyes. The silk ribbon accent drew attention to her slim waist.

"Good choice on the dress."

"Thanks. You look incredible in that. It hugs in all the right places. Frank's going to be all goo-goo eyes."

"I hope so. You traveling with us?"

"Nope. Dennis is picking me up here. I'll go back to his place, our place, after the party."

"I miss having you live here. Nine times out of ten, I'm the only kid home now that you three are in relationships."

"Honestly, sometimes I miss you guys, too. We should have monthly girls' nights and sleepovers."

"Great idea. We'll start right after Christmas. I'll bet Cynth and Amber will be in too." She moved from the wall mirror to the one over her dresser. "When are you getting married?" She leaned in and swept on some blush and then mascara over her lashes. She rarely wore cosmetics, but with her lack of sleep, she was pale and needed all the color she could paint on. She had already used some concealer and face powder, but it wasn't enough.

"We're thinking of having it on the spring solstice. It'll be small and simple. Just family and a few friends."

"That sounds perfect." She put her cosmetics away. No sense dragging them along, she probably wouldn't reapply them. "Shall we go?"

F rank had trouble keeping his eyes off Laz as they drove to the party. Her dress was incredible. His entire body had leaped to attention when she walked into the room. His inner caveman had demanded he carry her upstairs and remove it. He'd almost wept when she covered it with a long jacket.

He parked a block and a half away from the mayor's house. They were a bit late because he'd been held up at work. He didn't know the mayor well, though he'd met her several times, most recently at Cynth's birthday party.

Light spilled out of every window of the modest two-story house. The Christmas lights on the house and bushes were tasteful and elegant. As they walked up the sidewalk, he said, "I'd like to put up a Christmas tree for Rosie. Do you think your parents would mind?"

"Of course not. We usually have one, but we call it a Yule tree. They'll understand that she hasn't made the transition from Christmas to Yule beliefs. Santa always came to our house. Mom and Dad used it to show us the power of giving, of keeping good secrets, and doing nice things for others. It was special when I joined Cynth and Amber in knowing Santa wasn't real. That was the year I became Santa for Hazel." She smiled softly. "It was a treat to be in the know and to help choose the perfect gifts. I don't think any of us was traumatized by the truth."

"That's great."

"We should put up the tree this weekend."

"I'd appreciate it." Her family was so generous. Taking him and Rosie in, letting them stay, accommodating his wishes, even babysitting Rosie on occasion. Tonight, Rosie was with a friend from school, a young girl who was also magical and approved by Laz.

Music and laughter met them halfway up the walk. "This party is happening." She danced her way up the walk, hips swinging in time to the music.

"Is it the whole town, like regular people?" Being one of the few non-magicals at a party made him nervous.

"Probably not. Mayor Quinton usually has two parties. One for her political connections, and one for her friends. Most of whom are magical or know about magic. This is the magic one."

Frank stopped dead. "Have you had any premonitions about tonight?"

"No, why? I mean, I've had fantasies of what I'm going to do to you later, but no visions. My visions have been off...inconsistent, I guess. What are you thinking?"

"I don't know. Maybe I'm just worrying over nothing. But wouldn't a gathering of a bunch of magic people be the perfect place for an attack?"

"Definitely not. All this power in one place? Can you imagine the power it would take to take all these people down? There will probably be sixty or seventy magicals here. An attacker wouldn't stand a chance."

He didn't have a magical bone in his body, but logic told him she was wrong. This was the perfect place to attack. Didn't she pay attention to the action movies she loved? Strike while your enemies are gathered and distracted.

As they stepped inside, he threw a prayer to anyone who might be listening, God, the Goddess, the Universe, or Karma. He prayed that there would be no attack tonight and that everyone would get home safely.

Frank stood beside the buffet chatting with Dennis. Laz was across the room, talking to Mayor Quinton, or Gloria, as she asked to be called in private. It was all he could do to stay across the room, away from Laz, and pretend to be sociable. He wanted to haul her into his arms and slow dance the night away. Her dress was stunning and emphasized her soft curves. He couldn't wait to get her home.

"Why the frown?" Dennis asked.

"I'm not much for large parties. I'm okay with smaller events, but it's crowded in here. Laz is too far away, and I've got this shitty feeling nagging away at me. I feel like a damned Nervous Nellie, and I can't stand it."

"I'm done too. Except that Hazel is clearly having the time of her life. This is her favorite holiday event. Apparently, it has the best food, and if Hazel is anything, it's a foodie. All four sisters love their food." He said it with tender indulgence. "Can I grab you a beer?"

"Naw. But I'd take a cola." He wanted all his wits about him in case of the worst, and he was driving. He drank his soda and gave in to the urge to dance with Laz.

He strode across the room and took her by the hand. In the space between songs, he said, "Excuse us, Gloria. I believe this is our song." He tugged Laz onto the small space cleared for dancing. When the next song started, he groaned.

Laz laughed. "Really? *Thriller* is our song?"

"You know it." Her absolute joy in the moment lifted his darkening mood.

"I would have thought you'd pick something more romantic, or at least something magical or witchy."

"Honey, all I care about is that we're dancing. You've been miles away from me all night. I miss holding you." All around them, the guests were doing their own version of the Thriller Dance. He didn't care; he held her close and waltzed her around them without any care for the music's beat.

Oblivious to the others, they danced to the next song, and the next. He lost track of time, losing himself in her embrace. Abruptly, the music ended, and they stepped apart. The room was virtually empty. The caterers were clearing the food and dishes into the kitchen.

"Where did everyone go?"

Laz glanced at her watch. "Holy witches' broomsticks, it's after two. We've been dancing for hours." She slid her arm around his waist and leaned into him.

Across the room, Gloria and Leticia were deep in conversation with Hazel and Dennis. Nobody else remained in sight. Even Gloria's husband was gone. He was a morning person and not much for staying late. He'd probably gone to bed already.

"I guess the party's over," Frank muttered. "I wasn't finished dancing with you."

"You're adorable when you pout," she teased, popping up on her toes to drop a kiss on his lips. "We can continue this at home. Let's say our goodnights."

As they crossed the room, the front window exploded with a massive boom. Flames and broken glass flew everywhere, burning his arm with excruciating pain.

Frank grabbed Laz by the waist and threw her to the floor, covering her body with his. People screamed. "What the ever-loving fuck was that?" he growled, peering around to assess the situation.

Four men burst through the broken window, and another through the front door. "Stay down," Frank hissed and leaped to his feet. Diving across the room, he took down the guy who came through the door and smashed his fist into his face, knocking him out cold. He'd never appreciated his martial arts training more.

He whirled around to go after the others. Three were retreating out the window. Leticia was screaming hexes, and Hazel was putting out fires by pulling water from the air. Dennis had his hands on her back, probably feeding her his energy. Gloria had one man on the floor, her knee in his back, flames dancing between her open palms.

Just like that, it was over as fast as it had begun.

"Son of a bitch. I knew this would happen." He whirled around, taking in the entire room. "Where's Laz?" he demanded, panic cracking his voice and paralyzing him.

"Here!" She popped out from behind the buffet table. "I was putting out a fire." Red liquid dripped from her hands.

"Are you bleeding?" He raced to her side, his heart in his throat.

"What? No. That's punch." She laughed a bit hysterically and wiped her hands on the tablecloth, the red liquid leaving ominous streaks on the white linen.

Snatching her into his arms, he buried his face in her hair. "Jesus fucking Christ. I thought they got you." He shook her. "Don't ever do that to me again. That's it. You and I, and Rosie are packing up tonight. We're leaving this cursed town."

"Aw, isn't that sweet?" Hazel's voice intruded on his panic.

"Sh," Dennis hissed.

"Don't shush me."

"Hey," Laz stroked his cheek. "I'm okay." She looked him up and down. "Shit. You're covered in glass." Let me take it out for you." Using a napkin, she brushed the glass off his jacket and pants before gently pulling a piece out of his face and another from his hand. "I think you'll be okay. You're not bleeding badly. We'll clean you up properly at home." She glanced around the room. "We're all okay. They're gone now."

"I told you this would happen."

"You had a premonition?" Gloria demanded.

"I thought you were a mundane," Leticia said, glaring at him, hands on her hips. Somehow, while Laz was tending his wounds, the two remaining attackers had been bound and gagged. Probably more fucking magic.

"It doesn't take a damn witch to see that this was the perfect place to attack. I'm surprised it didn't come sooner. All you magicals in one place. One well-placed explosive would have wiped you all out."

Everyone stared at him like he'd lost his mind. Laz's face lost what little color she still had.

"This isn't rocket science, people. Any idiot who has watched an action movie would have seen this coming."

Nobody said anything. Laz just stared. Her mouth dropped open and she started laughing.

It was probably just relief that the attack was over because there wasn't a damn funny thing about that moment. He didn't care. He stormed toward the door. "I'll be in the truck."

"Freeze," Leticia demanded. "You're not going anywhere. This has to be reported to the council, and I have to make a police report. First, we have to get our stories straight for the public." The words were no sooner out of her mouth when a firetruck pulled up outside, with two police cruisers right behind it. "I'll handle this." She gave him one last look and said, "You might be mundane, but you're right, we should have seen this coming."

Laz slipped her arms around his waist from behind. "Hey, relax. I wasn't laughing at you."

He turned slowly to embrace her. "Are you okay?" he whispered, his voice breaking as he examined every inch of her beautiful face. His heart thundered in his chest, and hers beat almost as hard. He watched her pulse throbbing in her neck. He stroked a finger down the spot, and her pulse slowed. She had one tiny spot of blood on her forehead, but seemed unscathed otherwise.

"I really am okay. We need to check on the caterers. Thank the Goddess they're all magical and we won't have to explain anything. First, I have to check on Hazel. Can you call Mom and explain what happened?"

"Ya, I can do that."

She pulled up the hem of her dress and extracted her phone from a holster strapped to her thigh.

"Holy shit. I thought you left that at home."

"Gramma Pearl makes them. We sell a lot of them online. Perfect for these pocketless dresses." She grinned at him.

He yanked her back into his arms. "If I'd known those were stockings, we never would have left the damned house. I feel cheated."

She giggled. "Babe, I'll give you a proper view. Later." She filled the last word with unnecessary innuendo. "Call Mom."

Laz's heart was still pounding as she hurried to Hazel's side. Dennis had his arms around her sister and looked shell-shocked. "Hey, are you guys okay?"

"Just tired," Hazel muttered. "It took a shit-ton of energy to douse that fire."

"Oh, I forgot." Dennis frowned. "You need food. I'll raid the kitchen. You good for a minute?" He peered seriously at Hazel.

"I'm good." She dropped into the armchair behind her. "Mostly good," she added when he was out of earshot. "That was so damned fast. What did it take? A minute? Two tops?"

"I don't understand why they attacked. What purpose did it serve? What were they after?" Laz wrapped her arms around herself. She was chilled from the exertion of helping put out the fire. "I didn't even have time for real magic." She grinned weakly. "I did manage to pull in some water before I ran out of energy. I need more practice. I forgot how draining new skills are."

"Well, I'm praying to the Goddess that you never need to use it again. This bullshit has to end."

Laz felt Hazel's words right down to her soul. "You are so right, baby sister, so right."

"Hey." Frank stepped up to them. "Talked to your mom. She heard about the explosion on the radio after something woke her up. She'll call your sisters and wants a full report when we get home. She's very glad you're safe." He yanked her into his arms. "Not as glad as I am."

"Thank the Goddess this turned out so well." She squeezed his hand. "But you're right, it doesn't make sense why they didn't attack while there were more people here."

Four men in black suits and ties strode into the house.

"It's the fucking *Men in Black*," Frank muttered, half-stepping in front of Laz. "The only thing missing is the damned sunglasses.

She stepped back out beside him so she could see what was happening. He tried to push her behind him. "Quit pushing," she hissed, "I want to see." He grunted, but let her stand beside him, though he pulled her tight to his body.

"Mayor Quinton," the tallest of the men spoke. "Constable Stone. We're here for pickup." He pulled out a badge and flashed it too quickly for Laz to see.

"Go ahead," Leticia said. A deep frown formed between her brows. "We'll need someone to take statements. There are six of us here, and five more in the kitchen. We want this done quickly."

He nodded and turned toward the others. "You heard the lady."

Two men stepped forward and pressed something that looked like a *Star Trek* hypo-spray against the shoulders of the protesting men. They slumped to the floor, all fight gone, their eyes closed.

"Holy bloody sci-fi," Laz muttered. "What kind of tech was that?" Frank's entire body tensed at her side, and she knew his protective instincts were kicking into high gear.

With one man on each side, they flipped the men onto stretchers and rolled them outside and into ambulances as if they were injured, not captives. Through the missing window, Laz noticed a crowd gathering.

"Corporal Stone, you might want to do crowd control."

Leticia groaned in frustration.

Dennis came into the room. "Wait, take this." He thrust a cookie into her hand. She downed it in two bites and nodded her thanks. He carried the tray to the empty buffet table and hauled in some chairs from the kitchen. "Soup's on," he called cheerfully and led Hazel to the table. "Come on, guys. Eat."

Leaning heavily on Frank, Laz made her way to the table and dropped into a chair. Her knees were shaking, her fingers and toes tingling, and her head was pounding. The adrenaline of the moment was wearing off. Working her new water skill had taken a serious toll on her energy. Though the cookies called, she forced herself to eat some sliced ham and some cheese first. Sugar was fast, but protein lasted longer. They devoured the food and drank the juice Dennis had brought in. Nobody spoke until their energy was restored.

"I really didn't expect an attack. It never crossed my mind," Gloria grumbled.

Frank grunted and grunted again when Laz elbowed him to keep him quiet.

Leticia came back in. "More of my officers are here now. They've got the crowd under control. The official story is that the burner from a fondue pot exploded while being refilled. Our friends were burned and will be airlifted to the city. We'll pass them off as guests from out of town. Everyone who was here will know better, but I trust them to keep the truth quiet."

"Were they magical or not?" Dennis asked. "I know you guys can tell us apart, but Frank and I can't."

"I second that question," Frank growled.

Laz stroked his thigh. His overprotectiveness was adorable.

"The two left behind showed no signs of magic. I'm not sure about the others. I really didn't get a good look." She'd been caught up in fire control. "It would be reasonable for them to have non-magicals to do their dirty work."

His hand dropped on top of hers and squeezed gently. She rolled her hand over, so their fingers tangled as she leaned into him. He pulled his hand free and replaced it with his other one. He slung his arm over her shoulder and pulled her tight to his side.

She inhaled the soothing scent of his aftershave, and her nerves began to relax. With effort, she unbunched her shoulders and exhaled some tension. "Why now? Why tonight?"

"It was a test," Frank said. "If it's like you think and they need to act on the solstice, they're running out of time. They're testing your strength. You and those around you."

"Logical," Leticia agreed around a mouthful of food.

"And they took a blow for it," Gloria said. "They're two men down, and I know I burned one guy pretty badly."

"We'll get more out of them during interrogation. We'll try and learn about their final plan. It's gone far enough that the council won't be gentle."

Frank shuddered against Laz and muttered, "Geez."

She wholly agreed with his opinion. "When can we leave?"

"As soon as your statements are taken. The kitchen staff will go first, as none of them were in the room," Leticia said. "I know it's a pain in the ass, but there is a protocol we have to follow. Try and be patient."

"I'll do my best." He stood and pulled Laz to her feet.

"Where are we going?" She trusted him, she was just curious.

"To a comfortable seat." He sat on the couch, and she crawled onto his lap. She didn't want one millimeter of space between them.

"I'm scared," she whispered, for his ears only.

"Me too, babe. But we'll get through this. We'll fight this damned fight and come out on top. One thing I learned when I was taking mixed martial arts in university...the anticipation of a fight is always worse than the fight, even if you get your ass kicked."

Chapter Thirty-Two

"Don't make me go over it all again," Laz grumbled to her family.

"Me either," Hazel snapped. "We've told you what happened."

"You can try and analyze it to death, but it won't help," Dennis added from where he leaned against the kitchen doorjamb.

"Why does every meeting of this family take place in the kitchen?" Frank stood looking into the fridge. "Isn't there anything to eat?" Cynth had taken care of his wounds when they got home. Laz had been lucky to escape the flying glass, except for one tiny scrape, which Cynth healed. Both Dennis and Hazel had tiny cuts that she tended to as well.

Laz got up from the table. "I'll make you something." She joined him at the fridge. "How about an omelet?"

"I'd rather have a steak."

"It's eight in the morning." It had taken three hours to give their statements. Then two more to tell, and retell, all the details to her family.

"Ya, and I was up all night. My body thinks it's suppertime."

"Pizza would be good," Dennis said. "I make a mean pizza. If you have toppings, I can make the crust."

"Done," Laz said. "Our kitchen is your kitchen." She settled at the table beside Frank and watched Dennis, Hazel, and Cynth working. It was all so normal...like their lives weren't careening out of control.

"I can't get my head around my new powers. Have any of you heard about adult-onset magic skills?"

"Only in people whose magic was blocked, like Kody's parents did to him," Amber said.

Nobody else had heard of it either.

"I've been researching since you mentioned it the other day," her mom said. "I haven't found anything yet."

"It's like I was just given someone else's power. Like I have two people's magic." A memory leaped into her mind, making her laugh. "I used to dream that I was a twin, and that Mom and Dad had sent my sister away."

"That's not so odd," Cynth said. "I mean, Mom and Dad would never do that, but it isn't uncommon in a twin pregnancy for one fetus to absorb the other. It's estimated that about one in eight pregnancies start as twins but end up as a single birth."

"Gross." Hazel made a disgusted face.

"Did you have an ultrasound, Mom?" Laz looked at her mother.

"Sure, at about four months. I knew I was pregnant almost from the day I conceived. I knew early with every one of you. I didn't think seeing a doctor was necessary. Not until I got sick. A horrid case of pneumonia. They did an ultrasound when I was in the hospital in Edmonton. Just one baby."

"Are you saying I might have absorbed my sister?" Her stomach bounced, and she rushed to the bathroom to be sick.

Frank was waiting when she came out. "Hey, are you okay?"

"Ya, I think so. What if I ate my sibling?"

He shrugged. "Apparently, that happens. Nothing you can do about it."

"You don't think it's gross?" She shuddered.

"I think that the universe, or in your terms, the Goddess, has its path. What happened was meant to happen."

"I suppose." They hugged for several moments, and slowly the comfort of his arms returned her stomach to normal.

"It could be the goddess's plan to give you double magic for this fight. I mean, if the goddess knows everything, wouldn't it be logical that she would have foreseen this trouble?"

"Maybe. I mean, I guess that's possible...if I had a twin. If I absorbed her. If she were magic." It was too much to fully comprehend. Her brain hurt.

"Does that mean I have two girlfriends?" he teased.

She swatted him. "Jerk." His playful comment lightened the moment. He was right, fretting over it wouldn't change anything.

"I wonder," her mother said when they returned to the table, "what if that did happen, and you got a double dose of magic? Maybe all the stuff happening kicked that magic to life."

After a while, they concluded that the concept was plausible, but not likely.

"Do you remember when Riley attacked Baby Anna?" Hazel asked.

"How could we forget?" Cynth grumbled. "Which time?"

"When you were babysitting," Hazel clarified.

"What about it?" Laz asked, curious as to where her youngest sister was headed.

"Remember what Jeri said about her family? Every seventh generation, her family has a set of twins. Depending on how they're raised, they either turn out super good or incredibly evil. They had to have special protection to keep them safe from evil."

"What's the point? We aren't Jeri's family." Laz shook her head.

"The magic community is pretty tight-knit. A lot of us were killed off eons ago. The gene pool isn't that big. What if some of your ancestors were Jeri's ancestors?"

"Then Laz might be both sides of one of those powerful twin sets." Frank's eyes bugged out. "Okay, I was only joking when I said I had two girlfriends. I'm not sure I'm ready for this."

"Okay, suppose it's true," Laz injected, "how do we use my alleged superpowers?"

"There are five days left until the solstice, less if they make an early attack. That gives us time, or rather you, time to hone those skills. They won't be expecting that kind of power," Amber said. She'd been quiet all morning, as if she had something on her mind.

"All of us can work with you," Cynth said. "We'll show you our tricks, things that make using our skills easier, and tell you what the pitfalls are."

"I can show Frank how to push his magic into Laz, the way I did when Cynth saved Anna when she was born. Cynth and I can work on that with you." Earl suggested.

"Mundanes can do that?" Frank looked shocked.

"I thought it was rare, but if Earl did it, it can be done."

"We have to keep this quiet, from everyone not in this room," Trevor said. He looked at his wife. "Even from your mother. I don't like how weird she's acting. I don't disbelieve what she's told us about what she's doing, but it's so out of character that it worries me."

"She's my mother," Lily-Beth protested.

"I understand, dear. But until we know for sure..." he trailed off sadly.

"I get it. My lips are sealed."

"Sealed about what?" Gramma Pearl strode into the kitchen.

"Your Christmas present," Amber blurted after a ten-second silence. "We're going in together for something special."

"Don't tell her," Laz snapped the way she would have if her sister spilled the tea on a secret. "What part of secret don't you get, dipshit?"

"Girls, girls. No fighting," Trevor chided gently.

"First two pizzas are going in," Dennis called out, successfully distracting everyone.

Laz stared at her grandmother, wondering just how long she'd been lingering in the other room, eavesdropping.

Chapter Thirty-Three

F rank opened the door when Laz trudged up the steps. Her heavy jacket hung open, and her winter boots weren't properly tied. Even her hat was askew. She looked exhausted. He'd been waiting for her. For the past three days, she'd been out of bed super early, and had stayed up late...practicing. He made it his job to be there for her. Making sure she had breakfast and that she took a break to eat lunch. He'd made more cookies and energy balls than he thought possible.

"Hey, you." He helped her out of her jacket and drew her into his arms. "You ready for supper?"

"I think I'll just go to bed. I'm bushed."

Smiling to himself, he practiced the skill Earl and Cynth had taught him while Laz was honing her skills. Concentrating for all he was worth, he slowly pushed his energy into her.

"What the hell?" She jerked out of his arms.

"Did you just..."

"I did." His grin was big enough that it hurt his face. "I've been practicing." He made a come here motion. "Let me give you a bit more...just enough so you have the energy to eat and then give me a quick cuddle before you go to bed. I'm missing you."

She stepped back into the warmth of his arms. "You see me every day."

He gave her a bit of a boost. "True, but fifteen minutes three times a day doesn't cut it. Even Rosie is whining about you being gone. And she has your mother's undivided attention. You're my girlfriend." He kissed the top of her head. "That means I get hugs and cuddles. Frankly, I think you need them as much as I do."

"Thanks, Frank. I appreciate it. Where is everyone?"

"Amber and Kody went home for the night. His grandmother just got home. I guess she was gone for a few days. Hazel and Dennis are already in bed. So are Rosie, and your mom and dad." He shifted positions to lead her into the kitchen.

"Cynth and Earl?"

"Cynth is asleep. Earl went back to the bookstore to look something up." The microwave dinged. "Just in time, your dinner is ready. I started reheating it when you texted you were on the way."

They didn't see each other much, but he had nagged her until she agreed to text every time she left her shop. Sometimes, she practiced her emerging fire skills in the specially created brick-walled, sand-lined space where Amber learned to control fire.

"Pull up a chair. I'll grab your food."

"It smells amazing. What is it?"

"Beef pot roast with onion, carrots, turnips, and potatoes cooked with the meat. There's gravy and Yorkshire pudding too."

She groaned happily when he slid the plate in front of her. He grinned. "And, if you're a good girl and eat all of your dinner, you get dessert." He'd made dessert for her every night after work. She got hers the night it was made, and the family ate the rest the next day.

She picked up the Yorkshire pudding and dipped it in the gravy. "Oh, my Goddess, this is incredible." She devoured the whole pudding before eating anything else. "Is there more?"

"You betcha." He pulled another piece from the oven where it was keeping warm. It wasn't food that reheated well in the microwave, so he'd baked one batch for the family dinner, and another timed for when he expected her home. He was off a bit, but close enough. "How do you feel about chocolate caramel cheesecake for dessert?"

She smiled around her fork. After swallowing, she said, "I can't wait." Her grin fled, and the exhaustion showed again on her face. "Why do you do this?"

"Do what?"

"Wait up every night and have food ready? You don't have to." She looked down at her plate and stirred the food around with her fork.

"Eat, babe. I do it because I want to. Because you're important to me."

"Because you think I can defeat MacElroy?" Her voice cracked.

"To be one-hundred percent honest. That is a factor, but only a tiny one," he added before she had a chance to get upset. "I cook and wait up because I care about you. Because Rosie cares about, and we want you in our lives." He sat beside her and stroked the back of her hand. "You know how penguins bring each other small rocks as tokens of affection?"

She nodded. They'd watched a documentary on it one night when they couldn't sleep.

"This is my pebbling for you. Watching over you, feeding you, being a friendly face when you get home."

"I appreciate it."

The front door opened and closed almost soundlessly. A moment later, Earl strode into the kitchen. "Good, you're up. I'm glad I didn't have to keep this to myself until morning." He flapped a stack of papers onto the table.

"Keep what to yourself," Laz asked, her eyes bright with interest.

"Remember when I figured out approximately where Keres was hiding?"

Laz nodded. Frank had no idea but kept quiet.

"I thought we might be able to find MacElroy the same way. I've been working on it for nearly two weeks."

"Where is he?"

"I don't know, not exactly, but I found something else." He shuffled through the papers and pulled one out. "Cynth told me once that your house is built on one of Earth's natural power conduits, a ley line. Stonehenge is built on top of several. It is estimated that as many as 14 ley lines converge there." He pushed the paper closer. It was a map.

"If you look here," he stabbed the map with his finger. "This is your house. The network of red lines is ley lines."

"What's a ley line?" Frank asked.

"Ley lines are the earth's power conduits. The Earth's energy field has an invisible electromagnetic grid system composed of energy pathways or ley lines. Power runs along them. Where they intersect, that power is more accessible to channel," Laz said.

"I had no idea." Frank shook his head bewilderedly.

"Most people don't," Earl said, tapping his paper. "Typically, they run between significant historical places. Stonehenge sits on one. The pyramids of Giza and Machu Picchu are other sites."

"Alberta has only about eight or nine major ley lines. This one," he traced it, "runs from your house, past Chickadee falls, onto the next quarter of land before branching off again."

"Under your house, three lines meet." He touched the map at a point two-thirds of the way toward the first point. "But here, still on your land, is another three-point junction."

"The power of three," Frank muttered. "I thought that was television bullshit."

"Maybe it is," Earl said. "Maybe it isn't."

He unfolded a large map of the province. "Again, I've put the ley lines in red. Your land has three three-point junctions. It's probably the most powerful spot in the province."

"Meaning?" Frank raised one eyebrow in question. Laz kept eating but didn't take her eyes off the paper.

"I don't think your ancestors chose this land at random."

"So why build on this spot, and not the other intersection?" Laz muttered. "Why not exactly in the middle of the two?"

"My guess is, and I can't verify it, not even on the magical dark web, that this one is stronger."

"I still don't get it," Frank said. "Clarify it for us non-magicals."

"I'm not magic," Earl said, his tone dryly ironic.

"Dude."

Earl shuffled the papers and pulled out another folded paper. It was four sheets taped together. "This is the Hawk land. I've focused on the geography. Right here is where the second ley line junction is." He tapped the paper as if they would miss the red lines. "It's near the old quarry, it's wide open, there's a creek running through the quarry."

"Earth, air, and water. The only element missing is fire," Laz exclaimed, dropping her fork.

"And fire is the easiest to manufacture," Frank added.

"I think MacElroy is here," Earl said. "They've put up a block of some sort to stop you from finding them. That's why scrying doesn't work."

"It's in the direction that Marcy headed after she followed us home," Laz said. "She could have gone anywhere, but the guy tailing her lost her when he was cut off by another vehicle and went into the ditch."

"I can't believe those fuckers are hiding on our land." Laz slammed her fist on the table. "By the Goddess, I'll kill MacElroy if I get close enough."

"Hey, babe. Chill. We can't run off half-cocked."

"No," said Earl, "but we can attack them before they attack us. I'm guessing, and it is a total guess, that they still need something besides the pendant and chalice. Otherwise, they'd have attacked us to take them, since they seem certain we have them."

"Unless we're wrong and they're not doing their spell, whatever it is, on the solstice."

"I thought about that," Earl said. "I researched significant astrological events for next year. There is a full moon on March 2nd, and a full lunar eclipse March 3rd."

"If you consider the moon full for three days, like we do, that is one hell of a powerful alignment. Probably better than the solstice." Laz pushed away from the table to pace. Frank wanted to sit her back down and massage her shoulders to help her relax. Somehow, he was certain it wouldn't help.

"Who even thinks of this shit?" Frank asked.

"When I finally accepted that magic was real after Cynth saved Anna. I did a deep dive into all things magical. All the different sects and strands of magic beliefs. The significant calendar events. Moon phases. Ley lines. Every damn thing I could think of. It was like a YouTube rabbit hole. You start watching one thing, which sparks interest in something else. If it wasn't for Jeri, the bookstore would have run itself into the ground. She ran the place while I was lost in research. I felt so bad. I gave her a significant raise to go along with the increased duties."

Frank guided Laz back to the table, picked up her fork, and handed it to her. "You aren't solving this in the next ten minutes. Finishing eating, and I'll get your cheesecake."

"Cheesecake?" Earl piped in. "I wouldn't mind a piece of that. I can't believe you make dessert every day, man."

"Laz needs the calories. She's already lost too much weight. I figure catering to her sweet tooth is a good way to keep her from losing more."

"You're the one who's been baking?" Laz stared at him, caring and admiration in her eyes. "I had no idea."

Frank cast a look at Earl. "I had no intention of telling you either."

"Oops, my bad."

Surprisingly, Laz didn't grumble about him judging her weight. A lot of women would have. He would have understood if she got upset...which is exactly why he didn't make a big deal of being concerned for her health.

"We should wake everyone up," Laz said when she finished her second slice of cheesecake.

"No, we shouldn't. Earl is going to bed, and you and I are going to cuddle on the couch. With luck, we'll nap, at least for a little while."

"I don't think I can sleep."

"I know I can," Earl said, clearing their dishes. "I'm beat. I'm a researcher, not a planner. My work here is done. Goodnight."

"Go wash up. Brush your teeth and put on something more comfortable. I'll meet you in the living room. Bring a blanket."

H er mind was whirling. Ideas flew through her head like bits of debris in a tornado. She trudged back downstairs in her fuzzy pajamas with a jumbo fleece blanket in her arms. Her head hurt. Her body was exhausted. She could barely move. Magic took its toll. It wasn't meant to be used for hours every day. It was meant to be a tool, like a hammer or saw. Brought out when needed, not used constantly. And like a cordless tool, the battery could run out.

This bullshit couldn't end soon enough.

"Come on, babe. Lay with me." Frank was sprawled on the couch in his navy sweats. His shirt rode up just enough to reveal the flat planes of his stomach. Suddenly, she wasn't so tired. He patted the seat beside him. "I need you in my arms." His smile was rakish and sweetly charming.

"Me too." She climbed up beside him, lying half over his lap, her head resting on his shoulder, her face nuzzled into the sweet heat of his neck. She sighed.

"What?"

"That was a good sigh. This feels so right. So perfect. Thanks for being here for me." Tension slipped away, and surprisingly, she felt herself drifting into sleep. As she slipped under, she was almost certain she heard him whisper, "Always."

"I can't believe I slept." She stretched and yawned. "I thought I'd be up all night. I guess my body overrode my mind." She snuggled closer.

"I'm glad it did." He shifted under her.

"Stop moving. I'm comfy."

"You might be, but I've been awake and needing the bathroom for hours."

She jumped up. "Why didn't you wake me?"

"Because you were sleeping." He grinned and walked away, greeting someone as he walked through the kitchen.

"I guess it's morning." She finger-combed her hair before following him. Coffee. She really needed coffee. "Morning," she muttered on her way to the coffee pot. She didn't really notice who was there.

"Morning, darling," her mom responded. "Earl says you have something to tell us."

Earl! Right! It was a tribute to her exhaustion that she'd forgotten about last night. "Coffee first. Talk later." She tolerated mornings but wasn't a true morning person, especially when tired.

She poured coffee for herself and Frank before she turned around. "Holy shit. How are all of you here, and I didn't hear you come in."

"You were exhausted, babe." Frank wrapped his arm around her waist and urged her to sit.

"Where's Gramma Pearl?"

"She took off about five a.m.," Frank said.

"Weird." She didn't like that her grandmother was acting so odd. Usually, she stuck around and provided her opinion on everything, whether they wanted it or not.

"I think Earl should go first. He can explain what he found, then I'll tell you about my plan." Somehow, between the dead of night and the bright light of morning, her subconscious brain had formulated a plan.

"Are you out of your freaking mind?" Amber demanded. "That's insane."

"Is it though?" Laz asked. She had laid out her rough plan. "I think we can brainstorm the idea. We'll get the jump on them."

"At the very least, we should get Leticia in on the plan," Trevor suggested.

"I don't think so." She took a moment to organize her concerns into non-offensive words. "The Council has been unable to find Keres and MacElroy, even though there are rumors of sightings in the area. I would expect them to have some really talented seers who could scry for them...but they found nothing. The Council should also have the best magical researchers...again, no results. Earl did some basic research, not that it wasn't a lot of work, and figured out the most likely place for them to hide. That makes me...wary, I guess. Shouldn't the pros be better than a mundane?" She smiled at Earl to let him know she wasn't knocking his hard work.

There were murmurs of agreement around the table, so she threw out her big bombshell. "I don't think we should tell Gramma Pearl either." She held up a hand to their objections. "Look, she's acting weird. Doing stuff she wouldn't normally do and not doing things she always does. I doubt she's gone over, or turned dark, or whatever you want to call it, but I can't say for certain either way. That worries me. If we keep her out, she'll be pissed. If she's on our side, she'll get over it. If she's up to something, keeping her out is the wisest action."

Nobody spoke, but their frowns said they were struggling with the idea of leaving the family matriarch out of the plan, even though they didn't seem to like her plan.

Finally, after several minutes of uncomfortable silence, she said. "If they plan to act soon, we need to get the jump on them. If they plan to act on the full moon–lunar eclipse, not acting gives them time to find additional magic items and to turn more magicals to their side."

"Or steal their magic," Trevor said. "After years of chasing the magic thief and witch killer, we traced him here, then he vanished. That can't be coincidence. It has to be one of them."

"Judging by what you've told us," Lily-Beth added, "Keres showed up here about the time we thought our guy, or girl, was headed to Canada. It could be a coincidence, but after years of tailing him, I don't think it is." She swallowed audibly. "As much as I don't want to put this family in danger, I think that we need to act."

Chapter Thirty-Four

"This is the stupidest idea I've ever heard of," Cynth said. "We're walking right into their camp."

"If it's there," Laz corrected, climbing onto their snow machine. "We're just two girls out collecting rosehips to make wine." Besides, our scrying didn't find anything. We're probably wasting our time."

"And rosehips need a light frost to be at their peak, not to be damned well frozen solid." Cynth climbed on behind her. "I can't believe Frank let you go."

"He doesn't exactly know. He thinks he and I are going tomorrow." She gunned the engine, and Cynth clutched at her waist, shouting something Laz didn't catch. She drove them to the enormous wild rose patch close to where the ley lines connected. It was an area where they often collected medicinal herbs. Perhaps the ley lines were related to the abundance of herbs.

"I still say it's stupid."

"Shut up and pick. We'll wander their way and see if we discover anything.

"I don't get how we didn't know they were around. Maybe they aren't. None of the animals seems stressed."

"You mean none near the house are upset. Brenna refuses to leave Corbin. She's very protective, though I'm sure he's ready to fly." Using pruning snips, she cut off frozen rosehips and dropped them into a bucket. They didn't talk anymore; they just walked and picked.

Every snap of a branch, every gust of wind sent a shiver down her spine. Her nerves were on edge. She felt like she needed to pee, though she'd just gone. It was the nervous pees. Logic said it was her fight or flight response. The body tightened up, including the bladder, and you felt like you needed to pee even though you had just gone. It had been her nemesis during exam week at university.

They walked and picked, moving through the unnaturally silent woods. There were no bird calls, no chattering squirrels. Nothing moved. Even the air became still.

Twenty minutes later, their buckets were full, but there was no sign of human habitation. Laz was about to give up and go home when a vision slammed into her. She grunted with pain and doubled over, spilling her bucket.

"What?" Cynth was at her side in an instant.

"They're here. Close," she whispered. "About thirty yards that way. They're blocking their sound with some kind of spell. Like a ward but keeping sound in, and unwanted guests out. Similar to what we used that day in the shop." She straightened up. "Son of a bitch. We should go."

"I think not."

Laz whirled toward the voice. "What are you doing on our land?" Laz demanded, barely able to push the words past the lump in her throat.

The man laughed. His aura was pure black, and he radiated evil intention. He was bundled up in winter gear with half of his face covered. He lifted his walkie-talkie and called for assistance.

"You can leave now." She feigned bravery and wished Cynth were beside her instead of two steps behind.

"I'll do no such thing. A pitiful witch like you has no power over me."

"Maybe not," Cynth said, stepping up. "But two of us do."

"You!" he said gleefully. "You're the one I was waiting on. You have exactly what I need."

An ominous chill went down Laz's spine. "We've informed the council that you're in the area."

His laughter was like claws across her stomach. "That bunch of incompetents. They couldn't even hold me in jail. Useless twats the lot of them." He rubbed his hands together. "But this one," he pointed at Cynth. "Her babies have power. In another month, I'll take that power for my own, and end their lives, and nobody will stop me."

"I...I'm not...not pregnant," Cynth denied.

Laz admired her bravery in lying to him.

"Who are you?" Laz said, as if he were dirt on her shoe.

"You know who I am." He snarled. Her indifference seemed to aggravate him.

"No, actually, I don't."

Anger rolled off him in waves. It was the worst possible time for her visions to kick into overdrive. She pulled up a mental wall to block him. The pressure of his feelings eased, but didn't vanish.

"I am Vance MacElroy." He pronounced it Mac EL Roy. With the emphasis on El.

"Mackle Roy. Right. You're the idiot stupid enough to get caught stealing from the Council. Whatever. It's time for you to go." She whirled up a mini-tornado around him, blowing snow into his eyes. Cynth battered him with pinecones and small sticks.

"Enough!" He raised a hand, and the air went still. Everything they'd thrown up dropped straight to the ground.

Shit! He was stronger than Laz expected.

"You have twenty-four hours to bring me the chalice and the talisman."

"Or what?" Laz spat, wishing she were half as brave as she sounded. Her knees were like rubber, and she was pretty sure she'd peed a little. "What can a puny magician like you do to me?"

Energy slammed into her stomach like a baseball bat. She didn't even have enough air to grunt. She dropped to her knees. She felt bruises forming where the blow landed.

"I'll kill every member of your family. Every one of your friends. I'll torch this two-bit, mundane-filled town. You have no idea how much power I have." His voice rose with every word, and they hit her like physical stones. "My associate here," he pointed to a man who stepped out of the trees, his face scarred with burns.

Keres!

She gasped in unison with her sister.

"My associate," he repeated, "still has a mental connection with your fire witch sister. He can control her mind. You know that. You've seen it. He'll turn her insane in a minute. He can look through her eyes and see what she sees." He clapped his hands, and thunder reverberated through the trees. Lightning struck the ground thirty feet to their left. "Bring me that chalice."

"Fuck you! Even if I had it, I'd never give it to you."

He spread his hands to clap again, and the world went black.

Chapter Thirty-Five

She was freezing. Why was the heat so low? Laz reached out, patting the bed, trying to find her extra blanket. A crunchy rustling sound surprised her and made her head ache. What the hell?

She struggled to sit up. Her head pounded like someone was using it for bongos. She opened her eyes to blinding whiteness.

Snow?

Reality crept in slowly.

Cynth! Where was she? Hell, where were they?

She was on a road. She was surrounded by snowy gravel. It took a moment to determine she was on the ground, outside her workshop. Cynth lay beside her. *How the hell had they gotten there?* The last thing she remembered was MacElroy clapping.

"Cynth?"

No answer.

"Cynth," she shouted.

Her sister didn't move.

Laz rolled to her side. Every motion was like shards of glass cutting into her muscles, scarring her bones. "By the Goddess," she muttered, "this fucking hurts." She crawled to her sister, every motion agony to her body and mind.

Throwing off her glove, she pressed her fingers to Cynth's icy neck. It took twelve full seconds to find her pulse. Her panic subsided a bit. Gathering her mental and magical strength, she channeled a visual message to her family and slumped back on the ground. Waiting. No response came.

The next thing she knew, Frank was frantically whispering, "Come on, Laz. Wake up." He repeated the words over and over until she managed to crack her eyes open.

"Frank." Her voice was only a whisper through painfully parched lips.

"Don't you ever do that to me again," he snapped.

She was going to object to his demand until she recognized the fear in his eyes. "Okay," she muttered. He jerked aside, and Dr. Carter took his place.

"I see you're back."

She tried to sit up, but the living room ceiling swam overhead. "Where? How?"

"That's what we'd like to know," her mother asked.

"What the hell were you two thinking?" Frank demanded.

"Cynth?" She made another attempt to get up. The room spun.

"She's fine. A bit battered and cold, but she's fine. And the babies are too. Dr. Carter brought a portable ultrasound. She's having twins!"

Laz slumped back. She was home, her sister was safe. That was all that mattered. "My head."

"Cecily will be here any minute," Trevor said from somewhere behind them.

"How long was I out?"

"Three damned hours," Frank barked.

"Hon?" she whispered, her voice still slamming into her head like bricks.

"Ya?" He leaned in closely.

"Shut up. You're too loud."

He looked chagrined. "Sorry. I was worried. Rosie was frantic."

"Bring her. Let her see I'm okay." Exhaustion turned her vehemence to a trembling whisper.

Rosie came in and hugged her. "I was scared. I couldn't find you in the things that are going to happen. I thought you died."

That wasn't good.

"I'm fine." She smiled her best reassuring smile and kissed Rosie's cheek. "Just a headache, honey. I'm good. I promise." Rosie looked doubtful but backed away at Frank's urging.

"Two hours and twenty-eight minutes," Cecily declared, striding into the house. "That's a record. Where's the patient?" Her forest green eyes sparked, and her red hair flew about her head in uncontrolled waves.

"Hey ya, Laz. I hear you've been stirring up trouble." She didn't wait for a response. "What do you think, Doc?"

"A mild concussion. Bruising from being hit in the stomach. A bit of disorientation. Nothing you can't handle."

Laz recognized the envy in the doctor's voice.

"Okay, girlie. I'm going to start at the bottom and work my way up." Cec turned to face the room. "Everybody out."

"Not Frank."

"I want to stay," Rosie demanded.

"Except Frank and Rosie," Laz corrected.

Cec pulled off Laz's socks and pressed her icy hands to her feet. Laz jerked. "Sorry, forgot to warm them."

Laz focused on Frank and Rosie and the concern on their faces, rather than Cec's healing. Slowly, the ice and pain drifted from her body. Her stomach stopped hurting, and the bruising ebbed away.

Lily-Beth came in and shoved an energy ball into Cec's mouth. Gently, Cec buried her hands in Laz's hair until they were right against her scalp. The relief was immediate. The room stopped spinning, she could stop squinting to see properly, and the last of the pain flowed away.

Cec collapsed back onto her knees on the floor. Frank rushed to her and scooped her up. As he carried her to a chair, he called, "Cec needs food." Her mother rushed in with two plates of food. Amber followed with juice and restorative tea.

"Cec, you need to check Amber. Keres claims he is still connected to her mind. Probably just a lie."

"Better safe than sorry," Cec muttered. "As soon as I'm done with Cynth. I'll give you all a good check over. I swear I'm going to move here. I spend more time on the road than at work. You Hawks are a reckless bunch."

Eventually, Laz, Cynth, and Amber were declared clear. "I am one hundred percent sure that there is no way that guy is in Amber's head," Cec said as they ate supper.

"I'm going to kill him," Frank muttered.

Laz leaned against him. "Chill. We'll get him."

"And you, don't even talk to me. And don't snuggle up, trying to be all cute. You and I were supposed to do this tomorrow. How could you go behind my back like that?"

"How could I not? You have no magic, Frank. None. I don't want to hurt your feelings, but you'd be useless against MacElroy and Keres. Useless. I wasn't about to let you get hurt trying to protect me. It'd be like a mouse against a hungry hawk. Not. Happening. Why can't you understand that?"

"So, I should just let the woman I love rush off into danger alone?"

"I wasn't alone." She paused abruptly. "What did you say?"

"Not a damned thing. Not that you'd listen anyway." He stormed out of the room.

"Get back here, Frank Perrum. I'm not done talking to you." She chased after him.

"Too fricken bad, because I'm done talking to you. Rosie and I are moving out in the morning. We'll live in my office. I can't live like this. I can't keep wondering if the woman I love is going to get herself killed because she's reckless and stupid."

"I'm not stupid!"

Frank turned to face her. "Maybe not, but your actions are stupid. And reckless. My heart won't take it."

"I'll be careful," she said meekly.

"And you won't run off alone, right?"

She winced.

"Say it. Mean it. Or I'm gone."

"I'll try?" Her smile was more wince.

He grabbed her and pulled her into his arms. "Lazuli Rose Hawk, you're going to be the death of me." He gave her a little shake. "Do you know how scared I was when your mom screamed and bolted out of the house into the snow without shoes?"

"I love you too," she whispered. "I'll do better." She hoped he heard that she'd try not to put herself in danger; not what she meant...she had no intention of losing again.

Chapter Thirty-Six

"Off you go, Corbin. You two take care of yourselves," Laz called as her ravens, now almost pets, hopped a few feet and then soared into the air. Corbin's wing didn't move quite right; she hoped it was simple stiffness that would ebb now that he had freedom to fly. With Cynth's help, the bird had healed faster than normal. She couldn't do much but push healing energy to him, but Corbin had channeled it to his wing, as if he was magical too.

A lot of witches had familiars, animals who helped them perform magic. Laz did not. But she felt like Corbin and Brenna might be hers.

They swooped in joyous flight. Corbin spiraled gracefully to the ground and picked something up in his beak, then took off into the air and landed in front of her. He took three short hops toward her and dropped it on her boot. She picked it up. A pinecone. Just a small thing, but she took it for the token of appreciation it was.

"Thanks, Corbin."

He cawed loudly and flew away.

Brenna dropped a small stick at her feet.

"Aw, thanks."

Grinning, she returned to the house. She was starving. She'd delivered her last commission until the new year. Now, she could work on whatever she wanted and had more time to practice her skills. She'd been itching to take on MacElroy. She'd go herself, but she wasn't strong enough alone and didn't understand her family's insistence on waiting.

"What the hell are they waiting for?" They knew where he was and were pretty sure he was waiting for the right time. They just refused to act, and she couldn't do it alone.

Lily-Beth greeted Laz when she walked into the house. "Laz, I'm glad you're here. I was just about to call you."

"What's up, Mom?"

The living room was full. Frank and Rosie were there. As was her entire family, plus Kody's grandmother, Abigail. Mel, Jerry, Danica, Mayor Quinton, and Laz's cousin Cecily rounded out the group. "I sent your grandmother to town for groceries. We're ready to go. Your father and I managed to combine our energies and some skills we used while traveling to scry MacElroy's camp. Knowing exactly where it was made it easier. He has eighteen men and women with him. We read magic on most, but not all. There are four children in a cage. We need to free them and figure out who their parents are."

"What?"

Her mom nodded. "We assume they're being used to control the adults."

"One parent will be Marcy." She described Marcy.

"We're sending Mel, Jerry, Gloria, and Danica to get the kids out. We're hoping their parents won't fight, but if they do, those four should have enough magic to protect the children."

"Are you sure about this? Don't get me wrong, I'm tired of waiting, maybe we should turn this over to the council." She looked around the room. Nobody spoke. The brightly lit and decorated tree in the corner mocked the seriousness of their faces.

"We discussed this last night. The council is acting too slowly. They aren't doing what needs to be done. We have no idea what MacElroy is up to. Tomorrow is the solstice. If that's when he plans to attack us, we need to prevent it. He'll probably wait for the Lunar-Eclipse for whatever he needs the talisman for, but we need to be ahead of him." During their last meeting, her parents had stepped up and put themselves in charge of the upcoming fight.

Suddenly, the thought of the fight she'd been itching to have terrified her. This could go very wrong. Last night, after the family meeting, she'd dreamed of a fight. Faces were blurry, like she watched through thick fog. There was blood and bodies everywhere. She didn't dream an ending; she'd woken up in a cold sweat, certain the dream was a vision.

"I want to come," Rosie demanded.

Frank shushed her. "You and I are staying here. I have no magic, and you aren't strong enough to fight."

"I sawed it. They need me."

"Rosie Celine Perrum, do not argue with me on this. We're staying here with Abigail and Cecily. We'll play some games and maybe bake a cake."

She crossed her arms and glared. There was a stubbornness in her eyes that didn't bode well for her listening. He'd have to keep her well within sight and reach.

Cynth went into the kitchen and returned with a tray, and began handing out plastic baggies of energy balls to everyone. "Earl and I got up early to make these."

"Thanks, Cynth, and you too, Earl." Laz took a bag.

"I wish I could teleport," Laz grumbled to Hazel as they trudged through the snow. "Half a mile isn't far, but in this deep snow, it's a pain in the butt." They were following the remains of the snowmobile trail Laz and Cynth had made to get close to the camp, but the walk was still difficult.

"Me too," Hazel agreed. "We're going to need all our energy. I can feel it." Everyone else followed behind them.

The sky was overcast, but the air was warm. The odd flake of snow drifted down, which was good. It would be easier to pull moisture from the air if they needed it. A light breeze pushed the flakes slightly westward. Also good, it was easier to channel a breeze that already existed than to create one from nothing. Mother Earth was smiling on them.

Danica, Gloria, Mel, and Jerry had driven around to the back side of the camp in Jerry's four-by-four Jeep. They'd hike the last bit in. The rest of them were quiet but not overly focused on stealth. MacElroy would sense them coming. A mage as powerful as he wouldn't be caught unaware. He'd have sentinels or alarms set up for warning.

They stepped into a large, clear area at the edge of the gravel pit. Power throbbed through Laz. *The ley lines! She could feel their power.* There were several large canvas tents with smoking chimneys, the kind hunters used for winter camps. A cooking cauldron sat unattended over a large fire. Aside from that, the camp appeared abandoned.

"Where are they?" someone asked.

Laz's breath caught. They knew this wouldn't be a surprise, but they expected some resistance. This was bad. Really bad.

A firebolt shot out of the trees, landing in the firepit. Hot coals and ash exploded everywhere. Their group scattered. So much for a straight frontal attack. Only Laz stood her ground and extinguished the sparks on her jacket with her mittens, saving her magic for the fight.

MacElroy stepped out of a tent. His eyes glowed red, and he seemed to grow taller as he stood there. *What fresh hell of magic was this?*

"What the hell do you want?" he sneered at Laz.

"I want you off my land." She crossed her arms, just as defiant as Rosie had been earlier. "Pack your shit, and your minions, and leave before I call the RCMP."

His laughter sent chills down her spine. "As if those incompetent mundanes can do anything to me. Even the chief is useless. Nothing but a puppet of the Council."

"Get. Your. Shit. Together. And. Leave. My. Land."

"Give me the chalice and the pendant," he countered, stomping his foot. A shockwave shot across the ground, and she wobbled on her feet.

"Neat trick. Is that all you've got?" Concentrating, she mentally rolled a snowball and hurled it at him. He burned it out of the air with a fireball.

"Pathetic witchling. You don't have enough power to hurt me." He paused. "But you do have power. I think I'll have that power for myself."

"I think not." Her knees were shaking so bad she was certain he'd see it. She shifted her stance, widening her feet, bending her knees slightly, and balancing lightly on her toes to be more stable and ready to move.

"As soon as I finish taking the magic from the rest of your idiot family, I'm taking yours. Yours is special. Then, I'm going after that baby and the little girl."

Fucking hell!

Not Baby Anna and Rosie.

She'd have his balls hanging from her rearview mirror before she let him touch those innocents.

Where the hell was everyone?

"Your family, cowards that they are, are sneaking around in the bushes, trying to get the jump on me. All eight of them."

She did a mental head count. Mom, Dad, Earl, Cynth, Amber, Kody, Hazel, and Dennis. That was eight. She breathed a sigh of relief. There were twelve, if you counted the crew headed for the tent with the children. With her, there were thirteen. Her lucky number.

"Well," she smiled her best threatening smile, "I can beat you, and your pathetic helpers, by myself." She swirled snow around his ankles, up his body, and into his face.

Someone screamed to her left. She kept her focus on MacElroy.

From the corner of her eyes, she saw Amber stumble out of the trees, clutching her belly. Kody was right behind her. They hurried toward Laz.

"Keres," Amber groaned. "Scarred with burns, but him. He tried to get into my head. Something hit my body."

Kody wrapped his arm around Amber, and they turned toward the gap they'd come out of as Keres burst from the trees and shot a wave of water toward them. Amber threw up a wall of fire, evaporating the water.

A rock bounced off Laz's shoulder, bringing her attention back to MacElroy.

"Stupid witch. Your family will be your undoing," he gloated, tossing a fireball back and forth between his hands.

"My family is my strength." She ignored the pain in her shoulder and banked the urge to attack him. He was stronger than she was, even with her newly augmented strength. She'd let him wear himself out with his tricks. Then she'd take him down. "What's the matter, Mackle Boy. Didn't your mother love you enough?" She'd read the dossier Riley had on him. His father abandoned them, and his mother was abusive. *Was it any wonder he turned evil?* He'd been taken in by a magical family, who now wanted no part of him.

Back and forth they traded shots. Slowly, she retreated into the gravel pit toward the ley line junction. He might be more powerful there, but she'd have unlimited energy to call on.

"Leave that bitch out of it. This is between you and me. No family, no council. Just us." Snow whirled up around her, reducing her vision. She let it come, squinting to see through it. Fifteen feet to her left, Amber and Kody fought with Keres with a lot of cussing and grunting from all of them. Magical shots fired higgity-piggity between them. Linking hands, Amber and Kody buffeted him with flames until his screams stopped.

It was both sad and ironic that fire had taken Keres down twice. She forced away her regret over taking part in a living being's death. She revered all life. She'd deal with her conscience later. *Where in hell had Earl and Cynth disappeared to?*

A snowball smacked right into her face, blinding her. She brushed it away and used air to push the swirling snow to the ground so she could see clearly again.

"Aw, look at the big baby, throwing snow," she jeered. Keeping control of your emotions was critical in a fight, magical or not. Losing her temper would throw her magic off.

"I've got your back," her mother said, stepping up beside her. "Dad's behind us." Hazel and Dennis stepped into view. She winced. Dennis should be behind them, not out front. He had zero magic. He was supposed to stay out of sight and be a messenger if they needed to call Leticia. He'd refused to stay at the house.

Shit. They didn't plan this well enough.

A baby cried. Her head snapped in that direction. It must be one of the kids her mom had seen while scrying the camp. *No fucking way!*

Brown and Riley had Anna? It couldn't be. They walked up to stand beside MacElroy.

"Ah, there she is," Mac drawled. "The ultimate power source. Stolen right out of her bed while mommy was sleeping. This little one's power and life force will be delicious." His laugh stole Laz's breath.

"Touch her and die," she sucked the air away from his mouth. The color dropped from his face, and he gasped.

He slammed his hands together with a crack of thunder and a wave of energy, and she stumbled and lost her focus.

"Nice try," he taunted. "Shot and a miss." His laugh reverberated down her spine until it felt like her vertebrae were clacking together.

Rage raced through her. She took one step forward, intent on charging him. A hand grabbed her shoulder. "Don't," Hazel warned. "Lose the anger. Look...behind Brown."

Earl and Cynth crept over the edge of the pit. Walking slowly and carefully behind Riley and Brown, who carried Baby Annie. Earl's face was a mask of rage. Cynth didn't look much better.

Because they were behind and just to the right of Mac, Laz saw them clearly. Cynth bolted forward, around Brown, snagging the baby from his arms, and running like a scared rabbit for the woods. Brown tripped over Riley and kicked her solidly in the ribs. Earl dived onto Brown's back, bringing him to his knees. They wrestled as Riley hobbled after Cynth and Baby Anna.

Mac laughed. "I told you...your family will be your downfall. Watch me kill them." He shot a bolt of lightning toward where Earl rolled around on the ground with Brown. Laz gasped. *No! Not Earl!* The charge struck Brown in the back, and he slumped on top of Earl.

Earl struggled beneath him. Laz shot a gust of air their way, lifting the body's weight slightly. Earl pushed out from under him and limped toward where Cynth had disappeared.

Laz breathed a sigh of relief. At least now it was two-on-one trying to save Anna. They should have known not to leave Anna without more protection. She reminded herself that Earl and Cynth were a good team. They had defeated Riley once already, and nobody cared more about the baby than they did. They had it handled. She hoped.

Chapter Thirty-Seven

"Hey, Mackle Boy, you loser," Laz called. "Looks like they're getting away with your snack."

His eyes flared red, the ground shook, and a massive fireball came hurling her way. Hazel doused it with a sloosh of water, just as a group of men rushed over the incline behind Mac and down into the gravel pit where they were standing.

"Can you bind him?" Laz called her mother. "Like you bound me for misusing my magic?"

"Working on it," Trevor shouted. Her mom backed away out of sight. When they'd left home, Trevor had possessed only limited magic, but somewhere along the line, he'd been taught more.

One of the men rushed up to Mac and spoke.

Mac whirled toward him, his face a mask of anger. Reaching inside his jacket, he pulled out a dagger and stabbed the man in the heart. The man slumped to the ground, bright red blood spurting around the knife, and golden energy flowed into the air, straight into MacElroy's open mouth.

"Mother fucker," Laz groaned. "He stole his life force."

Hazel screamed in shock.

The rest of the men retreated, scattering back over the hill and disappearing out of sight.

"That was delicious," Mac laughed. "Not as delicious as you'll be." He raised his hands and waggled his fingers in a come here motion.

Unbidden, her feet obeyed.

"No." She fought against the pulling force. She wasn't going to let him win. She sucked the air from his mouth, then slammed it back in with all the force she could muster. While he gagged, she retreated several steps and stuffed an energy ball into her mouth. It did nothing. She grabbed another. Energy trickled in. *Were the balls faulty, or was this some magical side-effect?*

"Tell me, Mackle Boy, what's your end game? Why are you all pissy and having a temper tantrum?" She threw the words out in her best taunting tone...the one that drove her sisters ballistic.

Hazel snorted out a laugh and dumped more snow on his head.

"I'll tell you, witchling." He slammed her with air, leaving her winded. "The council, in their infinite wisdom, sent me to live with a family who didn't give a shit about me. They beat me as often as my mother had." His words were laden with hurt and rage.

She almost felt sorry for him. Nobody deserved to be abused.

"They didn't give a shit. Not my pseudo-parents, or the council. I may have been only twelve, just a babe, but I wasn't stupid. I knew what the council did. They stole artifacts from magical families and hoarded them for their own use. Wonderful, fabulous, powerful, amulets, jewels, cups, swords. Some were even presents from the Gods. With them, I could exact my revenge."

"Monologue much?" She waved her hand like she didn't care. He was losing control of his emotions, and she was going to hurry that along.

"Bitch, you asked." Another air punch, this one to the throat, left her gasping and down on one knee.

"I'll get back the things they stole from me. I'll use them to get more. I'll find and kill every magical on this planet. Those who know they're magic, and those who don't. I'll be undefeatable. Hell, I squashed your ability to see the future and messed with your ability to call your family. I was within two feet of you, and your pathetic skills couldn't find me. I touched you and you couldn't find me." He laughed.

Fiery anger sparked through Laz, shooting out her fingertips. She ruthlessly squelched her feelings. This wasn't the time nor the place.

"When I'm done with the magicals, I'll start on the mundanes."

"Huh. That's pretty stereotypical. Haven't you got anything original?" Hazel shouted. Dennis shushed her.

A geyser of gravel exploded up in front of them. Laz pushed it away without thought. Her magic level dropped. Her power was waning, and she was already almost out of energy balls.

"Left," Laz whispered, and Hazel looked left where two men were trying to sneak towards them. Apparently, not everyone had abandoned their leader. Laz stared in disbelief. Principal Tallus! He wasn't just creepy, he was evil. No wonder he'd made her skin crawl.

"On it." She peeled off toward them, Dennis hot on her heels.

"Mom?" Laz called. *What was taking so long with that damned spell? And where were Earl and Cynth? Was Anna okay? What about the kids their friends were trying to free?*

She pushed the questions and doubts aside and threw a fireball at Mac, catching him off guard. It hit him full in the chest. He staggered backward and put out the flames.

"So, the witchling has new skills. Interesting." Every damned word out of his mouth was a creepy as fuck.

She slammed him in the nose with an air bullet and asked the Goddess for forgiveness for hurting another person. So much for 'do as you will, with harm to none.' Surely the Goddess would understand.

She hoped.

She flung a snowball, followed by a fireball, then another air bullet. Back and forth, they fired shots. One of his went wide. Her mother grunted in pain.

Shit. Why hadn't they gone back into the woods, or further down into the gravel pit, out of the open? Did they need to be close to work that spell?

She tried to silence the doubts and fears in her mind, but they'd taken root and refused to be extracted.

He threw another fireball. Her hat and hair caught fire. She doused herself with water. Shivering, she called in hot air to warm herself.

They were going to lose this fight.

Hazel screamed.

"Nooo," Dennis's panicked shout tore through the air and Laz's heart. Her sister was hurt. Everyone was going down. She risked a glance toward the scream. Dennis scooped Hazel up in a fireman's hold and raced out of the pit, toward the trees.

MacElroy threw two fireballs at the men Hazel had been fighting. They dropped on the spot, their lifeforces whirled toward him. Then he began to laugh. Quietly at first. Then louder. "I see another Hawk is pregnant." He made a nonchalant gesture to where Dennis had taken Hazel. I'll dine on that one as well."

Son of a bitch. By the Goddess, this couldn't get worse. She wouldn't let anyone harm her sisters' babies.

"I've been playing your family for fools. Keres was my bitch. Traveling the world, stealing power. He wasn't smart enough to keep it for himself. He believed I'd raise his dead wife and that they'd rule by my side. He fed the magic to me in jail through my contacts. Trevor and Lily-Beth," he sneered their names, "were just as stupid and easy to dupe as you were."

He stood there smirking. The clearing fell silent. "Oh, look, you're all alone now. Like I said, your family will be your downfall."

Though she knew she shouldn't fall for the words, they were probably a trick, she whirled in a circle. They were alone.

Everyone was gone. Dennis, Hazel, Amber, Kody, her mom, and her dad. Cynth and Earl. Her heart sank.

She was truly alone. If what he said was true, she'd never defeat him alone.

No! Rosie said they'd win.

Okay, Goddess, I'm begging you....Let Rosie's visions be accurate.

It was her against MacElroy and the two men crouching behind him, trying to look invisible, but not coming to his aid. They radiated magic, and if they joined in, she was screwed.

Chapter Thirty-Eight

"**S**top."

Laz whirled toward Gramma Pearl's voice. Her grandmother stomped forward out of the trees, headed for MacElroy. "I've got the chalice." She held it in the air. "And the talisman pendant." The gold necklace glittered even in the dim afternoon light. *How in the hell had she gotten the talisman pendant? Didn't Dennis still have it locked up?*

"Gramma, what are you doing? No!"

"I want in. I want power."

Son of a...they were right. Pearl had gone dark.

Her grandmother tossed the chalice up and caught it. Not the fake chalice she'd created...the real one.

As Pearl walked by, she cast a wink at Laz.

What the—?

"Gramma, no. Don't give it to him. He'll kill you. He'll kill us all!"

"Good idea." Before the words finished leaving his mouth, a bolt of lightning shot straight into Pearl's chest. She went down hard, banging her head on the ground with an audible crack. The cup flew ten feet into the air and crashed to the ground before it rolled toward Mac, out of Laz's reach. He scooped it up, laughing triumphantly.

The pendant lay on the ground beside Pearl's hand, glittering in the light.

Mac dashed forward. An enormous black shape swooped in front of him toward Pearl. The raven snatched up the pendant and flew away. Corbin. Brenna followed him, cawing loudly. Mac shot fire after them. They dodged, and it fell harmlessly onto the snowy ground.

Laz ran to her grandmother's side. Dropping to her knees, she felt for a pulse. Nothing. She rolled her over. Her chest was a gaping hole.

Laz burst into tears. Her sobs rang through the air. Grief threatened to pull her under.

MacElroy's laughter seemed to rebound off the sky and shoot into her broken heart. "I win, witchling. Admit defeat and I'll kill you quickly."

"Fuck you, you son of a bitch." She rose slowly to her feet, burying her grief. Saving it for later. This son of a bitch wasn't taking her down. Not now. Not ever. She'd have retribution.

She might not have been the strongest witch in her family, but she was a double. If her sister was right and she'd absorbed her twin, that meant she had double power. Power fueled by grief and rage.

She popped her last four energy balls.

Air was her element. Pulling it to her, she gathered her strength for an attack.

F rank stared around the kitchen when he came in from shoveling to burn off energy. Waiting was killing him. Neither Abigail nor Cecily had any premonitions of what was happening. *Why hadn't they left a psychic behind?* "Where's Rosie?"

"She went to the bathroom," Abigail said.

"When?"

"Two minutes ago." Cecily didn't seem worried.

Dread raced through him. Rosie's capitulation to stay here had been too easy. He raced for the bathroom. It was empty. Her boots were missing from the back door.

His heart dropped to his toes. His breath whooshed out in a panicked rush. He knew exactly where she was. She was headed to the fight.

"She's gone," he screamed. "I'm going after her."

"We're coming." He didn't know which of them said it. He didn't give a shit. The only thing that mattered was that his daughter was in danger. He'd seen the map. He knew where they were headed.

Racing as fast as his legs would carry him, he exploded off the porch toward the trees on the far side of the yard. He knew exactly where the gravel pit was. Three years ago, they'd given him some rocks to fill a hole in his driveway.

He ran and ran. *How far could she have gotten?* Her legs weren't long. It had only been two minutes. Above him, a crow screamed.

One of Laz's pets?

It swooped past him, down a small path to his left. It circled back and dove at him before returning to the path.

"I got it," he shouted when the bird returned for another pass.

There! In the trees, small boot prints. *Thank the Goddess for ravens.*

Heart pounding, he doubled his pace, ignoring the stitch in his side. When he caught up with her, he ran on. Surely, he was getting close.

There, a flash of pink through the trees. "Rosie," he screamed.

She didn't look back, though her slight hesitation said she heard him.

Suddenly, he was out of the trees in a gravel clearing with a large pit in the center.

Rosie raced down into the pit toward Laz, who stood beside a body, firing fireballs and flinging dirt towards a towering, enraged man across from her. He fired back stones, branches, and ice pellets.

Rosie ignored it all, rushing to Laz's side.

"Rosie," he screamed. Laz whirled toward him and took a massive rock to her shoulder. She grunted and turned back toward her opponent.

He had to get his daughter out of here. But how could he leave Laz alone? Where the hell was everyone else? The only person left lay unmoving on the ground. He thundered toward his daughter.

"Daddy, no. Stop."

Something in her tone slowed him down. He stood between her and Laz, frozen with indecision. He loved Laz. He'd be lost without her. But Rosie was his child, his heart. He needed them both. How could he choose?

"Take the cup, Laz," Rosie called. "Use the wind."

Laz looked shocked.

"Use the air," she shouted again. "I'll help."

Wind whirled around the clearing, swooping past him, making his hair stand on end. Shivers raced down his spine. He should have grabbed a jacket. A small whirlwind grew in front of the man...what was his name? MacElroy! The magician backed away from the wind.

A silver cup in his hand jumped. He clutched it to his chest, screaming in defiance. The wind whirled faster and faster, higher and higher. It didn't go past Frank anymore. It descended from the sky, bringing snow and hail that pelted MacElroy.

"Use the power in the ground," Laz called.

"Now," Rosie screamed. She flung her hands forward. Blinding light shot out of the ground, sparking through them both, and out of their hands. It slammed into MacElroy.

He stumbled backward; the cup flew from his hands and landed at Laz's feet. Frank dropped to his knees. His daughter did that. Pride battled terror in his heart.

Laz clutched the cup and started chanting low, almost under her breath. Rosie ran to her side and joined in. She looked at him over her shoulder. "Daddy, help."

He rushed to their side, his body trembling, but no longer senseless with fear.

"Put your hands on us."

They needed his strength!

With one hand on Rosie's shoulder, the other on Laz's, he pushed his energy the way he'd been shown. His knees went weak, but he kept pushing.

A dark shadow blocked the light. He glanced up, prepared to fight off whatever it was. A raven swooped low with something glittering in its claws. It cawed once, and the object plummeted downward. Frank let go of Laz and snatched it out of the air.

"Put it on me," Rosie demanded.

"No. Laz says it's evil." They'd talked for hours about the amulet and why MacElroy might want it.

"Do it," Laz screamed. "I'm losing my strength."

"I'll kill you all," MacElroy threatened, his voice gleeful. He slammed his hands together, and a shockwave knocked them apart. Frank landed on his ass.

He stumbled up and staggered to Rosie and put the pendant around her neck. They better be right about this.

Fingers shaking like a willow in the wind, he fastened the catch. He grabbed her shoulder and reached out to grab Laz.

Another blow buffeted him. He could barely stand and nearly lost his grip. The two people he loved most in the world staggered with him.

"Goddess," he screamed, "help us. Save the women I love."

He'd heard enough prayers and chants over the past weeks, in their home, and while they were training. He should have been able to come up with something better.

"The Goddess won't save you, boy. She's nothing against me."

Abruptly, everything went still. No motion. No sound.

With the chalice in her right hand, Laz threw her hands forward again. Rosie did too. At the exact moment. Like they were connected. A sonic boom-like sound exploded through the air. MacElroy staggered back and dropped to the ground. Laz dropped to her knees.

Rosie flung her arms around her. "We did it."

Frank blinked stupidly and stared at them. "He's..."

"At least unconscious. Maybe more," Laz said. Her voice shook with exhaustion. Her skin was pale, and black circles drooped under her eyes. She dropped onto her backside. Rosie knelt beside her, with her arms around her neck.

Trevor staggered into the pit, Lily-Beth leaning heavily on his shoulder. They were both bloody and bruised, their clothing torn half off. They walked up to MacElroy and walked around him three times, clockwise, chanting in some foreign language. He bucked twice and went still.

"That should hold him. For now." Lily-Beth said. She stumbled to her mother's side and searched frantically for a pulse. Finding nothing, she wept. Slowly, one by one, her daughters and husband made their way to her side. Each wanting to comfort the other though they were torn by their own grief.

Trevor and Laz helped Lily-Beth to her feet. Standing beside Pearl, the family shared a long embrace, weeping aloud. They cried until the cold penetrated their bones and they had to seek warmth or risk exposure.

Laz stared up at the sky, "Dammit," she cursed the goddess, "why did you have to take her. She's our glue. She holds this damn family together."

From the corner of her eye, Laz saw Rosie ran up to Frank. "It's safe, Daddy. The bad man has gone into his mind. Laz and I did it."

Whatever it was, Frank thought.

He scooped her into his arms. "I'm glad you're safe. I'm proud of you, Rosie Posie. But if you ever run away on me again, I'll spank you." He had never hit her, not even one tap; but if there was ever something that would make him, running off to a magic fight was it. "I was so worried about you."

"Sorry, Daddy. I had to save her."

Took Laz into his arms. "Are you okay? Are we okay?"

"I don't think I'll ever be okay again. Gramma Pearl is...she's gone." After a moment of silent tears, she turned to their nemesis. "He's unconscious, and in a magic straitjacket." She closed her eyes for a moment. "He's...not all there anymore. We're safe."

Frank swallowed down the urge to puke. They'd messed up the guy's brain. "Um. How?"

"We pulled from the ley line. It was just enough to give us the edge." She shivered and seemed to wilt further into herself. "Honestly," she squeezed his hand. "He seemed insane when we started this. He's just...worse. I think he was losing his mind anyway. He'll be well cared for in a magical jail."

Frank snorted. After the guy put Rosie and Laz in danger, and killed Gramma Pearl. He didn't really care what happened to him, as long as he didn't ever come back to Three Moon Falls.

"Will it hold him this time?"

"Leticia says they caught the guy who instigated the break and fixed the problems he had manipulated to set them free. He won't escape again." She leaned into him. "Are we good?" Her tone implied she was talking about them personally.

"Yeah, we're good." He touched his forehead to hers.

"Good." She breathed out a breath that sounded relieved. "Rosie, honey. Take the necklace off. Put it in the cup."

Frank expected Rosie to resist. He'd heard over and over again how it called people in and made them do bad things. Rosie unfastened it and placed it gently in the cup.

"How come she can let it go? I thought it compelled you."

"It was made for me," Rosie said. "To win this fight. Its magic is sleeping now."

Jesus, thinking cups and sleeping jewelry, his entire life view had been destroyed.

"What will happen to it?" He asked. The question failed to express the depth of his fears.

"The council will take it and lock it up. I don't know why our family had it to start with. I'd better call Leticia."

Chapter Thirty-Nine

T he next morning, everyone gathered in the living room. They'd pulled in some kitchen chairs for more seating. It should have been a joyful moment. They'd won the day. But Gramma Pearl's death pressed heavily on their hearts and souls, despite their narrow victory.

Pulling herself from her grief, Laz looked around the room, mentally sorting the entire tragic event into coherence.

Cynth and Earl had defeated Riley and saved Baby Anna, who was now cuddled in her mother's arms under the watchful eye of her father.

MacElroy had killed Brown and several of his own minions. Leticia's people were looking after those poor souls.

Amber and Kody had taken out Keres.

The caged children were freed and reunited with their families with surprisingly little effort. Probably because MacElroy was distracted. Gloria reported that Marcy was okay, as was her son.

Rosie would get counseling. She seemed fine at the moment, but there was a lot to process. Better that she understood her feelings before they became a problem.

Hazel and Dennis were fine, though a bit battered.

Leticia and Gloria strode in with two stacks of pizza boxes. "Time for food, and statements," Leticia said in her official RCMP voice.

Rosie sat on Frank's lap beside Lazuli on the couch. Everyone crowded around to listen to tales of the fight from the other combatants.

"I'm going to record this. Tell it from the beginning." Leticia set her phone to record and placed it on the coffee table.

Laz barely had the strength to stay awake. Someone thrust a slice of pizza into her hand. She gobbled it down and started speaking. It was hard to find her voice. Slowly, she related the story from her perspective.

"I'm uncertain how you had the strength," Leticia said gently when she finished her story.

"It was the ley lines. There's power there. We suspected, and now we know just how much can be drawn from them. I'm not sure why MacElroy didn't tap into that power. He camped there for a reason." She shrugged. She didn't have the brain power to analyze anything at this point. She ate more pizza before continuing.

"I don't know what Gramma Pearl thought she was doing. I think...I think she planned to give me the chalice, but he stopped her. I mean, she winked as she passed me. She was trying to convey something." She brushed away tears and swallowed a lump of grief.

"MacElroy told me I had extra power. I mean, I knew. I felt it. It was my twin. I had the power of two witches, and I'm grateful. I wouldn't be here if I didn't."

Nobody moved or interrupted. This was the quietest her friends and family had ever been. She was rather surprised, but grateful. She didn't think she'd get through the retelling if they peppered her with questions.

Dennis piped up, "Gramma Pearl must have stolen Hazel's key to my house. That's how she got the pendant. It was hidden there."

"That makes sense. I couldn't figure out how I'd managed to lose my keys," Hazel grumbled lightly. "Gramma was always a sneaky one." Her tone was fond, but tears rolled down her cheeks and off her chin. Dennis passed her a tissue.

Laz closed her eyes and tried to shake off the lingering tension from yesterday's fight. Though she tried, she hadn't slept a wink, and she doubted anyone else had. "I managed to channel the ley line power through the chalice. Rosie did the same with the pendant."

"I did, but had its own power," Rosie piped in.

"Oh. Okay then." Laz had been guessing anyway. "He...MacElroy...He killed Gramma. He didn't even care." She broke down in shuddering sobs. Frank pulled her close and stroked her hair.

Rosie patted her hand. "She's not gone."

"Yes, she is, Rosie Posie," Frank said. "Gramma Pearl isn't coming back."

"She's here." She pointed to the corner of the room.

Everyone whirled to face the corner.

"Holy shit," Hazel muttered.

Pearl's ghost stood there grinning at them. "You aren't getting rid of me that easily."

Chaos erupted.

Laz curled into a ball. How would she ever come to terms with all that happened? She was grieving someone who was still there. Family ghosts were normal, but not immediately after death. Usually, they only surfaced a couple of years later, when the pain of grieving was less smothering. How could Pearl be here now?

"How? How are you here?" Laz demanded.

Pearl chuckled. "Do you think I was stupid enough to enter a fight like that without a backup plan? I spelled myself to keep me from crossing the veil into the next world."

"You can't do that!" Leticia chided.

"I can and I did." Her laugh landed somewhere between hilarity and maniacal. "I never had many visions in my life, but this time I knew I wasn't coming back. I did what I could to keep me here with you. For you."

"For how long?" Laz whispered.

"A while. In a few months, the normal death process will resume and I'll pass through the veil like anyone else."

Excited chatter burst out with everyone asking questions and demanding answers. In the end, everyone grew quiet when Pearl refused to reveal the spell she'd used, and informed them that she had destroyed all evidence of it.

E ventually, Leticia had statements from everyone. She stood up. "As far as we can tell, at least judging by MacElroy's journals, which were quite crazy, we've rounded up everyone. The parents and children who were prisoners will get counseling. All the spellbooks and magical items are safely in the vault for storage."

"That was fast," Frank muttered.

Laz snorted a small laugh.

"The council has ways of getting things done."

Except when it comes to catching killers. Laz kept the thought to herself. Instead, she said, "Our house will lose its magic with the chalice gone. We should be able to keep it. We created it."

"And its presence helped cause this disaster," Leticia said. "And I remind you; the jail has been fortified. There will be no more escapes. Before I go, I need to know if there are any more artifacts in your possession."

"None that we know of," Lily-Beth said. "I'll make sure all the books Mom borrowed from the library are returned to where they came from."

"See that you do." Leticia gave her a stern look. "And tell me if you learn of any other powerful relic."

"Yes, ma'am," Lily-Beth said.

Eventually, everyone was gone, leaving the family and their future spouses alone.

Laz looked at each of her sisters in turn. "Cynth, I'm glad the twins are safe. Amber, you should have told us you were pregnant. In hindsight, we never should have taken a pregnant woman into battle. All three of you should have been at home."

"I only became certain today," Amber said. "I thought it was heartburn. And I had no idea I was pregnant." She looked at Dennis. "I hope that's okay."

"Okay? It's fantastic." He swooped her into his arms, swung her around, and kissed her.

"I have a secret," Rosie whispered to her and Frank. He and Laz leaned in close.

"What's that?" she whispered back.

"The other cup is here."

Laz reared back. "What other cup?"

"Gramma Pearl made a new one. It works. It's in her room. We need to hide it where the first one was."

"Son of a gun. That wily old gal," Frank muttered.

"And one other thing." She grinned like she had an enormous secret.

"What's that?" Laz asked, almost dreading the answer.

"I saw a wedding."

"Oh," Frank said. "Who's getting married?"

"You guys."

Laz opened her mouth to respond, but nothing came out.

"I'm good with that," Frank said. "Lazuli Rose Hawk, I love you more than I've ever loved anyone, except Rosie. I want to spend the rest of my life with you. Will you marry me?"

"Yes. Yes. Yes."

In the corner, Gramma Pearl smiled. "About damn time."

Thanks for following the Hawk family through their battles. I hope you enjoyed the ride. I invite you to leave a review on the reading platform of your choice, and please tell your friends about my books. Please be sure to check out my other series, including Coyote Creek and Heart's Haven.

From the Author

In many ways, this was the hardest of the Three Moon Falls books to write, and not just because I had so many loose ends to wrap up and so many villains to include. Knowing that this was the last time I'd see the Hawk sisters was difficult for me. I'm going to miss them. Of course, the ending also cut out a bit of my heart. It's hard to kill off a character, especially one I've come to love. Knowing there are so many new Hawk babies coming along eases that grief.

Yes, I said grief. Through conception to completion, the characters in my books are as real to me as the living people in my life. I begin with an idea of where they'll go and what they'll do, but somewhere along the way, they develop minds of their own and branch away from what I intended. When I set a story on the back burner and deal with the rest of my life, the characters whisper to me, they nag at me, and demand I finish their story. If that doesn't make them real, or alive, I don't know what does.

I'm including a recipe for lemon fat bombs...not true energy balls, I only wish I had that recipe, but they are a good source of protein and healthy fat, and a treat if you are on a lower-carb eating plan. They're one of my go-to snacks.

As always, thanks for joining me on this fictional journey. I hope we can travel together again. Be sure to check out the companion novella to this series, Midnight Magic, available where ebooks are sold.

While I write this note to you, my dear readers, I can feel another magic series pushing at the back of my mind. I wonder where that idea will lead us, and I can't wait to find out.

Hugs,
Katie

About Katie

Alberta romance author Katie O'Connor can't live without her computer and eReader. Her favorite place to use them is in the woods while watching the deer frolic on her summer property, Sanctuary. Her passion, aside from romance and her grandbabies, is giving back to the writing community. She's always eager to share what she's learned about writing and romance. In 2025, she was a Story Coach in the Alexandra Writers' Centre's Author Development Program. She's fueled by coffee and steak, and is fluent in sarcasm, cussing, dad jokes, and romantic jargon. If you need her, she'll be cozied up by the coffee pot, eyeing the cookies.

Where to Find Katie

Website: https://katieohwrites.com
Email: katie@katieohwrites.com
Newsletter Signup: http://eepurl.com/Q2nRr
Facebook: https://www.facebook.com/katieohwrites
Bookbub: https://www.bookbub.com/profile/katie-o-connor
Instagram: https://www.instagram.com/katieohwrites/
Goodreads: https://www.goodreads.com/author/show/5362469.
Katie_O_Connor

Books by Katie O'Connor

Their Christmas Heart
Their Christmas Love
Their Perfect Christmas
A Silver Fox Christmas Box Set
Heart's Haven:
Running Home
Building Trust
Saving Grace
Loving Winter
Heart's Haven Box Set Books 1-3
Three Moon Falls:
Fire Magic
Water Magic
Earth Magic
Midnight Magic
Air Magic
Stand Alone Books:
Carly's Heart
Matchmaker Christmas
Cupid's Charm
Gingerbread Dreams
Christmas in Silver Creek
Fake Dating at Half Moon Bay
Playing for Keeps in Half Moon Bay
Sleigh Bells Inn
Hearts in the Spotlight
To a Tea
Bulletproof Heart
Protecting Josie
Rekindled Fire
Winning her Love

Ticket to Her Heart
KO'd by Love

Snickerdoodles

Ingredients
- 1 C unsalted butter (softened)

- 1½ C sugar

- 2 large eggs

- 2 tsp vanilla

- 2¾ C flour

- 1½ tsp cream of tartar (for less tang, use 1 tsp)

- ½ tsp baking soda

- ¾ tsp salt

Cinnamon-Sugar Mixture:
- ¼ C sugar

- 1½ Tbsp cinnamon

Instructions

- Preheat oven to 350ºF.

- In a large mixing bowl, cream butter and sugar for 4-5 minutes until light and fluffy. Scrape the sides of the bowl and add the eggs and vanilla. Cream for 1-2 minutes longer.

- Stir in flour, cream of tartar, baking soda, and salt, just until combined.

- In a small bowl, stir together sugar and cinnamon.

- If time allows, wrap the dough and let it refrigerate for 20-30 minutes. Roll into small balls until round and smooth. Drop into the cinnamon-sugar mixture and coat well. Using a spoon, coat the cookie balls for a second time, ensuring the cookie balls are completely covered. *To make flatter snickerdoodles, press down in the center of the ball before placing in the oven. This helps to keep them from puffing up in the middle.*

- Place on a baking sheet lined with parchment paper. Bake for 9-11 minutes. Let cool for several minutes on the baking sheet before removing from the pan.

Butterscotch Confetti

Ingredients

- ¼ C butter

- ½ C peanut butter

- 1 C butterscotch chips

- 8 oz multi-colored mini marshmallows

Instructions

- Grease and line a 9 x 9-inch pan with parchment.

- Place the butter and peanut butter in a pan over low to medium heat. Do not allow it to boil.

- Melt until smooth and combined.

- Add in the butterscotch chips and stir until melted.

- Remove from the heat and cool a little–you don't want it too hot, or it will melt the marshmallows.

- Mix in the marshmallows.

- Spoon into your prepared pan and press down.

- Run your clean hand under some cool water and then use it to finish pressing down the mixture–the water will stop it from sticking.

- Allow to cool until firm, remove from the pan, and cut into squares.

Lemon Fat Bombs

Ingredients

- 1 C cream cheese softened

- 8 tsp lemon juice

- 4 tsp lemon zest

- 2 C coarse almond flour

- 4 Tbsp coconut flour

- 16 Tbsp granulated erythritol, divided (or sweeten with another low-carb sweetener)

- 2 tsp vanilla extract

- ½ tsp sea salt

Instructions

Combine all except 2 Tbsp erythritol and beat until smooth. Roll into balls. Dip in remaining erythritol and roll to coat. Chill. Keeps in fridge for 2 weeks. Makes 10 balls.

NOTE: If you just want a protein-rich treat and don't care about sugar, you can use granulated sugar in place of erythritol. Reduce the sugar to 6-8 Tbsp.

www.ingramcontent.com/pod-product-compliance
Lightning Source LLC
Chambersburg PA
CBHW022141010726
47493CB00002B/297